Praise for *Doubt Your Doubts*

"In *Doubt Your Doubts*, Chad P. Conrad tackles some of the most challenging issues facing Latter-day Saints today. For those laboring with questions, he does not try to offer sweeping, definitive answers. What he does provide are timely explorations from a perspective of deep faith, informed study, and disarming personal honesty that are certain to assist in that all-important search for God and His truth."

—Matthew Holland, president of Utah Valley University

"We live in a frustrating yet fascinating age. Questions about faith and religion are all about us, and the Latter-day Saints are neither quarantined nor completely inoculated against hard issues in these hard times. Some have questions, some have genuine doubts, but everyone knows someone who has struggled. Chad Conrad addresses himself well to a host of difficult topics and responds meaningfully to them, and for this we owe him our gratitude. This book will help many people."

—Robert L. Millet, professor emeritus of Religious Education, Brigham Young University

"*Doubt Your Doubts* is a wonderful aid to all those who are seeking to strengthen their faith and receive the guidance of the Spirit as they deal with life's many challenges and trials. Drawing on his own personal experiences and those of his students, Chad Conrad has tackled many of the questions that often cause people to question and waver in their commitment to the Lord. By integrating personal experiences, the principles of the gospel, and the teachings of prophets (modern and ancient), this book provides an engaging and thoughtful guide for our journey to the Savior."

—Steven C. Wheelwright, president of Brigham Young University–Hawaii

DOUBT YOUR DOUBTS

DOUBT YOUR DOUBTS

SEEKING ANSWERS *to* DIFFICULT GOSPEL QUESTIONS

CHAD P. CONRAD

CFI
An Imprint of Cedar Fort, Inc.
Springville, Utah

ISBN 13: 978-1-4621-1592-1

Published by CFI, an imprint of Cedar Fort, Inc.
2373 W. 700 S., Springville, UT 84663
Distributed by Cedar Fort, Inc., www.cedarfort.com

LIBRARY OF CONGRESS CATALOGING-IN-PUBLICATION DATA

Conrad, Chad P., 1967- author.
Doubt your doubts / Chad P. Conrad.
pages cm
Includes bibliographical references and index.
ISBN 978-1-4621-1592-1 (alk. paper)
1. Faith. 2. Church of Jesus Christ of Latter-day Saints--Doctrines. 3. Mormon Church--Doctrines. I. Title.

BX8635.3.C66 2015
230'.9332--dc23

2015004547

Cover design by Shawnda T. Craig
Cover design © 2015 Lyle Mortimer
Edited and typeset by Kevin Haws

Printed in the United States of America

10 9 8 7 6 5 4 3 2 1

Printed on acid-free paper

Dedication

I dedicate this book to the ones who motivated me to write it—our children: Keely, Koby, Reese, Tessa, Megan, Sage, Lacy, and Seth. You all give me reasons to believe daily. May this book help you on your journey to the Savior.

Contents

Acknowledgments

While I alone am responsible for the answers in this book, I do thank several people for helping me ask better questions than I otherwise would have: Lisa Benson, Kevin Cox, Ben Dearden, Ted Gibbons, Chad Hancock, Cindy Harding, Josh Harding, Mike Harris, David Hoffman, Tom Hsueh, Rusty Jackson, David Jenkins, Jordan Jones, Greta Kelly, Kelly Lyman, Heather Moon, Chris Orr, Matt Peterson, Mike Peterson, Brian Rawlings, Rick Rawlins, Alex Reiter, Mike Rhea, Chauncey Riddle, Ian Sandland, Sharon Saunders, Bill Schlotthauer, Russ Thornley, David Thomson, Tom Tyler, and many other friends and colleagues. Walt Stone and Steve Nelson lovingly read and commented on the entire manuscript. Special thanks goes to Kevin Haws and Emily Chambers at Cedar Fort for their direction and encouragement. My wife, Stacy, continues to be my most faithful sounding board and loyal critic.

I've tried to be true to the doctrines of The Church of Jesus Christ of Latter-day Saints as I comprehended these questions, but this book is neither official nor authoritative. On all of these issues, I continue to seek better answers. I am confident they will come as I learn to ask better questions.

To protect privacy, I have changed many of the names that appear in my stories.

Introduction

This book is for believers. It's also for those who want to believe or want to help their loved ones believe. Even the most faithful disciples can be caught in riptides of questions or doubts that threaten to drown the soul. In those times of wavering, an outstretched hand of faith can be the lifeline to pulls the drowning soul back to the boat of belief.

Toward the end of His ministry, Christ took Peter, James, and John to the Mount of Transfiguration, where they enjoyed a temple experience that transformed their lives. Yet from the moment they came down from the mountain, they were "questioning one with another" what it all meant (Mark 9:10). The three of them rejoined the other Apostles, who were being pelted with questions by the unbelieving scribes.

When Christ finally arrived, the believers ran to Him for relief. Then the Master took over. "What question ye with them?" He asked the scribes (Mark 9:16). He was ready to answer the questions His Apostles could not. The man in the crowd who had stirred up the trouble stepped forward and said, "I have brought unto thee my son, which hath a dumb spirit" (Mark 9:17). This evil spirit had possessed and tormented the boy for years. So often there are troubling personal experiences that lie behind our doctrinal doubts and difficulties. The Apostles couldn't do anything to help. The man challenged Christ to solve what no one else could. The Lord's reply was a poignant one: "If thou canst believe, all things are possible to him that believeth" (Mark 9:23). If we can muster up enough faith to trust in Christ, He can answer all questions and heal all wounds. However, faith precedes the miracle, and the miracles come in His time and in His way.

This desperate father, at the point of tears, cried out, "Lord, I believe"; then, almost as if in reply to a penetrating, questioning gaze from the Savior (which isn't in the text), the man added, "Help thou mine unbelief" (Mark 9:24). Sometimes in a crisis we need help to buoy up our belief. We want to trust in the Lord and His gospel, but the questioning and mocking of skeptics deflate us, while we are also haunted by our own fears and insecurities.

In my twenty years of teaching the gospel to LDS youth, I have been both strengthened and challenged by the many thoughtful questions students have shared with me. Some are more general while others are deeply personal: Why don't I fit in at Church? Do I have a testimony? Where are the miracles in my life when I need them? Why must innocent people suffer? What about homosexuality? How can we make sense of evolution? How will I ever get married? Why do people say we're not Christians? Are women equal with men in the Church? Why would God ever command members to practice polygamy? Why couldn't blacks hold the priesthood for so long? Is there really life after death? Is Christ actually coming back? Can I ever be forgiven? Like the possessed boy's father, we cry out, "Lord, I believe; help thou mine unbelief."

This book is an attempt to address some of the issues that have come up most frequently among my students. I haven't tried to give a final answer to all these questions. Most of them continue to intrigue me. Sometimes what we need isn't an answer. Rather, what we need is an approach to help us carry on *in spite of* our questions and concerns. In a recent general conference address about the father and the son possessed by the evil spirit, Elder Jeffrey R. Holland declared,

> When problems come and questions arise, do not start your quest for faith by saying how much you do *not* have, leading as it were with your "unbelief." That is like trying to stuff a turkey through the beak! Let me be clear on this point: I am not asking you to pretend to faith you do not have. I *am* asking you to be true to the faith you *do* have. Sometimes we act as if an honest declaration of doubt is a higher

> manifestation of moral courage than is an honest declaration of faith. It is not! So let us all remember the clear message of this scriptural account: Be as candid about your questions as you need to be; life is full of them on one subject or another. But if you and your family want to be healed, don't let those questions stand in the way of faith working its miracle.[1]

My hope is to be as candid as I can about the real questions my students and I have had but to let my faith, as Elder Holland taught, work its miracle. I trust you'll forgive me if at times I seem to be trying to stuff the turkey through the beak. What I'm intending to do is to look at belief from different perspectives—discussing the flaws people think they see while still encouraging the feast.

In another recent general conference, President Dieter F. Uchtdorf assured us that there is a place in the Church for those with unanswered questions and concerns. He borrowed from the familiar metaphor of a seed to explain:

> It's natural to have questions—the acorn of honest inquiry has often sprouted and matured into a great oak of understanding. There are few members of the Church who, at one time or another, have not wrestled with serious or sensitive questions. One of the purposes of the Church is to nurture and cultivate the seed of faith—even in the sometimes sandy soil of doubt and uncertainty. Faith is to hope for things which are not seen but which are true.
>
> Therefore, my dear brothers and sisters—my dear friends—please, first doubt your doubts before you doubt your faith. We must never allow doubt to hold us prisoner and keep us from the divine love, peace, and gifts that come through faith in the Lord Jesus Christ.[2]

So while it's normal to question and struggle along the journey of discipleship, if we protect and nurture the fragile sapling of faith, it can grow into a productive Christian life that will fill us with joy and bless those around us for generations to come. It'd seem foolish to pull up the tree by its roots and throw it away just because we have concerns with how it looks or where it came from. The tree we are growing is the tree of life, and the tree of life is Christ in us.

When the Lord says, "Doubt not, but be believing" (Mormon 9:27), He's not saying don't ask questions. Asking good questions has always been an essential part of the gospel message. "Ask and ye shall receive" is the repeated promise. He's saying, "Look unto me in every thought; doubt not, fear not" (D&C 6:36). Our English word *doubt* comes from the Old French *douter*, which means "to be afraid." It's related to the Latin word *dubitare*, which means "to doubt, question, hesitate, or waver in opinion." Originally, it meant "to have to choose between two things."[3] Once we have chosen to follow the Lord as His disciples, we don't need to worry when alternatives to our faith are hurled at us. We can observe and understand them—maybe even wonder at their peculiarities at times—all the while marching forward with an eye single to the glory of God, who has blessed us so much.

If we do stumble over our questions and find ourselves hesitating and halting between two opinions (see 1 Kings 18:21), we don't need to panic. And we certainly don't need to panic if those we love seem stuck somewhere on or off the gospel path. The light of Christ is still shining, His love is still reaching, and His plan is still working—with or without our acknowledgement or theirs.

Ultimately, we won't resolve the deepest struggles of our souls by reading books, blogs, or websites—even inspired ones (see John 5:39–40). The answer is Christ. He is the Teacher. He is the Healer. I hope that what I share here can help you and your loved ones in some small measure on your journey back to the Lord.

Finding a Place in the Church

"You must be the change you wish to see in the world."[1]

—Mohandas K. Gandhi

Recently, I was walking out of a department store when I bumped into one of my former seminary students. I remembered her in ninth grade as a bright, inquisitive soul who wasn't afraid to speak her mind. I asked her how she was doing and, without too much prompting, she began to tell me an abbreviated story of her past several years in the Church. She said in high school she started hanging out with a different crowd and soon found herself involved in behaviors that alienated her from the members of her ward. She started smoking. When she came to Church smelling like smoke, no one would sit by her or talk to her, so she soon felt unwanted and stopped attending. She'd had a long struggle with depression and eventually attempted suicide. That just made matters worse, and she found herself the topic of considerable gossip at Church. She concluded by asking me why she should ever go back to her ward. She wasn't even sure the Church was true anymore.

In the thirty seconds I had before she dashed off, I weakly attempted a reply. I told her that her ward needed her. I said that even though the members weren't always true to the message, the message was still true. I expressed how sorry I was for the way she felt treated, conveyed to her my continued esteem, and assured her that the Lord still loved her and would hear her prayers if she shared her burden with Him. She smiled half-heartedly, but I could tell she wasn't convinced. In that moment, I wished I could somehow lift all her pain and suffering onto my own shoulders and wrap her up in the Savior's loving embrace, but of course I couldn't. All I could do was ache for her pain and pray for her soul—still as precious as ever in the Lord's sight. I wish I could've found a more effective way then to help carry her suffering.

During my years of teaching, I've met many students who didn't feel they fit into the cookie-cutter mold of Molly Mormons and Peter Priesthoods that they thought they saw in their wards. This made them wonder painfully if they'd ever really find a place. They felt too inferior or nonconformist to be part of the group. They sometimes would question if it's really worth the effort to keep looking. I understand such feelings. Many times, I have felt out of step and too unorthodox to be a full-fledged member. Still, over the years I've discovered that there are no perfect Latter-day Saints. By striving to serve others rather than judge them, I have found my place in the Church. I believe others can and should too—it's a large determining factor for our happiness, spiritual growth, and true success in life.

There's a classic story about a woman who learns the value of giving people the benefit of the doubt. While waiting at an airport for her flight, she goes to the snack bar and buys a package of cookies to munch on. The only available booth to sit at is occupied by a man, so she asks if he would mind sharing it with her. He consents, so she sits down and begins eating the cookies. Without warning, the man reaches over and takes one of the cookies and eats it while he reads. The woman considers this quite odd and extremely rude but says nothing. She simply takes another cookie herself. Shortly, the man reaches for another one and eats it, taking as little notice of the woman as before. Scowling, she grabs one herself. This goes on until there's only one remaining cookie. The man reaches for it, breaks it in two, gives the woman half, smiles, eats the other half, and then goes back to reading his newspaper. The woman gets up in a huff and marches away indignantly. As she reaches into her purse, looking for her plane ticket, she finds her bag of cookies. She had been eating the man's.

Choosing Charity

For too much of my own life, I've run around like the woman in the story. I'm always trying to get my fair share and to get others to respect and appreciate my efforts. I'm hurt when they don't, and I want to throw a tantrum or pity party. Yet it seems to me that the entire point of the gospel of Jesus Christ is to teach us to be more like the man in the story. Marvin J. Ashton described that attitude as charity. He said,

> Perhaps the greatest charity comes when we are kind to each other, when we don't judge or categorize someone else, when we simply give each other the benefit of the doubt or remain quiet. Charity is accepting someone's differences, weaknesses, and shortcomings; having patience with someone who has let us down; or resisting the impulse to become offended when someone doesn't handle something the way we might have hoped. Charity is refusing to take advantage of another's weakness and being willing to forgive someone who has hurt us. Charity is expecting the best of each other.[2]

To expect the best in others and give them the benefit of the doubt when we don't think we're seeing their best is a tall order.

Throughout many years of serving in the Church, I've often wondered about my ability to fit in. I've questioned my competency and doctrinal orthodoxy. Still my fellow ward members have been patient with me and have given me the benefit of the doubt. Acting with that gift of charity, they've ignored my foibles and quirks, for which I am highly appreciative. Sometimes, however, they have failed to lovingly correct me when they could have, which has kept me from opportunities to grow and improve that I probably needed. Peter said that "charity shall cover [a] multitude of sins" (1 Peter 4:8), but, as the Prophet Joseph Smith clarified, charity doesn't just cover sins; it prevents them (see JST 1 Peter 4:8). Because secrecy sustains sin, covered sins only sit, fester, and erode away spiritual defenses until they plunge us into temptations we're no longer prepared to resist. True charity appropriately exposes sin and invites the sinner to accept the responsibility for changing. Some observant ward members have seen all too clearly my sins and weaknesses, and I must beg their forgiveness.

Any choice we make that keeps us from being close to God is sin, or spiritual separation from God. But sin is also anything we do that separates us from being close to each other. One reason the "whole world lieth in sin, and groaneth under darkness" (D&C 84:49) is because we try to make it on our own while remaining spiritually, emotionally, and physically separated from each other. We hesitate to carry each other's burdens or let them help us carry ours. We'll never find unity with our heavenly family until we find unity with an earthly family because if we're not one, we're not His (see D&C 38:27). We can't be one with Christ without seeking unity with those He has called us to serve.

I've heard members of the Church say that they can feel the Spirit more during a Sunday nature walk than they can in a priesthood meeting or Relief Society. That may be true, but that could be more because of their own attitudes and efforts than any fault of Church programs or other members. Still, what about all the hypocritical members of the Church? How are we supposed to tolerate them? Former BYU professor Eugene England explained the folly of saying, "I know the gospel is true, but the Church is just full of imperfect people." Of course it is! That's why it's such a marvelous instrument for helping us reach perfection. The Church forces us to work together with other imperfect people we'd likely never associate with of our own choosing. As we work with each other, we bring out each other's faults as well as our strengths, which gives us the opportunity to repent, forgive, and transform one other.[3] The gospel message is one of love and forgiveness, and the Lord's Church is the workshop for developing those attributes. Joseph Smith taught that the "greatest temporal and spiritual blessings which always come from faithfulness and concerted effort, never attended individual exertion or enterprise."[4] Perhaps we need in the Church the unique voices of these more restless souls to help call us to repentance. How can they help us if they're off in the woods worshipping by themselves?

On Labeling

When people do see weaknesses in other members, they often are not as Christlike in their observations and corrections as they should be. As a result, many in the Church feel unfairly judged, labeled, and rejected. Some of the members of my own family have felt that way. I often feel compelled to plead their causes. Still, we have to get over the bitterness and resentment that comes from being unfairly judged. It does no good to get angry at others for not measuring up to our expectations of true Christians. If we don't, then we're guilty of judging them for being judgmental! The only Christlike response is to gently correct them, if appropriate, and to continue to love them.

In his classic book *I and Thou*, the Jewish theologian Martin Buber, said that you can never hate a whole person. All you can do is take a few encounters with them that went bad, generalize them into a negative attribute or two, and then hate your generalizations of them as if they *were* the whole person. He says when you really get to know the person, the only sincere response to them is love.[5] That's why God can love us all—because he knows us each perfectly. As President Monson succinctly put it, "Charity is . . . resisting the impulse to categorize others."[6] It is assuming that people have a good heart even when their actions say otherwise. President Monson also explained, "There is really no way we can know the heart, the intentions, or the circumstances of someone who might say or do something we find reason to criticize. Thus the commandment: 'Judge not.' "[7] Unrighteous judgment is when we try to judge a person's heart or motivations.

Of course, we need to judge behavior. Christ said, "Judge righteous judgment" (JST Matthew 7:2). Righteous judgment is when we focus on the rightness or wrongness of people's actions. The prophet Mormon gave this counsel: "Wherefore, I show unto you the way to judge; for every *thing* which inviteth to do good, and to persuade to believe in Christ, is sent forth by the power and gift of Christ. . . . But whatsoever *thing* persuadeth men to do evil, and believe not in Christ, and deny him, and serve not God, then ye may know with a perfect knowledge it is of the devil" (Moroni 7:16–17; emphasis added). Mormon teaches us that righteous judgment focuses on things, not people. And Christ taught in the Sermon on the Mount that "by their fruits ye shall know them" (Matthew 7:20). In other words, while the Lord judges people by their hearts, we can judge only their actions. We need to judge situations, activities, behaviors, and observable attitudes.

Even labels like member and nonmember or active and inactive can do considerable damage and alienate people. Don't judge or label the people next to you on the pew, because no matter how familiar you think you are with their circumstances, you don't really know them at all. If you were to see all that's inside them, you probably wouldn't even recognize them. So judge actions when appropriate, but never think you know people well enough to judge their hearts. Joseph Smith explained once that God judges His children based on the light and knowledge He gives them. "For of him unto whom much is given much is required" (D&C 82:3), so inversely unto whom little is given, little is required. We have no idea how much light and truth the Lord has given them and therefore have no idea what He requires of them.

President Boyd K. Packer made it clear that each life comes with its own handpicked tests and trials: "Some are tested by poor health, some by a body that is deformed or homely. Others are tested by handsome and healthy bodies; some by the passion of youth; others by the erosions of age. Some suffer disappointment in marriage, family problems; others live in poverty and obscurity. Some (perhaps this is the hardest test) find ease and luxury. All are part of the test, and there is more equality in this testing than sometimes we suspect."[8] My own family seems to struggle more than usual under the debilitating burden of depression. My great-great-grandmother, great-grandfather, grandmother, and uncle all committed suicide. And many others in the family have wrestled with suicidal tendencies. We all must struggle to overcome feelings of inadequacy and insecurity or feelings of superiority and the fear that no one will understand our concerns. Sometimes we simply have to fight against the temptation to be offended.

What's at Stake

My mother is descended from pioneer stock. Her third great-grandfather served in the Mormon Battalion. Her parents were active in the Church for the first part of their married lives. But one Sunday, my grandpa took offense at a thoughtless comment by a member of the bishopric and vowed never to return. He kept his word. From then on, he played golf on Sundays. He became quite a good golfer. (We do spend a lot of time at meetings that could be used for other things!) Grandma and their three oldest children left the Church as well.

My mother was four years old when she decided she wanted to go to Church with or without her family. She made her father drive her every Sunday. Her mother smoked like a chimney at home, so my mother often smelled like smoke when she attended Church, but she didn't care. When she was in high school, she made her father drive her to early morning seminary every morning.

In her senior year, my mother had a science teacher she greatly admired who was an atheist. He was one of the kindest, most thoughtful people she had ever met. Her parents had the restored gospel but didn't seem to get much out of it. Her teacher didn't have any religious backing for his values, yet he seemed to be happily living a meaningful life of service to others. My mother began to wonder if religion really helped or hindered in the pursuit of a good life. She decided she needed to investigate the claims of religion for herself, so she began attending as many different churches as she could find and reading their scriptures and literature. She went to her science teacher's home, met his wife and children, and saw how they lived. She also went to her seminary teacher's home and saw his family, then compared the two. She came to realize that the contention and strife in her home was because of their failure to live the gospel message. She concluded that, despite all her concerns and unanswered questions, she really was feeling the Lord's influence on her journey and she needed to stay with the Church.

Eventually, my mother married in the temple and raised four children in the Church. Despite lingering ambiguities, she found enough answers to stay her course in the faith and she endured joyfully to the end. Today, she has fifteen grandchildren who call her blessed because of the legacy she left behind.

I don't know how my mother found the strength and determination to attend Church week after week with people mocking her there and often at home. I guess she discovered early in life that the only approval that really matters is that of the Lord when He sends His Spirit to let us know we're on the right path. This is His work, and The Church of Jesus Christ of Latter-day Saints is His kingdom that offers the ordinances of salvation. My mother saw firsthand what can happen to good people who—for whatever reason—leave the Church. The light and joy of gospel living dissipates, and they lose that distinctive Mormon sparkle in their eye. They also lose their connection with the ordinances of salvation and the accompanying promises of peace in this life and eternal life in the world to come.

When my mother embarked on her journey, she had to rummage through libraries and go out actively to find people to help her. Today, the faith quests that people are taking are often beginning and ending online. Folks are going on the Internet and finding critics taking issue with the history and doctrine of the Church. What most fail to realize is the new issues they think they are discovering have been around for a long time, but they are just now getting retreaded and recycled with the ubiquitous power of the Internet. Just as the questions have been around for a long time, so have many of the answers. The Church hasn't been hiding anything—it just hasn't been advertising for its detractors. Almost every argument used against the Church has been dealt with in the *Ensign* or *BYU Studies* over the years. Now inquirers can go to lds.org/topics or fairmormon.org and find thoughtful rebuttals to most anti-Mormon claims. It can be comforting to know that other intelligent people have grappled with similar questions and yet have managed to continue in the faith. Estrangement is one of Satan's ultimate weapons.

Many feel that they are the strange ones and don't fit in with the mainstream members of the Church because of the uniqueness of their circumstances or their thinking. But there is a place for them. In President Dieter F. Uchtdorf's conference address "Come, Join with Us," he made this plea to those who feel they don't fit in: "If you could see into our hearts, you would probably find that you fit in better than you suppose. You might be surprised to find that we have yearnings and struggles and hopes similar to yours. Your background or upbringing might seem different from what you perceive in many Latter-day Saints, but that could be a blessing. Brothers and sisters, dear friends, we need your unique talents and perspectives. The diversity of persons and peoples all around the globe is a strength of this Church."[9]

At times as a Mormon, I have felt like a flute-playing giraffe at a piano recital. Despite our challenges though, there is a place for all of God's children in His Church and kingdom. The Lord's message is "at-one-ment"—the overcoming of differences to find peace in a unity amid diversity. Whatever our questions may be, there is a place for us (and our broken families) in the Church. And it's the ordinances and covenants of the Church that will help us overcome our differences and bring us back into the Lord's presence. Through the Atonement of Christ, we can be made whole. Only He can do it. Only we can let Him.

Discovering Testimony and Resolving Doubts

"Whatever choice we make, we make it at our peril."[1]

—William James

When I was a senior in high school, I had a crush on Amy Weiss. She was bright, funny, and always tried to include everyone in Church activities. She was a strong member of our ward youth group and worked hard to keep us together against all the opposition to our values that we faced at the high school.

Toward the end of our senior year, Amy stood up on a fast Sunday to bear her testimony. I remember thinking how awesome it was that she was getting up in front of the whole ward and realized I had never heard her bear her testimony. I think I even took out a pen and got prepared to take notes.

Then Amy began to speak and proceeded to blow me away. She said that she didn't have a testimony of the gospel. She loved the Church and hoped it was true. She was trying to find out for herself. Then she closed and sat down.

I didn't take any notes. I remember wondering if she had broken some sort of rule. Can you really say that in testimony meeting? I don't think I would've been more shocked if she had stood up and declared that she'd decided she was a kosher pickle! Yet as I reflected on what she had done, I began to admire her for her honesty and sincerity. Later, I discovered that her father wasn't a member of the Church and was rather hostile toward it. He had filled Amy with a lot of doubts, and she finally decided it was time to resolve them for herself.

After graduation, I didn't see Amy again for a few years. I went on my mission and afterward reenrolled at BYU. One of the first weeks of the new semester, I saw a young lady coming toward me near the administration building and recognized her immediately. It was Amy, and she was floating down the walkway with an angelic smile. We greeted each other warmly and I asked how she was. She declared triumphantly that she was getting married in the temple in two weeks. I didn't have to ask her if she'd ever discovered her testimony. She wore it in her countenance. I could see the love of the Lord sparkling in her eyes.

Seeking Answers

While we all must struggle with our own questions and issues, the answer is the same for each of us. Our only hope is to find and develop a personal relationship with the Lord, who is mighty to save. Job of the Old Testament was unjustly labeled and criticized by his wife and friends. He struggled bitterly, trying to understand why he had to suffer so much. Apparently he never found an explanation in this life. God finally did answer his prayers though. He spoke to him from a whirlwind and assured him that there was a place for him in the divine plan. That was enough of an answer to satisfy Job: "I have heard of thee by the hearing of the ear: but now mine eye seeth thee" (Job 42:5). His whole life Job had heard about God and His plan, but now he had a prayer answered for himself and he knew God was really there. As Dennis Rasmussen wrote, "Deeper than the desire to know is the desire to be known. Man's fundamental need is not to ask a question but to respond to one. Only by responding do I learn to be responsible; only by responding do I learn to care about something beyond myself."[2] Sometimes communication with the Lord is slow in developing. But if we persist, answers do come. It's our relationship with the Answerer that makes all the difference.

At times, the Lord gives us answers to different questions than to the ones we are seeking. After the Fall, Adam asked the Lord, "Why is it that men must repent and be baptized in water?" The answer came, but to a different question: "Behold I have forgiven thee thy transgression in the Garden of Eden" (Moses 6:53). Why this answer? Perhaps Adam was using a doctrinal question as a smokescreen for the real issue. He was terrified that, through his transgression, perhaps he had blown everything. The Lord answered, reassuring him that all was not lost and that things would turn out well in the end. Whatever we think our issues are, our greatest need is to reconnect with the loving Lord, who *will* provide comfort and answers.

The real sin is when we allow fear, apathy, or disbelief to keep us from asking our questions. The Lord was "weary" with the wicked King Ahaz because he said, "I will not ask" (Isaiah 7:12–13). And when Laman and Lemuel refused to go the Lord with their questions about Lehi's dream, Nephi replied, "Do ye not remember the things which the Lord hath said?—If ye will not harden your hearts, and ask me in faith, believing that ye shall receive, with diligence in keeping my commandments, surely these things shall be made known unto you" (1 Nephi 15:11). The Lord wants us to ask Him our questions so He can help us find answers and, more important, so we can find Him.

When we do find Him, we can be sure that He will send us out to find our brothers and sisters. The Jewish theologian Martin Buber shared his conviction that "all revelation is a summons and a sending."[3] In other words, the Lord calls us to Him first and then sends us out to minister to others. President Henry B. Eyring said, "If you trust God enough to listen for His message in every sermon, song, and prayer in this conference, you will find it. And if you then go and do what He would have you do, your power to trust Him will grow, and in time you will be overwhelmed with gratitude to find that He has come to trust you."[4] The Lord invites us to wear out our lives in His service, and throughout our seemingly endless meetings and conferences, He will show us what He expects of us, which is nothing less than a total sacrifice. As President Howard W. Hunter once said, "Ultimately, what our Father in Heaven will require of us is more than a contribution; it is a total commitment, a complete devotion, all that we are and all that we can be."[5] That commitment will always include service in His Church, as well as in our families and communities.

Difficult Journeys

As a child, I was a victim of abuse. Fortunately, my experiences were isolated incidents by strangers and not the repeated abuse by family members that has scarred the lives of too many of God's children. Still, over the years I had to deal with the severe effects of another's sins on my own life. I've had to deal with emotional baggage that has made it hard to connect with others. I've had to learn to deny myself of rationalizations and self-justifications to take responsibility for my own growth. I've had to learn to serve others despite my natural tendency to withdraw. Yet I've also had to simply accept some things about myself and be tolerant of my own weaknesses. As I have repented of my own mistakes and turned to the Lord for help in forgiving myself and others, I've watched my faith grow. As someone once said, "Today's tests are tomorrow's testimony."

While there may have been times when I felt like giving up on myself, the Church, or the Lord's promises to help me change, in the end I keep returning to the faith of my fathers. One reason is because of the strong testimonies others have shared with me. Alma taught Korihor that all of us have multiple witnesses of God's presence in our lives. Our families, our ward members, the prophets, the scriptures, and even God's natural creations around us call out to us, witnessing of God's redeeming love (see Alma 30:44), though eventually we have to discover our own testimonies. The storms and sorrows of life are too overwhelming to simply take the word of others that living the gospel is going to be worth it in the end.

As I have marched along the gospel trail in search of testimony, I've encountered four vital components of it that I wish to share briefly with you. They are experience, reason, the Spirit, and choice.

Experience

In one of John's Epistles, he explained his testimony in this way: "That which was from the beginning, which we have heard, which we have seen with our eyes, which we have looked upon, and our hands have handled, of the Word of life . . . declare we unto you, that ye also may have fellowship with us" (1 John 1:1–3). John's testimony was sharing with others the truths he had seen and heard from the Savior. He was a witness of the goodness of God.

Like John, I've seen and heard much of God's goodness, and one of the most important aspects of my testimony is all that experience. I've seen the Church work in my life. I've seen it work in the lives of others. It hasn't always worked perfectly—after all, it is a volunteer organization. Yet it has functioned well enough to convince me that it's an effective instrument for carrying out God's work. (That it is the only true and living church upon the face of the whole earth is something I've learned by revelation and will discuss in a moment.) I've had prayers answered. I've seen His hand working miracles all around me. I saw a man in Mexico who had drunk alcohol every day for twenty years start reading the Book of Mormon. Over a period of months, he gave up drinking entirely and joined the Church with his grateful family. I'm sure their challenges were just beginning, but the change was real. I've seen over and over the redeeming love of Jesus Christ improving people's lives.

This testimony is not some mysterious thing inside me that I possess, but rather it's articulations of experiences that I share with others.

Reason

The restored gospel of Jesus Christ makes sense. I have spent many years as an armchair philosopher. I studied philosophy and theology in graduate school and received a master's degree in philosophy from Boston University. I even taught philosophy at BYU for seven years. In all that time, I've found the gospel to be resilient to virtually every critique from philosophical and anti-Mormon circles. It's remarkably consistent, persuasive, and relevant to the questions of old and of today.

Take for example the age-old question of the problem of evil. Philosophers and theologians have been wrangling for centuries over the issue of how an all-loving, all-powerful God, who creates everything out of nothing, could allow so much evil in the world. The gospel helps me make more sense of this issue. Joseph taught that God didn't create everything out of nothing, as many other Christians, Jews, and Muslims believe. God took intelligences that have always existed alongside Himself and gave us spirit bodies and every other opportunity to grow into beings like Him. But the possibility of suffering and other evils has always existed. God's omnipotence is the ability to do everything within the limits of eternal truths and eternal beings to entice His children to love and follow Him. If I don't like who I am, I can't blame God because He didn't create my intelligence. All He has been doing is giving me blessing upon blessing to add to what I've always been. He gives me the agency to choose for myself how much I want to become like Him. Evil happens because we're forever agents unto ourselves.

I know that the Prophet's inspired insights into this ancient debate lead to more questions. I find that exciting. Some of the questions I uncover may even seem troubling at first, but the answers I've found fill me with hope that there will be even more forthcoming if I simply hold on tenaciously to my quest. The restored gospel really does make sense, and it helps me make sense of the questions that matter most.

However, what the gospel does best is inspire me to continue to act with faith even when I can't reason through all the problems at hand. While Christ was hanging on the cross, He cried out, "My God, my God, why hast thou forsaken me?" (Matthew 27:46). In that moment, there was no reply. All He could do was to finish His work without an answer. When Joseph and other Saints were rotting in Liberty Jail while the members of the Church were being persecuted and driven from Missouri, Joseph cried out, "O God, where art thou? And where is the pavilion that covereth thy hiding place?" (D&C 121:1). He pleaded to know why the Saints had to suffer and when the Lord would fight back for them. Again, there were no answers given—just the reassurance that He was still with them through all the suffering and they would one day rise above it, that "thine adversity and thine afflictions shall be but a small moment; and then, if thou endure it well, God shall exalt thee on high" (D&C 121:7–8). God reassures us that all this evil and suffering is, in fact, necessary for our growth and that Christ went through it too (D&C 122:7–8).

In a 2014 general conference address, Elder Larry S. Kacher of the Seventy shared his struggles with family, friends, and his own insecurities after joining the Church. Everyone seemed to pelt him with questions he couldn't answer. Even after considering the peace and joy the gospel had brought into his life, he was troubled:

> Still, there were many questions I could not answer. How would I address the uncertainty they created? Rather than allow them to destroy the peace and happiness that had come into my life, I chose to set them aside for a season, trusting that in the Lord's time, He would reveal all things. I found solace in His statement to the Prophet Joseph: "Behold, ye are little children and ye cannot bear all things now; ye must grow in grace and in the knowledge of the truth." I chose not to forsake what I knew to be true by following an unknown and a questionable current—a potential "riptide."[6]

Ultimately, it's because the world doesn't always make sense that I'm driven beyond my own ability to reason. Perhaps it's these incompletely answered puzzles and perplexities that drive my soul to God for answers. They prepare me to hear the things of the Spirit.

The Spirit

The spiritual element of my testimony comes through the confirmation of the Holy Ghost. When I was in ninth-grade seminary, our teacher challenged us to read and pray about the Book of Mormon. I read Alma's simple description of how he discovered the truth of the gospel: "I testify unto you that I do know that these things whereof I have spoken are true. And how do ye suppose that I know of their surety? Behold, I say unto you they are made known unto me by the Holy Spirit of God. Behold, I have fasted and prayed many days that I might know these things of myself. And now I do know of myself that they are true; for the Lord God hath made them manifest unto me by his Holy Spirit; and this is the spirit of revelation which is in me" (Alma 5:45–46). I thought if Alma could find out for himself, why couldn't I?

I read the entire Book of Mormon during the summer after ninth grade. I reached the end while I was attending scout camp near San Diego, California, with ten thousand scouts. Toward the end of the week, we had a meeting that I wasn't resonating with, so I did something I didn't do very often as a kid—I ditched. I returned to our empty tent, zipped myself in, and finished reading Moroni 10. Then I got on my knees and prayed. I told the Lord I had read His book and now needed to know if it was true. I said I wasn't in too much of a hurry to get back to my meeting, so I would just wait for an answer. I can't recall how long I was there, but I do recall exactly what happened next. It was as if someone unzipped the roof of the tent and poured a bucket of love over my head. I felt a tangible rush of energy that went down my spine and out the tips of my fingers and toes. With the feeling came a mental assurance that it's all true. Joseph Smith really was a prophet. The Lord's promise was true: "Yea, behold, I will tell you in your mind and in your heart, by the Holy Ghost, which shall come upon you" (D&C 8:2). It happened to me.

Now, I don't have dramatic, spiritual experiences like that often, but frequently when I read the Book of Mormon I do feel something. The feeling comes in different ways, and I do sometimes have difficulty discerning what the Lord is trying to communicate. Still, I recognize that the Spirit is working with me. My heart has been warmed, my mind has been enlightened, and my body has been invigorated by the mighty Spirit of God.

I understand that many people struggle to recognize the Spirit working in their lives. They're in good company. The repentant Lamanites in Nephi's day, right before the Savior's visit, were "baptized with fire and with the Holy Ghost, and they knew it not" (3 Nephi 9:20). In Joseph Smith's day, Oliver Cowdery struggled to recognize the Spirit working in his life. Even after seeing miracles, he began to wonder if it was real. It troubled him that he was having these concerns, but the Lord's answer was reassuring: "Verily, verily, I say unto thee, blessed art thou for what thou hast done; for thou hast inquired of me, and behold, as often as thou hast inquired thou hast received instruction of my Spirit. If it had not been so, thou wouldst not have come to the place where thou art at this time" (D&C 6:14). In our lives, the Lord seems to be reassuring us that we really have been guided by His Spirit all along the way—even if we haven't recognized it. If we search our memories, we'll find that there were times when we felt God's love for us. It was His Spirit communicating the Lord's presence to us. He asks us, "Did I not speak peace to your mind concerning the matter? What greater witness can you have than from God?" (D&C 6:23). If we don't give up the quest, peace will eventually come again.

We must not be discouraged if that peace is slow in arriving. President Howard W. Hunter made this comforting statement:

> I have sympathy for young men and young women when honest doubts enter their minds and they engage in the great conflict of resolving doubts. These doubts can be resolved, if they have an honest desire to know the truth, by exercising moral, spiritual, and mental effort. They will emerge from the conflict into a firmer, stronger, larger faith because of the struggle. They have gone from a simple, trusting faith, through doubt and conflict, into a solid substantial faith which ripens into testimony.[7]

Questioning doesn't have to be antagonistic to the things of the Spirit. If pursued in the right way, it can actually further our quest. It may take time, effort, sorrow, and great patience, but if we learn to rely on what we know while struggling with our concerns, answers will come. Perhaps, as with a butterfly struggling to get out of its cocoon, the effort will make us all the stronger.

Once while teaching at the MTC in Provo, I met a remarkable woman I'll call Susan. She was preparing to serve a Spanish-speaking mission and was "thrusting in [her] sickle with all [her] might." But she had a heavy load of resistance working against her at home. Her parents and older siblings had become disaffected from the Church for "doctrinal reasons" and had their names removed from the records of the Church. They were diametrically opposed to her serving a mission and bombarded her with all the anti-Mormon literature they could find or cook up themselves. With this background, Susan had sought out her own testimony of the gospel. She read, fasted, and prayed—and came up empty. She decided to go on a mission anyway, trusting that if the Church were true, somehow the Lord would let her know along the way.

I saw this courageous young lady at BYU a few months after her mission. Through her self-sacrificing service, Susan had found the testimony she was seeking. It wasn't the "burning bush" type that I had experienced, but, like Oliver Cowdery, she finally recognized that the Spirit *was* working in her life and she could dedicate herself to building the Lord's kingdom in spite of her family's rejection. Her testimony—her witnessing of how the Lord had worked in her life—was different than mine, but it was just as real and was inspiring her and others through her unique life's mission.

Choice

The fourth element of my testimony, the one that permeates and packages all the others, is choice. It may be the most difficult for some people to understand, but I really do believe it plays an essential role in my witness of the gospel. Elder Neil L. Andersen said once in general conference that "faith is not only a feeling; it is a decision."[8] I agree. Elder Richard G. Scott highlighted the role of choice in testimony when he said, "A testimony is not emotion. It is the very essence of character woven from threads born of countless correct decisions."[9] Because no amount of evidence will be convincing if I choose to reject it, there will always be the need for me to *choose* a life of faith.

Elder Andersen went on to explain further the role of choice in religious living in a later general conference address:

> I promise you, as you choose not to be offended or ashamed, you will feel His love and approval. You will know that you are becoming more like Him.
>
> Will we understand everything? Of course not. We will put some issues on the shelf to be understood at a later time.
>
> Will everything be fair? It will not. We will accept some things we cannot fix and forgive others when it hurts.
>
> Will we feel separated on occasion from those around us? Absolutely.
>
> Will we be astonished at times to see the anger a few feel toward the Lord's Church and their efforts to steal the struggling faith of the weak? Yes. But this will not deter the growth or destiny of the Church, nor need it impede the spiritual progress of each of us as disciples of the Lord Jesus Christ.[10]

When my experience, my intellect, or the Spirit fails to solve my problems the way I want now, I have the choice of believing and living the life of a faithful Saint anyway. That's why I was sent here to experience mortality: "And we will prove them herewith, to see if they will do all things whatsoever the Lord their God shall command them" (Abraham 3:25), especially when things get complicated.

Much has been said in general conference about the role of choice in testimony. Bishop Richard C. Edgley, formerly of the Presiding

Bishopric, highlighted this connection: "If your testimony is immature, untested, and insecure, *choose* to 'exercise [even] a particle of faith'; *choose* to 'experiment upon [His] words' (Alma 32:27)."[11] And President Henry B. Eyring told the young women of the Church that choice is as essential as prayer in the discovery of testimony. As we choose to act on the doctrines of the gospel, their fruits begin to grow in our lives, which confirms their truthfulness.[12] Why is choice such an elemental part of a testimony? Perhaps it's because the knowledge that saves and transforms us isn't a passive collection of facts that we accumulate. It's an interaction with people (mortal and divine). It's an orientation toward the world. It's a way of life.

I've voluntarily chosen a particular worldview and way of life. As a teenager in seminary studying, later in the temple and as a missionary, and repeatedly since those events, I've chosen the Mormon way as my way. I've given my life to the Lord and to The Church of Jesus Christ of Latter-day Saints. I've never regretted that decision and had to repeat it often in the face of opposition. I resolved to be in this for the long haul. To paraphrase the Apostle Paul, I'm persuaded that neither death, nor life, nor friend, nor family, nor career, nor monetary concerns, nor textual deconstruction, nor biblical criticism, nor historical anomaly, nor petty personal affront, nor global social concern, nor any other distraction shall be able to separate me from the love of God, which is in Christ Jesus and in His Church (see Romans 8:38–39).

I have *chosen* that, even if it ultimately turns out that we were all deceived and death really does end everything like the secularists tell us (and I must admit that even with all my gospel-confirming experiences, the thought has crossed my mind). My life is happier, more meaningful, and more fulfilled for believing and living the gospel. I would *not* be happier if I were to eat, drink, and be merry with the rest of the world. I would *not* be happier if I were to dedicate myself to the humanistic quest for a social utopia. I would *not* be happier in a simple, non-denominational Christian church somewhere, just trying to be good. My life is blessed beyond compare here and now for the LDS stories, ordinances, and doctrines that ennoble, empower, and exalt individuals and families. It really is worth the sacrifice to be a Latter-day Saint.

As I read Alma's account of growing faith and testimony in Alma 32:28, I wonder if he didn't have in mind something like these four aspects of testimony I've discussed. He describes the word of God that begins to "swell within your breasts" (the Spirit), to "enlarge my soul" (experience), to "enlighten my understanding" (reason), and to "be delicious to me" (choice). Even if I've taken Alma too much out of context, his point is still that there are multiple witnesses for our faith if we look for them.

Believing

So with my experience, reasoning, spirit, and decisions, I can testify that I *believe* God lives and loves us all as His family. I believe—and there is nothing less respectable about belief than knowledge. In their religious forms, they are both gifts of the Spirit (see D&C 46:13–14). In fact, sometimes the only difference in saying "I believe" and "I know" is that the latter statement can refuse to recognize human fallibility. Belief at times can be more passionate, more personal, and more committed than knowledge. And Paul warned us about claiming to know too much. He said, "Knowledge puffeth up, but charity edifieth. And if any man think that he knoweth any thing, he knoweth nothing yet as he ought to know" (1 Corinthians 8:1–2). Why? Perhaps it's because the knowledge that matters most is not the understanding of a proposition, but rather the familiarity with a person. "If any man love God, the same is known of him" (1 Corinthians 8:3). In a recent general conference, Jeffrey R. Holland emphasized the power of belief: "I [tell you] with all the fervor of my soul that *belief* is a precious word, an even more precious act, and [you] need never apologize for 'only believing.' I [tell you] that Christ Himself said, 'Be not afraid, only believe.'"[13]

So I'm comfortable saying I believe in The Church of Jesus Christ of Latter-day Saints. I believe in the Bible and the Book of Mormon. I believe in the divine calling of Joseph Smith and of the living prophet. I believe in the reality of personal revelation; I have received it. My testimony is my sharing of these beliefs with you. The knowledge that saves and exalts is my familiarity and closeness with Christ and with you.

Remembering

I'm convinced that the greatest threat to my testimony is that I'll forget what I've experienced, what I've done, what I've promised at holy altars, or what I've believed. President Spencer W. Kimball often said that the most important word in the English language is *remember*.[14] He wasn't talking about simple recall; his usage was more sacramental. If to *dis*-member is to pull apart, perhaps to *re*-member is to put back together again to recreate a prior wholeness. Such remembrance can be a part of redemption. It's our part to play in the "at-one-ment" with Christ.[15]

So I strive to remember. I search and ponder the scriptures. I write my own "scriptures" in my journal. I talk repeatedly with you about the same solemn issues—not because I am spending my "time in nothing else, but either to tell, or to hear some new thing," as the philosophical Athenians were doing in Paul's day (Acts 17:21). It's because I desperately desire to remember the questions, answers, feelings, promises, and experiences so that the Lord can put them all back together again in a redeemed life that includes you.

The greatest thing you could ever do for me is to win my trust and to ask me to share my burdens with you. It is our fellowship with the Saints that provides us such opportunities.

I resonate with the Apostle Paul's last words in Robert Frost's play entitled "A Masque of Mercy":

> The root of [it all is this:]
> We have to stay afraid deep in our souls
> [That] our sacrifice—the best we have to offer,
> And not our worst nor second best, our best,
> Our very best, our lives laid down like Jonah's,
> Our lives laid down in war and peace—may not
> Be found acceptable in Heaven's sight.
> And that they may be is the only prayer
> Worth praying. May my sacrifice
> Be found acceptable in Heaven's sight.[16]

I echo Frost's sentiment: May we do our best to see that our sacrifice be found acceptable in Heaven's sight. May we give the best we have to our families, the Church, and the Lord. May we, as Amaleki encouraged, offer our "whole souls as an offering unto him" (Omni 1:26). And may we give each other the benefit of the doubt—that they are doing their best too.

Reading and Writing Scripture

"First we make our habits, then our habits make us."[1]

—Charles C. Noble

I recently had a student with serious struggles in her life. This sweet young lady's parents had divorced, remarried, and were suffering from serious financial woes. On top of that, her mother was diagnosed with cancer. My student began to question if the Lord really cared about her and her family. She kept hearing about the power of the word of God, so she wrote me a note wondering if the scriptures really could help with any of her personal challenges.

"Can the scriptures answer all of my problems?" That seems like a legitimate question. After all, they were written so long ago in such different cultural contexts. Sometimes the scriptures can even seem boring when I read them. Mark Twain famously quipped that the Book of Mormon was "chloroform in print." He went on to ridicule it by saying that if "Joseph Smith composed this book, the act was a miracle—keeping awake while he did it was, at any rate."[2] Some young people might agree with Twain, using scripture study as a mild sedative to get them peacefully to sleep at night. Yet here's a promise from President Boyd K. Packer: "If [you] are acquainted with the revelations, there is no question—personal or political or occupational—that need go unanswered. Therein is contained the fullness of the everlasting gospel. Therein we find principles of truth that will resolve every confusion and every problem and every dilemma that will face the human family or any individual in it."[3] So if I believe President Packer's promise—and I do—the question transforms from "How do I stay awake?" to "How do I use the scriptures to solve all my problems?"

I'm constantly seeking new ways to make my scripture study more meaningful. Yet too often I resort to the standby method of scripture "study" where I just open the book randomly, point to a verse, and start reading. My hope is that I will be mysteriously guided to the right verse that will speak to my problems. You might recognize this primitive approach to scripture study. It's a popular one with my students because it requires little effort.

A friend of mine at one point was trying to decide whether to buy a BMW or a Honda. He opened his Book of Mormon randomly and landed on 1 Nephi 10:13: "Wherefore, he said it must needs be that we should be led with *one accord* into the land of promise" (emphasis added). That was enough to convince him to buy the Honda!

Sometimes this method seems to work, so we often go back to it. One of the weaknesses of this kind of approach, however, is that it deals too much with the spirit of sign-seeking. It says, in essence, "I'm desperate for divine inspiration that'll work out the messes and challenges of my life, but I'm not willing to pay the price to get it. I just want the Lord to give it to me on a silver platter." The Lord is merciful enough with our weaknesses to sometimes give us help when we seek it this way. But if this is the *only* tool in our box of scripture study skills, we have a pathetic toolbox. Perhaps the Lord's rebuke to Oliver Cowdery is appropriate here: "you took no thought save it was to ask me" (D&C 9:7). Asking isn't enough. He says that, in the process of getting revelation, "you must study it out in your mind" (D&C 9:8).

Study Tips

Fortunately, Church leaders have given us tips on how to improve our scripture studying. In a CES fireside, Elder David A. Bednar spoke about "a reservoir of living water."[4] The reservoir is, of course, the scriptures, which we are already familiar with. Yet, according to Elder Bednar, we have to learn better ways of drawing out the water.

The water is personal revelation. He taught that we must first get in the habit of reading the standard works from beginning to end. This will help us become better acquainted with the language, characters, and stories of the books. Simply skimming a random verse now and then isn't enough. We must also study the scriptures by topic, learning to use the Topical Guide to answer questions that arise from our reading. Finally, we must learn how to search the scriptures for connections, patterns, and themes that will broaden and deepen our understanding of God's plan. Only then will we learn what it means to truly feast on the word rather than merely nibble. In other words, we need to get in the habit of reading the scriptures chapter by chapter. Still, that will not be enough to draw out the living water to quench our thirsty spirits—we have to learn to dig deeper.

A few years after Elder Bednar's talk, President Henry B. Eyring spoke in general conference about serving with the Spirit. He said we must learn to move beyond reading and studying the scriptures, which are merely tools to a greater end: "Reading, studying, and pondering are not the same. We read words and we may get ideas. We study and we may discover patterns and connections in scripture. But when we ponder, we invite revelation by the Spirit. Pondering, to me, is the thinking and the praying I do after reading and studying in the scriptures carefully."[5] President Eyring went on to say that as we ponder on what we've studied in the scriptures, we invite the Spirit to guide us in our service to others during the day, which is the main purpose of scripture study.

In another general conference address, Primary General President Cheryl C. Lant gave some tips for going deeper into the scriptures. She taught us to delight in them, to ponder them, and to even learn (in a way) to write them. She suggested that we read them a little in the morning as well as at night to invite the Spirit to be with us throughout the day. She recommended we pray as we read—not only to have a witness that the scriptures are true, but also to have the Spirit teach us what we need to do and become in our lives. Sister Lant urged us to apply the doctrines and principles we gleaned from the scriptures so that they could become "written in [our lives]."[6] As we learn to really ponder the scriptures we read throughout the day and throughout our lives, they'll begin to transform our thoughts, feelings, and actions in ways that will bring us closer to Christ. Effective scripture study invites the Holy Ghost, who refashions us in the Savior's image.

A Personal Urim and Thummim

While acting as scribe for Joseph during the translation of the Book of Mormon, Oliver Cowdery asked for the Lord's help. In reply, he received the promise that the Lord would speak to him by revelation and he was promised another gift as well. "Now this is not all thy gift; for you have another gift, which is the gift of Aaron; behold, it has told you many things" (D&C 8:6). The Lord promised that this gift was something tangible, that "you shall hold it in your hands, and do marvelous works" (D&C 8:8) and "therefore, whatsoever you shall ask me to tell you by that means, that will I grant unto you" (D&C 8:9). And with this gift Oliver could even "know the mysteries of God" (D&C 8:11). What was this powerful gift of Aaron that'd bring Oliver such mighty answers?

The Lord designed high priest's clothing for Aaron to represent the House of Israel in the Tabernacle. It included a "breastplate of judgment" that was to be worn over the chest. The breastplate had a little pocket for carrying two stones. "And thou shalt put in the breastplate of judgment the Urim and the Thummim; and they shall be upon Aaron's heart, when he goeth in before the Lord" (Exodus 28:30). The Urim and Thummim were two precious stones that Aaron could use as if they were receivers for picking up revelations from God (see Numbers 27:21 and 1 Samuel 28:6). A seer was someone who could use the Urim and Thummim (see Mosiah 8:13 and Joseph Smith—History 1:35). It was this ancient gift of seership—being able to use the Urim and Thummim—that the Lord promised to Oliver.[7]

You may be thinking, *That's great for him, but what does that have to do with me and the assistance I need for the problems I face?* Elder Dallin H. Oaks said, "We do not overstate the point when we say that the scriptures can be a Urim and Thummim to assist each of us to receive personal revelation."[8] Just as Aaron wore the Urim and Thummim next to his heart, if we treasure up the word in our minds and hearts, it can become a receiver for spiritual reception as well.

When we learn to use the scriptures that way, we'll share in Aaron and Oliver's gift. As Brigham Young explained,

> My knowledge is, if you will follow the teachings of Jesus Christ and his Apostles, as recorded in the New Testament, every man and woman will be put in possession of the Holy Ghost; every person will become a Prophet, Seer, and Revelator, and an expounder of truth. They will know things that are, that will be, and that have been. They will understand things in heaven, things on the earth, and things under the earth, things of time, and things of eternity, according to their several callings and capacities.[9]

We won't start receiving revelations for the Church—only the prophet is entitled to that. But in our own "callings and capacities," in our own stewardships, we will become prophets, seers, and revelators. That's quite a promise! To receive these blessings, we have to learn to use our scriptures the way Joseph, Oliver, and Aaron used the Urim and Thummim: as spiritual intensifiers to pick up revelation in order to solve problems we're facing. So how do we do that?

Memorizing Scriptures

Memorizing scriptural passages can help. Elder Vaughn J. Featherstone, an emeritus member of the Seventy, gave this suggestion for maximizing scripture power: "When you memorize something, it becomes a part of you and can be called upon at will to give you strength when there seems to be no strength left."[10] If we want the word "written in [our lives]," to really plant the word in our hearts and let it grow and take over who we are and what we become, there is no better way than to work out a system of regularly memorizing key passages of scripture. It takes persistent effort and determination, and everyone has to find a system that works for them. I knew a woman who memorized a passage every day. Each morning, she would write it on a card and repeat it aloud several times, reviewing it throughout the day. It worked great for her. I feel successful if I learn one or two new ones a year!

Some time ago, I was teaching institute in another state at a city college. Every day as I rode my bike to work, I'd meet interesting people. One of those was a young woman riding her electric wheelchair to the college. Her body seemed badly distorted, but she always had a bright smile on her face. I stopped and chatted with her one day, and she shared her story with me in a greatly slurred but cheerful voice.

She said her name was Mercy Flyer. She had grown up a Christian and had always believed in God. But as an older teenager, she began to struggle with depression and feelings of worthlessness. One day, she decided her life was no longer worth living, so she devised a plan to end it. She entered her car and began accelerating toward a brick wall. Just before impact, however, a memory of a scripture she'd memorized as a child in her Baptist Sunday School class came racing through her mind: "Thou shalt not kill!" She slammed on her brakes, which slowed her down enough before hitting the wall to save her life. She was in a coma for six months and came out a quadriplegic, but she survived. Now she'd dedicated her life to spreading her conviction that God indeed lives and loves us as His children and that life is worth living.

The more scriptures we've memorized and have floating through our minds and hearts, the more the Lord can draw upon them at the right moment to bless us in countless ways. Most of those ways will likely turn out to be less dramatic than Mercy Flyer's experience. But we may be surprised at how directly the memorized word of God will apply to the situations of our day-to-day affairs—even possibly saving our physical or spiritual lives.

Likening Scriptures

Nephi explained one of the more powerful study tools for getting the most out of the scriptures. He knew the background and culture of the Jews, so he understood the ancient prophets in context. But when it came time to teach his people the word, he reported that he simply "did liken all scriptures unto us, that it might be for our profit and learning" (1 Nephi 19:23). He knew that to get the most out of the scriptures, we have to learn to apply them—first to see ourselves in them, and then to pull out the principles we find and relate them to our day-to-day lives. One way of doing this is to read our own names into the scriptures.

When I returned from my mission to Mexico City, I wanted nothing more than to get married in the temple and start raising a family. In fact, I was so eager that my family started placing friendly bets on how many months it'd take before I was married. But I was shy around women and clueless about courting; four years later, I was still just as single as ever and not making any real progress. I began to wonder if there was any hope for me. I prayed, fasted, spoke with trusted family members and friends, and I spent a lot of time questioning my ability to maintain a serious relationship.

Then one day a friend pointed me to a passage in the Doctrine and Covenants that spoke to my heart. It was D&C 98:1–3. As I read, I was surprised to see my own name and my own experience jump off the page at me. This is how I read it:

> Verily I say unto you my friend, Chad, fear not, let your heart be comforted; yea, rejoice evermore, and in everything give thanks, including your several years of post-mission bachelorhood;
>
> Waiting patiently on the Lord, for your prayers, Chad, have entered into the ears of the Lord of Sabaoth, and are recorded with this seal and testament—the Lord hath sworn and decreed that they shall be granted.
>
> Therefore, he giveth this promise unto you, Chad, with an immutable covenant that they shall be fulfilled; and all things wherewith you feel like you have been afflicted in your single state shall work together for your good, and to my name's glory, saith the Lord.

I felt a little like young Joseph Smith in that never before did any passage of scripture come with more power to the heart of man than this did at this time to mine. I knew that the Lord was still with me in my journey and that things were going to work out.

It still took a few years for me to find Stacy. Yet this scripture—just as I read it with all the personalizing touches—was literally fulfilled. And it infused me with the hope and courage to continue until I got there. Only the Spirit can help us appropriately apply scripture to our individual situations, but placing our names there can be a powerful study tool. Using the footnotes is another.

Footnotes

A few years ago, I was struggling with feelings of stagnation in both my life and my scripture study. One day, I was straightening desks in my classroom when I discovered a blue missionary edition of the Book of Mormon under a chair on the back row. I opened it up, looking for a name so I could return it. There was no name, so I began flipping through the book.

I quickly noticed that the book had been marked up considerably from cover to cover. As I read the underlined passages and the comments written in the margins, I began to form a mental profile of the book's owner. I envisioned a bright young man (the handwriting didn't seem neat enough to be a young woman's) who had grown up in the Church and had a lot of unanswered questions. Perhaps someone challenged him to read the Book of Mormon for himself and gain a testimony of it. He seemed to take this challenge seriously. He cross-referenced the things he found with verses on nearby pages. He underlined references in the footnotes. He put question marks in the margins next to difficult passages. And he put stars by thoughts he seemed to particularly like.

Page after page, I followed this unknown student's journey through the Book of Mormon. I even found myself opening my own copy, marking passages he had marked in his. For an hour or two, I became absorbed in this thoughtful, sincere search, hoping he'd found his answers.

Then I got to 3 Nephi 20:37. He'd underlined three adjacent words and drawn big question marks in the margin. He was clearly puzzled. The words were "arise, sit down." Immediately, I could empathize with his confusion. Which was it—get up or sit down? It almost sounds like a high school football cheer: "Stand up, sit down, fight, fight, fight!" I knew from all his careful markings in the book up to then that the first thing he'd do is look at the footnotes. So I went down and discovered there are no footnotes for verse 37! Unfortunately, that's probably where he gave up. I could tell he was genuinely stumped and that this frustration seemed to have taken the wind out of his sails. There was no more highlighting in chapter 20 and little more throughout the remainder of the book. He'd clearly finished the book because he still underlined an occasional word or two now and then, but all the cross-referencing and marginal commentary were gone. My young investigator let this one seemingly unsolvable puzzle drain all the passion from his project.

Yet *my* enthusiasm was just awakening. I was determined to find out whether I could make sense of the stumbling block that'd hindered my student. My first thought was to reread the verse in its context, looking for clues as to its meaning. Verse 36 reads, "Awake, awake again, and put on thy strength, O Zion; put on thy beautiful garments, O Jerusalem, the holy city, for henceforth there shall no more come into thee the uncircumcised and the unclean." I thought that the passage sounded like something out of Isaiah. So I looked down at the footnotes for verse 36 and, sure enough, there it was: Isaiah 52:1.

By this time I was really getting excited. My fingers trembling with anticipation, I turned in my Old Testament to that reference. "Awake, awake; put on thy strength, O Zion. . ." It was the same verse. I guessed that Jesus must have been quoting Isaiah to the Nephites during His visit. So I continued with the following verse: "Shake thyself from the dust; arise, and sit down, O Jerusalem: loose thyself from the bands of thy neck, O captive daughter of Zion." It was almost exactly the same troubling passage in 3 Nephi 20. This time, however, I looked at the footnote and there was the answer! In the interpretive comment, I read the explanation of the peculiar wording in Isaiah: "Arise from the dust and sit down in dignity, being redeemed at last."

The Lord's chosen people, Israel, are a royal family. They're destined to sit on thrones and rule with God in heaven. Yet for their sins, they've sold themselves into slavery. They're wallowing in the muck and mire of self-indulgent transgression. The Lord is telling them to pick themselves up out of the sludge of sin and sit down in dignity on the throne symbolically waiting for them in the temple.

Wow! How much does that passage apply to me? I too am from the house of Israel. My patriarchal blessing assures me of that. I too have received promises of thrones, principalities, and powers. Yet I, like ancient Israel, have wasted too much time wallowing in the sludge of sin and despair, failing to recognize and claim my royal heritage. Isn't it time that I "arise and sit down in dignity"?

How grateful I am now for the journey my anonymous student led me on through the scripture footnotes. Since then, I've been striving to act more worthily of the royal heritage I come from. I've also been searching the writings of Isaiah more and finding an ever-increasing number of scriptural gems like this one. I sincerely hope my student went on to continue his spiritual quest. Far too many people bump into stumbling blocks along the way and abandon their journey before they find their place in God's plan. They give up their search of the scriptures. They let go of the rod.

Failure to Study

I saw an example of this kind of floundering caused by a lack of regular scripture study when my family and I were living in another state. A sister in our ward asked my wife and me if we'd speak with her mother, whom I'll call Sister Smith. Sister Smith had helped convert her husband thirty years before. They'd been sealed in the temple and raised all three of their children in the Church. Brother Smith was serving as a counselor in their bishopric. Sister Smith was a temple worker. All three of their children served missions, married in the temple, and were raising their own kids in the gospel. One day, Brother and Sister Smith announced to their children and grandchildren that they'd turned in their temple recommends, resigned from their callings, and left the Church. They no longer believed.

The family was devastated. They asked me to talk with their mother to see if I could help. So one Sunday afternoon when Sister Smith was in town visiting her grandkids, we sat down and talked.

The Smiths had some Evangelical Christian friends who were heavily into anti-Mormon literature. They eventually convinced the Smiths to meet with them to go over some anti-Mormon claims and they invited over some "experts" from their church for this "friendly" discussion. The Smiths were blown out of their spiritual water. Many of the attacks were on the doctrine and history of the temple. They were all issues the Smiths had never heard of and for which they had no response. In one sitting, they were convinced that the Church was a hoax and were ready to leave it. Once they resigned their membership, the first thing they did was go out and start drinking together, as if they had been missing out on the good life all those years.

That Sunday afternoon, I addressed Sister Smith's specific concerns one by one. Still, I could tell there were underlying problems that went much deeper. After probing a bit, I learned that in thirty years of Church attendance, the Smiths had never studied the scriptures for themselves. They never had a habit of regular couple prayer. They'd raised their kids in the Church but had never let the gospel sink into their own hearts. The first time they ever took scripture study seriously was with these expert anti-Mormons. No wonder she was so confused!

We read Moroni's promise in Moroni 10:4–5 together and I challenged her to actually study the Book of Mormon for herself. She said she would, but I could tell her future with the Church was still on sandy, uncertain ground. Shortly after that encounter with Sister Smith, my wife and I moved out of state. We never heard what happened, but the whole experience reinforced to me the uncompromising need to feed my testimony with regular scripture study. Sheri Dew, a counselor in the Relief Society General Presidency, said, "Conversion is immersion. Immersion in truth. Immersion in the scriptures. Immersion in the teachings of prophets, seers, and revelators. And immersion in the Spirit."[11] Without that daily immersion, we are left unprepared to face the faith-sapping experiences of the world around us.

Dealing with Scriptural Puzzles

At times, we may come across passages that look to us like anomalies or that don't seem to fit with our modern sensibilities. One approach is to say, somewhat ostrich-like, "That's not relevant to my salvation." That really is like sticking one's head in the sand. Of course unanswered criticisms of my religion are relevant to my salvation if they make it more difficult to believe and have faith in the knowledge and love of God. It's not that I need answers to every question raised against the scriptures, but I have to know that there *are* answers that can be found. "Though argument does not create conviction," one theologian said, "the lack of it destroys belief. What seems to be proved may not be embraced; but what no one shows the ability to defend is quickly abandoned. Rational argument does not create belief, but it maintains a climate in which belief may flourish."[12] Sometimes just knowing that there are other smart people out there who have grappled with these issues and still maintained the faith can inspire me to keep going as well.

Matt is a friend of mine with a returned missionary son named Peter. About the time Peter graduated from BYU, he was in a serious car wreck without a seat belt that should've killed him. He was fortunate to walk away from the accident. He recovered from severe head trauma, got married, and started a family. A few years and a couple of children later, this bright young man read a critique of the Bible by Thomas Paine and believed it. Peter consequently gave up his belief in God and the gospel, but he continued attending Church for his family's sake. He called his father and announced that he'd finally seen the light of reason dispelling the darkness of superstitious religion. Matt decided to read Paine's book to help his son look for answers to the criticisms it raised. They discussed and argued but could come to no agreement.

About this time, President Hinckley challenged all the members of the Church to read or reread the Book of Mormon. Matt was serving in a branch at the MTC in Provo and didn't get to hear the letter read in sacrament meetings everywhere else. He heard about the reading challenge from his wife and others, but he decided they could just keep on reading as they had been. They were then in the book of Mosiah. When he read the letter in the September *Ensign*, he was impressed to start reading the book again from the beginning with his wife. In the October general conference of that year, President Eyring said he was reading a little bit extra every day to make sure he could complete the prophet's challenge by the end of the year. Matt and his wife decided to follow President Eyring's example and read a little bit extra every day.

On October 12, they were reading in Alma that "on the twelfth day, in the tenth month, in the tenth year of the reign of the judges over the people of Nephi that the chief judge" (Alma 14:23) had Alma and Amulek bound with cords. They noticed it was quite a coincidence that they were reading that on the twelfth day of the tenth month. They also realized it was the anniversary of Peter's car accident. They decided to call him up and invite him and his wife out to dinner to celebrate their wedding anniversary that had just past.

At the restaurant, Matt asked his son if he knew what day it was. He reminded his son that it was the anniversary of his accident. Matt also told him about the coincidence they'd had that morning reading in the Book of Mormon. Later that night, Matt's son called and asked what the reference was again to the passage Matt and his wife had read. Then he hung up. Two hours later, he called again and said, "I'm back."

His son had looked up the passage his parents had read. Then he kept reading to the end of the chapter. On the next page, he came across where Alma and Amulek had prayed and asked the Lord how long they would have to suffer in bondage. When this young man was recovering from his accident, he was unemployed, unmarried, and was feeling lost and without direction. He'd prayed and felt the Spirit strongly that all would work out. He wrote about the experience in the margins of his scriptures right there in Alma 14. Within a few months, he found a great job and was happily married in the temple. Now, he felt the Lord's love for him again and could not deny the power of the scriptures speaking to him.

Eventually, this bright young man began to discover possible responses to Thomas Paine's criticisms of the Bible and was able to return wholeheartedly to the faith. Yet more than anything else, it was my friend's willingness to take his son's questioning seriously that convinced him his father was still on his side. Today, Matt's son is a bishop, helping the members of his ward find the power of the scriptures in their own lives.

Because the scriptures are true, they can stand up against critics and detractors. However, sometimes it takes patience and faith to forge onward until answers come.

A few years ago, I was teaching an institute class when a student brought up an intriguing question. He asked about an apparent inconsistency in the official Joseph Smith story of the First Vision. In Joseph Smith—History 1:10, the Prophet wrote, "In the midst of this war of words and tumult of opinions, I often said to myself: What is to be done? Who of all these parties are right; or, are they all wrong together?" But later, when the Father and Son appeared and Joseph asked which of all the churches he should join, he wrote, "At this time it had never entered into my heart that all were wrong" (Joseph Smith—History 1:18). It may seem a trivial point, but either young Joseph had thought of the possibility that all the churches were wrong or he hadn't. In his account, the Prophet appears to contradict himself. If he contradicts himself on simple historical points in his story, how can we trust that he's telling the truth about the rest of the story?

In my own study, I'd seen and wondered about this apparent discrepancy in the Prophet's writing before. I hadn't discovered a good answer to the question. I just assumed that in retelling the events eighteen years after they happened, perhaps the Prophet had forgotten a small detail. We can't expect him to be perfectly consistent in everything he says. Even prophets can make mistakes. In the title page of the Book of Mormon, Moroni wrote that "if there are faults [in this book,] they are the mistakes of men." Perhaps this discrepancy in the Joseph Smith—History was likewise just one of those mistakes of men.

However, one of the other students in the class raised his hand meekly and offered a possible explanation. He said he didn't pretend to know much about Church history, but perhaps the answer to the apparent contradiction had to do with *where* young Joseph was asking the question. When Joseph described his search for the truth, the questions he asked were all in his mind: "my mind became somewhat partial to the Methodist sect," "my mind at times was greatly excited," and so forth (Joseph Smith—History 1:8–9). But when the answer finally came from the Lord, it came to his heart: "At this time it had never entered into my heart that all were wrong" (Joseph Smith—History 1:18). In other words, he could've thought about the logical possibility that all the churches of his day were wrong altogether but never really considered in his heart that that might be the real answer. He was still expecting to be told to join a preexisting church.

When my student shared this simple explanation, it made sense. We all accepted that explanation as a plausible solution to our exegetical puzzle. Our discussion was then able to proceed to other topics. Later, someone helped me see that Joseph's question in verse ten ("Who of all these parties are right; or, are they all wrong together?") probably referred only to the Presbyterians, Baptists, and Methodists Joseph was investigating in verse nine. Perhaps he had considered that the true church might not be one of those three, but he hadn't considered the possibility that *all* the churches on earth were wrong.

Whatever the real explanation may turn out to be, my experiences with these verses have served as reminders to me that there are forthcoming answers to the apparent "problems" of the scriptures if I'll just be patient. I mustn't let a current difficulty in my understanding block my memory of the tremendous stockpile of spiritual strength I've garnered from the scriptures in the past.

Is the Book of Mormon a Historical Record?

Sometimes the adversary uses perplexing puzzles that can arise from a critical examination of scriptures to sap their influence from our lives. He tries to convince us that the scriptures are not a reliable record of actual events, so we don't need to do everything they instruct us to do. If the Book of Mormon is merely a creative invention of Joseph Smith, we're free to pick and choose from the lessons it contains—as we would from a novel.

This Satanic ploy has been around for a long time. Laman and Lemuel tried using a version of it to diminish the significance of hell in Lehi's vision of the tree of life. Of all the amazing things their father saw in his dream and related to the family, Laman and Lemuel focused on the river of filthy water. (We can see what their minds were attracted to!) Nephi explained that the river was "a representation of that awful hell, which the angel said unto me was prepared for the wicked" (1 Nephi 15:29). Laman and Lemuel next wanted to know if Lehi was addressing things that were "temporal" or "spiritual." In other words, is this hell something literal that the wicked suffer now or something symbolic of a judgment to come in the next life? Nephi answered them that the river of filthy water was "both temporal and spiritual" (1 Nephi 15:32). He told them to take the suffering of the wicked to be both literal (in the here and now) *and* symbolic (greater suffering to come in the hereafter). He refused to let them justify their behavior by "spiritualizing" the scriptures and robbing them of their authority and urgency.

Today, it has become fashionable among many bright, intellectual Saints to accept the claim that the Book of Mormon was written by Joseph Smith to articulate his thinking on the religious debates of his day. They want to claim that the book can still be considered "scripture" in the sense that it provides a foundational narrative and can offer food for thought and symbols for our religious worship. But since they don't believe it to be an ancient document about real people, anything in it that conflicts with modern sensibilities is discountable.

Though I believe there's ample textual and archeological evidence that the Book of Mormon truly is an ancient document about real people, in the end I doubt if anyone will be convinced by the evidence. I have on my bookshelf a five hundred-page book written by a group of scholars, each arguing that the Book of Mormon was a nineteenth-century document written by Joseph Smith.[13] Right next to that compilation of essays by brilliant but skeptical scholars I have another five hundred-page book written by similarly competent but believing scholars that refutes the arguments of the first.[14] It's full of evidence, footnotes, and persuasive arguments to match and refute all the scholarship of the first one. Ultimately, I have to choose which book I'm going to believe. As the philosopher and psychologist William James taught, "We merely muster up rational arguments after the fact to justify our temperament, which decides these controversial issues for us."[15] I'm grateful for the witness of the Holy Ghost that has reassured me time and again the Book of Mormon is a faithful record—what Joseph Smith said it was. Still, I recognize that my acceptance of it as true scripture is a choice. I've wagered my life on that choice.

I have a few friends in the Church who are of a different temperament than I am and have chosen to believe the Book of Mormon is a nineteenth-century document. They still enjoy living as Latter-day Saints, recognize the fruits of Mormonism, and have no intention of leaving the Church. It's as if they want to be "in the Church but not of the Church" so that they can relate better to their non-LDS friends and colleagues. While I'm skeptical of that position, I'm fine allowing them their position—as long as they don't start preaching it to others. However, that viewpoint seems to sap the scriptures of their spiritual strength to secure a person in their times of trial. If the iron rod isn't attached to anything, it's going to prove to be a flimsy protection against falling into the river of filthy water.

In a revealing essay entitled "Scripture as Incarnation," James E. Faulconer argued that the scriptures become our guide to life when we accept their symbolic ordering of the world. To accept someone's challenge to prove that the scriptures are an actual historical account is to be sucked into their understanding of truth defined by rational, scholarly guidelines. The scriptures were never written with that intention. They deal with real people and events from real history, but they were never meant to be historical (to satisfy the canons of modern history). The purpose of the scriptures is to help order our lives around God by seeing His symbolism everywhere.[16]

When we accept the scriptures as our "standard works" to judge life's experiences and choices that we make, we may still find rational evidence for them along the way. But our acceptance of them shouldn't be based solely on rational evidence.

When I was attending graduate school, I had a friend in a doctoral program in political science who was studying with some brilliant academic atheists. They took a sort of fiendish delight in dismantling all of his treasured religious beliefs. Their attacks rattled him to the core. One day as we were talking about his experiences, I asked him if he still believed in Mormonism. He said that these critics had succeeded in refuting every argument he ever had for the truthfulness of the Church except one: chiasmus in the Book of Mormon.

Chiasmus is a form of ancient Hebrew poetry. It's where an author makes a series of declarations and repeats them in reverse order. Instead of repeating sounds in rhyme, there are repeating conceptual ideas. A classic example of the style can be seen in Isaiah 60:1–3.

a *Arise,*
  b *shine;*
    c for thy *light* is come,
      d and the *glory*
        e of the *Lord is risen* upon thee.
          f For, behold, the *darkness* shall cover the earth,
          f and gross *darkness* the people:
        e but the *Lord shall arise* upon thee,
      d and his *glory* shall be seen upon thee.
    c And the Gentiles shall come to thy *light,*
  b and kings to the *brightness*
a of thy *rising.*

Chiasmus wasn't discovered in the Bible and discussed by scholars until the last half of the nineteenth century. Turns out that it makes frequent appearances all over the Old Testament. In the late 1960s, it was discovered in the Book of Mormon.[17] Alma 36 is a nearly perfect example of the form (verses are paraphrased to reflect overall ideas):

a My son, give ear to my words (1)
b Keep the commandments and ye shall prosper in the land (1)
c Do as I have done (2)
d Remembering the captivity of our fathers (2)
e They were in bondage (2)
f He surely did deliver them (2)
g Trust in God (3)
h Supported in trials, troubles, and afflictions (3)
i Lifted up at the last day (3)
j I know this not of myself but of God (4)
k Born of God (5)
l I sought to destroy the church (6–9)
m My limbs were paralyzed (10)
n Fear of being in the presence of God (14–15)
o Pains of a damned soul (16)
p Harrowed up by the memory of sins (17)
q I remembered Jesus Christ, a Son of God (17)
q I cried, Jesus, Son of God (18)
p Harrowed up by the memory of sins no more (19)
o Joy as exceeding as was the pain (20)
n Long to be in the presence of God (22)
m My limbs received strength again (23)
l I labored to bring souls to repentance (24)
k Born of God (26)
j Therefore, my knowledge is of God (26)
h Supported under trials, troubles, and afflictions (27)
g Trust in him (27)
f He will deliver me (27)
i and raise me up at the last day (28)
e God brought our fathers out of bondage and captivity (28–29)
d Retain in remembrance their captivity (28–29)
c Know as I do know (30)
b Keep the commandments and ye shall prosper in the land (30)
a This according to his word (30)

There are hundreds of these chiasmic structures in the Book of Mormon.[18] To think that they appeared accidentally seems beyond belief. The best that critics can make of all this is to say perhaps Joseph Smith read the Bible so much that the chiasmic forms subconsciously entered his thinking and writing. But that seems a preposterous idea to me. Chiasmus stands as a powerful witness that the Book of Mormon really is a translation of an ancient text, as Joseph Smith claimed. It was sufficient evidence to help my friend cling to his belief in Mormonism until he could work through his doubts. I saw him a few years later as a professor at BYU, firm again in the faith. Chiasmus doesn't prove that the Book of Mormon is an ancient record, but to those who have taken it as their guide, it can be evidence that supports their leap of faith.

Keeping focused on the things we know and have experienced for ourselves can protect us from being distracted by trivialities. Once when I was teaching missionaries at the MTC, a group of them came up to me after class. They obviously had an important question they needed to ask, and they didn't want any other missionaries to hear it. They waited until everyone else had left for the dorms, shut the door, and unloaded their bomb: In 1 Nephi 11:8, Nephi says that the "whiteness thereof [of the tree] did exceed the whiteness of the driven snow." Their question was, "How did Nephi know what snow was? He lived his whole life in the desert!" I could tell that this was truly a mini crisis of faith for these sincere servants of the Lord. So I tried to take their question as seriously as I could.

I drew a dot on the blackboard and said something like, "What do you see?"

They replied, "A dot."

I answered, "No. There is an entire board in front of you, but all you're looking at is the tiny dot in the center that's drawing your attention. Peculiar gospel or scriptural questions can become like this dot. They seem so significant and unexplainable that they can distract us from all the positive gospel experiences around us."

In Alma 7:8, the prophet demonstrated how to handle troubling issues that arise. When dealing with the people's question of whether Christ would visit them while in the flesh, he replied, "Now as to this thing I do not know; but this much I do know, that the Lord God hath power to do all things which are according to his word." Instead of getting caught up with unanswered questions, Alma focused on the essential gospel truths he'd already discovered.

As it turned out, this particular issue for the missionaries was easy to resolve. Of course Nephi knew what snow was. Even though Israel is mostly a dry desert wasteland, there was snow at the top of Mount Hermon, just over a hundred miles north of Jerusalem. Besides, Nephi was writing on the small plates thirty years after coming to the promised land (see 2 Nephi 5:28–31). Certainly he'd seen snow here. And he would have read about snow in the scriptures many times.[19] The point wasn't that this particular question was easy to answer. It was about how to keep questions and issues in perspective when they arise so we don't get too distracted by them. These missionaries had been feeling the Spirit every day in their MTC experience, but they let one perplexity throw them offtrack. All they really needed to do was get back to work and let the Spirit continue to teach them, trusting that further answers would come.

Elder Jeffrey R. Holland made a similar point in general conference. He declared, "When those moments come and issues surface, the resolution of which is not immediately forthcoming, *hold fast to what you already know and stand strong until additional knowledge comes.*"[20] He went on to say we should lead with our faith, not with our doubts. We should acknowledge when we have questions and concerns, but we have no need to get too caught up with them. "*In this Church, what we know will always trump what we do not know. And remember, in this world, everyone is to walk by faith.*"[21]

At times, the troubling questions life hurls at us will not be easy to answer. The resulting tidal waves of concerns can truly rock us. But if we've learned how to deal with them, they need not capsize our precious boat of faith.

Keeping a Personal Record

Sometimes even Saints who've had spiritual experiences with the scriptures and had their prayers answered in the past (such as my good friend in graduate school and these missionaries at the MTC) can forget and lose their way in the face of current challenges. It's hard to remember the faith-confirming experiences we've accumulated over the years. So along with feasting on the scriptures and praying, the Lord has given us another invitation.

In Moses, we read about our first parents: "And a book of remembrance was kept, in the which was recorded, in the language of Adam, for it was given unto as many as called upon God to write by the spirit of inspiration" (Moses 6:5). From the beginning, anyone who sincerely prayed was supposed to write down the resulting inspiration in a book of remembrance.

We learn the most about this process in the Book of Mormon. The Lord explained, "For I command all men, both in the east and in the west, and in the north, and in the south, and in the islands of the sea [are we getting the picture here? He means everyone!], that they shall write the words which I speak unto them" (2 Nephi 29:11). If He commands us all to write the words He speaks to us, what does that imply? He said in the following verse, "For behold, I shall speak unto the Jews and they shall write it [the Bible]; and I shall also speak unto the Nephites and they shall write it [the Book of Mormon]; and I shall also speak unto the other tribes of the house of Israel, which I have led away, and they shall write it [the Doctrine and Covenants? Some other book of scripture yet to be revealed?]; and I shall also speak unto all nations of the earth and they shall write it." Clearly, the Lord is going to communicate with all of us; when He does, He wants us to write down what we learn.

Why is it so imperative to record our inspiration? One reason may be that it'll be easier to see the Lord working in our lives. President Kimball was emphatic about the need for every Latter-day Saint to keep a journal: "We hope you will begin as of this date. If you have not already commenced this important duty in your lives, get a good notebook, a good book that will last through time and into eternity for the angels to look upon. Begin today and write in it your goings and your comings, your deeper thoughts, your achievements, and your failures, your associations and your triumphs, your impressions and your testimonies. We hope you will do this, our brothers and sisters, for this is what the Lord has commanded, and those who keep a personal journal are more likely to keep the Lord in remembrance in their daily lives."[22] We write to acknowledge the Lord's blessings in our individual lives.

When counseling the Twelve Apostles on the importance of record-keeping, Joseph Smith was even more emphatic: "For neglecting to write these things when God had revealed them, not esteeming them of sufficient worth, the Spirit may withdraw and God may be angry. . . . Here let me prophesy. The time will come, when, if you neglect to do this thing, you will fall by the hands of unrighteous men."[23] So another reason for journal writing may be to show the Lord that we esteem His words and want to remember them. Then He may be inclined to send us more. Still another reason may be to fortify us against attacks on our faith in the future. When we face trials and opposition, we can go back to our journals and recollect experiences to help us weather the storm.

Whatever the reasons the Lord has for wanting us to keep a record of our dealings with Him, He's certainly made it clear how important it is in His eyes: "Then they that feared the Lord spake often one to another, and the Lord hearkened and heard; and a book of remembrance was written before him for them that feared the Lord, and that thought upon his name. And they shall be mine, saith the Lord of Hosts, in that day when I make up my jewels; and I will spare them as a man spareth his own son that serveth him. Then shall ye return and discern between the righteous and the wicked, between him that serveth God and him that serveth him not" (3 Nephi 24:16–18). It'd seem that the righteous who will be spared at the Second Coming are those who are serving the Lord and keeping a book of remembrance of His dealings with them. The wicked are—at least in some sense—those who are not keeping such a record.

There's another long-term benefit of keeping a journal that extends beyond mortality. Back in 2 Nephi, the Lord gives a fascinating promise: "For out of the books which shall be written I will judge the world, every man according to their works, according to that which is written" (2 Nephi 29:11). We could say this means that the standard works will be used as a touchstone or measuring rod against our own deeds, and that would be true. In context, however, the Lord is saying that He's going to speak to all people and have them write down His words. Then, according to those records that they themselves have kept, they will be judged. In other words, our journals may somehow be a part of our final judgment. How embarrassing will it be when that time arrives, if the Savior invites me to bring out my journal to review my life, and all I can say is I was too busy to write one!

Doesn't God keep a record of everything? He does. To the Nephites who had neglected their record-keeping, the Savior said that "all things are written by the Father" (3 Nephi 27:26). The scriptures refer to this record as the book of life (see Revelation 20:12). Yet that doesn't excuse us from keeping our own record. It's just the opposite. The Lord said, "Write the things which ye have seen and heard. . . . For behold, out of the books which have been written, and which shall be written, shall this people be judged, for by them shall their works be known unto men. . . . Therefore, what manner of men ought ye to be? Verily I say unto you, even as I am" (3 Nephi 27:23, 25, 27). This famous passage is all about keeping journals. If we're ever going to become like God, we're going to have to learn how to keep records like He does.

My journal can become a sacred record of God's dealings with me and my family, just as the Book of Mormon is a record of God's dealings with Lehi and his family. "And we talk of Christ," Nephi wrote, "we rejoice in Christ, we preach of Christ, we prophesy of Christ, and we write according to our prophecies, that our children may know to what source they may look for a remission of their sins" (2 Nephi 25:26). If I don't keep such a record, I'll be depriving my descendants of the benefit of my experience. "Joseph Smith . . . advised the elders all to keep daily journals. 'For,' said he, 'your journals will be sought after as history and scripture.' " As I learn to write with the Spirit, my record will become a sacred message for me and my posterity.[24]

My Record

I was thirteen when I started keeping a journal. I heard President Kimball teach that we all should have one and decided to take his counsel to heart. I didn't really understand the difference between a diary and a journal, so I mostly wrote about the simple, routine comings and goings of my life. "I played in a soccer game today. We won. Afterward, we went as a family to see a movie. My friend came with me. It was a fun day." Yet every now and then, I made a funny comment or insightful observation on those happenings. Here's one from December 15, 1981: "I'm on an interesting program to treat my acne. My mom found it in a magazine article. Since Saturday, when I started, I've noticed improvement already. Hope for the cure of the teenage nightmare!" As an adult still dealing with acne, I can empathize with my struggle as a teenager. Five months later, on May 6, 1982, I wrote: "Yesterday I started shaving. Dad showed me how to cut the whiskers. I'm going to let them grow back to see if I'll have a fluffy mustache."

Is this stuff corny? Sure. Are my children ever going to be interested in it? You could bet your life on it. Fortunately, even without too much instruction on journal-keeping, I was able to figure out that what matters most to write about are those experiences that make a difference, that are life-changing (even in small ways), and that could help someone else. Here's an entry from that same first journal of mine:

> Tonight, I was reading the Doctrine and Covenants. I read one section in particular that had a large impact on me. I've never read *anything* in my entire life that had more meaning to me than section 19 in the D&C. After reading that, I knew I had to pray to my Father in Heaven. I asked for forgiveness of my sins and the strength to live more the principle of repentance. After I read that section and prayed, I felt a spirit that burned within me stronger than anything I've ever felt before. Tears came to my eyes in joy. I could see God the Father and Christ our Savior before me in my mind's eye. The love I feel for them is beyond anything I could ever explain.

I was fourteen. I totally forgot that experience until I read it again thirty years later. Thanks to my journal, I can remember what I felt like that evening.

When we have experiences reading the scriptures—with promptings from the Spirit, answered prayers, or in seeing God's hand in our lives—and write them down, we're stockpiling homemade bricks of faith that we, and others of our family, can draw upon again in the future. They are the building blocks of a testimony.

Is this the same as writing scripture? I'm not deluded enough to think that the prophet is going to ask to publish selections of my journal in the standard works. But I'm egotistical enough to imagine a future day when my children or grandchildren just might take an interest in my doings enough to dust off these old books I wrote with some reverence. If the timing is right, perhaps they may find power in the words that'll help them forge connections with the Lord to transform their lives. Isn't that the meaning of scriptures: sacred, inspired writings that bring us closer to God and to holiness?

Even if no one else ever becomes interested in my record, it will not have been kept in vain. As Nephi said of his journal, "I know that the record which I make is true; and I make it with mine own hand; and I make it according to my knowledge" (1 Nephi 1:3). These are experiences I can't easily deny, and they will continue to transform me as long as the record survives. There is a saying that "if the world had more historians, we wouldn't need as many prophets." If we'd simply record more of the promptings the Lord gives us and strive to act on them, perhaps in the future we wouldn't find ourselves in so many predicaments and needing His help to get out of them.

So what is the study project the gospel proposes? First of all, I must establish the habit of daily scripture reading. Next, I must learn how to use the scriptures as a Urim and Thummim to receive personal revelation. Then I must get in the habit of writing down in a journal the insights, promptings, and observations of God's hand working in my life. It all could seem kind of daunting—reading, writing, and living a sacred story. Still, this is what prophets and gods do, and it's my destiny to join in their company. The reward is almost unimaginable: "All that my father hath shall be given unto him" (D&C 84:38). Quite the incentive for such a small price to pay!

Writing Glory

Ignited by a prompting,
I take up this tool of creation
And begin to write a soul.
But scarce a pair of words escapes
And something cries correction.
It isn't I but we—you, me, and a sky full of them, like stars.

But like a falling star, I break the path.
An exploding supernova,
My sin threatens to leave behind a black hole in its wake.
Thankfully I'm only a comet, ripped out of orbit—
Dismembered but not obliterated.

There is One who re-members me.
Rewritten by the Word of words.
Put back on course—
A celestial turn round the universe.
Holy fire cleanses, transforms, and blazes the night sky
With glory.
The story shines
Because the light is His.

How Miracles Help

"There are only two ways to live your life. One is as though nothing is a miracle. The other is as though everything is a miracle."[1]

—Albert Einstein

When I was younger and thought I knew a lot, I taught an introductory philosophy course at BYU. One year, I had an extremely bright freshman sign up for my class. He'd been raised in the Church and considered himself a believer, but he also had many unanswered questions. He was scientifically minded—not at all inclined to believe in the fairy tale-like stories of miracles he'd heard in the Church his whole life. How could an intelligent, rational being actually believe in miracles? It was a challenging question to answer. But Peter said that we should be ready always to give a reason for the hope that's within us (see 1 Peter 3:15). I certainly had a hope in Christ, so I wrote down a simple response to his inquiry. Later, I adapted that response into this chapter. It may take a miracle, but I'll do my best to explain how my belief in the Lord and in His Church is strengthened by the ongoing occurrence of miracles.

First of all, let me say that I don't know "beyond a shadow of a doubt." I know that some do, and perhaps that is a gift. However, I've had both shadows of doubt and genuine doubt in my thirty-year struggle to believe. My doubts don't really trouble me though. Elder Hugh B. Brown often quoted the great historian Will Durant, saying,

"No one deserves to believe unless he has served an apprenticeship of doubt."[2] This may be a bit of an overstatement. While there must be "an opposition in all things" (2 Nephi 2:11) to truly value what we have, I don't think we have to personally experience the opposite of every good thing. I don't have to cheat on my wife to appreciate the loving relationship I enjoy with her. Fortunately, I can learn vicariously from the sad experience of others. I can appreciate the value of my belief simply through seeing others struggle with doubt.

Still, an appropriate amount of skepticism may not be a bad thing. President Howard W. Hunter stated,

> I have sympathy for young men and young women when honest doubts enter their minds and they engage in the great conflict of resolving doubts. These doubts can be resolved, if they have an honest desire to know the truth, by exercising moral, spiritual, and mental effort. They will emerge from the conflict into a firmer, stronger, larger faith because of the struggle. They have gone from a simple, trusting faith, through doubt and conflict, into a solid substantial faith which ripens into testimony.[3]

We cannot always control the circumstances that may lead to doubts, so everything depends on what we do with them when they arise. Do we let them fester and eat away at our peace and faith, or do we go about using them to learn more about Heavenly Father and His plan? Do we seek guidance from skeptics and Church critics who are all too ready to magnify our concerns by exposing odd-shaped pieces of the theological puzzle, or do we humbly take our puzzle to the one who can help us put all the pieces together? If we turn to the Lord, the experiences that once raised doubts can become the key pieces of a well-built testimony.

So what exactly are miracles? The Bible Dictionary defines them as "manifestations of divine or spiritual power."[4] The Latin *miraculum* means "an object of wonder." In Mark 16:17–18, the Savior said that signs would follow them that believe. So we could say that a miracle is something extraordinary that happens to believers, which also becomes a sign of God's power working in their lives. Some agnostics and nonbelievers would like signs *before* they believe, but that's not the way the Lord works. He condemns such an attitude as sign-seeking. He says if you will act on the gospel message, then you will know it's true (see John 7:17), but usually the proof won't come until after the belief. Miracles are evidence after the fact that the Lord is there and intervening to better the lives of His children.

Many people are suspicious about any claims to miracles. While I was in college, I came across the writings of the famous skeptic of the Scottish Enlightenment named David Hume. He presented himself as a believer in Christianity, but he seemed more loyal to human reason than to the testimony of scripture. His arguments intrigued me, however. In his classic work *An Inquiry Concerning Human Understanding*, he gave five reasons for not believing in Christian miracles:

1. There are no miracles with enough reliable witnesses.

2. We love too much the passion and surprise of telling and hearing about miracles to not be skeptical of any accounts of them.

3. Miracles are more often reported among the "ignorant and barbarous" people of the world, so you have to be stupid and gullible to believe in them.

4. If miracles happened in the time of Christ and His Apostles, shouldn't we expect them in our day?

5. There are as many reports of miracles supporting other religions' claim to validity as there are supporting Christianity.[5]

While these are strong objections to believing in miracles, as a young LDS wannabe scholar, I found possible answers to each of Hume's concerns.

Not Enough Reliable Witnesses

To avoid this charge, the Lord set up the law of witnesses: "In the mouth of two or three witnesses shall every word be established" (2 Corinthians 13:1). The whole point behind the Three Witnesses and the Eight Witnesses to the Book of Mormon was to have a sufficient number of trustworthy, first-hand testators to the miraculous origins of the keystone of our religion. A teacher, a military sergeant, and a successful farmer each said they handled the plates, saw an angel, and heard a divine voice. Even after they left the Church, they never denied their testimony, which makes them even stronger witnesses. If it all had been a hoax, surely they would've exposed it when they became disaffected. But they were honest men and, because they really *had* seen the plates and heard an angel, they couldn't deny it, even when they were alienated from the Prophet Joseph Smith. Cowdery and Harris came back into the Church after some time and died as faithful members. Whitmer spent forty years giving interviews to reporters and consistently testifying that he handled the plates and saw an angel.[6]

Today, fifteen men are called to be special witnesses of the reality of the Savior's Resurrection—the essential miracle of human history. Here are some examples of what these special witnesses have said about the role of an Apostle:

President Howard W. Hunter: "Indeed, the call to the holy apostleship is one of bearing witness to the world of the divinity of the Lord Jesus Christ. 'Am I not an apostle? Am I not free? Have I not seen Jesus Christ our Lord? Are not ye my work in the Lord? . . . For the seal of mine apostleship are ye in the Lord' (1 Corinthians 9:1–2). This always has been the testimony of the Apostles, to which I add my witness, in the name of Jesus Christ."[7]

President Spencer W. Kimball: " 'I know that God lives. I know that Jesus Christ lives,' said John Taylor, my predecessor, 'for I have seen him.' I bear this testimony to you brethren in the name of Jesus Christ. Amen."[8]

President Gordon B. Hinckley: " 'For we saw him, even on the right hand of God; and we heard the voice bearing record that he is the Only Begotten of the Father' [D&C 76:23]. It is in this spirit that I add my own witness. Our Eternal Father lives. . . . Jesus is the Christ."[9]

President Boyd K. Packer: "After all the years that I have lived and taught and served . . . there is one great truth that I would share. That is my witness of the Savior Jesus Christ. Joseph Smith and Sidney Rigdon recorded the following after a sacred experience: 'And now, after the many testimonies which have been given of him, this is the testimony, last of all, which we give of him: That he lives! For we saw him' (D&C 76:22–23). Their words are my words. *I* believe and *I* am sure that Jesus is the Christ, the Son of God, and that He lives. . . . I *know* the Lord. I am His witness."[10]

Are these men fraudulent or delusional? I've never encountered wiser, more collected, or more sincere voices in my life. They're guarded in what they say, perhaps trying to avoid casting their pearls before swine. But it's clear that they have firsthand spiritual knowledge that makes their witnesses sure.

We Like Them Too Much

It's true that we're intrigued by miracles and we ought to be a bit more cautious in the way we talk about them. Oftentimes, we pass on Mormon folk stories to each other without ever seeking corroborating evidence of their veracity. I've been guilty of this error myself. Have you heard the one about the missionary who has a broken leg, gets a blessing from a Protestant minister, and is supposedly healed? His mission president finds out about it and gives the elder another blessing, rebuking the power of Satan. His broken leg reappears and needs to be set in a cast. Why do we tell these stories? We do because, as Hume noted, they're exciting and we think that they "build faith." In actuality, they're at best sentimental and probably detract from accounts of true miracles by increasing skepticism among thoughtful people. Faith is "hope for things which are not seen, which are true" (Alma 32:21). Therefore, false stories can't build faith. They can only give people a false sense of security while setting them up for disillusionment later. Certainly we should be more careful and refrain from passing around spurious accounts of miracles.

All this being acknowledged, the fact that we like to talk and hear about miracle stories doesn't mean that some of them can't be true. We like to hear about pompous politicians being caught in scandalous behavior and are often predisposed to believe rumors spread about them, but that doesn't mean that some of them aren't guilty. It just means we should be suspicious of these reports until there's good evidence to back them up. The same could be said of miracles.

Miracles Reported More in Ignorant Nations

It may be true that, in general, less-educated people are more believing in miracles than more-educated people. Education teaches us to be less gullible and to recognize the need for good evidence to make strong claims. I served a mission among poor, uneducated people in southern Mexico, and they were much less skeptical than Americans. But to say they more easily believe in miracles *because* they're less educated is to commit the fallacy of false cause, claiming that because two events happen together, one causes the other. Perhaps they more easily believe because they're more humble. In any case, while in many religions, belief and commitment diminish with higher levels of education, among Latter-day Saints they actually increase! On average, the higher the education a Latter-day Saint has, the greater their activity in the Church.[11] So in a sense, perhaps you have to be smart to believe in Mormonism and all its miracles.

If Miracles Happened in Christ's Day, Shouldn't They Happen Today?

Latter-day Saints couldn't agree more. If God is the same yesterday, today, and forever, then you'd expect to see signs following believers in any age—even the modern, technological world we live in. President Kimball once wrote,

> A question often asked is: "If miracles are a part of the Gospel program, why do we not have such today?" The answer is a simple one: We do have miracles today—beyond imagination! If all the miracles of our own lifetime were recorded, it would take many library shelves to hold the books which would contain them. What kinds of miracles do we have? All kinds—revelations, visions, tongues, healings, special guidance and direction, evil spirits cast out. Where are they recorded? In the records of the Church, in journals, in news and magazine articles and in the minds and memories of many people.[12]

President Kimball certainly knew what he was talking about. By the time he died, he had entire bookshelves filled with journals of his experiences, including hundreds of miracles. He even published a book on how to experience miracles.[13]

Here's one simple miracle from his life, recorded in his biography. While in Arizona, President Kimball had heard that an old friend of his was losing his faith in the gospel. He called up his friend and suggested they go on a weekend camping trip. President Kimball talked extensively with this friend about his intellectual concerns with the Church, but to no avail. As they were preparing to leave, they couldn't get the car to start after several tries. Finally, President Kimball suggested they pray, and his friend consented. The car started up immediately and they made it home. Over several years, the friend's faith was strengthened, and he and his wife eventually served many missions for the Church.[14] The skeptic will always call such events lucky coincidences, but the thoughtful believer can see the strong possibility of a higher power at work.

If a Church member has gone his or her entire life without experiencing any miracles, he or she would understandably feel a bit left out. We hear so many accounts of miracles every week at Church that a person in this position might begin to wonder, "What's wrong with me? Why don't I have those experiences in my life?" But if that member doesn't give up and simply continues his or her religious journey, hoping to find answers—even if all that can be mustered up in the realm of faith is a small desire to believe—he or she will eventually discover the sought-after evidence (see Alma 32:21–43).

There Are Many Claims of Miracles That Support Other Religions

For me, this is the most difficult challenge to answer. Certainly there are miracles performed among members of many churches and religions. Some of those that are reported are spurious (as are many reported among ourselves, like the missionary's broken leg). Still, I have no reason to believe that *none* of them could be genuine simply because they didn't occur among Latter-day Saints. The Lord loves all His children and rewards faith wherever it is found.

On my mission in Mexico, I heard a sincere fourteen-year-old girl share the most sacred experience of her life. She said she'd never really believed in God until one day, while playing in the ocean, she saw a vision of the cross appear above a wave and she knew then and there that Christ really had died for her. We in the Church are not accustomed to revering the image of the cross. In fact, we were tempted to tell her that her so-called miracle might have been a Satanic counterfeit. Fortunately, we refrained from sharing any disparaging remarks. We simply went on teaching her the restored gospel. She accepted it wholeheartedly and was baptized along with her entire family. Since "every thing which inviteth and enticeth to do good, and to love God, and to serve him, is inspired of God" (Moroni 7:13), who am I to say that the Lord couldn't convert this young lady to Christianity and eventually to the LDS faith through a symbol she was familiar with? Perhaps there's more miraculous power in the symbol of the cross than we Latter-day Saints are acquainted with.

We need not be unsettled by miracles performed in other religions as long as we're not looking to miracles for proof that the Church's beliefs are true. During His visit to the Nephites, the Savior explained that "if it so be that the church is built upon my gospel then will the Father show forth his own works in it" (3 Nephi 27:10). To His Apostles in Jerusalem, He declared that "signs shall follow them that believe" (Mark 16:17). He consistently taught that signs would *follow* believers, not that they'd prove to others that their religion was true. Miracles are a sign to the people involved that the Lord is with them; they have little merit in converting a nonbeliever to a particular religion. In fact, the Lord said, "Require not miracles" (D&C 24:13). It's not that miracles aren't going to happen, but rather that they'll usually come after—not before—we take the leap of faith.

In 1831, a Methodist preacher named Ezra Booth attended a meeting with his friends John and Elsa Johnson. They'd come to hear the Mormon leader, Joseph Smith. Elsa had an arm that'd been partially paralyzed for six years. She couldn't raise it on her own. During the meeting, someone asked the Prophet if there was something that could be done to help Elsa. Joseph took Elsa by the hand and said, "Woman, in the name of the Lord Jesus Christ, I command thee to be whole." Elsa could immediately lift her arm. The next day, she was seen outside using her arm freely while hanging laundry. Elsa and John were both baptized into the Church, as was Ezra. In fact, Ezra was quickly ordained an elder and sent by the Prophet on a mission in Ohio.

However, Ezra's mission was hard and not all that successful. He didn't see any more miracles. Ezra grew discouraged and left the Church. He even started writing letters to local newspapers attacking the Saints. What happened to Ezra? Apparently his entire conversion to the Church had been based on one miracle, but he didn't experience the miraculous change of heart that comes with true conversion. When the miracles ceased, so did his interest in the Church.[15]

President Joseph F. Smith gave this warning to the Ezra Booths of the Church:

> Show me Latter-day Saints who have to feed upon miracles, signs and visions in order to keep them steadfast in the Church, and I will show you members of the Church who are not in good standing before God, and who are walking in slippery paths. It is not by marvelous manifestations unto us that we shall be established in the truth, but it is by humility and faithful obedience to the commandments and laws of God.[16]

The Lord never intended to use miracles to prove the Church is true. In fact, sometimes it's the sacrifice required for belief (in the absence of immediate evidence) that builds trust in the Lord. That trust always pays off down the road.

Different Kinds of Miracles

A friend once asked me if I sincerely believed that miracles of biblical proportions really happened today. I told him I certainly did believe that God still intervenes in the lives of His children, but that most miracles aren't as spectacular as parting the Red Sea or raising the dead. Those are just the ones that get written down and passed on for thousands of years—precisely because they *don't* happen every day! But for those who have eyes to see and ears to hear, there are all kinds of miracles happening in our day. I'd like to share some of those different kinds of miracles that I've found.

The first kind of miracle is the ability to see the Lord's hand in all things. My wife and I recently experienced the birth of our eighth child, Seth. Letting him curl his little fingers around my finger thrills me to the soul and is a powerful witness to me of God's love. The heavens declare the glory of God to all those who have eyes to see it. Of course, seeing these kinds of miracles is mostly a matter of choice. People can appreciate newborns and marvel at the starry night sky without seeing evidence of God's handiwork. The Lord says, "Wo unto the blind that will not [that choose not to] see" (2 Nephi 9:32). Either we choose to see God at the center of everything or we don't, and we'll see two distinct worlds depending on what we're looking for.

On this point, a quote attributed to C. S. Lewis impressed me greatly: "I believe in Christianity as I believe in the rising sun; not because I can see it, but by it I can see all else."[17] My belief in God's goodness becomes a lens through which I view the world and interpret my existence. Sharing this vision with someone who can see only pain and suffering in the world becomes a difficult task. Dennis Rasmussen wrote, "My language sets the limits of my world; I call things around me by the names I have learned. Fortunate are they who have learned the language that teaches of God, for their world will be filled with His presence."[18] What we see is determined by what we look for and by the language we use to describe it. Alma said that "even if ye can no more than desire to believe, let this desire work in you" (Alma 32:27). But we must at least *want* to see God's goodness. Without a desire to believe, no degree of divine intervention can convert our vision. But once converted, we begin to see God's tender mercies everywhere.

A second kind of miracle is answers to prayers. I could never begin to count how many times I've lost something, prayed, and easily recovered it. To those who care to interpret these events with the eye of faith, they are miracles. Surely the skeptic could explain away such coincidences. They might say that prayer is merely a form of personal meditation that allows the mind to clear itself of distractions and solve its own problems. I've considered this possibility myself. But when you have these kinds of answers over and over again (and record them in your journal to remember them), the psychological explanations begin to seem less and less convincing.

My friend's mother, Sister Phillips, worked in the Church Office Building in Salt Lake City for over twenty years and was excited about her upcoming retirement. Over the years, she had seen and met many General Authorities, which was the highlight of her work experience. A few days before her retirement, Sister Phillips started praying that she could meet the prophet, President Monson. She admitted to the Lord that her desire was a purely selfish request and not too important, but she pled for this tender mercy anyway.

The day before she left, Sister Phillips walked down a hall, looked up, and saw the prophet coming around the corner! He walked right up to her, said hello, and shook her hand. He started talking with her as if he didn't have another care in the world. She told him she was retiring the next day and was so happy to see him. As they shook hands to part, President Monson thanked her for her many years of service, and then took her little face in his big hands, leaned down, and kissed her on the forehead. She was shocked and delighted. With that, the prophet disappeared around the corner, leaving her standing there, a bit overwhelmed. A second later, President Monson peeked his head back around the corner at her and said, with a twinkle in his eye, "You got more than you prayed for, didn't you, Sister Phillips?" She was speechless. She just smiled as the tears rolled down her cheeks. She knew Heavenly Father knew her and had heard her prayer. And she knew that President Monson knew as well.

Another kind of miracle is the healing of the sick through prayer or priesthood blessings. In a double-blind randomized study of the power of prayer, a cardiologist arranged to have groups of people pray for the well-being of half the coronary care patients at a San Francisco hospital while no prayers were said for the other half. The study found that even though they didn't know anyone was praying for them, the first group had considerably fewer complications than the second group (fewer required intubation, suffered pulmonary edema, or needed antibiotics). The cardiologist who conducted the study reached the conclusion that prayer is "effective and beneficial" in the clinical treatment of patients.[19] The medical profession usually just chalks up these miracles to what they call "spontaneous remission," an inexplicable, sudden cure. But the believer sees a higher power intervening in His children's affairs.

A fourth category of miracles is dreams, visions, and prophecies. In 1964, Joseph Johnson, a preacher in Accra, Ghana, found a copy of the Book of Mormon. He read it, prayed about it, and knew from the Spirit that it was true. The problem was that there was no LDS presence in Ghana. Joseph didn't know what to do. One evening, he had a vision and heard a voice. It said, "Johnson, Johnson, Johnson, take up my work, and I will bless your land." He replied to the voice, "With thy help, I will do whatever you command me." Joseph began going from street to street, preaching from the Book of Mormon. Immediately, the persecution began. Despite heavy opposition, he started up ten congregations of unbaptized believers during the next fourteen years. He had no help, no missionaries, and no priesthood—just the Book of Mormon and some additional literature sent from Church headquarters in Salt Lake City.

One day, during a time of great frustration and trial, Joseph had a dream. His brother, who had died a few years previously, appeared and spoke with him. He told Joseph not to worry, that he had found the one true church on the earth and that he himself was learning about it where he was in the world of spirits. Joseph didn't know anything about the spirit world and was astonished. His brother said he'd prove the truth of his words by singing Joseph a song from his Church. He began to sing "Come, Come Ye Saints." Joseph had never heard it before but remained silent. His brother concluded the visit by insisting that, come what may, Joseph never leave the Church. He pleaded with Joseph to make sure his baptism was performed. Joseph knew nothing about baptisms for the dead, but he kept the entire experience close to his heart and used it to find the motivation to continue his work through the hard years that came.

Then in 1978, President Spencer W. Kimball received the revelation that all worthy males could now hold the priesthood, regardless of race. Joseph knew that missionaries would be coming to Ghana. Eventually they did, and the work exploded in Accra. Joseph Johnson became the first branch president in the city. He later served several missions and eventually became an ordained patriarch. When the temple was built in Accra, Ghana, Joseph Johnson attended there often, always singing his favorite hymn: "Come, Come Ye Saints."[20]

While these kinds of experiences may seem remarkable to us, they're actually quite common in the records of the Church. The Lord communicates with His children in miraculous ways.

A fifth kind of miracle is controlling the elements. In 1969, President Gordon B. Hinckley visited Chile during a terrible drought. He dedicated two meetinghouses, pleading with the Lord for rain in each dedicatory prayer. The day after he left, it started to rain, and the drought ended. In 1999, President Hinckley again visited Chile during a severe drought. Members had been praying that the rain might come when he arrived. It did, and 57,000 members listened to the prophet as it sprinkled on the soccer stadium in Santiago. When he finished his talk, President Hinckley said, "Now it can rain." The drizzle quickly turned into a downpour. The drought was over. For those 57,000 members, the event became a powerful witness that they were being led by a modern-day Moses.[21]

The last kind of miracle I'll be listing here is the various experiences of directly parting the veil. In the October 2000 general conference, Elder Robert D. Hales shared some health struggles he had, during which he experienced bouts of depression. However, he was sustained by angelic visitations. He testified, "On occasion, when the Lord so desired, I was to be comforted with visitations of heavenly hosts that brought comfort and eternal reassurances in my time of need."[22] These incredible manifestations aren't limited to a few leaders. As Moroni expounded on the Brother of Jared's experience when the premortal Christ appeared to him, he says that "there were many whose faith was so exceedingly strong, even before Christ came, who could not be kept from within the veil, but truly saw with their eyes the things which they had beheld with an eye of faith, and they were glad" (Ether 12:19). The Lord went on to explain in the Doctrine and Covenants that "every soul who forsaketh his sins and cometh unto me, and calleth on my name, and obeyeth my voice, and keepeth my commandments, shall see my face and know that I am" (D&C 93:1).

I've often fretted that I don't seem ready for such a witness. Then the Lord comforts me with this assurance: "Ye are not able to abide the presence of God now, neither the ministering of angels; wherefore, continue in patience until ye are perfected. Let not your minds turn back; and when ye are worthy, in mine own due time, ye shall see and know" (D&C 67:13–14). There'll be opportunities for each seeker to part the veil, so let's just be patient for now.

My Witness

Well-meaning people in the Church sometimes attempt to reassure others about their lack of visions and manifestations by saying that these things happen only when there's a specific need for them. There may be some truth in that. Yet if we could grasp clearly the gravity of our mission here, I wonder if we wouldn't see that we all stand in need of such power. Joseph Smith said, "Thy mind, O man, if thou wilt lead a soul to salvation, must stretch as high as the utmost heavens, and search into and contemplate the darkest abyss, and the broad expanse of eternity."[23] When the Lord appeared to the Nephites at Bountiful, he declared unequivocally the need for everyone to be encouraged to seek these experiences: "And ye see that I have commanded that none of you should go away, but rather have commanded that ye should come unto me, that ye might feel and see; even so shall ye do unto the world" (3 Nephi 18:25). Ultimately, each of us could seek manifestations of the Lord's presence in our lives and encourage others to do the same. Going to Church, paying tithing, and trying to be a good person are wonderful starts. But the commandment is to "seek the face of the Lord always" (D&C 101:38). This is the purpose of temple worship.

In the JST footnote of 1 John 1:1–3, John says that his testimony is "that which was from the beginning, which we have heard, which we have seen with our eyes, which we have looked upon, and our hands have handled, of the Word of life." So what is my testimony? What have I personally heard, seen, and handled of Christ's power that I can declare unto you?

First of all, I'm learning to see the Lord's hand in all things. Moreover, visions, revelation, prophecy, speaking in tongues, interpretation of tongues, the lame made whole, sight to the blind, dramatic weather changes, and daily answers to prayers have all been a part of my personal experiences and fill up my journals. Could it all be attributed to coincidence, schizophrenia, or wishful thinking? A skeptic is always free to believe this. But if it is, it's still just as real to me as my day-to-day walk and talk in the world. In fact, it's *become* my walk and talk in the world.

Let me be so bold as to share one such miracle that I've experienced. In sharing it, I'm not trying to convince anyone that God exists, the Church is true, or much less to give anyone the idea that I consider myself anything special. I simply wish to give an example of the miraculous evidence I have that the Lord is indeed real and working in the lives of His children. My memory is deplorable, so fortunately I've recorded these experiences in my journal. This one comes from my journal exactly as I wrote it down the evening of the day that it occurred: July 27, 1996. I changed only one of the names, for obvious reasons.

I saw the Lord save a boy's life today.

Last night, Blair Jensen, Ryan Beatty, and myself took a group of our young men on a camping / hiking trip. We made camp up in Provo Canyon above Aspen Grove, and then got everyone up at 3:30 a.m. to hike up Mt. Timpanogos and slide down the glacier. The boys had a great time, and everything went well—except for Larry.

Larry comes from a single-parent home and is only partially active and has been hanging out with the wrong crowd lately, so we've begun trying hard to get him to our activities this summer. He missed our hike down Nutty Putty Cave last week but came on this one.

I found out up on the mountain side this morning that this was only the second hike Larry had ever been on (the other being our hike up to Stewart Falls last summer). Larry really struggled. He had terrible balance, unsure footing, and, I realized only as we were coming down, shoes that were too big. He stumbled and fell quite a lot.

I was concerned for his safety, so I sent the others on ahead and stayed back with Larry. We only made it to Emerald Lake, while everyone else reached the top and slid down the glacier. (I did convince Larry though that reaching the lake was a big accomplishment.)

After the others came back down to the lake again, I stayed in the back with Larry as the others forged back down the trail. Larry was exhausted and careless and stumbled and fell even more going down than coming up. I was so concerned about him that I walked just a step behind him, hoping I'd be able to reach him before he tripped off the side of the trail and plunged a hundred feet to a rocky death. I also prayed that the Lord would protect him.

In an unusually flat and rockless part of the trail, I had let Larry get a few feet ahead of me as I stopped to fill my water bottle in the stream. As I rushed to catch up with him, I was stunned to see a miracle occur. Larry had gotten even more careless than usual and had taken a misstep off the side of the trail. He began to fall off a steep precipice when out of nowhere a huge hiker coming up the trail the other way, who was positioned perfectly, reacted instinctively, reached out, and caught Larry's arm before his whole body could go over the side toward almost certain disaster. I thanked the passerby, Larry stumbled on down the trail, apparently oblivious of how near catastrophe he had come, and the hiker quickly disappeared up the trail.

I believe the Lord was watching over that thirteen-year-old fatherless child today, and I was grateful to see the Lord's hand at work.

Again, it'd be easy for someone to see this as merely a happy coincidence. Even faithful members of the Church could reasonably smile at my willingness to see more than what's on the surface. Still, others could get overly excited and shout, "It must have been one of the Three Nephites!" I think either interpretation misses the mark. I choose to see the experience simply as evidence that a loving Heavenly Father at times intervenes in our lives. This is the point I'm trying to make about miracles: Until the day when every knee shall bow and every tongue confess that Jesus is the Christ, the essential ingredient of all miracles will always be choice. Either we choose to see God's hand in our lives or we don't. And the recurrence of intervention depends on how willing we are to accept it and remember it. As Elizabeth Barrett Browning wrote, "Earth's crammed with heaven, / And every common bush afire with God; / But only he who sees, takes off his shoes."[24]

Why Miracles Happen

Miracles will rarely convert nonbelievers. Joseph wanted to silence the early critics of the Restoration by showing people the gold plates. Yet the Lord explained, "Behold, if they will not believe my words, they would not believe you, my servant Joseph, if it were possible that you should show them all these things which I have committed unto you" (D&C 5:7). Consider the classic case of Laman and Lemuel. They saw angels, felt prophetic thunderbolts, and heard the divine voice speaking from the heavens. Still they couldn't muster up enough faith to follow the Lord, even with Nephi praying for them the whole time. But miracles can be a powerful reconfirmation of belief to those who already have faith.

Ultimately, there's an even greater value of miracles. In the days before Christ appearing to the Nephites, the prophet Nephi, son of Nephi and grandson of Helaman, went about doing many miracles among the people. They knew Nephi was a just man because he performed all these wonders and "there was not any man who could do a miracle in the name of Jesus save he were cleansed every whit from his iniquity" (3 Nephi 8:1). We can understand that passage to mean no one can perform a miracle until he is first cleansed. But we could also construe it to mean no one can take part in a miracle without the miracle cleansing them of their sins. This latter interpretation seems to be supported by the New Testament Apostle James: "And the prayer of faith shall save the sick, and the Lord shall raise him up; and if he have committed sins, they shall be forgiven him" (James 5:15). The miracle that heals the body will also heal the soul—of both the recipient and the instrument of the miracle! How does that happen?

The authority that qualifies a person to act in the name of the Lord is the priesthood, but the power that enables mortals to act with superhuman abilities is the Spirit. President Boyd K. Packer said, "Your authority comes through your ordination; your power comes through obedience and worthiness."[25] So miracles require that we have the Spirit. Bruce R. McConkie taught, "Whenever faithful saints gain the companionship of the Holy Spirit, they are clean and pure before the Lord, for the Spirit will not dwell in an unclean tabernacle. Hence, they thereby receive a remission of those sins committed after baptism."[26] The same Spirit that comes into our lives to heal sick or battered bodies; to enlighten with dreams, visions, and revelations; to teach us new languages; or to comfort, prompt, and direct will at the same time heal our sick souls and make us clean.

Apparently, the main reason the Savior performed miracles while in mortality was to get the people's attention long enough to convince them that He could heal them spiritually. When the scribes silently accused the Savior of blasphemy for forgiving the sins of the man "sick of the palsy" (paralyzed), the Lord replied, "For whether is easier, to say, Thy sins be forgiven thee; or to say, Arise, and walk? But that ye may know that the Son of man hath power on earth to forgive sins, (then saith he to the sick of the palsy,) Arise, take up thy bed, and go unto thine house" (Matthew 9:5–6). Certainly the Savior healing a man of his paralysis was a phenomenal miracle. Yet His point seems to be what He cares about the most is changing who we are—planting a new seed in us. When we see He can heal our bodies, maybe we'll trust Him to heal our sins as well. All we have to do is stop denying His power and let Him in.

When Miracles Don't Happen

How do we make sense of the fact that sometimes the miracles we seek don't happen? If the Lord really loves us so much, why does

He seem to leave so many of our heartfelt pleas unanswered? This is a tough question to tackle. Some of the most significant petitions I've ever sent to heaven have come back apparently unfulfilled. I don't know all the answers here, but I think that an experience Nephi had can provide us with some clues.

After Lehi died, Nephi sank into a temporary depression. His strongest ally was gone, and now nothing but the power of God stood between him and his angry brothers. Nephi prayed for help: "Behold, it came to pass that I, Nephi, did cry much unto the Lord my God, because of the anger of my brethren" (2 Nephi 5:1). Nephi didn't tell us what he asked the Lord to do on this occasion, but we can speculate that it was probably what he'd been praying for all along, namely for "the power of God" to "soften their hearts" (1 Nephi 18:20). All he ever wanted was for God to touch their lives so they could have a change of heart and live the gospel in peace and happiness with the rest of the family. But it wasn't to be. What was the result of Nephi's prayer? "But behold, their anger did increase against me, insomuch that they did seek to take away my life" (2 Nephi 5:2). All the faith Nephi could muster wasn't enough to evoke the miracle he sought in the lives of his brothers.

That's not to say the Lord was ignoring Nephi's petitions, however. In verse five of that same chapter, we find out that He had different plans: "And it came to pass that the Lord did warn me, that I, Nephi, should depart from them and flee into the wilderness, and all those who would go with me." Things didn't turn out the way Nephi wanted, but the Lord was still leading him. He and his followers were spared.

Our own desires aren't the only factor in bringing about a miracle. The will of the Lord and the agency of others always come into play as well. Sometimes the best we can do is hold on and trust that the Lord is still in charge: "Therefore, let your hearts be comforted concerning [whatever is troubling you]; for all flesh is in mine hands; be still and know that I am God" (D&C 101:16). Eventually, the Lord always comes through with His assistance, even though it's usually on His timetable and not ours.

Sometimes the hardest trials to overcome are the ones of our own making. When we're suffering the natural consequences of our own bad judgments or choices, at times we still desire or even expect the Lord to come in and solve our problems. It's a hard lesson to allow the Lord to prune us so we can be humble enough for Him to build us back up. The Lord's power is great enough to help us even here, but only when we're willing to let Him in to reconstruct our lives. It starts with a change of heart and mind. That kind of total refashioning can hurt, but it can also heal. The miracle isn't always the ceasing of the storm; sometimes it's the Lord's hand pulling us through the wind and waves.

One More Look

At the conclusion of this discussion on miracles, I'd like to humbly submit one more for your consideration. I originally wrote this chapter as an essay to give to a student of mine at BYU many years ago who was struggling with the idea of miracles. I saved it in case I ever had use for it again. Then about a year ago, I decided I wanted to include it in this book, but I couldn't find my only hard-copy of it. I assumed it was lost, and I had no electronic version. A few months ago, I felt a strong desire to find this essay. I spent a week praying to the Lord, pleading with him to help me find it. At the end of the week, I was in our basement, going through an old filing cabinet we rarely open. I was looking for materials to use with our children for general conference, but I couldn't find them in any of our labeled hanging files. So I opened the bottom drawer, which turned up some unmarked files with old tax papers in them. I wasn't even going to bother looking in them, but then—out of the blue—there it was!

It wasn't the conference bingo I was looking for. It was my old essay on miracles, sticking out of one of the unmarked files. I don't think it would've ever occurred to me to look in that spot for the essay, but there it was, like a little basket of manna from heaven. The Lord says that He gives us "grace for grace" (D&C 93:20). We give our simple gifts to the Lord, and He gives us His in return, pouring out blessing after blessing. He likely doesn't even care all that much about my little essay. But He cares about *me* and wants me to trust Him so He can heal my broken heart and soiled hands and make me clean.

So yes, I do believe in a loving God who looks after His children. I believe that The Church of Jesus Christ of Latter-day Saints is the Lord's instrument of salvation on the earth today. I believe that miracles happen. I've seen them. They're for the benefit of those who keep all of God's commandments—but also for those who "seeketh so to do" (D&C 46:9). That means that, as imperfect as I am, I can still qualify to have His power work in my life. The greatest miracle of all that I've seen is the change of heart the Lord is working in my life and in the lives of my family. One day, I hope to behold His face and see that I have become like Him. It'll take a miracle, but I believe in miracles.

Marriage and the Fragility of Revelation

"Real difficulties can be overcome, it is only the imaginary ones that are unconquerable."[1]

—Theodore N. Vail

For someone to say, "But the Spirit told me I should marry you" can be the epitome of perplexity—until you think it yourself. Someone did say this to me once. We were friends in college; she wanted to be more than friends. She informed me that the Lord had told her I was the one. I was befuddled. She was a sincere member of the Church trying to follow the Lord, but I had no desire to marry her. How could she be so wrong about revelation on the most important decision of her life? Or was I the one out of tune? A few years later, the tables were turned, and I was the one thinking I had a revelation. Over the years, I've come to realize that it's not uncommon for Latter-day Saint young adults to struggle and agonize over the issue of personal revelation and the marriage decision. I think it's clear that the Lord is willing to help us, but in the end He's going to leave the choosing up to us. If we keep an open mind and don't get overly attached to someone too soon, we can be more receptive to His help.

The Most Important Decision

No one wants to mess up when choosing a marriage partner. In Shakespeare's *Twelfth Night*, the Clown comments to Maria, "Many a good hanging prevents a bad marriage."[2] While we might find that a bit irreverent, as Latter-day Saints with a belief in forever families, we can certainly empathize with the sentiment. President Hinckley once said that it "will be the most important decision of your life, the individual whom you marry."[3] We feel the weight of this momentous choice and desperately feel the need for divine assistance. Surely the Lord will help us in our decision, right? Of course He will, though maybe not in the way we'd expect.

The Lord has always given help in choosing a spouse to those who are prayerful and active in their search. When it was time for Isaac to marry, Abraham sent his servant away from the unbelieving Canaanites, where they were living, back to the covenant people of his birth to search for possibilities. Abraham testified that he knew the Lord would "send his angel before thee" (Genesis 24:7) and help them in this essential matter. The servant told the Lord what he was looking for. Rebekah appeared and fit the bill perfectly. After the servant chose Rebekah as the best candidate, he explained how the inspiration came: "I being in the way, the Lord led me to the house of my master's brethren" (Genesis 24:27). Because his feet were moving along the path, the Lord was able to guide him to a good place to search. Yet even after the Lord helped Isaac's cause, it was up to Rebekah to make her choice. She did so courageously, saying in words reminiscent of Nephi's famous declaration, "I will go" (Genesis 24:58). Because of faith and committed action, the Lord helped Isaac and Rebekah get together.

We read stories like this one and feel strongly that we need divine assistance too. Most of the time, we don't really want to go back to the days of arranged marriages, but won't the Lord send *us* revelation on finding a spouse? He will. He says, "Be thou humble; and the Lord thy God shall lead thee by the hand, and give thee answer to thy prayers" (D&C 112:10). The most oft repeated promise in all the standard works is "ask and ye shall receive." The Lord is intimately concerned with our marriage decision and is willing to assist us, but there's still the challenge of our limitations.

Interpreting Revelation

How good do we think we are at receiving and interpreting revelation? The Lord wants to help us in these crucial life decisions as well as the more mundane ones, but He has to work with our imperfections. The Lord introduced the Doctrine and Covenants by saying, "Behold, I am God and have spoken it; these commandments are of me, and were given unto my servants in their weakness, after the manner of their language, that they might come to understanding" (D&C 1:24). The Lord here is speaking as plainly as He can to us, yet in our weakness we often misunderstand Him. Brigham Young described our plight this way: "I do not even believe that there is a single revelation, among the many God has given to the Church, that is perfect in its fulness. The revelations of God contain correct doctrine and principle, . . . but it is impossible for . . . [us] to receive a revelation from the Almighty in all its perfections. He has to speak to us in a manner to meet the extent of our capacities."[4] I understand President Young to be saying that while God's communication to us is perfect, our ability to receive, understand, and apply it never is. Therefore, we must always stay open the possibility that we're interpreting something wrong.

The Apostle Paul also recognized our limitations in understanding, even while receiving divine assistance. He said, "For we know in part, and we prophesy in part. But when that which is perfect is come, then that which is in part shall be done away. . . . For now we see through a glass, darkly; but then face to face: now I know in part; but then shall I know even as also I am known" (1 Corinthians 13:9–10, 12). We think we're looking at the world and seeing things the way they are. In reality, we see only a distorted reflection of ourselves and a subsequent projection of ourselves onto the world. All this happens with even the most spiritually in-tune Latter-day Saint who's acting under the spirit of revelation.

What does this mean for the young adult trying to receive help on the marriage decision? There's going to be a lot of trial and error in the process. So we better keep an open mind about the whole thing and stay tentative about the conclusions we come to. Like circus elephants learning to tightrope walk, we're bound to make a lot of mistakes along the way. But there's always the Lord's safety net underneath, ready to catch us when we fall.

One of these errors we're likely to make is letting our emotions take too large a role in the process. Elder Richard G. Scott explained, "The inspiring influence of the Holy Spirit can be overcome or masked by strong emotions, such as anger, hate, passion, fear, or pride. When such influences are present, it is like trying to savor the delicate flavor of a grape while eating a jalapeño pepper. Both flavors are present, but one completely overpowers the other. In like manner, strong emotions overcome the delicate promptings of the Holy Spirit."[5] Here is a similar caution from President Boyd K. Packer: "The spiritual part of us and the emotional part of us are so closely linked that it is possible to mistake an emotional impulse for something spiritual. We occasionally find people who receive what they assume to be spiritual promptings from God, when those promptings are . . . centered in the emotions."[6] Because emotions so often blur our vision, we should be looking for ways to check the inspiration we think we're receiving against other sources: our reason, our experience, trusted advisers, and further prayer. The uncertainty that comes from this process is going to make courtship a stressful and difficult time—sometimes excruciatingly so.

Making a Choice

A typical courtship for a Latter-day Saint young adult might go like this: I start hanging out socially with lots of people. I go on a few dates with different people. I find someone I'm attracted to and who seems to reciprocate my interest. I like this person a lot. I stop dating other people to focus just on this one possibility. I think maybe I could love them, so I start praying and asking the Lord, "Is he (or she) the one?" But perhaps there's a problem with the question I'm asking and in the way I'm narrowing the field.

President Kimball taught that the idea of a "one-and-only" out there for us to find is misguided. "'Soul mates' are a fiction and an illusion; and while every young man and young woman will seek with all diligence and prayerfulness to find a mate with whom life can be most compatible and beautiful, yet it is certain that almost any good man and any good woman can have happiness and a successful marriage if both are willing to pay the price."[7] So I've been praying to ask the Lord if my sweetheart is *the one*, and the Lord has been answering me by saying that I've made a good choice. The problem seems to be that I want Him to tell me whom to marry. This is the scariest decision I'll likely ever make. Joseph Smith once said,

"There is no pain so awful as the pain of suspense."[8] I'm desperately looking for some way out of that pain. In addition, I don't want to be responsible if something goes wrong. I've heard that half of all marriages end in divorce, and I don't want mine to be another casualty. I want the Lord to somehow guarantee that this is a match made in heaven that's going to last forever. But if the idea of soul mates is a fiction as President Kimball said, then matches aren't made in heaven—they're made on earth. Perhaps the risks are unavoidable.

President Packer seemed to support this idea when he said,

> While I am sure some young couples have some special guidance in getting together, I do not believe in predestined love. If you desire the inspiration of the Lord in this crucial decision, you must live the standards of the Church, and you must pray constantly for the wisdom to recognize those qualities upon which a successful union may be based. You must do the choosing, rather than to seek for some one-and-only so-called soul mate, chosen for you by someone else and waiting for you. You are to do the choosing.[9]

That reasoning puts all the pressure back on me. I can ask for the Lord's help, but since it's *my* eternity that's resting on this decision; it has to be *my* choice.

Perhaps in some respects, the Lord doesn't care whom I marry. After all, *He* won't have to live with him or her for all eternity—I will! Perhaps all He truly cares about is that I pick someone who's headed in the right direction. Bruce R. McConkie was an Apostle in the 1970s and 80s and was well-known for always striving to be on the same page as the Spirit. He gave this revealing account of selecting a marriage partner:

> How do you choose a wife? I've heard a lot of young people from Brigham Young University and elsewhere say, 'I've got to get a feeling of inspiration. I've got to get some revelation. I've got to fast and pray and get the Lord to manifest to me whom I should marry.' Well, maybe it will be a little shock to you, but never in my life did I ever ask the Lord whom I ought to marry. It never occurred to me to ask him. I went out and found the girl I wanted; she suited me; I evaluated and weighed the proposition, and it just seemed a hundred percent to me as though this ought to be. Now, if I'd done things perfectly, I'd have done some counseling with the Lord, which I didn't

> do; but all I did was pray to the Lord and ask for some guidance and direction in connection with the decision that I'd reached.[10]

So perhaps I should expect nudges and promptings along the way but not a definite answer like, "This is the person you should marry."

Wait a minute! Doesn't Nephi say that if you "receive the Holy Ghost, it will show unto you all things what ye should do" (2 Nephi 32:5)? Certainly, as long as there is a *should* among the choices. If it's the case, however—as President Kimball and President Packer taught—that there is no soul mate out there for me to find, then there are perhaps a number of excellent choices I could choose for my spouse. Who's going to make the decision? I will. But then, even if the Lord approves of my choice, I have to wait and see if that person picks me in return.

Where Is the Lord?

Perhaps like you, I've heard stories in the Church of people who claimed they didn't choose their spouse. The Spirit somehow led them to a singles' dance and seemed to knock them over the head with a lightning bolt, saying, "Here's the one!" How could that happen if there are no soul mates?

Is it possible the Spirit was trying to help, but they misinterpreted the message? Could it be that what the Spirit was really trying to tell them was something more like: "Look, I know you're struggling with this marriage thing, so I'm going to help you out a bit. Here's someone who would be an excellent choice for a companion—if they'll have you. Why don't you ask them?" Because of weakness in interpreting revelation, they thought the Spirit was saying, "There's the one!" But wouldn't the Lord have to respect "the one's" agency in this whole thing as well? Hugh B. Brown, a former counselor in the First Presidency, declared, "I think that as a rule the Lord does not come down and take us by the ear and turn us around and lead us to somebody and say, 'This is your future husband or wife.'"[11] Whatever exceptions there may be, normally we have to make the decision ourselves and simply seek for the Lord's encouragement along the way.

This doesn't mean that I should stop seeking for inspiration on the marriage decision. While the Lord may not care so much which of several right choices I might make, He certainly will warn me if I'm going to make a *wrong* choice. Too many young people seem to rely mainly on the romantic tuggings of the heart and fail to be careful enough. Craig Horton, a marriage and family therapist in southern California, conducted a survey among Church members whose marriages had failed and discovered that most people cited a major flaw in the spouse's character or irreconcilable differences. What surprised him was that virtually all of those he talked with sensed these differences or flaws *before* marriage, yet they'd relied upon love and romance to overcome them.[12] So I'd better be listening to input from all sources about reasons *not* to marry someone, to be safe.

Would the Lord prompt me to pursue a marriage possibility with someone He knows is eventually not going to reciprocate my interest? That's a good question. Why did the Lord tell the early Saints to build a temple in Jackson County, Missouri, when He knew it wasn't going to be built in their lifetime? Sometimes we have important lessons to learn through rejection and disappointment. The Lord doesn't set us up for failure, but He does allow for individual agency.

Keeping Personal Revelation Personal

One thing I must *not* do if I think I received inspiration is to tell the other person about it. Here's a warning from Randy Hall, a former assistant administrator for seminaries and institutes in the Church Educational System: "We should be cautious of using phrases such as 'The Spirit told me to . . .' or, 'The Spirit said I should. . . .' Intentionally or unintentionally, these phrases can be used to eliminate discussion or disagreement. When prompted by the Spirit, it is generally sufficient to act on the prompting without announcing that we are doing so."[13] Brother Hall seems to be saying that personal revelation is, well, just that—personal. To start telling others about it, particularly those I don't have stewardship over, is a risky business under any circumstances. But to use my prompting that I feel is a personal revelation to try to persuade someone else to do what I want them to do is manipulation. It may be unrighteous dominion.

President Boyd K. Packer gave a similar warning: "I have learned that strong, impressive spiritual experiences do not come to us very frequently. And when they do, they are generally for our own edification, instruction, or correction. Unless we are called by proper authority to do so, they do not position us to counsel or to correct others."[14] That would include not counseling someone we felt prompted to marry. They have to get their own inspiration on this all-important decision. As Elder Robert D. Hales wrote, "No young woman should ever marry a young man based on revelation or inspiration he has received. She has the right to receive her own revelation regarding this matter of eternal consequence."[15] Of course, that warning applies to young men as well.

I had a college roommate named Peter who fell in love during our freshman year. But Peter was supposed to go on a mission first. I think he really didn't want to leave because he was so sure his girlfriend, Samantha, would marry someone else if he did. (This was a pretty good example of why the prophets teach us not to date seriously until after the young man gets off his mission.) Peter was a good guy though, and he wanted to do the right thing. He prayed and felt he got an answer: If he served a faithful mission, he could marry Samantha when he got back. He was so excited that he went and told Samantha all about it.

I don't know if he got that revelation or not. Perhaps the Lord was trying to tell him something and he misinterpreted it. Maybe what the Lord was saying was something like, "Yes, you should go on a mission and things will work out with Samantha." Then Peter interpreted that to mean, "Things will work out with Samantha *the way I want them to*." Whatever happened between him and the Lord, I don't think he should have told Samantha. But the deed was done. Peter left on his mission.

Almost two years later, I saw Samantha on campus at BYU. She said she'd been writing Peter all through his mission and now he was almost home. She was afraid that when he came back, they would start dating again and she'd have to marry him because of the revelation he had. She wanted advice.

I was in a precarious position. The last thing I wanted to do was "mess things up" for my former roommate, but I strongly felt that he'd put her in an unfair position. Anyway, how in the world should I have known whether Samantha should marry Peter? Though I was sorely tempted to tell her to dump him and go find someone else, I refrained. I knew this had to be her decision. I simply listened to her concerns and assured her that the Lord would help her figure things out. The one piece of advice that I *did* give her was that she didn't have to worry about acting against someone else's personal revelation.

Samantha started dating a young man toward the end of Peter's mission and married him shortly after Peter returned. Peter was devastated, of course, but he later married someone else in the temple and now is raising a happy family. Things did indeed work out with Samantha, just not how he'd pictured them.

As far as I can tell, dilemmas like this one aren't that uncommon for righteous, thoughtful young adults trying to get married. This whole courtship and marriage thing is rarely smooth sailing for anyone—even for the best of Latter-day Saints.

I had an institute student once who was dating a nice returned missionary. They fell in love and began talking about getting married. But then my student's sister received her patriarchal blessing, which said that she should go on a mission and that one of her sisters would follow her example. She shared her blessing with her sister; my student decided that she was the one her sister's blessing was referring to, so she broke up with the nice young man and went on a mission. I'm all in favor of everyone making his or her own decisions about who and when to marry, and I hope things turned out well for my student and this young man. Yet I think it's a serious mistake to use someone else's revelation as a sign of how you should make the important decisions in *your* life.

The Follies of Sign-Seeking

It seems as though many of us are looking for some sort of sign from heaven to ensure we don't mess up, and we're willing to take a sign wherever we can find one. Perhaps this sign-seeking is what's confusing the issue the most. The Lord says that "he that seeketh signs shall see signs, but not unto salvation" and "behold, faith cometh not by signs, but signs follow those that believe" (D&C 63:7, 9). We shouldn't wait for a sign *before* we act. As we ask for guidance and make our own decisions, we may expect to see signs along the way indicating that we are on the right path.

Monte J. Brough of the Seventy once taught a powerful lesson about how the Spirit works. At a BYU devotional, he compared the

Spirit to the onboard navigating system of a jet plane. Before taking off, the pilot programs in the desired destination. The navigational computer sends radar signals to the preprogrammed destination. As long as the plane is on course, nothing happens. When the plane starts to veer off course, however, the radar triggers an alarm to warn the pilot to make a course correction. Elder Brough suggested that perhaps this is how the Spirit often works with us. Being on course guarantees that I'll eventually make it to my destination—as long as I never give up. Yet this does not do anything to prevent obstacles from blocking my path. If I can feel the Spirit with me in my life, that's the Lord's way of telling me that I'm on course. That isn't the same thing as a guarantee that the person I like is going to become my eternal companion.

As confusing as sign-seeking can be before marriage, it can get even more confusing down the road.

A few years ago, an incredibly distraught woman of my acquaintance came to me in tears. Her husband had committed adultery. She hammered me with the question that was smashing her soul: "Why in the world did the Lord prompt me to marry him if He knew my husband would do this to me later on?" Somehow, it was God's fault she was in this mess. Realizing that she was in no state of mind to be lectured to, I just listened to her. Later, I did have several thoughts about her situation. How could she be so sure she understood what the Lord was trying to tell her all those years ago? Even if the Lord had approved her decision to marry her husband, was that the same thing as guaranteeing that he'd never betray her? Her husband still had his agency. Even if she did get the inspiration right, maybe she was too caught up in her sorrow to see a larger design. Why would the Lord prompt Joseph Smith to marry Emma, knowing that she would end up having great challenges later in life that would stretch their marriage to the breaking point?

The Lord isn't there to make everything work out for us the way we want it to. He's there to guide us as we make our own decisions along a path that'll eventually lead us to become as He is. Still, that path may require disappointment and even betrayal along the way. It'll *always* require that we make difficult decisions ourselves and be responsible for the outcomes. Even though we may be looking for the security of a sign that our marriages will work out happily ever after, the Lord doesn't give guarantees that we'll be spared from crushing disappointments: "The Son of Man hath descended below them all. Art thou greater than he?" (D&C 122:8).

Growing Greener Grass

A friend of mine named Jeff returned from his mission eager to find his eternal companion and be married in the temple. He drew close to marriage several times and even got engaged once, but each time he backed away, fearing he was making the wrong choice. What if there was someone better out there he simply hadn't met yet? Was he settling for less than he might find later? What if his "dream girl" was just around the corner?

Jeff finally talked to his bishop and was referred to an LDS counselor to help him work through these fears and the resulting difficulties in his relationships. Jeff was able to see through his negative thought patterns and discovered that his fear came from "the grass is always greener on the other side" syndrome. Instead of looking for potential, he was looking for perfection. His counselor taught him that perfect matches aren't found—they're made, and not in heaven. They're made on earth with two imperfect people who decide to move ahead in spite of fears and weaknesses and simply make a go of it.

The night before his temple sealing, Jeff was assaulted by the adversary. He stayed up all night, battered by his old doubts and insecurities. At four in the morning, he finally asked for a priesthood blessing. Satan was rebuked and cast out for the day. Jeff was able to get a little rest and eventually enjoy a beautiful day with family and friends in the temple. He is now content and happy in his marriage and is on the path that eventually leads to eternal joy.

Of course, Jeff and his wife will still have challenges. A key to success in their marriage (and all marriages) will be their willingness to communicate with each other and work through those challenges. His wise therapist taught him, "You don't find greener grass; you grow it!" Certainly there will be a lot of weeding and watering along the way. By working together, they have the potential to *create* the ideal match that before he was trying to *discover*.

Ruining Good Relationships

As hard as it is to receive and interpret revelation on dating and courtship, we often make it much harder by the way we go about it all.

One of the biggest problems General Authorities have been warning young single adults about is the decline of courtship and the rise of "hanging out." For instance, Elder M. Russell Ballard counseled returned missionaries to "go on dates. Hanging out is not the way, nor is it enough! Courting seems to be a lost art. Rediscover it. It really works."[16] While hanging out in place of serious dating is a problem on the one extreme, there's another mistake on the other extreme: getting too serious too soon.

While I was in a BYU singles ward, I received what I consider the best dating and courtship advice I ever heard. Bishop Rogers delivered a fireside address one evening called "Seven Ways to Ruin a Perfectly Good Relationship." Of his seven ways, the one he seemed to condemn the most was to date exclusively. He tried to convince us that as soon as you start to date someone exclusively, you begin the process of ruining that relationship. That advice seemed counterintuitive. I always thought having a girlfriend was a necessary step for me along the path to courtship and marriage. That seems to be what everyone else did.

Yet Bishop Rogers had my attention. He said that dating is the time to compare qualities that people have that could make them potential marriage candidates. To remain objective, you need to keep your independence as long as possible—while still moving toward marriage. Engagement is the time to cut off all other relationships and begin to meld your life with your intended. Even then, you should be cautious and a bit tentative, because engagements can be broken. Bishop Rogers said even after he'd started getting serious about his wife, he continued to date other young women until she said, "Yes."

While it took me time to understand and evaluate what Bishop Rogers was trying to teach us, I've now come to agree with him strongly. The dumbest thing that a youth or young single adult can do is have a boyfriend or girlfriend! That might be an unpopular thing to say, I know. Yet I am convinced of it. Nothing will get in the way of personal revelation more than having a boyfriend or girlfriend. Two people start to intertwine their lives together before ever committing to do so permanently. Then, after emotionally investing so much into a relationship, they go to the Lord and ask for revelation on whether they should make it permanent. At that point, they're so invested that it's almost impossible to discern between inspiration and emotion.

A healthy dose of the law of witnesses might be helpful here. Joseph Smith said that "by proving contraries, truth is made manifest,"[17] and Lehi said that there must needs be an opposition in all things (see 2 Nephi 2:11). The best way to do that during courtship is keep dating other people until you get engaged. That way you'll always have another option to consider against the one you're thinking about. When you finally make your choice, ask the Lord for confirmation. Then ask the person (or wait to be asked). If they choose you, it's time to get engaged. That's the time to break off all other dating options and start focusing on creating a relationship with just one person.

To start getting seriously involved with someone before you've both made the official commitment of engagement is like creating a counterfeit marriage. You start sharing intimate feelings, dreams, and desires with someone you may not end up pursuing them with. Then if you break up, you have to go through what amounts to a mini-divorce. You have to pull apart and extricate yourself from the person you've just spent weeks, months, or even years intertwining your life with. Almost inevitably, you go through much of the same feelings of heartbreak, betrayal, and anger that accompany a divorce. And there was no good reason for setting yourself up for this in the first place.

But don't I have to get to know others intimately to determine if I want to spend eternity with them? Well, I do need to get to know them. I ought to see how they react in different situations with different groups of people. I should definitely see how they interact with their families, if possible. But if I can do those things without getting too intimate, I can keep a little objective distance from which I can evaluate the relationships better. The more intimate we become, the closer the relationships, and the stronger the ties of sharing, the harder it's going to be to make objective decisions about the rightness of the relationships. And the harder it's going to be to break off the relationships if I decide it's not wise to pursue them further.

President Kimball explained, "Missionaries should begin to think marriage—when they return from their missions, to begin to get acquainted with many young women so that they will have a better basis for selection of a life's companion."[18] The key there is to have *many* people you're pursuing. How can you make an informed choice if there's only one selection from which to choose? In a special address to youth and young adults, President Hinckley similarly warned, "Steady dating . . . leads so often to tragedy. Studies have shown that the longer a boy and girl date one another, the more likely they are to get into trouble. It is better, my friends, to date a variety of companions until you are ready to marry. Have a wonderful time, but stay away from familiarity. Keep your hands to yourself. It may not be easy, but it is possible."[19] Engagement means you're ready to marry.

Don't we need to spend time as boyfriend and girlfriend before getting engaged to see if we love each other? As strange as it may seem to say, falling in love is easy! The whole experience of collapsing the ego boundaries and feeling all the emotional rush that goes along with it can happen to almost any couple if placed in the right (or wrong) circumstances for long enough. What we need is enough emotional distance to make an objective decision about whom we want to *choose* to love before we allow ourselves to *fall* in love. The best way to do that is not date exclusively until officially engaged.

My Journey

I thought I'd fallen in love once. I had been off my mission for a couple of years and felt it was time to get married. Jane was everything I thought I was looking for in a wife. And wonder of wonders—she seemed to like me too. I went to the temple and prayed about asking her to marry me. I seemed to get a good feeling, so I thought I was set. However, I once listened to George Durrant give a talk on marriage. He taught that if you think you received a revelation about whom to marry, simply ask. If she says yes, you got the revelation right. If she says no, you got it wrong. I asked Jane about her feelings and she said the infamous words, "Let's just be friends."

I was devastated. For a while after that, I doubted my own worthiness. I doubted my ability to receive revelation. I doubted everything. I assumed she prayed about her decision and felt like the Lord was helping her with it. Did that mean the Lord told her I wasn't the right person? What did that say about me?

Fortunately, I came to see this simply as a matter of choice. The Lord isn't going to choose spouses for us. He sent us here precisely so we could choose partners to love completely. But they also have to choose us! If they do, then we spend the rest of our lives trying to love them more than ourselves. But first, you both have got to make your own individual choices. Jean-Paul Sartre said that man is forever condemned to be free. As much as we might want someone to make the important choices in life for us or make those choices for someone else, ultimately the choice will always be up to the individual. Even if we mistakenly *do* allow others to decide for us or try to force our own decisions on others, each person involved will have to live with the consequences.

With time, I came to see how wise Jane's decision was not to get married. We barely knew each other at all. I was so immature that I didn't know how to develop a relationship. I was infatuated with the idea of being in love and getting married, but I didn't know how to talk with a woman and share feelings and affection. I was still so egotistical that I had little idea about how to relate lovingly with another human being. I projected an image of my ideal self onto a person I admired and fell in love with that image. In a real sense, I fell in love with myself.

So what was the Lord trying to tell me in the temple? I don't really know. Perhaps it was something like, "Yes, Jane is a special one of my daughters. It shows your good taste that you'd be interested in her. If she'll have you, go for it!" Of course, the Lord knew that I wasn't ready for marriage and that she wasn't really that interested, but perhaps He was trying to teach those things to me—things that I wasn't ready to hear—in a way I could understand. He let *her* tell me no so I could learn about agency. It was *her* decision.

A few years later after maturing a bit, I almost fell in love again. Rachel was incredible—bright, energetic, talented, and from a remarkable family. She was a returned missionary who was obviously going places with her life. We hit it off from the first date. A General Authority had set us up on a blind date. Certainly she must be the one! What stronger sign could I ask for? After a summer of picnics in the park, we started talking about the possibility of marriage. She was obviously interested in me, and unlike my one-way, mirror-like relationship with Jane, this was a reciprocal interest and concern that felt real.

There was one serious problem though. I wasn't attracted to Rachel physically. That bothered me to no end. I wanted to take our relationship to another level and perhaps give her a kiss goodnight, but I simply couldn't bring myself to do it. I fasted and prayed about my dilemma and finally took my issue to the Lord in the temple. I prayed seriously for some kind of divine intervention.

It came. The next time I picked up Rachel for a date, she seemed different to me. And on each subsequent date, I found Rachel more and more attractive. Eventually, Rachel seemed almost irresistible to me. It was just about the strangest phenomenon I've ever experienced. The Lord had truly parted a Red Sea for me, and I was sure that the promised land—eternal marriage—would be waiting for me on the other side.

Then on one date, we had a serious talk. We discussed our different views on money and lifestyles and other relevant topics. There were so many issues we hadn't been able to examine because we were caught up in the physical aspects of our relationship. We recognized that we had irreconcilable differences and eventually we went our separate ways.

But now I was a bit upset with the Lord. I almost felt betrayed. The reason I'd petitioned the Lord so fervently to change my physical feelings for Rachel was so I could marry her and get on with the business of creating a family. What was He thinking? Why would He play games with my emotions like that?

I still had a lot to learn. Perhaps He answered my prayers about physical attraction because I was so sincere. Maybe He wanted me to discover that He really is omnipotent in the sense that He can overcome all obstacles to His plan. Maybe I needed help in overcoming my physical barriers so I could see that there were other obstacles to our getting married I wasn't looking at. Perhaps part and parcel to the Lord's plan is our own individual agency, and that's an obstacle He simply will not overpower. Perhaps most of the time for us mortals, as the Jainist saying goes, "truth is the way of the perhaps."

I had a lot of time to think about these questions. I was the blind date king of Utah County for the next five years. During this time, I often resorted to poetry, trying to express the anguish of my search:

A Fragile Find
There is a space
Where fingers do not run through my hair
Like gentle rain,
Where sunsets and ice cream shakes
Do not overflow evening skies,
Where children do not run and shout
And wear out carpet,
A space only you can fill
But only I can find
—May 1998

In the summer of 1998, I was in Mexico City speaking at a young adult conference. After a day of talks, I was up late drinking chicken broth and hot sauce to calm my cold symptoms. I felt drawn to a copy of the priesthood manual sitting on the table. I opened it and read Brigham Young addressing single adult males and calling on all of us within the reach of his voice. He said it was time to repent and simply go find a wife, and then wear out our lives in making her happy. I felt a strong directive from the Spirit that this was the Lord's message for me right then and there. I graciously accepted those promptings as a revelation.

But the experience didn't end there. Next, I did something that surprised me. I made a decision sitting in that kitchen in Mexico City. I decided that my choice was Stacy Harding. I'd never dated Stacy. I didn't even know her that well. I knew she was a hard worker, loved the Lord, and seemed to have her head on straight. To top it off, she was quite attractive to me. But I felt the Lord was serious about me getting married, so I made a momentous—if somewhat presumptuous—decision.

I went home to Orem and asked Stacy out three times in the same week. She started to panic. She knew I was serious and told her mother that she didn't want to marry me. Her mother just smiled and said, "Your feelings might change, dear." Stacy ran into her bedroom, got on her knees, and entreated the Lord, saying, "Please don't let my feelings change. Please don't let my feelings change." Despite all her pleading, her feelings changed! I don't feel that the Lord changed her heart so she'd fall in love with me. He helped her discover the space to make the choice to change her own heart.

Before I officially asked Stacy's dad for her hand in marriage, I went to the temple to pray about it. There were no burning bushes—not even a burning in the bosom. There was just a peaceful assurance that I was on track. That was good enough for me.

Even after choosing Stacy and having her choose me, we tried to keep our emotional independence for as long as possible. We weren't dating exclusively. Two days before I planned to propose to Stacy, I took out another young lady on a date. I told Stacy I was going and told her all about it when I got back. I didn't want to hurt Stacy, but the fact was that we hadn't yet committed ourselves to marriage, so there was no reason to act like we *were* married and had to be loyal to each other before any real commitments were made. Going out with another nice, kind woman only reconfirmed in my mind that Stacy was the one with whom I wanted to spend eternity. I decided to ask Stacy's parents for her hand.

We both experienced last-minute doubts and questions about our decision. What if the other didn't measure up? What if there was someone else out there who'd be better? What if *I* didn't measure up? We prevailed over our doubts and fears, however, and finally made it to the temple. It was worth the effort. December 18, 1998, kneeling across the altar in the Manti Temple, was the greatest moment of my life.

I don't consider myself an expert on getting married. I've done it only once. All I know is that the Lord is truly interested in this most important decision of our lives and will help us through the difficult journey if we let Him.

Staying Single . . . for Now

It took me ten years after my mission and plenty of miracles to reach the goal of a happy marriage. What about those who never get the opportunity to marry in this life? The prophets have given repeated assurances that a merciful Father in Heaven will provide a way in the next life. The Lord will deprive no one who is worthy. Here is President Kimball's message of hope:

> I am aware of some young men and women who seemingly have not been successful in total fulfillment. Some have been on missions; some have completed their education. And yet they have passed the period of their greatest opportunity for marriage. The time has passed, and while still attractive and desirable and efficient, they find themselves alone.
>
> To you we say this: You are making a great contribution to the world as you serve your families and the Church and the world. You must remember that the Lord loves you and the Church loves you. To you women, we can only say we have no control over the heartbeats or the affections of men, but pray that you may find fulfillment. And in the meantime, we promise you that insofar as eternity is concerned, no soul will be deprived of rich and high and eternal blessings for anything which that person could not help, that the Lord never fails in his promises, and that every righteous person will receive eventually all to which the person is entitled and which he or she has not forfeited through any fault of his or her own.[20]

How can Saints get married after they die? The Savior said that "in the resurrection they neither marry, nor are given in marriage" (Matthew 22:30). Commenting on that passage, Elder James E. Talmage explained, "All questions of marital status must be settled before that time."[21] So it looks like any post-mortal matchmaking will have to be done in the spirit world before the resurrection. Perhaps there will be some spirit mix n' mingles or singles dances! Somehow, they will have the opportunity they didn't receive in mortal life.

Heber J. Grant once shared a story in general conference illustrating this possibility. While growing up, President Grant's best friend was Feramorz Young. President Grant said that Feramorz was the kindest, gentlest soul he ever knew. At the age of eighteen, Feramorz was called on a mission to serve with Apostle Moses Thatcher and open up missionary work in Mexico. They held the first conference of the Church in Mexico on April 6, 1881, at the top of Mount Popocatepetl just a few miles outside of Mexico City. They baptized sixty-one people. Then Feramorz got sick with typhoid fever. Elder Thatcher decided he needed to get Feramorz back home, and they headed for the Gulf of Mexico. On route to Florida, Feramorz came down with pneumonia and died. He was buried at sea.

President Grant recounted later what happened. A woman came to Feramorz's mother in Salt Lake City, carrying with her a photograph of this woman's dearest friend. Here is what she said to Sister Young:

> Now, Mrs. Young, I do not believe a thing of what I am going to tell you. This girl friend of mine was one of the noblest, finest, choicest kind of girls and young women that ever lived. She has come to me in this city of Salt Lake on three separate occasions at night in dreams, and has given me this information: the date of her birth, the date of her death, and all that is necessary, she says, for a record in the temple; and she has told me that your son, Feramorz L. Young, has converted her, and that in addition to converting her he has proposed marriage to her. 'I want you to go to Mrs. Young and give her this information and vouch for my honesty, virtue, integrity and upright life, and have the work done for me and have me married for eternity to her son, Feramorz Young.'
>
> This woman who was speaking to Sister Young then concluded, "I do not believe a word of it, but the last time this friend of mine came—which was the third time—she said, 'There is nobody in Salt Lake City who knows me and can vouch for me except you. You are the only individual that I know in Salt Lake City.'" She continued her incredulous explanation to Sister Young: "I can furnish you any references you may wish regarding my character, from the place where I formerly lived. The last time this young woman came to me, she said, 'You might just as well go to Mrs. Young and give her this information, because I am going to come, and come, and come, until you do it.' " Then the woman concluded, "I just cannot bear to have her come again; it is so uncanny, and I do not believe a thing of it."

Well, Sister Young *did* believe it, got permission, and had her son married vicariously to the woman he'd chosen in the spirit world.[22] Either in this life or in the next, the Lord will provide a way if we're willing to choose it.

The Bottom Line

Let me state clearly that there's nothing we need more divine help with than in choosing an eternal companion. There's also nothing more difficult to correctly interpret than inspiration on that choice. First of all, I shouldn't expect the Lord to make the decision for me. I have to make the choice. Second, I'd better be open to the possibility that I've misunderstood what the Spirit is trying to tell me. That doesn't mean that I have to go around constantly second-guessing every prompting I receive. Still, I do need a healthy skepticism about my own decisions and a large dose of charity about the other person's right to receive inspiration. Third, because receiving and interpreting inspiration on this decision is so difficult, I need to maintain as objective a stance as I can before jumping in. The best way I know to do this is to actively try to date and court, but not to date exclusively until after getting engaged.

Choosing an eternal companion is the most important decision we'll ever make. Even with good intentions, it's easy to commit some egregious mistakes. The Lord's Atonement is broad enough to rescue us from our own dumb decisions—or the dumb decisions of others—on this most important matter of choosing an eternal companion. There's so much that's confusing and uncertain in this whole matchmaking endeavor.[23] In this life, we see through a glass darkly. But I'm certain that if we're worthy of an eternal companion and desire that with all our heart (and if we stay on the path where that blessing is most likely to occur), then one day—either here or in the spirit world—the Lord will provide the way by which we may choose and enjoy that blessing. I know. He has done it for me. And it was well worth the struggle. I'll close this chapter with a poem from my inspired and inspiring sister:

No Island
By Shoni Conrad

There will be tears and kisses
and children's freckled faces
and crystal choir voices
and returns to favorite places
There will be gentle mornings
and poetic evening skies
and you will need someone
with whom to share your sighs

Women and the Priesthood

"To keep your marriage brimming / With love in the marriage cup, / Whenever you're wrong, admit it; / Whenever you're right, shut up."[1]

—Ogden Nash

One day, I was sitting on the couch reading the paper while our four-year-old daughter, Keely, played with her doll in the other room. Suddenly, she burst into the room, ripped the newspaper out of my hands, and asked with great earnestness, "Why can't women hold the priesthood?"

I'd expected our children to ask questions like this at age fourteen, not at four!

From the kitchen, Stacy watched me squirm a bit to reach for an answer without much success. Then, with a warm smile, she came over to where we were, knelt down to look into Keely's eyes, and said something along the lines of, "Oh, Keely, what a great question to ask. Heavenly Father loves when we ask thoughtful questions like that. It means you're smart and want to learn about His plan."

Keely glared at her as if to say, "Stop stalling and get on with it!"

Then Stacy said, "After Heavenly Father created this beautiful world for us, He gave women the greatest power in the universe. Do you know what that is?"

Keely thought about the question for a moment and replied, "To have babies?"

"That's right," Stacy said, "To have babies. And then He had to give the men something so they wouldn't feel left out. Do you know what he gave them?"

"The priesthood?" Keely answered, a bit skeptically.

"That's right!" replied Stacy. "Since women can have babies and men have the priesthood, a husband and wife can work together to create families that'll be together forever. Isn't that wonderful?"

Keely looked at Stacy inquisitively, looked at me skeptically, and then looked back at her mother and said, "That's cool." And she was off in a flash, playing with her doll again. Stacy smiled, winked at me, and went back to her project in the kitchen. I picked up my paper again, though I was in too much shock to read anything.

In another bolt of energy, Keely ripped the paper out of my hands again and said, "But Daddy, next time you talk to Jesus, you tell Him we want the priesthood too!" And then off she went again.

She was four. I couldn't wait to see what she'd be thinking about at fourteen. At four, fourteen, or forty, hers is still a good question that calls for discussion. Why do men hold the priesthood in the Church? What exactly are the expected roles for men and women? Are they merely culturally determined or does the Lord really expect us to be different in the powers we wield? How can we be different and still be equal? Should women hold the priesthood too? These are all issues that thoughtful Latter-day Saints must address at some time or another.

The Church's answers to these questions differ greatly from mainstream America's answers. Once while teaching institute at a small community college, I had a young lady visit who wanted to know more about the Church. She was bright and seeking religious enlightenment and fulfillment. She started taking the missionary lessons, read the Book of Mormon, attended Church, and was progressing toward baptism. One day, she came into my office and wanted to know the Church's stance on feminism and women's rights. She had stumbled onto some anti-Mormon websites and wanted to investigate some of the claims being made against us.

I started my explanation by reading the words of Nephi about the universality of the Lord's love: "He inviteth them all to come unto him and partake of his goodness; and he denieth none that come unto him, black and white, bond and free, male and female; and he remembereth the heathen; and all are alike unto God" (2 Nephi 26:33). I explained that the Church supports total equality in politics, education, and the workplace, but we also support traditional roles for men and women that sustain the family at home. In the public sphere, we support total equality; in the private sphere, we encourage divinely appointed gender roles with mutual support and respect. As a fledgling feminist, she wasn't impressed and quickly ended her involvement with the Church. After all, how could this be the true Church of God if it didn't treat women exactly the same as men?

While on this occasion I (a man) was trying to teach a woman about the issue, I believe that women in the Church have much to teach men about it. This has been true ever since the Fall.

The Fortunate Fall

For millennia, men have used the story of the Fall to justify their "superior" position over women in society. Because Eve was deceived, and not Adam, and because she fell first, all womankind has "rightfully" been made to suffer for her mistake. Yet as Latter-day Saints, we view the Fall differently than other Judeo-Christian faiths. Thanks to latter-day scripture, we understand the Fall to be a great blessing—a gift from Adam and Eve to us, which is the gift of mortality. It was a fortunate Fall. So because it was a blessing, Eve should be thanked and honored for taking the initiative.

After partaking of the fruit, Adam began "to prophesy concerning all the families of the earth" (Moses 5:10). But his focus seems to be just a bit off: "because of *my* transgression *my* eyes are opened, and in this life *I* shall . . . see God" (Moses 5:10; emphasis added). Adam was supposed to be prophesying about the families of the earth, but all he seemed to see were the positive consequences of the Fall for *his* life.

At this point, Eve could've easily chided Adam a bit for his self-focus, but apparently she didn't. Adam wasn't wrong in his analysis of the Fall; he just wasn't seeing the bigger picture yet, so Eve delicately broadened his perspective. In the most loving way imaginable, she joined in Adam's reverie over the rightness of their choice to embrace mortality, but she added the family perspective into his prophecy about their family.

"And Eve, his wife, heard all these things and was glad" (Moses 5:11). First of all, Eve was content to let Adam go first. Righteous women want their husband to take the lead in the spiritual affairs of their family. Much of the time, it'd be easier to do things themselves, but they know that, for the husband's sake (and for the family's sake), he needs to lead.

It's significant that Eve listened to Adam. That was her covenant with God—to hearken to her husband. She didn't always have to agree with him, but if she wanted him to take the lead, she was wise to listen to and respect his point of view—even when (as in this case) he was limited by his typically male, self-centered focus. Eve didn't merely listen to Adam to be polite though; she was genuinely glad. She rejoiced along with her husband for his spiritual focus, his leadership, and for his love of God and His plan.

Now Eve was going to take a turn rejoicing in the blessings of the Fall, as it would affect their family, but unlike Adam, she actually focused on the family. "Were it not for *our* transgression . . ." she began in verse 11. Basically, she was saying, *Remember, Adam, this was a joint effort. In fact, you weren't even going to go through with it until I pushed things along. But that's a trifling detail, so let's not dwell on it.* "We never should have had seed. . . ." *Remember, this whole mortality thing was about having children. Children will bring out the worst in us, but that was part of the plan so we could have our weaknesses exposed and eventually be perfected in Christ. Without falling, we never would've known "the joy of* our *redemption*" (emphasis added). If we're going to be saved, we're going to do it together. And it'll come through childbearing and child-rearing. In fact, the Apostle Paul said of our choice to accept the conditions of mortality, "Notwithstanding they shall be saved in childbearing" (JST 1 Timothy 2:15).

The woman often has to remind the man that the central experience of mortality (and eternity) is the perfection of the family. In fact, the eternal life—the Godlike life—that they aspire to is simply the "continuation of the seeds forever and ever" (D&C 132:19). Children aren't obstacles to personal fulfillment, as Satan seems to have brainwashed modern society into believing. They are the essence of fulfillment. The possibility of bearing and raising children is the reason for mortality: "Adam fell that men might be" (2 Nephi 2:25). The fortunate Fall was all about the possibility of having families: in mortality as a dry run-through and, more significantly, for all eternity as gods. Proper family life requires that both man and woman sacrifice individual aspirations to accomplish something together of a much greater value.

Sheri L. Dew, a remarkable single sister who served in the general Relief Society presidency, outlined her view of the complementary roles of womanhood and priesthood in a classic general conference address entitled "Are We Not All Mothers?" She declared,

> Of all the words they could have chosen to define her role and her essence, both God the Father and Adam called Eve "the mother of all living"—and they did so *before* she ever bore a child. Like Eve, our motherhood began before we were born. Just as worthy men were foreordained to hold the priesthood in mortality, righteous women were endowed premortally with the privilege of motherhood. Motherhood is more than bearing children, though it is certainly that. It is the essence of who we are as women. It defines our very identity, our divine stature and nature, and the unique traits our Father gave us.
>
> President Gordon B. Hinckley stated that "God planted within women something divine." That something is the gift and the gifts of motherhood. Elder Matthew Cowley taught that "men have to have something given to them [in mortality] to make them saviors of men, but not mothers, not women. [They] are born with an inherent right, an inherent authority, to be the saviors of human souls . . . and the regenerating force in the lives of God's children."[2]

According to Sheri Dew's interpretation of President Hinckley and Elder Cowley, men are given the priesthood to narrow the gap between them and women and to make *them* more equal with their partners. For some women, that explanation—the same one my wife gave to our daughter at age four—may sound too patronizing. For many of us who are men (who see all too often how superior our wives are to us in most spiritual measures), there is some sense in it.

I know there are exceptions, but from my limited experience, I'd say that most women in the Church want their husbands to take the lead in the spiritual affairs of the home. Here's what some women said to Elder David A. Bednar when he was a stake president:

> Please help my husband understand his responsibility as a priesthood leader in our home. I am happy to take the lead in scripture study, family prayer, and family home evening, and I will continue to do so. But I wish my husband would be an equal partner and provide the strong priesthood leadership only he can give. Please help my husband learn how to become a patriarch and a priesthood leader in our home who presides and protects.[3]

Perhaps without the priesthood duties given to men, too many of us would be content to let our more spiritually mature wives take the lead in everything. The divinely appointed roles for men and women are designed to nurture, promote, and protect the family. Complete fulfillment for the individual comes only as an interdependent part of the family whole, and the priesthood ordination given to men helps them stay up with their wives in fulfilling their obligations to their families.

Power and Authority

This complementariness doesn't mean women are entirely dependent on men for their experience of God's power in their lives. There is a sense in which women share equally with their husbands in the priesthood. That realm is in priesthood power. Single women in the Church enjoy it equally as well. Priesthood is both the authority and power of God. President Packer said, "Your authority comes through your ordination; your power comes through obedience and worthiness."[4] By faithful covenant keeping, women become direct partakers of the power of the priesthood—the "power of godliness" (D&C 84:21). Such faith and obedience fills them with the Spirit and enables them to act and speak for Christ. This is the power of the priesthood that women have equal access to along with men. Just as it's possible for men to have the authority without the power if they are *not* worthy, it's possible for women to have the power of the priesthood if they're worthy.

Julie B. Beck, former Relief Society General President, addressed the topic of priesthood power being available to women in a BYU women's conference:

> Don't confuse the power of the priesthood with the keys and offices of the priesthood. . . . The power is limitless and is shared with those who make and keep covenants. Too much is said and misunderstood about

> what brothers have and sisters don't. This is Satan's way of confusing men and women so that neither understands what they really have.
>
> Our responsibility . . . is to make sure that our homes are blessed with priesthood power, as the Primary song says, "every hour" (Children's Songbook, 190). It isn't just when Dad is there. It isn't just when Mom is there. It isn't just when a priesthood ordination or blessing is being performed. It's *every hour* as covenants are made and kept.[5]

As long as we're keeping our covenants, we all have equal access to the power of the priesthood.

Self-proclaimed Mormon feminist Valerie Hudson Cassler wrote about the equality and complementarity of men's and women's roles this way: "Priesthood is not something extra given to men and denied to women. Priesthood is a man's apprenticeship to become a heavenly father, and I believe that women have their own apprenticeship to become like their heavenly mother. . . . Pregnancy, childbirth, lactation . . . [that women provide] are not less powerful or spiritual than the ordinances . . . [that men provide]. Women have their own godly power."[6] Cassler's point is that husbands and wives work together with an equal responsibility to protect and bless the family with priesthood power, even while functioning in separate roles to do so.

Sheri Dew made a similar point. She stated,

> Sisters, some will try to persuade you that because you are not ordained to the priesthood you have been shortchanged. They are simply wrong, and they do not understand the gospel of Jesus Christ. The blessings of the priesthood are available to every righteous man and woman. We may all receive the Holy Ghost, obtain personal revelation, and be endowed in the temple, from which we emerge "armed" with power. The power of the priesthood heals, protects, and inoculates all of the righteous against the powers of darkness. Most significantly, the fulness of the priesthood contained in the highest ordinances of the house of the Lord can only be received by a man and woman together.[7]

The gender complementarity with which the Lord has created us assures that we each need the other to exercise our divinely endowed powers. What a perfect plan!

Presiding in an Equal Relationship

What's the proper gospel-centered relationship for a husband and wife to be equally yoked? "The Family: A Proclamation to the World" states that by "divine design, fathers are to preside over their families in love and righteousness and are responsible to provide the necessities of life and protection for their families. Mothers are primarily responsible for the nurture of their children. In these sacred responsibilities, fathers and mothers are obligated to help one another as equal partners." So they have distinct roles and the father presides, but they're to be equal partners. How can that be?

What does it mean to preside? A dictionary definition is to act as chairperson or to be in charge. It comes from the Latin root meaning "to stand guard." *Prae* means "before" and *sedere* means "to sit." So to preside literally means "to sit in front of." Somehow the husband is supposed to stand guard over the family and lead. He's supposed to be a patriarch. A patriarch is a father-ruler. The word comes from the Greek words *pater* (father) and *arkein* (to rule). But before the father can "rule," the word becomes *patria*, which means "family." So for the father to preside, he has to put the family first. So must the wife. She becomes the matriarch to rule in the family alongside her husband. The husband and the wife agree to this for the sake of their jointly created family.

So how can the man properly preside without belittling his wife and her role? Obviously way too many men botch their job as provider and protector and falsely see themselves as superior to women. The Lord acknowledges as much: "We have learned by sad experience that it is the nature and disposition of almost all men, as soon as they get a little authority, as they suppose, they will immediately begin to exercise unrighteous dominion. Hence many are called, but few are chosen" (D&C 121:39–40). As soon as they make this classic male blunder, they cut themselves off from God's power and place themselves in opposition to his plan (see verses 37–38). In this section, the Lord is trying to teach us a more delicate balance between strength and deference.

Paul described the appropriate relationship that should exist between husband and wife in his Epistle to the Corinthians: "The head of every man is Christ; and the head of the woman is the man; and the head of Christ is God" (1 Corinthians 11:3). So the way the husband is supposed to preside over the woman is the same way the Father presides over the Son in the Godhead. The scriptures repeatedly declare that the Father and the Son are one (for example, see John 10:30). How are They one? They are perfectly united in purpose, thought, and word. Technically, the Son defers to the Father as the one who presides (see 1 Corinthians 15:28). But because They are unified in all Their plans, this presiding by the Father seems mostly symbolic and honorific rather than anything that'd affect Their day-to-day operations. It'd be hard to argue that the Father's place at the head of the Godhead in any way belittles the Savior in His place. This relationship between the Father and the Son as the model for the husband and the wife is enhanced if we look at the Savior's Intercessory Prayer.

In John 17, Christ prays for unity among His disciples. If we consider a couple sealed in the temple and striving to follow the Savior to be the epitome of discipleship, the Savior's prayer becomes quite revealing: "That they [both] may be one; as thou, Father, art in me, and I in thee, that they also may be one in us: that the world may believe that thou hast sent me. And the glory which thou gavest me I have given them; that they may be one, even as we are one" (John 17:21–22). The perfect unity portrayed in the relationship between the Father and the Son becomes the model to follow. The Father loves the Son and gives Him honor, letting Him speak for the Father in all things. Yet to provide order, the Son still honors the Father and defers to Him as the presiding authority.

In another famous New Testament passage, Paul compared the relationship we should strive for between husband and wife with the one between Christ and the Church. "Wives," Paul said, "submit yourselves unto your own husbands, as unto the Lord. For the husband is the head of the wife, even as Christ is the head of the church: and he is the saviour of the body. Therefore as the church is subject unto Christ, so let the wives be to their own husbands in every thing. Husbands, love your wives, even as Christ also loved the church, and gave himself for it" (Ephesians 5:22–25). If a wife had a husband who sacrificed for her the way Christ sacrificed for the Church, why would she not be willing to submit ultimately to his position as the one who presides in the home? Yet how many husbands treat their wives with that level of self-sacrifice?

In any case, the operative term in "The Family: A Proclamation to the World" is *equal partners*. For years, the leaders of the Church have been trying to teach the Saints (both men and women need to understand this) that equality is key to marital success. Perhaps one example will suffice. Richard G. Scott wrote, "The way of the Lord is that you make every decision together—period. And if you can't do that, you work until you do. You pray about it."[8]

Like stargazers waiting to catch a glimpse of a falling star, women may need a lot of patience waiting for men to step into their proper role. Some are tired of waiting and perhaps become feminists as they feel they need to actively advocate for institutional change until women are simply allowed to take their equal, undifferentiated role in the Church and the family. I understand and sympathize with those who feel this way and allow them their right to those feelings. Finding the right avenue to express those views may prove to be a bit of a challenge. It certainly has thus far.

Heavenly Mother

While Mormonism's preservation of somewhat traditional complementary roles for husbands and wives might leave the Church open to critique by modern feministic views, our unique belief in a Heavenly Mother could possibly soften the blow a bit.

> In the heav'ns are parents single?
> No, the thought makes reason stare!
> Truth is reason; truth eternal
> Tells me I've a mother there. . . .
> When I leave this frail existence,
> When I lay this mortal by,
> Father, Mother, may I meet you
> In your royal courts on high?[9]

These words come from the hymn by Eliza R. Snow, who was sealed to the Prophet Joseph Smith during his lifetime. Wilford Woodruff later declared them to be a revelation.[10] Brigham Young also taught of our Heavenly Mother: "We were created upright, pure, and holy, in the image of our father and our mother, the image of our God."[11] So the title *God* actually means "heavenly parents." That insight radically alters my own view of divinity. Anytime I interact with Heavenly Father, I'm also interacting with Heavenly Mother. They share everything together, including interaction with me as Their child.

The scriptures also offer some veiled hints about our Mother in Heaven. A messianic psalm praising God seems to acknowledge Heavenly Mother's position next to Her husband: "Kings' daughters were among thy honourable women: upon thy right hand did stand the queen in gold of Ophir" (Psalms 45:9). When we understand the doctrine of Heavenly Mother, it seems a natural impulse to want to worship her and pray to her. Jeremiah had to deal with this challenge among the Israelites. The Israelites, particularly the wives, were burning incense to the "queen of heaven" (Jeremiah 44:15–30). Jeremiah didn't condemn their belief in the queen of heaven, just their perverting the Lord's plan by worshiping Her.

In "The Family: A Proclamation to the World," we read that the official doctrine of the Church includes a belief in Heavenly Mother: "All human beings—male and female—are created in the image of God. Each is a beloved spirit son or daughter of heavenly parents, and, as such, each has a divine nature and destiny."

This doctrine of our Mother in Heaven places the Church in a unique position among contemporary religions. In a remarkable essay entitled "I Am a Mormon Because I Am a Feminist," LDS scholar Valerie Hudson Cassler articulated the strength of our position in this way: "The restored gospel teaches that the term 'God' means an exalted woman and an exalted man married in the new and everlasting covenant (D&C 132:19–20). We are taught that there is no God without men and women loving each other as equals. Heavenly Father is not an eternal bachelor; he is married to our Heavenly Mother. In fact, the one who's an eternal bachelor is Satan."[12] Our divine destiny is attained only through unity between a husband and a wife. Everything that fosters the interdependence of marriage and family can lead us closer to that destiny. Everything that fosters separation and independence can actually lead us closer to Satan.

Heavenly Gallantry?

Since the existence of a Mother in Heaven is official doctrine of the Church, why don't we know more about Her? The traditional explanation of our ignorance about Heavenly Mother is that Heavenly Father is protecting Her good name. We see how His name is dragged through the mud in blasphemous expressions. Perhaps He doesn't want Her name treated that same way. The idea holds that Heavenly Father is basically just being gallant.

I understand the need to have explanations for things we don't understand, but this popular folk explanation has little justification in the scriptures, in the writings of the prophets, or even in common sense. Would the fact that teenagers often disrespect their fathers be justification for a father to refuse access or knowledge of their mother in order to shield her from slander? "No, I don't want you to have a relationship with your mother because you might not respect her—just like how you don't respect me." That'd be a ludicrous explanation. The benefit of knowing, loving, and being loved by a mother would far outweigh any risks of disrespect.

As a Church, I think we simply don't know why we don't know more about Heavenly Mother. And yet we know we have one and want to know more about Her, so it seems natural to wonder if we should try to communicate with her in prayer. Leaders have clarified the Church's position on this matter. President Gordon B. Hinckley declared,

> Logic and reason would certainly suggest that if we have a Father in Heaven, we have a Mother in Heaven. That doctrine rests well with me. However, in light of the instruction we have received from the Lord Himself, I regard it as inappropriate for anyone in the Church to pray to our Mother in Heaven. The Lord Jesus Christ set the pattern for our prayers. In the Sermon on the Mount, He declared: "After this manner therefore pray ye: Our *Father* which art in heaven, Hallowed be thy name."[13]

The message is clear—we have a Heavenly Mother, but we shouldn't pray to her. The Lord has instructed otherwise.

When I was teaching missionaries in the MTC in Provo, I had an elder in one district who was raised by a single LDS feminist mother. He was in the habit of praying in public to Heavenly Mother. After he tried this in class, I pulled him aside privately to talk with him about the practice. He said that was simply how he was raised. I explained to him that the teachings of the Church actually discourage praying to Heavenly Mother, that Christ Himself instructed us to pray only to the Father (3 Nephi 18:23), and that He didn't even want us praying to Him (3 Nephi 19:17–22). I suggested that if he felt the need to include Heavenly Mother in his prayer, perhaps he could pray to the Father *about* her. My explanation and invitation seemed to help this elder at the time, but I'm sure his struggle to understand and relate with our heavenly parents has continued. My own quest to understand and please my heavenly parents continues as well.

A Woman Prophet?

Some people in and out of the Church feel that it's sexist because women can't be bishops or stake presidents, that women don't have enough say in what happens. If they had more of a voice and a leadership role, women's needs would be more adequately addressed. Women do serve in presidencies over women and children and they teach men and women in Sunday School, but they don't preside over men in congregations as women do in some other churches. Would they feel more fulfilled and less oppressed if they did?

One woman in the Church thought so. Her name is Maxine Hanks. Sister Hanks grew up in the Church from pioneer stock, but she considered herself a feminist. In 1992, she published a book on feminism and the Church and she was excommunicated for apostasy. She spent the next twenty years out of the Church. She ended up affiliating with a non-denominational Christian church in Salt Lake City for a number of years and was trained to become an ordained minister. She'd always felt like she needed priesthood ordination to legitimize her service. But after twenty years out of the Church, she decided it was time to return. When the local bishop asked her to come back, Maxine Hanks was rebaptized in 2012. She decided that there was enough power and authority in the LDS priesthood to reach everyone.[14]

The Church is "feminist" to the degree that it empowers women to rise to their greatest heights. Where it differs with the world is on where those heights lie. Nothing sets out a clearer picture of women's divine roles than section 25 of the Doctrine and Covenants. It was originally given to Joseph Smith's wife, Emma, but the Lord makes clear that it's to be a guide for all women in the Church as it said, "This is my voice unto all" (D&C 25:16).

The Lord's first instruction to Emma isn't to reproach her husband for the things that "are withheld from thee" (D&C 25:4). With Emma, the Lord was probably referring to the gold plates, which she never got to see. With some women today, this verse could apply to priesthood ordination. Emma was to be a comfort to her husband and to "go with him" (D&C 25:5). She was to teach the scriptures, exhort the Church, learn and write much, and be supported by her husband (see verses 7–9). And she was to do it all under the direction of the priesthood (verse 8). The Lord specifically warned Emma to "beware of pride" and to "delight in thy husband, and the glory which shall come upon him" (D&C 25:14). The Lord even went so far as to say that "except thou do this, where I am you cannot come" (D&C 25:15). The implication seems to be that unless women in the Church can humble themselves and rejoice in their God-given roles in marriage and family, they'll miss the "crown of righteousness" that awaits them as an eternal queen in heaven (D&C 25:15). That's a hard pill to swallow for a traditional feminist demanding absolute equality and independence from male subordination. But for a humble daughter of God seeking the ideal of unity in an interdependent family relationship, the possibilities are endless.

Certainly there's still room for us to grow as a people toward greater gender equality. The Church has made great efforts to empower Relief Society leaders with more input and direction in ward councils. In April 2013, women were invited to offer prayers in general conference for the first time. More needs to be done so all feel that their input is valued. Perhaps young women could be greeters at the door for sacrament meeting and hand out programs along with the young men, as this is not a scripturally defined priesthood duty like passing the sacrament. This would be a small gain indeed for those holding out for a revelation that'll ordain women to the priesthood. That might take some time. It may well never happen. It's up to the Lord.

One thing is clear, however. The role of women in the Church seems designed to complement the role of women and men in the family.

Equally Yoked

Over the years, I've asked many couples and individuals what they thought the key to a successful gospel-based marriage is. I've learned much. The answers I received all seem to be variations of a single theme, which is learning to sacrifice your own needs and desires to satisfy those of your spouse so that they can do the same for you. Then rely on the Atonement of Christ to cement your every effort, fill in every gap, and smooth over every conflict along the way.

One good friend reminded me of the experience that couples enjoy after their temple sealing where they gaze into the endless reflections in the parallel mirrors in the sealing room. If you look at yourself in the mirror, all you can see is your own reflection looking back at you. But if you look at the reflection of your spouse, you can see eternity in both directions. It's our focus on ourselves that becomes the biggest distraction in marriage. When we aim to please and support our spouse, he or she is then free to do the same for us. This cycle creates a healthy interdependence that binds a couple together.

Years ago while I was working as a teaching assistant for a distinguished professor, he invited me over to his home to have dinner with him and his wife. He knew I'd served a mission in Mexico, so while his wife was finishing with the meal preparations, he pulled a set of maracas off his bookshelf and replaced his wife's small flower display with them as a centerpiece on the table. He seemed quite pleased with his Mexican "touch" to the table. But when his wife returned to the dining room to put out more food, she saw the maracas and said under her breath, "Who put these silly things here?" As soon as she returned to the kitchen, this dedicated husband quickly and quietly switched back the flower display and returned the maracas to the bookshelf. He wanted to make me feel like an honored guest at their table, but pleasing his wife was much more important to him. What I'm sure he didn't realize was he was teaching me a lesson in that small moment of self-sacrifice and humility that continues to teach me over twenty years later.

Shortly after we were married, my wife and I had a stake president who suggested that every night we kneel together at our bedside, hold hands, and offer couple prayer before having individual prayer. It's hard to hold hands and pray with and for each other and still hang onto resentment or anger from the tensions of the day. This one tradition has done more to solidify our relationship than almost anything else. Consistently putting our relationship before our personal needs and wants is what cements us to each other, and reporting together to the Lord on our relationship every evening reminds us of this priority.

A friend of mine shared the story of his hero, a man who seemed to finally understand his duty to his wife in the big things. His colleague was the head of the library at Texas Tech University. He'd spent much of his career trying to get funding and approvals for the construction of a new university library. The last thirteen years of his career were spent on fulfilling this lifelong dream. Finally, the library was almost complete and was scheduled to be dedicated in June. Then to the surprise of all his friends and colleagues, this librarian secretly retired six months early. His friends all wanted to know why he hadn't waited six more months for the dedication of his lifelong dream and then to go out with a blaze of glory. He balked and dismissed their badgering him, but eventually he felt compelled to explain himself.

He said that thirty-five years earlier when he and his sweetheart were first married, they were struggling students at BYU. His wife was soon pregnant and felt like she needed to drop out of school to start raising their children. She never got the chance to realize her dream of graduating from college. This good husband retired early so they could move back to Provo, where his wife was enrolling as a sixty-two-year-old sophomore at BYU. He was sacrificing his dream so she could finally realize hers.

While there are times in a marriage that call for big sacrifices, they're usually overshadowed by the small, daily opportunities to put the needs of your spouse ahead of your own. Another friend of mine who hates running took up the sport and now runs three to four times a week because his wife loves it. It's become a form of marriage and family therapy where they address all the concerns of the day.

An academic study designed to predict the stability of marriages over time included a survey given to recently married couples. Nine years later, the researchers followed up to see if the couples were still together. The single survey item that best predicted success for the marriage was "the husband voluntarily and cheerfully participates in housework."[15] Wives seem to naturally understand better how to put the needs and desires of their husbands before their own. But when the husband can figure this out as well—particularly in the little daily conflicts that arise—the marriage usually lasts.

When husbands and wives make mutual sacrifices for each other and their family, a healthy interdependence grows that can bind them inextricably to each other. Those sacrifices can lift them way beyond the narrow walls of self-identity and self-fulfillment into an interconnected family unit that has the potential to grow eternally. Yet to avoid resentment and regret, those sacrifices must be made voluntarily by both parties, out of desire and love.

"Nevertheless neither is the man without the woman, neither the woman without the man, in the Lord" (1 Corinthians 11:11). The Lord's plan includes mutually essential, interdependent roles for husbands and wives that allow for families to be safely created, nurtured, and perfected. Though the struggle for gender equality will likely continue through this life and into the next, when a couple is moving in the right direction on this path—focusing on the partner and the relationship rather than individual needs and wants—there's a light that shines and dispels skeptical darkness. Questions may remain, but with each act of self-sacrifice, those questions become less and less significant. That light that shineth grows brighter and brighter until the perfect day when their calling and election will be made sure together and the Lord "makes them equal in power, and in might, and in dominion" (D&C 76:95).

The Perplexing Question of Polygamy

"No man knows my history. I cannot tell it: I shall never undertake it. I don't blame any one for not believing my history. If I had not experienced what I have, I would not have believed it myself."[1]

—Joseph Smith

My wife once told me that, if necessary, she could handle polygamy. It's not that she likes the idea; it's just that she could accept it if she had to. To me, the idea pretty much stinks. I couldn't imagine trying to share the emotional and physical intimacy I enjoy with my wife with someone else. Because the entire plan of happiness hinges on the sacred relationship between husband and wife, why would the Lord ever command anything like plural marriage, which could seemingly jeopardize that? This is a good question without any immediate, easy answers.

After Joseph Smith finished translating the Book of Mormon and restored the Church on April 6, 1830, the Lord had him begin working on a revision of the Bible that came to be known as the Joseph Smith Translation. It was a project that engaged Joseph with the scriptures in an intimate way, which sparked questions leading to further revelation. Many of the sections of the Doctrine and Covenants came about as a result of Joseph's study. One of the perplexing questions that arose concerned the practice of plural marriage among the patriarchs of the Bible. Polygamy is the generic term for having more than one spouse. Polygyny is specifically a husband who has more than one wife. Polyandry is a wife who has more than one husband. Although polygyny historically is far more common than polyandry, both were practiced in the Bible and in the early days of the Church. Why?

In 2013, Brian C. Hales published a landmark three-volume comprehensive study entitled *Joseph Smith's Polygamy*. In it, he addressed every contemporary document up to the 1890s regarding Joseph Smith's involvement in polygamy. He tries to look objectively at all the evidence used by both defenders and critics of the Prophet in order to allow readers to come to their own conclusions about this difficult issue. Hales clearly felt the evidence showed Joseph was an honorable man who sincerely did what he felt God had commanded him to do.

Polygamy Revealed

As early as 1831, the Lord revealed to the Prophet that plural marriage was a true principle. Sometimes in order to raise up a righteous posterity, the Lord commands His people, through His prophet, to practice it. Joseph was instituting the Restoration of the fulness of the gospel and would also be required to restore plural marriage among the people. He knew that this would not be a popular teaching, just as he knew the Victorian sensibilities of his own wife, Emma, would be repulsed by such a doctrine. As a result, Joseph kept it to himself. It wasn't until 1834 when an angel appeared and commanded that he move forward with the practice that he began to try to figure out how to live it.[2]

When the Lord gives commandments, He rarely lays out all the particulars of how we're supposed to apply them in our lives. That's part of our agency. Sometime in late 1835 or early 1836 in Kirtland, Ohio, Joseph decided to try to start a relationship with a young woman named Fanny Alger, who worked in their home. He instructed a close friend, Levi Hancock, to approach Fanny's parents, teach them the principle of plural marriage, and then do the same with Fanny. They all accepted the principle. Levi married Joseph to Fanny in the presence of her parents.[3]

As careful and obedient to the Lord as Joseph tried to be, the entire experience turned out disastrously. Joseph knew that his wife, Emma, would reject this principle, so he didn't tell her about it. When she discovered what'd happened, she felt that Joseph had cheated on her and threw Fanny out of the house. Because he hadn't let Oliver Cowdery or Martin Harris in on his actions, when they found out about it they sided with Emma, which caused a rift in the leadership of the Church. Fanny left Kirtland in disgrace and lived the rest of her life outside the Church, though her family remained loyal to Joseph and the Church and came out west to Utah.[4]

Joseph clearly felt horrible about what happened to Fanny and felt like a failure. He didn't act on the commandment to practice plural marriage again for several years. In 1841, the angel appeared again to Joseph and demanded that he move forward with his practice of this principle.[5] Still stinging from his failure with Fanny, Joseph decided to go about it differently this time. With the sealing power of the priesthood he received in the Kirtland Temple in 1836, he'd seal himself for eternity to women who already had husbands but leave them to live with their husbands for mortality. There's no record that any of these polyandrous marriages were consummated.[6] The husbands gave their consent and were often present at the sealing. Many of them weren't members of the Church and didn't share their wives' view of the importance of eternal marriage in the afterlife. To Joseph, it seemed to be a safe way to fulfill the commandment of plural marriage without having to face all the backlash of actually having relationships with other women.[7]

But early in 1842, the angel appeared again and commanded that Joseph move forward with the commandment. Apparently, Joseph's attempts at non-sexual polyandry weren't good enough. The angel expected him to live the commandment as the patriarchs of old did—with the possibility of children. So in 1842 and 1843, Joseph married several single women and consummated the marriages.[8] Interestingly, from all Joseph's plural marriages, at most only two children were born, which shows that he really didn't spend much time with any of them in that way.[9] Reliable birth control wasn't available until after his death.

With all of Joseph's thirty-five plural wives, including the polyandrous ones, not one of them ever claimed later that Joseph seduced her, tricked her, or coerced her. He always had multiple witnesses to the events and tried to get Emma's approval on many of them.[10] With those that struggled with accepting the principle (which were most of them), Joseph was patient and allowed them the right to receive their own testimony before entering the practice. Most of his plural wives who later talked about their experience reported receiving divine manifestations of its truthfulness. Some even reported having angels appear to instruct them on the principle.[11] Two of his wives were as young as fourteen, but he didn't consummate those marriages, and one of them was at the young woman's father's request.[12] Over half of Joseph's marriages were only for eternity without any other relationship on earth.

As historian Richard L. Bushman put it, "Joseph did not marry women to form a warm, human companionship, but to create a network of related wives, children, and kinsmen that would endure into the eternities. . . . Like Abraham of old, Joseph yearned for familial plentitude. He did not lust for women so much as he lusted for kin."[13] Those few who did accuse Joseph of debaucheries were the ones guilty themselves, like John C. Bennett[14] and Joseph H. Jackson,[15] who both had been excommunicated for scandalous behavior and tried to get revenge on the Church by publishing sensational exposés. Yet these are the sources that anti-Mormons typically rely on for their accounts of Joseph's polygamy.

Response of the Faithful

Those who knew Joseph best had no trouble seeing past the lies of his enemies, but the inherent challenges proposed by polygamy still rocked the world of even Joseph's most loyal followers. Like Joseph, few of the faithful had any desire to live this law. Brigham Young later confessed upon learning the doctrine that "it was the first time in my life that I had desired the grave, and I could hardly get over it for a long time. And when I saw a funeral, I felt to envy the corpse its situation, and to regret that I was not in the coffin."[16] John Taylor later described how some of the Apostles felt upon learning about polygamy after returning from a successful mission to England: "[At] the time when men were commanded to take more wives. It made us all pull pretty long faces sometimes. It was not so easy as one might think. When it was revealed to us it looked like the last end of Mormonism. For a man to ask another woman to marry him required more self-confidence than we had."[17] Joseph knew that his brother Hyrum would struggle so much with the commandment that Joseph postponed revealing it to him as long as he felt he could.[18]

Yet Joseph promised everyone he taught the principle to that the Lord would confirm it to them, as He had to the Prophet himself. And one by one, they each received their own witness that it was from God. James Allred, a member of the stake high council in Nauvoo, later explained that "he did not believe it at first, it was so contrary to his feelings, but he said he knew Joseph was a prophet of God so he made a covenant that he would not eat, drink or sleep until he knew for himself, that he had got a testimony that it was true, that he had even heard the voice of God concerning it."[19] As it did to many others, that witness came.

Emma's Response

Understandably, Emma Smith struggled to accept plural marriage as much as anyone. At first, she saw it as little more than adultery. Her strict Protestant upbringing just wouldn't allow her to embrace this new and alien doctrine. At one point, Hyrum, who had to struggle himself to gain a testimony of the doctrine, told Joseph to write down the revelation and he'd persuade Emma of its truthfulness. Joseph said Hyrum didn't know Emma the way he did, but he complied at Hyrum's insistence. The resulting revelation was section 132 of the Doctrine and Covenants. Hyrum took it to Emma. He returned a few hours later, saying he'd just received the worst tongue lashing of his life.[20] Emma eventually burned the original revelation, but Joseph had anticipated her rejection of it and had a copy made.[21]

One time, a woman visiting Nauvoo asked Emma where the Church got the doctrine of polygamy. Her reply was, "Straight from hell, madam."[22] Yet other times Emma's heart softened toward Joseph and the doctrine of plural marriage. On more than one occasion, she selected wives for him to marry and brought them into their home to live with them.[23] But then she would have fits of jealously and throw them out of the house.[24] Historian Richard L. Bushman said of their struggle, "They were in impossible positions: Joseph caught between his revelation and his wife, Emma, between a practice she detested and belief in her husband."[25]

In the end, Emma couldn't quite bring herself to fully embrace plural marriage. She'd gained a testimony of the principle and never stopped trying to accept and live it, but she never found peace with it. Once when explaining some harsh words spoken in anger against her husband, she confided in Maria Jane Woodward: "What I said I have got to repent of. The principle is right but I am jealous hearted. Now never tell anybody that you heard me find fault with Joseph on that principle. The principle is right and if I or you or anyone else find fault with that principle we have got to humble ourselves and repent of it."[26] Joseph never gave up on her. She was the love of his life, and he catered to her wishes as much as he felt he could.

Brigham Young did give up on Emma. He later recalled struggles over plural marriage by saying, "Joseph used to say that he would have her hereafter, if he had to go to hell for her, and he will have to go to hell for her as sure as he ever gets her."[27] When the majority of the Saints followed Brigham west after the martyrdom, Emma refused to go. Instead, she remarried a non-Mormon, Louis Bidamon, and spent the rest of her life in Nauvoo, raising her children as pious Protestants. She taught them that Joseph never practiced polygamy, which became the official position of the Reorganized Church of Jesus Christ of Latter-day Saints, founded in 1860 by Mormons who'd been excommunicated in Nauvoo and led by her son Joseph III. Though for years the Reorganized Church taught that Brigham invented plural marriage, today the renamed Community of Christ Church officially recognizes that Joseph Smith was the founder of it.[28]

The Lord, however, never gave up on Emma. In her patriarchal blessing (pronounced by her father-in-law, Joseph Smith Sr.), she was promised, "Thou shalt see many days, yea, the Lord will spare thee till thou art satisfied, for thou shalt see thy Redeemer." On her deathbed, she saw a vision that she afterward recounted to her nurse. Joseph came for her and told her it was time for them to be together again. He showed her their lost babies and assured her she'd soon be with them. "Then she saw standing by his side a personage of light, even the Lord Jesus Christ." Two days later, she reached up toward heaven, saying, "Joseph! Joseph! I am coming," and passed away.[29]

Brigham Publicizes and Expands on Polygamy

Most of the twenty-nine men who had entered into polygamous relationships by the time of the Prophet's death followed Brigham Young out west. Brigham Young married many of Joseph's plural wives—at Joseph's request—to care for them. Those marriages were for this life only.[30] In 1852, the Church (now settled outside of the United States in the Utah Territory) began to officially announce to the world its practice of plural marriage. Brigham eventually married fifty-five wives and had fifty-six children.

The United States government, backed by popular opinion, opposed the Church's practice of polygamy for many years. The Church claimed its right to freedom of religion and defied the laws of the land as an act of civil disobedience. They appealed every law and every court decision until they'd exhausted all legal avenues. As leaders and fathers were being hounded by government officials and hauled off to prison, many Saints resorted to deception to protect the polygamists. They'd shelter them, hide them, and lie about their whereabouts. They almost seem like Europeans during the reign of the Nazis who harbored Jews and then lied about it to the Gestapo to protect them. These faithful, otherwise law-abiding Saints felt they had to protect those who had put obedience to God ahead of obedience to their country.

Finally, it was clear that the government was set on destroying the Church over this practice. Yet the Saints proved they were willing to be destroyed rather than disobey the Lord. He accepted their sacrifice and called for an end to it. In 1890, President Wilford Woodruff received a revelation that became known as the Manifesto, officially putting an end to the Church's practice of plural marriage. But the practice had become so entrenched in the doctrine and daily life of the Church that both members and leaders struggled to comply with the government and with the Manifesto, and more plural marriages were performed.

In 1904, President Joseph F. Smith issued a "Second Manifesto," stating the Church's complete cessation of plural marriage, making it an excommunicable offense. Still, it took some time before everyone in the Church gave it up. It'd taken such a monumental force of effort to practice it in the face of so much societal and governmental pressure that it took some time to get it out of everyone's psyche. As late as 1943, Apostle Richard R. Lyman was excommunicated for practicing polygamy. Today, anyone who practices it is indeed excommunicated. Even in countries where polygamy is legal (such as the Middle East and Africa), potential members must cease living it before they can become members. The Church hasn't repudiated the doctrine behind it, but it has ended its practice.

Why Polygamy?

Over and over again, as Joseph privately taught the principle of plural marriage, he testified that he was merely trying to fulfill the commandments of God. Those who knew him best knew he was sincere, and those who sought for the Lord's witness knew he was indeed inspired by the Almighty. So why would God command His people to participate in a practice that seems so anti-family to our way of thinking?

The traditional LDS response usually starts with the clarification that it's not just polygamy with Joseph Smith and Brigham Young that needs explaining. Abraham, Isaac, and Jacob were all polygamous prophets, as was Moses. So anyone who condemns early Church leaders has to throw away the Bible as an authority on proper marriage relationships as well. In the Bible, plural marriage was practiced to ensure the production of offspring (see Genesis 16:2–4; 30:1–3), but it never provides a justification or defense of the principle. For that, we have to turn to the Book of Mormon.

In Jacob's day (500 BC), the Nephites were using stories of David and Solomon practicing plural marriage as justification for seeking multiple wives themselves. Jacob clarified the Church's position on marriage, upholding monogamy as the standard: "Wherefore, I the Lord God will not suffer that this people shall do like unto them of old. Wherefore, my brethren, hear me, and hearken to the word of the Lord: For there shall not any man among you have save it be one wife; and concubines he shall have none; for I, the Lord God, delight in the chastity of women. And whoredoms are an abomination before me; thus saith the Lord of Hosts" (Jacob 2:26–28). But in the same breath, the Lord made it clear that plural marriage can at times be justified: "For if I will, saith the Lord of Hosts, raise up seed unto me, I will command my people; otherwise they shall hearken unto these things" (Jacob 2:30). So for plural marriage to be justified, it must be commanded by the Lord and it'll be for the purpose of raising up a righteous generation of children.

This is precisely what happened with the family of Israel in Old Testament times. The Twelve Tribes came from Jacob's (Israel's) four wives. It happened again in the days of the early pioneers. A good number of Latter-day Saints today with Utah heritage (like me, Mitt Romney, and many others) can trace their lineage back to polygamous marriages.

In the late nineteenth century, plural marriage stirred up resistance against the Church. The press and eventually the federal government took an aggressive stance in condemning Mormon polygamy. The result of this cultural and political backlash was that the Church had to unify together to survive. In his book *Evidences and Reconciliations*, Apostle John A. Widtsoe suggested that the opposition generated against plural marriage in the nineteenth century might have been the influence that bound those families together and allowed the Church to survive into the twentieth century.[31]

Ultimate Tests

The primary purpose of plural marriage, however, is found in the revelation on marriage: section 132 of the Doctrine and Covenants. The first half of the revelation (verses 1–28) outlines the requirements for eternal life. They are that one man and one woman be sealed in the temple and keep their covenants—"then shall they be gods" (132:20).

It's the second half of the revelation (verses 29–66) that addresses the purposes of plural marriage. The issue is being obedient to the Lord at all hazards. At the end of the revelation, the Lord sums up why he gave the Saints this unpopular and counterintuitive commandment: "To prove you all, as I did Abraham, and that I might require an offering at your hand, by covenant and sacrifice" (D&C 132:51). Just as Abraham had to be willing to sacrifice everything, even his sense of right and wrong, to prove that he was willing to follow the Lord, the early Saints had to be willing to sacrifice their conventional ideals of marriage to prove themselves willing to follow the Lord at all costs. Many of them passed the test; some didn't. Perhaps those who didn't will have an opportunity to face other tests in the next life. Because families are at the heart of the gospel plan, tugging at the heartstrings of family seems to almost be the ultimate test of faithfulness the Lord uses with His most loyal disciples.

Abraham's wife, Sarah, had to go through just such a test of her own—twice! While in Egypt with the pharaoh (in Genesis 12) and later in Gerar with King Abimelech (in Genesis 20), Sarah was desired for her beauty. Both times, Abraham asked her to say she was his sister so they wouldn't kill him in order to steal her. Both times, the kings took her into their households as a part of their harems. Against her will—but with her consent—Sarah became a polyandrist.

The Pearl of Great Price clarifies who came up with this awful strategy for saving Abraham's skin: the Lord Himself (see Abraham 2:21–25). Certainly the Lord could've devised another way to save Abraham from the jealousy of rival kings, but He chose to do it through this dreadful test of Sarah's faithfulness. Both times, the Lord smote the kings' households with disease until they gave Sarah back. Both times, Sarah's virtue was divinely protected. She must have been a remarkable woman to endure all this humiliation without complaint.

What was the Lord teaching here? The kings learned they couldn't have any woman they wanted simply because she was pretty. Abraham learned that, just as he was dependent on the Lord for the protection and survival of his family and his life, he was also dependent on the faithfulness and courage of his wife for what he treasured most. But what did Sarah learn from these horrendous ordeals? Was she tempted to consummate her marriages with these kings? Was she tempted to reveal her prior marriage to Abraham to keep from being married off again? Either would've ruined her and her marriage. The Lord showed her that He could protect her virtue and honor, even when the world was treating her like a prize to be won and used. "For them that honour me I will honour" (1 Samuel 2:30). Sarah passed her test as a loyal wife at all costs before Abraham faced his own sacrificial test with Isaac on the altar.[32]

Some historians and anti-Mormons have claimed that the introduction of plural marriage was just a doctrinal cover-up for Joseph lusting after other women. Any thoughtful inquirer does consider that possibility. But the evidence is clear that both Joseph and those who helped him practice this doctrine sincerely believed they were following the Lord's will. Each time Joseph would introduce the practice to a woman and propose marriage, he'd meet their resistance with a promise that the Lord would grant them their own witness of the truthfulness of the doctrine. Almost every time, that witness came and was received. Of the thirty-five or so women Joseph was sealed to, none of them or their families ever claimed that Joseph seduced them. They were all sure that they were following the Lord's command.[33]

One classic example of hearts being changed to accept the principle of plural marriage is Heber and Vilate Kimball. Rarely has there been a couple more devoted to each other than this stalwart husband and wife. On a similar level was their test keenly felt. The first part of their test occurred in 1841. Joseph told Heber that it was the will of the Lord that he give his beloved Vilate to him, the Prophet, to marry. Heber stewed and stewed. He prayed, wept, and fasted for three days. Then he led his beloved Vilate to the Prophet's side and put her hand in his. Joseph wept at his friend's devotion and said it was enough. By virtue of the sealing power, he sealed Heber and Vilate together as husband and wife for all eternity.[34] Just like Abraham putting Isaac on the altar, Heber had put his beloved and willing Vilate on the altar—but in the end (again like with Abraham), their willingness was enough.

For all their proven faithfulness, their tests were just beginning. In 1842, there'd be no ram in the thicket to bail them out as there was the year before. They would have to go through with the sacrifice. Here's how their daughter later described their Herculean challenge:

> My mother had noticed a change in his [Heber's] looks and appearance [since the command to practice plural marriage], and when she enquired the cause, he tried to evade her question, saying it was only her imagination, or that he was not feeling well, etc. But it so worked upon his mind that his anxious and haggard looks betrayed him daily and hourly, and finally his misery became so unbearable that it was impossible to control his feelings. He became sick in body, but his mental wretchedness was too great to allow of his retiring at night,

> and instead of going to bed he would walk the floor; and the agony of his mind was so terrible that he would wring his hands and weep, beseeching the Lord with his whole soul to be merciful and reveal to his wife the cause of his great sorrow, for he himself could not break his vow of secrecy. His anguish and my mother's, were indescribable and when unable to endure it longer, she retired to her room, where with a broken and contrite heart, she poured out her grief to [God]. . . .
>
> My father's heart was raised at the same time in supplication, and while pleading as one would plead for life, the vision of her mind was opened, and she saw the principle of celestial marriage illustrated in all its beauty and glory, together with the great exaltation and honor it would confer upon her in that immortal and celestial sphere if she would but accept it and stand in her place by her husband's side. She was also shown the woman he had taken to wife, and contemplated with joy the vast and boundless love and union which this order would bring about, as well as the increase of kingdoms, power, and glory extending throughout the eternities, worlds without end.
>
> Her soul was satisfied and filled with the Spirit of God. With a countenance beaming with joy she returned to my father, saying, "Heber, what you have kept from me the Lord has shown me."
>
> She related the scene to me and to many others, and told me she never saw so happy a man as father was, when she described the vision and told him she was satisfied and knew that it was from God. She covenanted to stand by him and honor the principle, which covenant she faithfully kept, and though her trials were often heavy and grievous to bear, her integrity was unflinching to the end.[35]

Heber and Vilate went on to welcome forty-three additional wives to their family. Heber served faithfully as a counselor to Brigham Young in the First Presidency for many years.

As faithful and blessed as Abraham, Sarah, Joseph, Brigham, Heber, Vilate, and so many were for their sacrifices, I for one am immensely grateful that plural marriage is no longer a test of faithfulness for the Saints. Bruce R. McConkie explained:

> Plural marriage is not essential to salvation or exaltation. Nephi and his people were denied the power to have more than one wife and yet they could gain every blessing in eternity that the Lord ever offered to any people. In our day, the Lord summarized by revelation the whole doctrine of exaltation and predicated it upon the marriage of one man

> to one woman (D&C 132:1–28). Thereafter he added the principles relative to plurality of wives with the express stipulation that any such marriages would be valid only if authorized by the President of the Church (D&C 132:7, 29–66).
>
> All who pretend or assume to engage in plural marriage in this day, when the one holding the keys has withdrawn the power by which they are performed, are guilty of gross wickedness.[36]

Facing Tests Today

The Lord hasn't asked me to sacrifice my son on an altar or share my affection with another spouse. In fact, for me to try to pass someone else's test would lead to disaster. But I understand that I too must face my own Abrahamic test if I wish to inherit the blessings he did. "Therefore," the Lord said of His Saints, "they must needs be chastened and tried, even as Abraham, who was commanded to offer up his only son. For all those who will not endure chastening, but deny me, cannot be sanctified" (D&C 101:4–5). In His own way, the Lord will put me to the test and allow me to discover the degree of my willingness to submit to His sovereignty. Plural marriage is one of the ways He has done that in the past.

These partial answers don't resolve all the concerns about plural marriage. For some bright Latter-day Saints today, accepting the Lord's use of plural marriage in the past to test others' faithfulness might be part of their own Abrahamic test. When the angel Moroni appeared to Joseph Smith to announce the Restoration and the Book of Mormon, he warned Joseph that his "name should be had for good and evil among all nations, kindreds, and tongues, or that it should be both good and evil spoken of among all people" (Joseph Smith—History 1:33). Today, the Internet is full of trash being hurled at Joseph, accusing him of atrocious crimes committed in the name of polygamy.

Joseph himself never claimed to be perfect. In 1842, he said, "Altho' I do wrong, I do not the wrongs that I am charg'd with doing—the wrong that I do is thro' the frailty of human nature like other men. No man lives without fault."[37] Even the Lord acknowledged Joseph's faults, but He still gave him an ultimate stamp of approval: "Let no one, therefore, set on my servant Joseph; for I will justify him; for he shall do the sacrifice which I require at his hands for his transgressions, saith the Lord your God" (D&C 132:60). If that isn't enough of a divine endorsement, in the same revelation, the Lord said, "I seal upon you your exaltation, and prepare a throne for you in the kingdom of my Father. . . . Behold, I have seen your sacrifices, and will forgive all your sins" (D&C 132:49–50). Joseph had plenty of faults and made many mistakes, but his heart was ever dedicated toward doing the will of the Lord. In the end, he succeeded.

One time while my wife was trying to help me see why she could accept polygamy if she had to, she explained it this way. She said to suppose a husband and a wife were married in the temple, loved each other more than anything, and had children together. Then the wife died. The husband might want to remain true to his wife's memory and not remarry. But the wife, on the other side of the veil, would likely want her husband to remarry and provide a mother for their children. Suppose that after the children were raised, his second wife died. Should he spend the last twenty years of his life a lonely bachelor? No, certainly both his wives would want him to marry again and have companionship, friendship, and love to fill his remaining life with joy. When they all passed away and found each other on the other side of the veil, would there be jealousy or rivalry among the wives? No, they would love and respect each other and likely become good friends. They might even be sealed together as one big, happy family.

Then my wife asked me to consider that if I could accept that scenario, how was it different if all the wives were alive at the same time? She said she was glad I wasn't excited about the idea. Because the command of the Lord today is monogamy, it's probably a good thing that we're mostly repulsed by the idea of polygamy. If He ever asked us to live it again, He would have to change our hearts the same way He changed the hearts of the early Saints who were commanded to live it. We don't have to like the idea or want it to return, but "my thoughts are not your thoughts, neither are your ways my ways, saith the Lord" (Isaiah 55:8).

I'm grateful for a wife who is patient with me and continues to encourage me to pass my own tests and trials faithfully. I'm grateful for the Prophet Joseph Smith, who was willing to sacrifice everything to be obedient to the Lord at all hazards. Since he could forgive Emma for her difficulties in accepting polygamy, so can I. Since she could forgive *him* for his weaknesses in trying to adopt and live this principle, so can I. I believe Joseph passed his tests nobly, notwithstanding his weaknesses. He really was a prophet who spoke with God and led the Church by revelation. Time and again, the Spirit has confirmed that witness to me. Despite my weaknesses, I can pass my tests as well. As with Joseph and Emma, for most of us, our greatest tests are still going to come through marriage and family life—just in different ways. To paraphrase Martin Luther, "Marriage is the school of love."[38] And what a tough curriculum!

Evolution, Creation, and Consequences of Belief

"The greater danger for most of us is not that our aim is too high and we miss it, but that it is too low and we reach it."[1]

—Michelangelo

Many people in the Church think there are only two options when it comes to LDS doctrine and evolution: "We have either to reconcile our beliefs in science and religion and ignore the apparent discrepancies, or reject either science or our religion."[2]

In this chapter, I'd like to present a third alternative. Perhaps it's possible to prioritize our knowledge in such a way that we don't have to pit our religious beliefs against our understanding of science. Perhaps we can learn to hold fast to our religion and use our scientific knowledge. We can be believing Latter-day Saints at all times who understand and use science whenever appropriate—without placing our ultimate trust in it.

The Theory

Often when discussing a controversial topic, we have a tendency to jump into a debate right away without ever clarifying what the disagreement even really is. We argue on and on, defending our positions to the death without ever really understanding what the other person is saying or where they're coming from. It makes sense, then, to begin with a basic outline of our topic. The theory of organic evolution teaches that all life on this planet has developed from simpler lifeforms over the course of billions of years. The two basic mechanisms for this development are random variation and natural selection.

Random variation states that as living things reproduce, slight changes can occur in the replication of genetic material from one generation to the next. Some of these random changes are fatal to the resulting offspring; others are insignificant. But occasionally, a mutation occurs in the genetic material of the offspring that *modifies* its physical or behavioral characteristics that give it a distinct advantage for survival over other members of its species.

Natural selection states that, over time, nature "selects" some species of organisms for survival because they've better adapted to their changing environment. All species must compete with others for limited resources. If a random mutation occurs in one member of a species that gives it an advantage, it's then more likely to survive and pass that trait onto the next generation. Over time, this process allows a species to survive by adapting to its new environment. Those that don't evolve run the risk of dying off and becoming extinct. This process can occur quickly, altering a species in just a few years; more commonly though, the changes occur gradually over the course of hundreds, thousands, or even millions of years.

Scientists use the theory of organic evolution to assert that the multiplicity of life on our planet originated from a simple, primordial organism that existed four billion years ago.

An often-used example of such organic evolution at work is the peppered moth. In England two hundred years ago, most peppered moths had a light color with dark spots that afforded them camouflage among the trees where they lived. With the onset of the Industrial Revolution in the nineteenth century, the trees all over the country began to turn black from pollution. Subsequently, the black-bodied peppered moth rose in frequency in nature. Moths with darker bodies had a greater chance of survival among all the blackened trees. As pollution control laws came into effect in the twentieth century, the trees started lightening up again. Now the light-bodied peppered moth is much more common than the black.

As a description of what we observe in nature, the law of organic evolution explains this phenomenon quite well.

Another example is found in medicine. In a laboratory, you can watch as bacteria change to resist antibiotics, creating new drug-resistant strains. Each alteration in the environment—each new drug—precipitates a change in the organism that allows it to survive and pass on its resistance to the next generation. This is why scientists must continually develop new antibiotics.

These are just two of thousands of examples of the law of change that are studied in nature and in scientific laboratories. What Darwin's theory of organic evolution did when it exploded in the world's intellectual communities in the middle of the nineteenth century was eliminate the great Designer of the universe as a necessary explanation for the reality we see around us. According to the theory, it all occurred by chance without anyone or anything to give it direction or purpose. This is what seems most troubling to the religious mind.

So what should believing members of the Church do with such a theory?

Creationism

Sometimes in dealing with the sticky issue of organic evolution and LDS beliefs, well-meaning individuals counsel students to study science, learn all they can about it, and then just throw out the theory of evolution when they come to it because we "know" it must be wrong. Creationists are Christians who reject Darwin's theory of gradual descent over millions of years in favor of a more literal reading of the Bible. They typically teach that earth is only six thousand years old and that God created each species of life independently of all others in an act known as "special creation." Darwinism is rejected outright as a dangerous atheistic attempt to explain away the need for God and lead young people astray. Being strongly religious myself, I can empathize with this impulse to want to reject evolution altogether. But I fear that doing so sets up unnecessary confrontation.

Organic evolution isn't simply one of many theories in science that we're free to pick and choose from. It's the overarching theory that organizes many branches of science: zoology, botany, geology, archeology, anthropology, and genetics, to name a few. The eminent geneticist Theodosius Dobzhansky said, "Nothing in biology makes sense except in the light of evolution."[3] In some ways, to reject evolution is to reject science altogether, which simply becomes too big a demand to make of bright, young, scholastic minds. We do them a disservice if we force them into a corner where, like my uncle, they feel that they have to make a choice between faith and reason. Then we're shocked if they choose reason and abandon religion.

Besides, the Lord makes it clear in the Doctrine and Covenants that He wants us to study everything that science teaches. He wants us to learn "of things both in heaven and in the earth, and under the earth; things which have been, things which are, things which must shortly come to pass" (D&C 88:79). And He tells us why too: "That ye may be prepared in all things when I shall send you again to magnify the calling whereunto I have called you, and the mission with which I have commissioned you" (D&C 88:80). If I'm going to have any success in sharing the gospel with intelligent people, I'm going to have to be able to converse with them on secular topics as well as religious ones.

The 1960 classic movie *Inherit the Wind* with Spencer Tracy was based on the 1925 court trial of John Scopes. Scopes was accused of breaking a state law by teaching evolution in his biology class. The case captured the nation's attention and became known as the Scopes Monkey Trial. Scopes was found guilty but was fined only a hundred dollars. In the movie, the overzealous local preacher offends, alienates, and eventually rejects his own daughter because she loves and defends the accused biology teacher. The prosecutor, Matthew Brady, though also committed to defending the Bible, recognizes that the preacher has gone too far. In an attempt to rein in the preacher's wrath against his daughter, he quotes Proverbs: "he that troubleth his own house shall inherit the wind" (Proverbs 11:29). Sometimes in an attempt to stand up for what we believe is true, we can unnecessarily offend and alienate those we love. We can't save our children by condemning them for their allegiances. The Savior taught the Nephites that "this is not my doctrine, to stir up the hearts of men with anger, one against another; but this is my doctrine, that such things should be done away" (3 Nephi 11:30).

Inherit the Wind shows the consequences of the fight between creationists and evolutionists: young people are left disillusioned and hopeless. At a climactic moment in the movie, the prosecuting attorney explains the motivation for enforcing the law and prohibiting the teaching of evolution in the schools: "A victory here would be a monument to God that would last a thousand years." The true believer wants to protect children from the godless theories of science that would lead them away from their "old time religion." But the prosecutor's wife wisely responds: "Every man has to build his own monument. You can't do it for him. If you do, it becomes your monument—not theirs. And they'll topple it the minute they find a flaw in it."[4]

The point here is that we can't simply shield people from dangerous theories. All we can do is instruct them and trust them to figure out these issues for themselves. At the end of the movie, the defense attorney walks out of the courtroom carrying the Bible and Darwin's *On the Origin of Species* together. The point is clearly that an intelligent person can believe in both.

Theistic Evolution

In trying to be good Latter-day Saints and still be respectable in academic or other intellectual communities, some have tried following the path of Spencer Tracy's character by believing in a version of theistic evolution. This is the belief that God created the world, but that he used evolution as the mechanism for creation. People who subscribe to this theory are impressed—even convinced—by the preponderance of evidence in support of evolution and are persuaded that it accurately accounts for the diversity of life on the planet. These committed Saints want to say that God created the universe using organic evolution. That way, they can believe in everything science teaches about evolution and just add at the end, "but God did it all."

I understand the inclination some might feel to want to try combining both perspectives. They love and believe in the gospel. They also believe in current scientific theories of our day, so they try to work out a harmony between them. This is what the Catholic Church has done.[5] Many intelligent Latter-day Saints have gone this route as well.

The Lord says, "Seek ye first the kingdom of God, and his righteousness; and all these [other necessary] things shall be added unto you" (Matthew 6:33). Our job is to serve God and *use* science. We can't use it unless we understand it and even master it.

Scientific Challenges to Evolution

For all the explanatory power the theory of organic evolution provides, it's not without weaknesses. Besides the threat it seems to pose to religious belief, there are at least four other serious objections to the theory's legitimacy: irreducible complexity, missing links, spontaneous generation, and the development of higher culture.

The first one I'll discuss is irreducible complexity. It seems pretty easy to conceptualize how something like a fin on a fish could evolve slowly over time with slight variations, each alteration giving the subsequent generation a survival advantage. It's a much bigger stretch to envision how an organ such as an eye or an ear could develop over time. Such organs are so complex and so perfectly "designed" with a single purpose that it's baffling to imagine them arising randomly and piecemeal, and then coming together to make a perfectly interconnected organ. Darwin himself recognized this challenge to his theory: "If it could be demonstrated that any complex organ existed, which could not possibly have been formed by numerous, successive, slight modifications, my theory would absolutely break down." Yet he goes on to state quite confidently, "I can find no such case."[6]

It turns out that each part of complex organs like the eye actually *can* be shown to add survival value for the organism. The proposed evolutionary chain starts with the development of simple photoreceptor cells that can discern between light and dark. These cells could give the organism a slight survival advantage over less-developed relatives. Subsequent random variations in its offspring could continue, eventually resulting in the complex interconnected neurochemical pathways of the human eye. Biologists can string an entire chain of similar species together, showing each developmental step along the way.[7] So this challenge to organic evolution seems rebutted.

Another classic critique of evolution is the glaring absence of "missing links." Darwin called them "transitional links"—organisms that show common features of two species supposedly connected in the evolutionary chain. Theoretically, fossil records should be full of them. Darwin acknowledged that their absence constituted "the most obvious and serious objection which can be urged against the theory."[8] Darwin's answer was simply that fossil records are imperfect, but he predicted that eventually the transitional fossils would begin to appear.

They have. Just two years after the publication of *On the Origin of Species* in 1859, paleontologists discovered the first fossil remains of an archaeopteryx, or the proposed link between dinosaurs and birds. Over time, many such transitional fossils have appeared. So this objection seems to have been overcome, but creationists continue using to attack the theory.[9]

A third (and more serious) difficulty for the theory of organic evolution is the notion of spontaneous generation. Scientists can line up species and show their chain of descent on chart after chart. Yet eventually, all this genealogy comes to a dead end. Where and how did the first organism come into existence? All evolutionists can offer is spontaneous generation, or more accurately abiogenesis. This is the process by which non-living materials supposedly come together to form a living organism. The problem is that it's never been seen in nature or artificially re-created in a laboratory. Everything science can demonstrate shows that life only comes from life. But science has to assume that at some point in history, at least once (but perhaps several times), all the pieces just fell together in the right sequence and—with a bolt of lightning or some other major catalyst—came to life. To declare that this is how it all happened when there's no evidence of it is quite a piece of imagination.

A fourth challenge for evolution—and perhaps the most baffling—is the development of human culture. How can survival of the fittest explain things like music, art, beauty, taste, morality, consciousness, or the search for the meaning of life? None of these endeavors appears to have any reproductive survival value at all, yet they're the things that separate us from animals and make us human. Evolution paints a portrait that says the development of humanity operated purely by chance. That ultimately, it has no purpose but survival. If the theory of organic evolution is true, then the development of higher culture all came about by chance. If so, then ironically even our human sense of a higher purpose was determined by the purposeless, random drive for survival. The field of evolutionary psychology studies this phemonenon. It's an interesting and vibrant field of study that tries to address and explain evolutionary principles of psychology and culture.

For a believer in the gospel, the strict evolutionist's view that replaces God with randomness as the driving force behind the creation of life is out of the question. Yet with our divinely appointed quest to seek all truth, the creationist's view that rejects science seems almost equally untenable. The theistic evolutionist's view that harmonizes the two positions would seem like the happy medium, and many faithful Latter-day Saints have adopted this solution to the dilemma. Still, theistic evolution leads to some serious objections as well.

Challenges to Theistic Evolution

There are some Church doctrines that don't seem compatible with the theory of organic evolution, as taught by the scientists—and even as modified by the theistic evolutionists. Here are some of those challenges:

Death before the Fall. Many Saints believe that there was no death of any kind for any living thing on the earth until Adam and Eve partook of the forbidden fruit and became mortal. Their justification is 2 Nephi 2:22: "And now, behold, if Adam had not transgressed he would not have fallen, but he would have remained in the garden of Eden. And all things which were created must have remained in the same state in which they were after they were created; and they must have remained forever, and had no end." Yet evolution requires an uninterrupted cycle of birth and death for millions of years before humans ever appeared on the planet. There seems to be a conflict here.[10]

Procreation before the Fall. This related clash comes from the same chapter in 2 Nephi. Lehi explained that if Adam and Eve had remained in the Garden, "they would have had no children" (2 Nephi 2:23). Many assume this passage implies that no living being on the planet could reproduce until after the Fall.

There are possible explanations for those who want to combine belief in the Fall story with belief in organic evolution. We could say that conditions in the Garden were unique and that there could've been a lone and dreary world outside the Garden where the cycle of birth and death had already been going on for countless ages. But that idea seems to go against the teaching that some take from Moses 3:7, that Adam was the "first flesh upon the earth," or the first to become mortal after the Fall. The belief is that when Adam and Eve chose to fall, their choice caused all living things on the earth to fall and become mortal as well.

Special creation of each species. The scriptures teach that "God, said: Let the earth bring forth the living creature after his kind, cattle, and creeping things, and beasts of the earth after their kind, and it was so" (Moses 2:24). Some interpret passages such as this one to mean that God created each species in a special creation patterned after a spiritual creation done first in heaven. The Lord says, "I, the Lord God, created all things, of which I have spoken, spiritually, before they were naturally upon the face of the earth" (Moses 3:5). This special creation of each "kind" of plant and animal doesn't seem to allow for the possibility of a gradual, chance development of various species over millions of years.

Age of the earth. Scientists have theorized that the earth has been around for four to five billion years and that the multitudinous species on the earth today were millions of years in the making. The scriptures teach that God created the earth in six days and on the seventh, He rested. They also teach that a thousand years to man is as a single day to the Lord (Abraham 3:4; 2 Peter 3:8). Some want to interpret such passages literally to mean that it took exactly six thousand years for the Lord to create the earth, and that it has been around for another six thousand years since then. After all, in D&C 77:6, the Lord talks about "this earth during the seven thousand years of its continuance, or its temporal existence" (including a thousand years for the Millennium). Others would say the Lord just means that creation took a long time and that the numbers are not meant to be interpreted literally. The number *billion* (let alone the concept or need for such a high value) didn't exist at the time. As has been pointed out, the word *day* in the Old Testament could just as easily be translated as "period of time."

Age of man. Some use the chronology of the Bible to argue that man has been on the earth for around six thousand years. Yet scientists use carbon dating on skeletal remains found all over the planet to argue that humans have been on the earth for two hundred thousand years and that humanlike creatures have been around for four to five million years. This leaves some believers to speculate that perhaps there were Pre-Adamites—other races of humans that existed before Adam and Eve, our first parents, were placed in the Garden. But then, what is their relation to Adam and Eve? Are they children of God or merely creatures of His creating?

Dinosaurs. Where in the world do the dinosaurs fit in with what the scriptures teach about the creation? This is another tough one. There are basically three approaches that believing Latter-day Saints have taken on this issue. The first possibility is that dinosaurs didn't live on our planet—that their fossil remains are leftover from fragments of other planets that God used to create this earth from preexisting matter. The trouble with this belief is that the fossil record is so orderly that it looks much more like a long, continuous line of development rather than the hodgepodge of scattered remnants we'd expect if they were from other planets.

Another belief is that dinosaurs must have been some of the animals created by the Lord before Adam and Eve made their appearance on the earth. They must've fallen and become mortal at the same time Adam and Eve did, and all the scientific dating methods that place them millions of years ago must be wrong.

A third belief is that there must've been death before Adam and Eve's fall. Dinosaurs just came and went just as the paleontologists tell us they did. The experience of Adam and Eve in the Garden of Eden could've been a special case of events added later "on top" of a world already teeming with life-and-death struggles that'd been going on for millions of years in preparation for their arrival.

Some Latter-day Saints have followed the ways of the secular world entirely and given up their belief in a historical Adam and Eve. They want to keep that story as a religious myth that exists to teach us moral lessons but has no historical accuracy. Yet faithful Latter-day Saints have a hard time bending their beliefs that far. The First Presidency issued an official statement in 1909, saying, "It is held by some that Adam was not the first man upon this earth and that the original human being was a development from lower orders of the animal creation. These, however, are the theories of men. The word of the Lord declared that Adam was 'the first man of all men' (Moses 1:34), and we are therefore in duty bound to regard him as the primal parent of our race."[11] So to give up belief in a literal Adam and Eve, you'd have to reject an official First Presidency statement.

These are just some of the apparently irreconcilable claims of science and religion that the thoughtful Latter-day Saint must face. The theistic evolutionist typically responds to the apparent contradictions between the scriptures and science by saying that the creationists have misinterpreted or misapplied the scriptures. For instance, the scriptures don't actually say that Adam and Eve were the first living things on the planet to experience mortality, have children, and become subject to death. They simply state that "man became a living soul, the first flesh upon the earth" (Moses 3:7). What that verse means could be open to reinterpretation. The problems that science has with religion—from the point of view of the believing scientist—are not with what the scriptures say, but with how the theologians interpret the scriptures.

Consequences of Belief

Philosopher and psychologist William James argued that the meaning of any idea is the consequence for believing it.[12] If he is right, the meaning of organic evolution is simply the consequences of believing in it. What, then, are the consequences of believing in organic evolution?

There's a Jewish story about a rabbi sitting next to an atheist on an airplane. Every few minutes, one of the rabbi's children or grandchildren would inquire about his need for food, drink, or comfort. The atheist comments, "The respect your children and grandchildren show you is wonderful. Mine don't show me that respect." The rabbi responds, "Think about it. To my children and grandchildren, I'm one step closer in a chain of tradition to the time when God spoke to the whole Jewish people on Mount Sinai. To your children and grandchildren, you are one step closer to being an ape."

To believe in the LDS God is to believe that we're literally His sons and daughters. It's to believe that we have all the necessary seeds of divinity planted within us and that we have inherited from our heavenly parents the nature and predisposition to eventually become as They are. That belief can bring great hope while we struggle with the inevitable challenges and disappointments of life.

If evolutionism, creationism, and theistic evolutionism all leave significant questions unanswered, what option *am* I left with? I think Elder Neal A. Maxwell gave us a valuable key in an address to the BYU faculty many years ago. "The LDS scholar has his citizenship in the kingdom, but carries his passport into the professional world—not the other way around."[13] I think we can fruitfully apply this provocative statement by an Apostle trained in academia to the issue at hand. I'm going to study all I can about organic evolution and seek to understand and even master it, if possible. It is, after all, the foundational structure of all the life and earth sciences. But I don't have to *believe* in it. I don't have to put all my faith and trust in it. My citizenship is still in the kingdom. I can rely on the word of God as the foundation for building my life. I can trust in God's creative power to protect the universe and me.

This seems to be the approach suggested more recently by another Apostle, Dallin H. Oaks. In his book *Life's Lessons Learned*, the former university president and Utah Supreme Court justice has a short chapter on science and religion. In it, he warned against trying to compartmentalize our search for truth by studying religion on Sundays and pursuing pure science Monday through Saturday.[14] But he also warned against trying to prematurely harmonize our studies in science and religion. Finally, he suggested a plan of engagement for the thoughtful Latter-day Saint:

> I am confident that when we progress to the point where we know all things, we will find a harmony of all truth. Until that time, it is wise for us to admit that our understanding—in religion and in science—is incomplete and that the resolution of most seeming conflicts is best postponed. In the meantime, we do the best we can to act upon our scientific knowledge, where that is required, and always upon our religious faith, placing our ultimate reliance for the big questions and expectations of life on the eternal truths revealed by our Creator, which transcend human reason, "for with God nothing shall be impossible" (Luke 1:37).[15]

Elder Oaks's strategy seems to be clear: learn and use science but trust in and rely on the scriptures for finding the answers when we need them. And throughout the journey, keep an open mind.

President Packer's Concerns

Over the course of his nearly forty-year ministry as a General Authority, President Boyd K. Packer has expressed from time to time his concerns about belief in organic evolution. "This secular doctrine," he has said, "holds that man is not a child of God, but basically an animal, his behavior inescapably controlled by natural impulse, exempt from moral judgments and unaccountable for moral conduct." He's warned that "in time, the consequences of following [. . . it] will become visible enough."[16]

In another address, President Packer emphasized the negative consequences of believing that man is merely an animal:

> The comprehension of man as no more than a specialized animal cannot help but affect how one behaves. A conviction that man did evolve from animals fosters the mentality that man is not responsible for moral conduct. Animals are controlled to a very large extent by physical urges. Promiscuity is a common pattern in the reproduction of animals. In many subtle ways, the perception that man is an animal and likewise controlled by urges invites that kind of behavior so apparent in society today. A self-image in which we regard ourselves as children of God sponsors one kind of behavior. A conclusion which equates man to animals fosters another kind of behavior entirely. Consequences of which spring from that single false premise account for much of what society now suffers. I do not speak in theoretical terms; it matters very much in practical ways.[17]

In other words, if someone can convince me that organic evolution adequately explains my origins, they can readily convince me that I'm merely an animal that needs to learn to adapt to my physical surroundings. Conscience and morality become hang-ups to be overcome so I can learn to get more out of the world.

In the same address, President Packer went on to say, "You should not be hesitant to pursue knowledge; indeed you should excel in fields of scientific inquiry. . . . Study to your heart's content any worthy field of inquiry, just remember that all knowledge is not equal in value."[18] So in all your studies, resist the urge to buy into the theories that equate man with animals. "Have faith *in* the revelations; *leave man in the place the revelations have put him!*"[19]

So where have the scriptures placed man? In Moses 6:22, we read, "And this is the genealogy of the sons of Adam, who was the son of God, with whom God, himself, conversed." Adam is our literal ancestor and he was literally a son of God. Even as my understanding of the meaning of this doctrine continues to develop over time, it's a truth I can put my faith in and build my life around. It'll never let me down. Rather than dumping all knowledge together on the same plane, President Packer has urged that we prioritize our knowledge. Gospel knowledge gathered from the treasure troves of the scriptures should come first. This is where we should put our faith. Then we should feel free to gather knowledge from all other sources around us as possibilities to consider. The reason the scriptures are called the standard works is because they are supposed to be the standard by which we judge and sift through all other knowledge.

President Packer tried to show the negative consequences that can come from putting your faith in organic evolution by quoting from the autobiography of Charles Darwin himself:

> I have said that in one respect my mind has changed during the last twenty or thirty years. Up to the age of thirty, or beyond it, poetry of many kinds, such as the works of Milton, Gray, Byron, Wordsworth, Coleridge, and Shelley, gave me great pleasure, and even as a schoolboy I took intense delight in Shakespeare, especially in the historical plays. I have also said that formerly pictures gave me considerable, and music very great delight. But now for many years I cannot endure to read a line of poetry: I have tried lately to read Shakespeare, and found it so intolerably dull that it nauseated me. I have also almost lost any taste for pictures or music.—Music generally set me thinking too energetically on what I have been at work on, instead of giving me pleasure. I retain some taste for fine scenery, but it does not cause me the exquisite delight which it formerly did.
>
> This curious and lamentable loss of the higher aesthetic tastes is all the odder, as books on history, biographies and travels (independently of any scientific facts which they may contain), and essays on all sorts of subjects interest me as much as ever they did. My mind seems to have become a kind of machine for grinding general laws out of large collections of facts, but why this should have caused the atrophy of that part of the brain alone, on which the *higher tastes*

> depend, I cannot conceive. A man with a mind more highly organized or better constituted than mine, would not I suppose have thus suffered; and if I had to live my life again I would have made a rule to read some poetry and listen to some music at least once every week; for perhaps the parts of my brain now atrophied could thus have been kept active through use. The loss of these tastes is a loss of happiness, and may possibly be injurious to the intellect, and more probably to the moral character, by enfeebling the emotional part of our nature.
>
> Let me repeat that last sentence, "The loss of these tastes is a loss of happiness, and may possibly be injurious to the intellect, and more probably to the moral character, by enfeebling the emotional part of our nature."[20]

Darwin himself pointed to many of the most refined and exquisite aspects of civilization that evolution seems to fail to explain adequately: morality, art, music, poetry, drama, literature, and, I might add, religion. According to evolutionary theory, these are merely unintentional offshoots of higher brain functioning that developed accidentally in the natural selection process. Darwin suggested that his belief in and pursuit of evolutionary theory are what led to a loss of these hallmarks of culture from his life.

It's not *learning* about evolution that worries President Packer, but rather *buying into* it as a replacement to the Creator:

> We may safely study and learn about the theories and philosophies of men, but if they contradict the plan of redemption, the great plan of happiness, do not "buy into" them as truth. If you do, you may be putting a mortgage on your testimony, on your knowledge of premortal life, on the creation of man, on the Fall and the Atonement, on your Redeemer, the Resurrection, and exaltation; for "every plant, which my heavenly Father hath not planted, shall be rooted up" (Matthew 15:13). If you "buy into" the philosophies of men, you may have your testimony repossessed. Your respect for moral law may go with it, and you will end up with nothing.[21]

Will we ever know exactly how evolution fits in with the Lord's plan? Of course we will, though it may not be until after the Second Coming, or even later. The Lord makes this promise: "Yea, verily I say unto you, in that day when the Lord shall come, he shall reveal all things—things which have passed, and hidden things which no man knew, things of the earth, by which it was made, and the purpose and the end thereof—things most precious, things that are above, and things that are beneath, things that are in the earth, and upon the earth, and in heaven" (D&C 101:32–34). It's interesting to me that the Lord seems to include the way the earth was made as one of those "hidden things which no man knew." This verse teaches me to be skeptical of anyone who pretends to have all the answers to how everything fits together.

Laws, Theories, and Gospel Principles

The biggest challenge belief in organic evolution poses is its threat to a *bona fide* belief and trust in God. The law of natural selection can be shown quite readily in the laboratory, in a backyard, and in the natural history museums. But the claim that random variation is the sole source of change on the planet is what seems to threaten religion. John A. Widtsoe was an Apostle and a respected scientist. His view, articulated in *Science and Your Faith in God,*[22] was that we need to distinguish between the law of evolution and the theory of evolution. He believed that evidence for the law of evolution was ubiquitous. Everywhere we look, we see that living things change and develop from one generation to the next. He actually compared this law of evolution with the gospel doctrine of eternal progression. Yet he said that's a far cry from proving that all living things on the planet have a common ancestor, derived through pure chance. That's the theory of evolution, which is merely an inference made from the facts. It's constantly being changed, revised, and is subject to question.

Before Darwin, people looked at the marvelous interconnectedness of all living things and saw the hand of a benevolent God holding everything together. After Darwin, it became fashionable to see all the beauty and interconnectedness of life as evidence of random forces at work.

The prophet Jacob left a warning against such hubris: "O that cunning plan of the evil one! O the vainness, and the frailties, and the foolishness of men! When they are learned they think they are wise, and they hearken not unto the counsel of God, for they set it aside, supposing they know of themselves, wherefore, their wisdom is foolishness and it profiteth them not. And they shall perish. But to be learned is good if they hearken unto the counsels of God" (2 Nephi 9:28–29). So the danger, as Jacob wrote it, is when we think we can explain away everything and no longer need to believe in or obey God and His commandments.

The Book of Mormon also shows us a potential outcome of believing in the survival of the fittest doctrine codified by the theory of organic evolution. Korihor, one of the great anti-Christs of the book, came to Zarahemla with an influential new doctrine. He taught that "every man fared in this life according to the management of the creature; therefore every man prospered according to his genius, and that every man conquered according to his strength" (Alma 30:17). The natural consequence of Korihor's version of survival of the fittest was that "whatsoever a man did was no crime" (Alma 30:17). Once he convinced people that they were simply doing what comes naturally, Korihor got what he really wanted: "And thus he did preach unto them, leading away the hearts of many, causing them to lift up their heads in their wickedness, yea, leading away many women, and also men, to commit whoredoms—telling them that when a man was dead, that was the end thereof" (Alma 30:18). Once again, what seems to be at stake is nothing less than a believer's commitment to life-sustaining moral values.

I'm still not sure what to make of Darwin's analysis in *On the Origin of Species*. He doesn't seem like a godless man trying to create excuses for those who want to give up their religious background, as Korihor does. He seems like a brilliant scientist who was fascinated by the obvious interconnectedness of living things and was sincerely trying to make sense of the data nature amply provides. He outlined the evidence for the law of evolution that surrounds us. Organisms do mutate and species do adapt, and Darwin gave us some explanations as to how that happens. But the theory of organic evolution—which teaches that all life on the planet came from a single lifeform through random changes over billions of years—seems like too much for a believer in the gospel to swallow. Even adding at the end that God is somehow behind it all doesn't seem convincing enough.

Fortunately, I don't have to believe in organic evolution to be intelligent. I can study it and try to make sense of it the best I can. I can even learn to use it to explain natural phenomena around me. Then I can go about my life with faith in the Lord and in His word, merely using my added understanding of science when appropriate. That's how I study philosophy, psychology, history, and literature as well—not as sources of ultimate truth, but instead as sources of interesting possibilities to consider and sift through. Eventually, as the First Presidency taught in a message to the Church, our destiny is to "evolve into a God."[23] When that happens, no doubt I'll understand how to create planets and lifeforms. Ultimately, it'll require that I understand all the philosophies of the world along with all the doctrines of the gospel, and I'll be thrilled with how all truth can be connected together into one great whole. But that is a long, long way off. In the meantime, I trust in the Lord with all my heart and lean not unto my own understanding. In all my ways, I'll acknowledge Him and trust that He will direct my paths (see Proverbs 3:5–6).

Homosexuality, the Plan of Salvation, and the Moment of Truth

"You can't move forward unless you're willing to accept where you are."[1]
—Patrick Henry Hughes

While I was going to graduate school, I had the privilege of attending a university ward that was teeming with bright, enthusiastic students. With my sheltered LDS upbringing, I was astonished by the number of people I met there who considered themselves gay. I was assigned as a home teacher to a young man who was dealing with same-sex attraction and who wanted desperately to marry in the temple and raise a family someday. I was a bit shocked each time a ward member would declare their homosexuality in Church settings. When I was made a counselor in the bishopric, I served on disciplinary councils encouraging the repentance process for members acting on their same-sex attraction. I felt the Savior's love for these beloved children of God in their struggles, but nothing prepared me for Sam.

Sam and I spent a year together as counselors in the ward bishopric. I was quite fond of Sam. He was strong and opinionated, but he was also thoughtful and sensitive. In ward council meetings, he was always insightful when sharing ideas on how to help people. He was a good listener and was always the first one to lend a helping hand to someone in need. Sam was the epitome of a good Christian and Latter-day Saint. He was a hero to me and I wanted to be more like him.

After serving in the bishopric together for a year, Sam told me he was gay. After Sam confided in me, he spent a lot of time trying to help me understand what he went through as a Mormon with homosexual feelings. He said that from the first time he ever felt sexual attraction, it was toward males. He'd been sexually abused as a child, so he didn't really feel that he could claim his orientation was by nature or by nurture. All he knew was that he didn't choose to be that way. He'd spent fifteen years of his life trying to hide or change his sexuality. He worked with bishops and counselors and spent hundreds of hours in prayer and fasting. He even submitted himself to shock therapy (which used to be a common treatment). But it was all to no avail. When he finally told his parents about his struggle, they rejected him. That wasn't the worst of it—he felt rejected by God. Why wasn't his earnest desire, coupled with the Savior's Atonement, enough to bring about the change he so desperately sought?

Still, Sam carried on. He'd served a faithful mission, was a thirty-year-old virgin, and tried to do everything our religion required of him. Now he was trying to decide if he could spend the rest of his life single. He spent some time talking with Catholic priests to get a perspective on what it would be like to live a life of celibacy. I personally have never known another human being who struggled so much—against all odds—to try to do what was right.

Was Sam a worthy Latter-day Saint? Of course he was—as worthy as any of us ever are in this life. President Hinckley taught that having same-sex attraction isn't a sin. Sam didn't choose to have the drives he had, but because of his love for the Lord and his desire to follow the plan, he chose not to act on them. Once I learned of Sam's ceaseless struggle, he became an even greater hero in my eyes.

The Church's stance on homosexuality is quite different from current cultural trends. The cultural message of the gay community is that homosexuality is an inborn trait and that change is impossible and undesirable. Even more, their message suggests that churches who reject homosexuality lead believers who struggle with it to suicide as their only option. Because no one with an ounce of compassion can possibly want suicide as the only option, churches should be pressured to change their stance and simply accept same-sex relationships.

As I write this chapter, thirty-five states have legalized same-sex marriage. In 2013, the U.S. Supreme Court overturned the Defense of Marriage Act and essentially overturned on a technicality California's constitutional ban on same-sex marriage—which the Church helped to get passed. Next, federal judges started overturning state bans as well. In December 2013, same-sex marriages became legal in Utah for a few weeks until the U.S. Supreme Court put a temporary stay on a district judge's decision. In 2014, the Supreme Court refused to look at the lower court's decisions, again legalizing same-sex marriage in Utah. This same process has legalized the practice in many other states. The majority of Americans polled are now in favor of same-sex marriage, and our current president has publicly supported the practice as well. In 2015, the Supreme Court has decided to weigh in on the matter definitively. The handwriting on the wall is pretty clear as to which way our country is headed.

The Church has been vilified in the liberal press for not following the trend. We're labelled as being homophobic, intolerant, anti-gay, and on the wrong side of history. The Church has replied that it's not anti-gay, but rather pro-family and simply promoting the law of chastity taught by God in the scriptures. But that doesn't satisfy the critics. Many young people in the Church, moved by a sense of compassion, can't see any reason not to support gay marriage rights. So the question I've agonized over is this: How can I support the Church's stance on homosexual issues (which I agree with) and still be understanding and compassionate toward those who deal with these issues—especially as same-sex marriage becomes the law of the land?

When Latter-day Saint families are confronted with issues of same-sex attraction, they encounter several moments of truth. These are moments when our prejudices, biases, and ideals come head-to-head with uncomfortable realities. These moments demand a response and provide us with opportunities to rise to the challenge or cower in fear, denial, or superficial conformity to someone else's expectations. How we deal with these moments could have long-lasting—perhaps even eternal—consequences.

In this respect, I must confess that writing this chapter worries me more than any other in this book. I feel a keen responsibility to accurately represent and sustain the standards of the Church, in which I so deeply believe. I also feel an acute need to recognize and validate the intense and heroic struggles that so many families and individuals in the Church go through as they deal with the challenge of same-sex attraction. I'm sure that, in the end, my ruminations will offend people on both sides of the issue, but please believe me when I say that my only intent is to reach out with help toward those who deal with this issue and to do so from within the guidelines of the Church and the Lord's plan of happiness. Perhaps writing this chapter is a moment of truth for me.

Defining Our Experience

For Latter-day Saints, it's important to begin this discussion with a clarification of the Church's stance on the issue. Regardless of the laws of the land where we reside, to live in or to encourage a homosexual relationship is wrong in the sight of God. On November 14, 1991, in a letter to members, the First Presidency declared the Church's position on the law of chastity: "Sexual relations are proper only between husband and wife appropriately expressed within the bonds of marriage. Any other sexual contact, including fornication, adultery, and homosexual and lesbian behavior, is sinful."[2] The Church has never varied on this stance.

Yet it's also wrong to unfairly discriminate against those who believe differently than we do and choose to live in homosexual relationships. President Gordon B. Hinckley explained,

> People inquire about our position on those who consider themselves so-called gays and lesbians. My response is that we love them as sons and daughters of God. They may have certain inclinations which are powerful and which may be difficult to control. Most people have inclinations of one kind or another at various times. If they do not act upon these inclinations, then they can go forward as do all other members of the Church. If they violate the law of chastity and the moral standards of the Church, then they are subject to the discipline of the Church, just as others are.
>
> We want to help these people, to strengthen them, to assist them with their problems and to help them with their difficulties. But we cannot stand idle if they indulge in immoral activity, if they try to

> uphold and defend and live in a so-called same-sex marriage situation. To permit such would be to make light of the very serious and sacred foundation of God-sanctioned marriage and its very purpose, the rearing of families.[3]

Clearly, for the prophet (and the Lord, for whom he speaks), same-sex attraction is *not* a sin, but same-sex behavior is. Recently, the Church clarified its position on homosexuality:

> As a church, our doctrinal position is clear: any sexual activity outside of marriage is wrong, and we define marriage as between a man and a woman. However, that should never, ever be used as justification for unkindness. Jesus Christ, whom we follow, was clear in His condemnation of sexual immorality, but never cruel. His interest was always to lift the individual, never to tear down.
>
> Further, while the Church is strongly on the record as opposing same-sex marriage, it has openly supported other rights for gays and lesbians such as protections in housing or employment.
>
> The Church's doctrine is based on love. We believe that our purpose in life is to learn, grow and develop, and that God's unreserved love enables each of us to reach our potential. None of us is limited by our feelings or inclinations. Ultimately, we are free to act for ourselves.
>
> The Church recognizes that those of its members who are attracted to others of the same sex experience deep emotional, social, and physical feelings. The Church distinguishes between feelings or inclinations on the one hand and behavior on the other. It's not a sin to have feelings, only in yielding to temptation.
>
> There is no question that this is difficult, but Church leaders and members are available to help lift, support, and encourage fellow members who wish to follow Church doctrine. Their struggle is our struggle. Those in the Church who are attracted to someone of the same sex but stay faithful to the Church's teachings can be happy during this life and perform meaningful service in the Church. They can enjoy full fellowship with other Church members, including attending and serving in temples, and ultimately receive all the blessings afforded to those who live the commandments of God.[4]

Even though the Church is seen by most of the world as anti-gay, it's done things recently to demonstrate understanding. In 2009, it supported legislation in Salt Lake City protecting housing and employment rights for those living in same-gender relationships. With the Church's support, the bill passed unanimously in the city council. The message was clear that the Church doesn't condone same-sex marriage in any way or sexual relations outside of marriage, but neither does it condone discrimination against anyone because of their sexual orientation.

In 2012, the Church launched a website to address the needs of individuals and families dealing with same-sex attraction. It is designed to offer encouragement while still supporting the Church's stance that sexual activity outside of heterosexual marriage is sinful.

Since 3–4 percent of the population deal with same-sex attraction,[5] it's likely that we will know someone who struggles with it. Fortunately, the Church has provided direction on how to deal with this question.

First of all, Elder Dallin H. Oaks said that Latter-day Saints should avoid labeling themselves or others as homosexual. He said, "We should note that the words *homosexual*, *lesbian*, and *gay* are adjectives to describe particular thoughts, feelings, or behaviors. We should refrain from using these words as nouns to identify particular conditions or specific persons. Our religious doctrine dictates this usage. It is wrong to use these words to denote a *condition*, because this implies that a person is consigned by birth to a circumstance in which he or she has no choice in respect to the critically important matter of sexual *behavior*."[6] When so many struggling with this challenge have found such relief in finally labeling themselves as gay, why would the Church be against using that label?

The Church wants to help people define themselves above all else as children of God. That is our fundamental identity. Using "gay" or "homosexual" as nouns implies a permanent condition. This is precisely the issue at stake. Activity or propensity is not the same as identity, and our identity is the issue here. To label oneself as gay is to identify with a community that often goes against the teachings and standards of the Church. It also increases the likelihood of acting on same-sex attraction. In one study, 96 percent of women and 87 percent of men who labeled themselves as homosexual or bisexual had participated in sex with someone of the same gender, but just

32 percent of women and 43 percent of men who admitted same-sex attraction had done so.[7] Whether or not labels cause or influence the behavior is debatable, but they do matter.

Recently, the Church has softened somewhat on its stance against labeling and seems to allow people to use commonly accepted labels like "gay" and "homosexual" as nouns if they want.[8] This seems to be a practical issue to increase our ability to engage in meaningful dialogue. But the reasoning and doctrine behind refusing to label oneself gay would seem to remain.

The gay community has successfully persuaded a majority of America that same-sex attraction is an inborn trait, is normal and healthy, and should be celebrated, as any other "diversity" would be.[9] In my opinion, some of the most telling evidence on the issue are the twin studies that have shown that 52 percent of the time when one identical twin labels himself as gay, the other one will also, and 48 percent of the time when one identical twin labels herself as lesbian, the other one will as well. Where 3–4 percent of the general population is affected, half of the time twins with the same genetic makeup are affected.[10] If there were *no* genetic influences involved, we'd expect closer to 3–4 percent of the twins of those experiencing same-sex attraction to also be affected. If there were *only* genetic influences involved, we'd expect closer to 100 percent. Apparently, both genetics and other factors are at work. Developmental issues, upbringings, and personal choices all probably play a role as well.

Still, even if science *could* prove that same-sex attraction was entirely genetic and thus natural, would that justify indulging in it? If science could prove that heterosexual attraction was genetically determined, would that justify fornication? "The natural man is an enemy to God" King Benjamin says, and our duty is to "putteth off the natural man . . . through the atonement of Christ" (Mosiah 3:19). Paul puts it this way: "There hath no temptation taken you but such as is common to man: but God is faithful, who will not suffer you to be tempted above that ye are able; but will with the temptation also make a way to escape, that ye may be able to bear it" (1 Corinthians 10:13). The Lord promises that He never allows us to suffer any challenge that we cannot bear and to give us His help. Similarly, He said through Nephi that "the Lord giveth no commandments unto the children of men, save he shall prepare a way for them that they may accomplish the thing which he commandeth them" (1 Nephi 3:7). The Lord has commanded, through His prophets, that any sexual relations outside of marriage are wrong, so there must be a way for anyone who experiences homosexual feelings to master them, modify them, or at least avoid them.

That's a hard pill to swallow, I know. Many are probably afraid they can't successfully fight off those impulses or may not even want to because the temptations seem so strong and incessant. It'd be a much easier route to find a culture that embraces and ennobles those impulses and encourages their full satisfaction. Yet a true Christian should never expect an easy path through life. Christ said, "Take up your cross, follow me" (D&C 112:14). The road to Golgotha can be a lonely and painful one. It can also be a fearful one. Surely Christ knows something of our fear and is able to help us through it.

On Homophobia

Are Latter-day Saints "homophobic"? Are we irrationally afraid of homosexuality? Many of us probably are to some degree. Same-sex attraction opposes the eternal plan of happiness as we understand it in that we almost don't know how to make sense of it at all. Yet all too often, from our principled rejection of same-sex relationships comes an irrational fear of them. Most of the time, it's easier not to talk about the topic and to pretend it doesn't really exist. When it comes up in Church circles, it's often dismissed with an insensitive wisecrack about Sodom and Gomorrah and that ends the need for any further discussion. But what should I do if a same-sex couple walked into sacrament meeting holding hands? Should I walk up to them, welcome them, and shake their hands? Or should I turn away in quiet disgust? Many Saints are already trying to deal with this issue in a loving, Christlike way, but perhaps some of us should be more willing to examine our homophobia.

As I struggle to make sense of this issue, I see how little I really understand it. Same-sex attraction is a topic that I think about often, but for many of my brothers and sisters in the faith, it's the burning reality of their day-to-day lives. The hypothetical becomes incarnated when I discover that someone I care about deals with same-sex attraction. Then I arrive at a moment of truth.

Moments of Truth

When someone I love tells me they experience same-sex attraction, how am I respond? It could be particularly challenging because they may not break the news the way I'd like them to, and there may be nothing to adequately prepare me for the shock of that moment. Still, I'll have a choice: I can either focus on my own disappointment and discomfort or I can focus on their need for love and acceptance. Many parents suffer denial, anger, and mourning when their children announce their same-gender attraction. Yet what about the children? They're hurting the most. This isn't something they did to their families. It's something that, in many respects, happened to them, and in many cases they've been struggling with it in silence for years out of fear of rejection. Just when they need acceptance and love the most, their parents confirm all their worst fears by rejecting them out of a sense of loss and failure.

What they want—what we all want and need—is someone to hug them and tell them they are okay and to be a listening ear. That tender acceptance doesn't require a call to repentance, but it does require a deliberate withholding of judgment long enough to try and understand what they're going through.

Born That Way?

A second moment of truth that we'll have to face is the question of origins. Where do these feelings come from? Were they born that way or was it a combination of upbringing and decisions? To tell those dealing with same-sex attraction that it's simply a choice and that if they wanted to, they could choose to be normal is to reveal our insensitivity and ignorance of the issue. In our culture, there's so much rejection, pain, and misery associated with any expressed homosexual feelings that it'd be ludicrous to believe someone would choose it as a way of life like the way you would a career or a place to live.

In my limited experience and surveying of the literature, I'd say that for males who deal with same-sex attraction, there's often a strong genetic factor. Family and friends often can see the feminine attributes in them from an early age. Usually, they report that, from the first feelings of sexual attraction, they found themselves drawn to other boys. They quickly learn society's condemnation of those feelings and learn to hide everything they experience.

With women who struggle with lesbianism, the situation is often different. They're often abused or abandoned by boyfriends, fathers, or other relatives. Around 50 percent of women seeking therapy for lesbianism report traumatic sexual abuse.[11] They learn to put up barriers between themselves and men. Lesbianism becomes a defense against further abuse. They find a relationship with a woman who understands and accepts them, finding the emotional fulfillment that they never could with a man. Emotional fulfillment eventually leads to sexual fulfillment.[12]

Of course, these are stereotypes and averages that ultimately fail to adequately describe the lives of individuals. The real opportunity is to earn their trust and to ask them to share their stories with you.

Hiding or Listening?

This brings us to another moment of truth. Will we talk about this challenge openly or keep it a secret? By now, it should be clear what my answer is to this question: I think we'd all be better off if we could learn to talk openly and frankly about this issue. Of course, there's a time and a place for sensitive topics. But if we spent less time condemning and more time asking questions and trying to learn from each other's experiences, those most affected by same-sex attraction could find happiness, peace, understanding, and a place to stay among loving friends and leaders under the gospel umbrella, where before they'd find it only in the gay community.

Bishops and therapists are there to discuss the issue behind closed doors, though friends and family need to be a part of the dialogue as well. Brothers and sisters need to be called on for support. Aunts, uncles, and grandparents need to be prepared and marshaled into a great army of advocates to help the individual feel connected in a community of love. We don't need to become obsessed with the topic, but it's essential that we learn how to listen compassionately when someone needs to talk.

To use a common metaphor, nothing is worse than ignoring or denying the elephant in the living room. So either we find a place for it in our homes and lives or it'll come out and find a place somewhere else. Many once-active Latter-day Saints have found liberation in labelling themselves as homosexual but have found sincerity, openness, and acceptance only in the gay community. I know a young man who returned home early from his mission because he was beginning to act on his same-sex feelings, but when friends asked his family what happened, they said he was struggling with pornography. The young man felt mortified and betrayed. If we want to keep a positive relationship with those struggling, we're going to have to be honest about the issue, be willing to discuss it frankly, and acknowledge there are things we can't change. As one man who deals with same-sex attraction expressed it, "Those who love most and love longest will be the ones who win the hearts of God's children."[13]

To Be or Not to Be Gay?

Another moment of truth will come when an individual who experiences same-sex attraction decides whether or not to keep the standards of the Church. The pressure and opposition are so great that we shouldn't be shocked if for a time our loved ones decide to experiment with the behavior or even a same-sex relationship. They'll still need our love and acceptance even though we can't embrace their decisions. The inexplicable tragedy is the fact that many otherwise good LDS families disown children who choose to live a life contrary to the gospel. A friend of mine has a daughter who is openly gay and has her daughter's friends over for Christmas every year because their LDS families have disowned them. Who did Christ disown as he traveled among us sinners? How can we learn to appreciate them if we just write them off?

If loved ones who deal with same-sex attraction choose to follow the standards of the Church, they'll need even more support. Ty Mansfield is an example of someone who has wrestled with same-sex attraction and has chosen to follow the gospel path. He humbly tells his story in two books he's published, *In Quiet Desperation* and *Voices of Hope*. Brother Mansfield grew up LDS and served a faithful mission. He wrestled all through adolescence and young adulthood with same-sex attraction. At times, he struggled with his commitment to the Church. Finally, he committed himself to keeping his gospel covenants at all costs. Eventually, he met a remarkable LDS woman. She understood and respected his unconventional journey, fell in love with him, and chose to marry him in the temple and be part of his journey. They're seeking to create an eternal family, despite his ongoing struggle with same-sex attraction. They've found the hope promised in the scriptures, which is that through faith we can overcome all things.

Clearly marriage by itself isn't the solution for someone experiencing same-sex attraction. It just comes back to haunt individuals and couples and it all too often ends up destroying families as one finally leaves to pursue a same-sex relationship, no longer able to "live a lie." But the Mansfields and many others have discovered that, with open eyes, therapy, mutual commitment, and support, truly all things are possible to them that believe.

Jeffrey W. Robinson, an LDS therapist working with men who want to temper same-sex attraction, wrote an article outlining steps he's used to help people change. His approach lies not in eliminating same-sex attraction, but in "changing the context in which it is experienced and interpreted."[14] He argues that the capacity for sexual arousal is genetically programmed but that the direction that arousal takes is mostly contextualized by circumstances and decisions. It's not a drive in the sense of a need or a necessity—like eating or sleeping—that forces us to act. It's a craving that can be directed and controlled with proper contextualization and training. He helps people stop over-focusing, look beyond themselves, connect with others, restore chastity, and connect with the Savior. His claim is that weak things can be made strong for those who want to change by applying the gospel in the right way. He doesn't claim to "heal" or "cure" anyone, but he's had success with hundreds of clients in tempering inclinations and modifying behaviors.

Scriptural Hope

There's much that could be said about the condemnation of homosexuality in the scriptures. The Apostle Paul, for instance, had some fairly harsh comments directed toward those who chose to give up the gospel to live in same-sex relationships (see Romans 1:18–28). He even listed sins of a homosexual nature in the same breath with murderers and adulterers (see 1 Timothy 1:9–10). But there's at least one passage of scripture that offers a ray of hope.

In Matthew 19, the Savior answered questions raised by the Pharisees about marriage and divorce. Christ made it clear that, from the beginning, the Lord intended that "a man leave father and mother, and shall cleave to his wife: and they twain shall be one flesh" (verse 5). Yet His disciples expressed concern about the gospel's high price for marriage, facetiously proposing that maybe it'd be better not to marry and just remain celibate. To this, Christ made an intriguing reply.

To understand the Savior's response, we first need to understand what a eunuch is. In the ancient world, there were effeminate men (usually castrated slaves) who were used in a master's home to care for and supervise the women of the household. They could be trusted because they were forced to be celibate. With that introduction, here's the Savior's response to His disciples: "For there are some eunuchs, which were so born from their mother's womb: and there are some eunuchs, which were made eunuchs of men: and there be eunuchs, which have made themselves eunuchs for the kingdom of heaven's sake. He that is able to receive it, let him receive it" (Matthew 19:12).

The context of the Savior's remarks is His discussion with the Pharisees and the disciples about marriage and divorce. Hence, He could've been talking about celibate divorcees. Some scriptural commentators say that Christ was praising a celibate life, because they believe He was single. That explanation seems hollow to Latter-day Saints, who assume that Christ was either married in mortality or is now married. Either way, marriage is required for a place in the kingdom of heaven. Perhaps, like Paul does in JST 1 Corinthians 7:29–33, Christ was referring to missionaries who, for a time, sacrifice marriage and dating opportunities to preach the gospel. Certainly the Lord's words would apply to single brothers and sisters who, due to circumstances out of their control, live their lives alone, without the intimacy and fulfillment of a sexual partner, because of their covenants with the Lord.

But maybe we could apply Christ's words to those who deal with same-sex attraction. Perhaps there are some who are simply born with that predisposition. And there are also those who are made that way by life's experience. He acknowledged both groups and didn't appear to condemn or praise either one. However, He implicitly praised another group: those who voluntarily choose to remain celibate because of their love of the gospel. Christ recognized the difficulty of the invitation. Not everyone is going to be "able to receive it."

Similarly, living polygamy was a soul-wrenching experience for many early Saints. Yet those who sacrificed all for the Lord and His gospel shall in the eternities inherit "thrones, kingdoms, principalities, and powers" (D&C 132:19). The Lord promises help along the way and gives the assurance that, in the end, it'll be worth the effort.

Institutional Changes?

Will the Church ever change its stance on homosexuality, as some strongly advocate? After all, it changed its position on blacks and the priesthood. Couldn't acceptance of homosexuality be just another such issue that's waiting for the right time, the right prophet, or the right amount of social pressure to make the change? Some have taken this position. While still believing in the Church, they're waiting for the day when it'll recognize that it's been wrong on these issues and begin to accommodate same-sex relationships. Some are waiting for the day when the enlightened Church will finally perform gay marriages in the temple.[15]

What I'm tempted to say in response is that homosexuality stands in opposition to the Father's plan of eternal families to such a degree that it could never be accommodated. The whole plan is centered on a man and a woman creating a union in this life, or the next, that results in the "continuation of the seeds forever and ever" (D&C132:19). Then again, I'd say that about polygamy if it hadn't been an essential part of the Church in the past. And that section I just used to justify heterosexual marriage includes verses justifying polygamy (D&C 132:31–39).

The Church's dealings with homosexual issues *have* changed. In 2012, the Church launched a website called mormonsandgays.org, designed to support those dealing with issues of same-sex attraction. And in the summer of 2013, the Church issued a statement supporting the Boy Scouts of America's decision to allow openly homosexual boys to participate in scouting. As gay marriage becomes more widely accepted in society, I have to find more charitable ways of dealing with it. In the summer of 2015, the U.S. Supreme Court is expected to make a decision on same-sex marriage that'll have strong implications for the entire nation.

Regardless of their decision, I can't see homosexuality ever becoming an accepted practice in the Church. I don't pretend to be a prophet or to have any business telling the prophet how to run the Church. We all need to be more aware of the dangers of priestcraft—making ourselves a light to the world. And we need to keep ourselves open to the possibility of major changes in the Church. After all, we believe that the Lord "will yet reveal many great and important things pertaining to the Kingdom of God" (Articles of Faith 1:9).

But to run around saying that the Church *should* change its stance on homosexuality is to go against the prophet and the Quorum of the Twelve Apostles. It's to start down the path of apostasy. That isn't to say that the Lord requires blind obedience. He wants us to consider prayerfully the words of our leaders and seek for the spiritual confirmation. Brigham Young stated,

> I am more afraid that this people have so much confidence in their leaders that they will not inquire for themselves of God whether they are led by Him. I am fearful they settle down in a state of blind self-security, trusting their eternal destiny in the hands of their leaders with a reckless confidence that in itself would thwart the purposes of God in their salvation, and weaken that influence they could give to their leaders, did they know for themselves, by the revelations of Jesus, that they are led in the right way. Let every man and woman know, by the whispering of the Spirit of God to themselves, whether their leaders are walking in the path the Lord dictates, or not. This has been my exhortation continually.[16]

More recently, Boyd K. Packer taught, "We are not obedient because we are blind, we are obedient because we can see."[17] The Lord wants me to study the issues and what the Church leaders have taught about them, and then take them to Him in prayer. But if the answers I think I'm receiving are going against the position of the Church and His prophet, I need to reconsider the source of my answers.

The options for Latter-day Saints who deal with same-sex attraction are daunting. Either they accept a life of celibacy—as any other unmarried Latter-day Saint must—or they seek help in adapting their sexual orientation so they can eventually be married in an eternal relationship. If they choose to remain single, they're going to face a life of unmet sexual inclinations and desires, as well as the loneliness of living without the emotional intimacy of marriage. Theirs is a similar plight to any single adult in the Church, only it'll be coupled with the discouragement of living without hope of a relationship in this life.

Those who choose to pursue the path of change will have a difficult road to follow as well. Opponents of the Church want to claim that this type of change is impossible—that homosexuality is an inborn, immutable part of one's identity. But there's ample evidence that this is simply not true.[18] Whatever the initial factors involved, in many cases people can and do change. As one who is successfully making that journey reported: "Yes, people like me do exist: people who have and do experience same-sex attraction but have also found helpful ways to address those feelings. We are your children, siblings, neighbors, friends, coworkers, and fellow Church members. For the most part, we are a quiet bunch; we do not march, protest, or publicize our private lives. It is sad to me that more people do not make the choice we have made, and sadder still that many people do not even know they have the choice to make."[19] The gospel of Jesus Christ is all about fostering change and becoming a new person. There are now several organizations, such as North Star, that are dedicated to helping Latter-day Saints successfully make this journey.

Change is often slow in coming. For many—perhaps most—who experience serious same-sex attraction, even with fervent and prolonged prayer, fasting, and counseling, it becomes a lifelong effort. If my interaction with loved ones dealing with this issue is limited to a focus on getting them to change, I'll miss many opportunities for Christlike love. Ty Mansfield has written about this narrow focus: "The problem with this approach is that it often leads people to anchor their hope in change of sexual orientation rather than in Christ. And then if efforts to change don't work or don't work as quickly as expected, this approach actually has the potential to increase despair rather than hope."[20] Whether our "thorn in the flesh" is removed in this life or (as it happened with Paul) it remains to our dying day, the issue is whether we'll remain true to our faith in Christ or not (see 2 Corinthians 12:7). My point is that if we would spend less time criticizing and demanding that people conform to our expectations and spend more time trying to understand, perhaps we could provide the support system that they need. As Mother Teresa is credited for saying, "If you judge people, you have no time to love them."[21]

Live and Let Live?

All right, let's suppose you can convince me that the LDS view on practicing homosexuality isn't going to change. Let's suppose you can convince me that it's diametrically opposed to the plan of happiness and as such could never be accommodated by the Lord's Church. Now comes another moment of truth. Does it follow that we should campaign against same-sex marriage in society? Wouldn't the more Christian thing to do be to live and let live? Why should we impose our morality on nonbelieving neighbors?

Again, these are questions I resonate with. I tend to be opinionated and dogmatic in my beliefs, but I try to respect other people's right to disagree with me. After all, we claim to "allow all men the same privilege, let them worship how, where, or what they may" (Articles of Faith 1:12). So why not just let any consenting adults marry and enjoy the same social protections and acceptance that I enjoy?

First, there are political concerns. Too often, civil law defines morality for society. If it's legal, it must be okay. So if same-sex marriages were legalized, churches could be punished for refusing to perform them. Schools could be forced to teach children to accept gay marriages. Private adoption agencies could be forced to give children to gay couples. All of these have happened to some degree in Massachusetts, for example, since the state legalized same-sex marriage. Catholic Charities was told that their refusal to place children with same-sex unions was discriminatory. They were unable to secure a religious exception and were forced out of the adoption business.[22] In the name of tolerance, public school curricula have been changed to teach that homosexual relations are normal and, at times, heroic. Wedding businesses are being forced to cater to same-sex marriages, regardless of their religious objections. And churches are regularly harassed for their pro-family stances without protection from government officials. The list of consequences goes on and on.[23]

What's ultimately at stake, however, is something that was suggested to me by an openly gay man. He explained that marriage is primarily a religious institution. Religions understandably want to safeguard it. Only individuals who still consider themselves religious and want religious sanction for their same-sex relationship care much about gay marriage. Many non-religious people living in gay relationships just want civil unions where their civil liberties can be protected, but they don't need the religious sanction of a church. They no longer believe in marriage anyway. Yet those who still believe in God want him to approve their same-sex relationships. So if they can legalize same-sex marriages, perhaps the churches will "see the light" as well (as the Episcopal Church has) and sanction their relationships.

This anti-marriage agenda can be seen clearly in a 2013 statement by lesbian activist Masha Gessen: "The fight for gay marriage generally involves lying about what we're going to do with marriage . . . because we lie that the institution of marriage is not going to change. . . . The institution of marriage is going to change. . . . I don't think it should exist."[24] There's more going on here than simply endorsing tolerance for people who are different.

What's at stake, then, is the definition of family, society, and religion. "The Family: A Proclamation to the World" makes this somber warning and appeal: "We warn that the disintegration of the family will bring upon individuals, communities, and nations the calamities foretold by ancient and modern prophets. We call upon responsible citizens and officers of government everywhere to promote those measures designed to maintain and strengthen the family as the fundamental unit of society." What are the calamities foretold? Mormon said, "And if the time comes that the voice of the people doth choose iniquity, then is the time that the judgments of God will come upon you; yea, then is the time he will visit you with great destruction even as he has hitherto visited this land" (Mosiah 29:27). So, as a dedicated Christian and Latter-day Saint, I can't simply live and let live. I feel as though I must fight for the right or watch in despair as all morality in society goes up in flames.

However, perhaps I can find a more enlightened, peaceful, and Christlike approach to defend the values I believe in. As the world changes to embrace and normalize same-sex relationships, I'll need great courage to be willing to stand for something. But I'll also need to be sensitive to changes going on around me. I'll need to listen and learn from them and be willing to acknowledge where I was wrong.

Perhaps I can learn from Tevye in *Fiddler on the Roof.* When his three daughters successively confront him about getting married outside their tradition, Tevye feels he has to choose between his faith and his love for his daughters. What he discovers is that much of what he thought was a part of his faith is merely tradition, which is susceptible to change. He tries to accommodate their right to choose their own paths, but eventually he has to draw the line or risk losing his faith altogether. He ends up disowning his youngest daughter because of her choice to marry out of the faith. Ultimately, he learns that his rejection of her choice can't cut the ties of love, responsibility for, and commitment to her as her father. He finds a way to accept her and her husband without embracing their marriage.[25]

Lines and Circles

Eventually, we too may have to draw the line somewhere, and even then we'll need to allow for a loving response to those who reject our lines. In 1 Corinthians 8:1, Paul said, "Knowledge puffeth up, but charity edifieth." In other words, when I think I know everything there is to know about a controversial issue, my pride can close me off to the needs and viewpoints of others. But when I seek first to love others, my goal is to understand and appreciate them—even if I initially disagree with their opinions on the matter. I can draw a line on an issue without drawing a line against a person.

In Spanish bull fighting, there comes a moment at the end where the matador makes the final sword thrust to kill the bull. That's the moment of truth, and by that time the demise of the bull is already a foregone conclusion. It used to be when people declared themselves as homosexual, the foregone conclusion was that they would leave the Church and go find same-sex relationships. But today, there's much more hope. My part and yours is to learn to embrace and accept those dealing with same-sex attraction as children of God, support them in their trials, and not judge them, just as I don't want others to judge me for my trials, struggles, and temptations.

My mother once taught me a classic little poem that I believe could help if I remembered to act on it more. It's called "Outwitted" by Edwin Markham:

> He drew a circle that shut me out—
> Heretic, rebel, a thing to flout.
> But Love and I had the wit to win:
> We drew a circle that took him in.[26]

Perhaps while I'm clarifying and solidifying my commitment to gospel standards of appropriate conduct, I can still learn to draw broader circles that'll help me win people over to the gospel cause. Whether they choose to live the message or not, my duty will always be to love.

Priesthood, Prejudice, and Racial Equality

"He inviteth them all to come unto him and partake of his goodness; and he denieth none that come unto him, black and white, bond and free, male and female; . . . and all are alike unto God."

—2 Nephi 26:33

One of my best friends in college was Federico Echeverria. His parents were from Nicaragua, and his skin was as dark as a moonless night. Even though Rico was born and raised in San Francisco, with his name and appearance, people often thought he was a foreigner. I once asked him why he always seemed so angry. He frankly told me it was his response to being discriminated against so much. A little insensitive, I asked him if he might be exaggerating a bit. I told him I didn't think people really cared what he looked like or where he was from.

Rico was determined to prove me wrong. He took me out to eat at a little diner. As we walked in, he stepped up and asked the young female hostess if we could have a table for two. She looked at him as if he were a leper and walked away without saying a word. He turned to me and said, "There, now you try." When she walked back toward the entrance where we were waiting, I stepped forward and requested a table for two. She smiled and said, "Sure, follow me please." Rico just smiled at me. He didn't have to say anything else. He assured me that he had to put up with that kind of treatment every day of his life—even occasionally in the Church.

I grew up in such an ethnically homogenous environment that, besides that day with Rico, I never really experienced or even witnessed the discrimination that so many of God's children have had to endure. It's one thing that His children have had to endure such prejudice from the ignorant and uncouth, but the fact that they've also experienced prejudice within the Church is even more troubling. Perhaps I shouldn't pretend to understand or much less try to explain an issue so puzzling and troubling. Perhaps I should just listen more to friends like Rico.

But I do have questions, and Rico didn't have many answers for me, so I feel compelled to seek them for myself. Why couldn't those of African descent hold the priesthood in the Church until 1978? Why would the Lord deny blessings to someone because of their lineage? Why was I born with so many advantages and Rico with so many disadvantages in our society? Perhaps by asking the questions and listening for answers, I can begin to empathize with those who struggle more regularly and personally with these issues.

Biblical Restrictions

Throughout scriptural history, there have always been restrictions on who could enjoy the blessings of the gospel. In the days of Adam and Eve, their son Cain slew his brother Abel out of greed. Cain and his descendants were cursed and not allowed to hold the priesthood. The Lord "set a mark upon Cain, lest any finding him should kill him" (Genesis 4:15). The scriptures are unclear as to the exact nature of the curse Cain brought to his family, but they declare that "a servant of servants shall he be unto his brethren" and "a veil of darkness shall cover him, that he shall be known among all men" (Genesis 9:25; JST Genesis 9:26). They were cut off from the things of the Lord and lived in spiritual darkness.

Ham, the second son of Noah, married a Canaanite (a descendant of Cain) and "from this descent sprang all the Egyptians, and thus the blood of the Canaanites was preserved in the land" (Abraham 1:22). Abraham described what happened: "Pharaoh, being a righteous man, established his kingdom and judged his people wisely and justly all his days, seeking earnestly to imitate that order established by the fathers in the first generations, in the days of the first patriarchal reign, even in the reign of Adam, and also of Noah, his father, who blessed him with the blessings of the earth, and with the blessings of wisdom, but cursed him as pertaining to the Priesthood." The scripture goes on, "Now, Pharaoh being of that lineage by which he could not have the right of Priesthood, notwithstanding the Pharaohs would fain claim it from Noah, through Ham, therefore my father was led away by their idolatry" (Abraham 1:26–27). Anciently, some of God's children were denied gospel or priesthood blessings due to their ancestry. Because of these verses, many in the Church assumed that blacks descended from a race that was denied the priesthood.

The descendants of Cain and the Egyptians aren't the only people who were denied access to the priesthood. In the days of Moses and Aaron, only the Levites could hold the priesthood. Israelites from any of the Twelve Tribes could enjoy the blessings of having the gospel and living in the covenant, but only those males of Levi could hold and exercise the priesthood. Everyone else enjoyed priesthood ordinances through their service (see Numbers 16:3–10, 40; 18:1).

In the days when Christ walked the earth, there were also restrictions on who could enjoy all the blessings of the gospel. Once while Jesus was visiting north of the land of Israel, a Canaanite woman approached him. She was a Gentile (a non-Jew), but she'd heard that Jesus of Nazareth was the Son of God and she believed. She needed His help because her daughter was possessed by an evil spirit. He refused to help her. His reason? "I am not sent but unto the lost sheep of the house of Israel" (Matthew 15:24). His mission was to the Jews, not to the Gentiles. The woman persisted and cried, "Lord, help me" (Matthew 15:25).

In what appears at first to be an almost heartless reply, the Savior of all mankind said, "It is not meet to take the children's bread, and to cast it to dogs" (Matthew 15:26). Yet this Gentile woman replied, "Truth, Lord: yet the dogs eat of the crumbs which fall from their masters' table" (Matthew 15:27).

The woman's faith and persistence impressed the Savior, and He declared, "O woman, great is thy faith: be it unto thee even as thou wilt. And her daughter was made whole from that very hour" (Matthew 15:28).

It'd be easy to misunderstand this event and accuse the Lord of being prejudiced against the woman because she was a Canaanite. But actually He was simply staying true to His mission call. He was called by the Father to teach and convert the lost tribes of Israel. Later, the gospel message would be preached to the Gentiles. According to the Lord's timetable, the Jews received it first. Despite what could've felt like a horribly unfair exclusion based solely on her ethnic background, the woman's tremendous faith was enough to procure a blessing for her daughter.

Of course the Lord wasn't being racist! He was operating within an apparently unexplained, preset timetable regarding who was going to get specific blessings and when they'd receive them. This one Gentile woman was able to jump the gun because of her exceeding faith.

Just before Christ left His apostles and offered His life as a sacrifice for all, He explained that they were then going to take His word to the Gentiles. "Go ye into all the world, and preach the gospel to every creature" (Mark 16:15). Still, that simple instruction didn't immediately overcome years of Jewish prejudice against the Gentiles. For some time after Christ's Resurrection, Peter and the other Apostles preached mainly to the Jews and focused their efforts only on converting the house of Israel to the cause of Christ.

It took a revelation to the Lord's prophet to change all this. Yet first, the Lord prepared a number of Gentiles to receive the gospel. Cornelius was a righteous Roman soldier, a "just man, and one that feareth God, and of good report" (Acts 10:22). The Lord sent an angelic messenger to Cornelius, instructing him to see the prophet. Meanwhile, the Lord sent Peter a vision to prepare him to accept the Gentiles. He repeated the vision three times to His prophet, but Peter still doubted its meaning until Cornelius showed up at his doorstep, ready to be taught the gospel. Cornelius had brought his "kinsmen and near friends" (Acts 10:24), and as Peter began teaching them, he "found many that were come together" (Acts 10:27). The Lord used Cornelius to prepare many Gentiles to hear the gospel message that was now available to them.

Why couldn't the Gentiles have the gospel blessings first, along with the Jews? The Lord doesn't ever really explain Himself on this one. He makes it clear that He calls some people—His chosen people—and grants them special blessings. Then He sends them out to share those gospel blessings with others. In the process, prejudices often arise and have to be overcome. Peter was met with intense opposition among the Saints of Jewish background to his revelation about bringing the gospel to the Gentiles.

Even Peter had to struggle with his own prejudices. In a letter to the Galatians, Paul described a time he felt he had to correct the prophet. Peter was eating with some Gentiles until some Jewish Church members arrived. Peter then separated himself from the Gentiles, afraid of offending the Jewish converts (see Galatians 2:11–14.) Paul didn't say in his letter if this incident happened before or after Peter's revelation to accept the Gentiles into the Church, but either way, it exposes the fact that even the Lord's prophet needed time and help to confront and overcome his own prejudices. Apparently, the entire Church needed time to deal with the Savior's message to love all people as brothers and sisters before they'd be ready to fully accept Gentiles into the fold. Throughout much of the rest of the New Testament, Paul tried to help the Jewish Christians overcome their prejudices against the Gentile converts.

Book of Mormon Curses

In the Book of Mormon, there are curses, markings, and restrictions, just as there are in the Bible. When Laman and Lemuel rejected the gospel and tried to murder Nephi, the Lord separated him and his family from the descendants of his brothers. The Lamanites were cursed by being cut off from the Lord's presence (see 2 Nephi 5:20), and the sign of their curse was that they were marked with a "skin of blackness" (2 Nephi 5:21). A superficial reading of the mark that came upon the Lamanites has led many to assume that the Lamanites were marked with a dark skin color as the sign of their curse. Yet at least some Book of Mormon scholars have seen it differently. Hugh Nibley, for instance, believed that the terms *Lamanite* and *Nephite* are never used to designate racial differences, but rather only cultural, political, military, and religious divisions. The skin of blackness in the Book of Mormon in his eyes seemed to be "the mark of a general way of life; it is a Gypsy or Bedouin type of darkness."[1]

In Alma 3:6–19, we get a more complete description of the curse that came upon the Lamanites. The initial reason for it was the transgression and rebellion of their fathers. The purpose was to keep nonbelievers separate from believers so the believers wouldn't mix with them and lose their faith. Anyone who married into the Lamanites would bring the mark of the curse upon the children. And those who chose to mingle with the nonbelievers would bring upon themselves their own curse, as the Amlicites did when they marked their own foreheads with red as a sign that they'd joined up with the Lamanites (see Alma 3:4).

There are events in the narrative that make it clear that the difference between Nephites and Lamanites wasn't literal skin color.[2] For example, when Captain Moroni looked for one of his soldiers of Lamanite ancestry to take wine to the Lamanite guards, he didn't use skin color to find him. And when the soldier (Laman) approached the guards, it wasn't until he started speaking with them that they could tell he was a Lamanite (see Alma 55:3–9). If it were skin color that differentiated Nephites and Lamanites, this entire exercise would've been a visual one, but it's always ancestry and cultural distinctions that seem to matter.

Jacob clarified that the mark on the Lamanites was merely symbolic. To his own rebellious Nephite brothers, he warned, "O my brethren, I fear that unless ye shall repent of your sins that their skins will be whiter than yours, when ye shall be brought with them before the throne of God" (Jacob 3:8). So white skin seems to be more of a *symbol* of purity, not a sign of it. It's always the "blackness" of the soul that the prophets worry about. Jacob went on to decry any discrimination based on their culture of origin: "Wherefore, a commandment I give unto you, which is the word of God, that ye revile no more against them because of the darkness of their skins; neither shall ye revile against them because of their filthiness; but ye shall remember your own filthiness, and remember that their filthiness came because of their fathers" (Jacob 3:9). Self-purification—including overcoming prejudices—is part of the test of mortality.

Yet repeatedly throughout the scriptures, the Lord says that "the last shall be first, and the first shall be last" (1 Nephi 13:42; see also Luke 13:30). In other words, the Lord does give the blessings of the gospel to some people before others, but then He turns the tables around and switches who gets the blessings. At different points in the Book of Mormon, the Lamanites repent and accept the gospel while the Nephites reject it. Then the Lamanites are the righteous ones and the Nephites are the wicked ones (see Helaman 6:34). By the time Christ came, only the more righteous of Lehi's descendants survived and there were no more cultural or ethnic distinctions (see 4 Nephi 1:17). Two hundred years later, the religious and cultural harmony faded and the people began to divide into cultural groups again. Once again, they broke up into religious groups, with Nephites being those who accepted the gospel and Lamanites being those who rejected it (see 4 Nephi 1:36–38). This wasn't a change in skin color; it was a change in association—in religion and culture.

Modern Restrictions

In the days of Brigham Young, ancestry again became a factor in who could enjoy all the blessings of the gospel. At least three black gentlemen—Elijah Abel, Joseph Ball, and Walker Lewis—were ordained to the priesthood in the days of Joseph Smith.[3] Elijah Abel was baptized in 1832, received the priesthood in 1836, and served three missions for the Church. He stayed faithful until his death and ordained his son to the priesthood. Joseph Ball served missions to Boston and New Jersey and was the branch president of Boston from 1844–45. Walker Lewis was a well-known abolitionist who joined the Church in 1842 and was ordained an elder in 1843.

When the Saints arrived in Utah with a small scattering of blacks, Brigham Young announced a ban on them holding the priesthood. This restriction, which included a denial of temple blessings, continued until the 1978 revelation that ended it. No one really knows exactly how the ban came about. Some people blame negative experiences the Church endured from the hands of a black convert named William McCary.[4] Regardless, the Lord allowed the ban to be implemented in the Church.

Over the years, Brigham Young made several comments condemning racism and defending the rights of blacks, but he was also adamant about the ban. In 1852, he declared that "any man having one drop of the seed of [Cain] . . . in him cannot hold the priesthood and if no other Prophet ever spake it before I will say it now in the name of Jesus Christ—I know it is true and others know it."[5] This priesthood ban was always based on ancestry, not skin color. Dark-skinned people from any region of the world except Africa were never denied priesthood or temple blessings, but light-skinned people from Africa were.[6]

Because the Lord has used ancestry to deny some groups of people certain blessings at certain times, it's natural for a thoughtful believer to ask if God is, well, racist. He assures us that He isn't (see 1 Nephi 17:35 and Romans 2:11) and says that envy, malice, and contention don't come from Him (see 2 Nephi 26:32). He also makes clear that "he inviteth them all to come unto him and partake of his goodness; and he denieth none that come unto him, black and white, bond and free, male and female; and he remembereth the heathen; and all are alike unto God, both Jew and Gentile" (2 Nephi 26:33). Even while He offers blessings for righteousness and curses for wickedness to individuals and their posterity (see Deuteronomy 5:9), He's willing to reverse those conditions when the descendants prove themselves worthy (see Deuteronomy 5:10), though sometimes the process takes a long time.

Preparing for Change: Joseph Johnson

Even as we struggle to understand why the Lord would allow ethnicity and skin color to be such a divisive cause of discrimination among His children throughout the years, we can see His tender mercies helping those who are discriminated against. Just as He'd prepared Cornelius and a host of Gentiles to accept the gospel message once Peter received the revelation to take it to them, in our day the Lord prepared a people in Africa to receive the gospel once the revelation unlocking gospel blessings to them was received.

Joseph Johnson was a young man living in Cape Coast, Ghana, in the 1960s. He started praying to the Lord for help in knowing which church to join. In 1964, he met someone with a pamphlet retelling the Joseph Smith story. He prayed about it and came to know it was true. Next, he read the Book of Mormon and gained a witness from the Holy Ghost that it was God's word. Then one morning as he was preparing for work, Joseph had a sacred experience. He heard a voice that said, "Johnson, Johnson, Johnson, if you will take up my work as I will command you, I will bless you and bless your land." Trembling and with tears flowing, he replied, "Lord, with thy help I will do whatsoever you will command me." From then on, Brother Johnson felt compelled to go door-to-door to meet people and tell them about the true Church. With no priesthood, and not even having been baptized himself, Joseph went around teaching and building up congregations all over Ghana. He ended up with ten congregations and over a thousand unofficial members.[7]

Brother Johnson faced great opposition in his work. People mocked his devotion to a church that wouldn't recognize his efforts or allow him to fully participate. They accused it of being racist and anti-Christ and published articles in local papers against his work. After a particularly hard day, Brother Johnson had a dream in which he saw both Joseph Smith and Brigham Young, who assured him that he was on the right track and that authorized missionaries would soon be sent to his country. He continued in his work and even named his next child Brigham.

Still the opposition continued to mount against Brother Johnson. The stress became too much for his wife, who left him. One night, while struggling with the grief of losing her, Brother Johnson had a dream. His only brother, who'd died seven years before, appeared to him and assured him he was doing a great work. He told Brother Johnson he'd sing a song from his church and proceeded to sing "Come, Come Ye Saints." Brother Johnson had never heard it before, but it became his instant favorite. His brother told him to stay true to the Church and to make sure he—his brother—was baptized someday. That was the first Brother Johnson had ever heard of the possibility of baptisms for the dead.

At one point, authorities of another Christian denomination approached Brother Johnson. They offered him ten thousand dollars and a trip to the United States if he'd bring his followers and join their church. Brother Johnson had always wanted to visit America and was tempted by the offer, but the Spirit prompted him to stay his course, assuring him that authorized missionaries from the true Church would be coming. He just needed to wait a little longer.

Brother Johnson continued to write to Church headquarters in Salt Lake City requesting missionaries, but he was repeatedly told that the time hadn't yet come. Then, early in the year 1978, Brother Johnson had a dream. He saw two missionaries enter one of his congregations. They addressed him and his followers as Latter-day Saints and said they had come to baptize them all. This sustained him in the midst of opposition and disappointment.

After one particularly long and frustrating day, Brother Johnson came home exhausted and discouraged. He felt inspired to turn on his old radio and tune into the BBC, which he hadn't listened to for several years. It took him over an hour to tune in to the station on his old short-wave set. He finally got reception just in time to hear the revolutionary news that the Church had announced to the world a revelation extending the priesthood to all worthy males. Less than a year later, the Church sent missionaries to Ghana and Joseph Johnson was one of the first to be baptized. Most of his followers joined with him.

As it turned out, Joseph Johnson was just one of many pioneers who embraced the gospel in Africa before the missionaries were allowed to come and baptize them. In the 1960s, what had started as a trickle of letters to Salt Lake requesting Church literature turned into a flood. More requests for literature came from Nigeria and Ghana than from all other countries combined.[8] People there started opening LDS bookstores to try to keep up with the demand. There were more than sixty congregations with over sixteen thousand participants in those two countries, and none of them had been baptized to that point.

LaMar Williams

In 1961, President David O. McKay assigned LaMar Williams (secretary to the Church Missionary Department responsible for responding to all requests) to go to Nigeria on a fact-finding mission to see if the people there were sincere. He was met at the airport and treated like royalty by ten ministers who had all been preaching Mormonism. None of them knew of anyone else's involvement in the Church. Brother Williams went from town to town, to where he'd been sending literature, and held informal firesides. Hundreds of people came to each one—all of them walking, some up to twenty-five miles just to get there.

At one such fireside, Brother Williams spoke for two hours, teaching the restored gospel, and tried to end the meeting. But a ripple of protests went through the congregation. The minister in charge said the people had something to say. For the next three hours, they held a testimony meeting. One old gentleman said, "I keep hearing you say, 'If we are sincere.' Elder Williams, I want you to know that I am sincere. I am an old man. . . . I am sick. But when I heard you were going to be here, I walked sixteen miles this morning to see you and to hear what you have to say. I still have to walk sixteen miles to get back home, and I am not well. I want you to know that I am sincere or I would not be here. I have not seen President McKay. I have not seen God. But I have seen you. And I will hold you personally accountable to tell President McKay that I am sincere." Brother Williams reported to the First Presidency that he felt thousands were ready for baptism.[9]

LaMar Williams was later called with his wife to be a mission president in Nigeria. For months, he tried to obtain the necessary government visas but was rebuffed because of the prejudice against the Church for its priesthood ban on blacks. Then without explanation, the First Presidency instructed Brother Williams and his wife to return to Salt Lake immediately. N. Eldon Tanner of the First Presidency told Brother Williams they didn't know why he was recalled, but they would both live to see the reason.

Within three weeks, on July 6, 1967, Africa's bloodiest civil war to date broke out in Nigeria: the Biafran War. The worst of the fighting occurred in the regions where the most unbaptized Mormons were located. Two ambassadors were shot on the steps of the embassy where Brother Williams had received the telegram ordering him back to the States weeks earlier. He was released from his mission and turned over lists with more than fifteen thousand names of unbaptized members to the Missionary Department.[10]

A General Authority from Africa

In 1975, the Church announced the construction of a temple in São Paulo, Brazil. There were many people in that country of African descent, which would deny them the right to hold the priesthood or enter the temple. One of these people was Helvecio Martins.

In 1972, Brother Martins was searching for the true religion with his wife, Ruda, in Rio de Janeiro, Brazil. One day, he was stuck in a downtown traffic jam and started pleading with the Lord to help him. A few nights later, LDS missionaries arrived at their door. Brother Martins invited them in. His first question was, "Are you racist?"

That first night with the missionaries, Helvecio and Ruda felt the Spirit testify that the missionaries' message was true. Two weeks later, they were baptized. In 1974, Brother Martins was called to be the public communications coordinator for the North Brazil Region.

When President Kimball announced the construction of the São Paulo Temple, Brother Martins served on the publicity committee for it. Sister Martins sold her jewelry to contribute to the construction of the temple they didn't plan to enter.

But their son, Marcus, received his patriarchal blessing in 1973. In his blessing, he was promised that one day he would serve a mission for the Church, which would require him having the Melchizedek Priesthood. After the blessing, Brother and Sister Martins wept in each other's arms as the Spirit confirmed the reality of that promise. They knew that changes were coming, but they kept their experiences to themselves. They started a mission fund for Marcus.

At the cornerstone ceremony of the São Paulo Temple, Brother Martins found himself standing near the prophet. At one point, President Kimball put his arm around Brother Martins and said, "All you need to do is remain faithful." The revelation was announced to the world June 9, 1978. That summer, Marcus was called as the first missionary for the Church of African descent and served in the Brazil São Paulo North mission. The São Paulo Temple was dedicated in 1979, and Helvecio and Ruda Martins were one of the first couples sealed there as an eternal family.[11]

In 1990, Helvecio was called as the first General Authority of African descent and served faithfully in the Second Quorum of the Seventy until he was honorably released in 1996.

The Lord says by two or three witnesses shall every word be established. Here are three believable witnesses who have all the needed credentials. Joseph Johnson, LaMar Williams, and Helvecio Martins were among literally thousands of people whom the Lord raised up and prepared to move His work forward among His children of color. They knew the Lord was in charge of the work and preparing the way.

The 1978 Revelation

The dedication of the São Paulo Temple seemed to have been the immediate impetus that moved President Kimball to feel that the time had come to lift the priesthood ban.[12] With so many in the area of different skin colors, how could the Church ever determine who had African ancestry and who didn't? President Kimball spent hundreds of hours on his knees in the Salt Lake Temple, pleading with the Lord to make His will known. Finally, on Thursday, June 1, 1978, the revelation was given.

The official historical account of the revelation, as updated by the Church in 2013, is brief but candid:

> The Book of Mormon teaches that "all are alike unto God," including "black and white, bond and free, male and female" (2 Nephi 26:33). Throughout the history of the Church, people of every race and ethnicity in many countries have been baptized and have lived as faithful members of the Church. During Joseph Smith's lifetime, a few black male members of the Church were ordained to the priesthood. Early in its history, Church leaders stopped conferring the priesthood on black males of African descent. Church records offer no clear insights into the origins of this practice. Church leaders believed that a revelation from God was needed to alter this practice and prayerfully sought guidance. The revelation came to Church President Spencer W. Kimball and was affirmed to other Church leaders in the Salt Lake Temple on June 1, 1978. The revelation removed all restrictions with regard to race that once applied to the priesthood. (Official Declaration 2)

The two-fold message is clear: The Lord loves and cares for all His children equally and we don't know why, but He held back some blessings from people of African descent. What happened in 1978 wasn't a policy change. It was a revelation of monumental proportions.

President Hinckley gave the most intimate account of the revelation when he said,

> The question of extending the blessings of the priesthood to blacks had been on the minds of many of the Brethren over a period of years. It had repeatedly been brought up by Presidents of the Church. It had become a matter of particular concern to President Spencer W. Kimball.
>
> Over a considerable period of time he had prayed concerning this serious and difficult question. He had spent many hours in that upper room in the temple by himself in prayer and meditation.
>
> On this occasion he raised the question before his Brethren—his Counselors and the Apostles. Following this discussion we joined in prayer in the most sacred of circumstances. President Kimball himself was voice in that prayer. I do not recall the exact words that he spoke. But I do recall my own feelings and the nature of the expressions of my Brethren. There was a hallowed and sanctified atmosphere in the room. For me, it felt as if a conduit opened between the heavenly throne and the kneeling, pleading prophet of God who was joined by his Brethren. The Spirit of God was there. And by the power of the Holy Ghost there came to that prophet an assurance that the thing for which he prayed was right, that the time had come, and that now the wondrous blessings of the priesthood should be extended to worthy men everywhere regardless of lineage.
>
> Every man in that circle, by the power of the Holy Ghost, knew the same thing.
>
> It was a quiet and sublime occasion.[13]

Anyone who has ever received a revelation knows how difficult it can be to describe it adequately to someone who's inexperienced in the ways of the Spirit. Yet President Hinckley was adamant that the event was real, profound, clear, and distinct. The Spirit spoke to their hearts and minds, and they each knew what God's will was.

Elder Bruce R. McConkie was also present when the revelation was given. He too struggled to describe it but was certain of its reality:

> Well, in that setting, on the first day of June in this year, 1978, the First Presidency and the Twelve, after full discussion of the proposition and all the premises and principles that are involved, importuned the Lord for a revelation. President Kimball was mouth, and he prayed with great faith and great fervor; this was one of those occasions when an inspired prayer was offered. You know the Doctrine and Covenants statement, that if we pray by the power of the Spirit

> we will receive answers to our prayers and it will be given us what we shall ask (see D&C 50:30). It was given President Kimball what he should ask. He prayed by the power of the Spirit, and there was perfect unity, total and complete harmony, between the Presidency and the Twelve on the issue involved.
>
> And when President Kimball finished his prayer, the Lord gave a revelation by the power of the Holy Ghost. . . .
>
> On this occasion, because of the importuning and the faith, and because the hour and the time had arrived, the Lord in his providences poured out the Holy Ghost upon the First Presidency and the Twelve in a miraculous and marvelous manner, beyond anything that any then present had ever experienced. The revelation came to the president of the Church; it also came to each individual present. There were ten members of the Council of the Twelve and three of the First Presidency there assembled. The result was that President Kimball knew, and each one of us knew, independent of any other person, by direct and personal revelation to us, that the time had now come to extend the gospel and all its blessings and all its obligations, including the priesthood and the blessings of the house of the Lord, to those of every nation, culture, and race, including the black race. There was no question whatsoever as to what happened or as to the word and message that came.[14]

Each of the Apostles received his own individual, sure witness by the Holy Ghost that the time had come to extend the priesthood to all worthy males throughout the world.

Personal Witnesses

Unlike President Hinckley and Elder McConkie, I wasn't present when the prophet received this revelation. But I've read the personal accounts. And what's more, I've read the scriptural account. I've read the "Official Declaration 2" in the Doctrine and Covenants: "[The Lord] has heard our prayers, and by revelation has confirmed that the long-promised day has come when every faithful, worthy man in the Church may receive the holy priesthood, with power to exercise its divine authority, and enjoy with his loved ones every blessing that flows therefrom, including the blessings of the temple. Accordingly, all worthy male members of the Church may be ordained to the priesthood without regard for race or color" (Official Declaration 2).

The Spirit has born witness to my mind and heart, independent of anyone else, that this was all somehow in accordance with the will of the Lord. So now I have my own revelation and can rely on that.

In the last chapter of the Book of Mormon, Moroni outlined a pattern for developing a testimony of the Lord's work. He said, "Behold, I would exhort you that when ye shall read these things, if it be wisdom in God that ye should read them, that ye would remember how merciful the Lord hath been unto the children of men, from the creation of Adam even down until the time that ye shall receive these things, and ponder it in your hearts" (Moroni 10:3). So he invites us to read the scriptures and ponder over the tender mercies of the Lord interacting with His children through the ages, "even down until the time that ye shall receive these things." His promise is that the Holy Ghost will then confirm that this is the Lord's work.

Passing Tests and Carrying Crosses

If we want to look at all the perceived injustices of mortality and focus on what others have and we don't, or on what we have and others don't, we can get quite worked up. The Lord says, "My thoughts are not your thoughts, neither are your ways my ways" (Isaiah 55:8). But at times, we still want to judge God by our standards of fairness, of right and wrong.

Darius Gray is a black Latter-day Saint who leads the Genesis Group in Salt Lake City. The Genesis Group is a group of black Saints who meet once a month under the direction of the Apostles to strengthen and edify each other in light of their shared challenges. Once while struggling to make sense of this complete denial of the priesthood from his people for so many years, Gray had a revelation:

> During the night of August 9, 1998, Darius Gray, president of the Genesis branch, received an overwhelming flood of insights. He arose to write, and over the following days the concepts developed further. At their heart lay the understanding that being born black was not a penalty but a challenge. In the premortal life, race in mortality was one of the conditions agreed upon in a covenant between premortal spirits and God. It was a calling that would test the ability of men and women who were denied priesthood and temple blessings to set aside any impulse to anger and rebellion. It would also test the ability

> of men and women given access to priesthood and temple to resist thinking themselves of greater worth than those subjected to limitations. Just as the blind man whom Jesus healed was not born blind because of his own sins or because of the sins of his parents, but "that the works of God should be made manifest in him" (John 9:3), so those born under priesthood restriction were not limited because of their own premortal sins or because of the sins of their ancestors, but as part of God's plan for the perfection of his children. He reported this inspiration to his General Authority supervisors and after a short time was advised that he could teach what he had learned, carefully prefaced with this statement: That which I am about to share should not be considered as doctrine, in that it does not appear in the standard works of the Church. It is, however, consistent with the scriptures and permission has been granted by "the brethren" for me to teach this.[15]

Life is a test. Being born with darker skin in a world that denigrates people based on their color isn't a punishment or a curse, but rather is part of the test for some of God's children.

As Christ was carrying His cross from Herod's palace to Golgotha to be crucified, He stumbled along the path. The Roman soldiers found a man named Simon from the city of Cyrene to finish carrying the cross to the place of the Crucifixion (see Matthew 27:32). Cyrene was a town in Libya on the northern coast of Africa, so when artists have portrayed this moment in Christ's life, they usually paint Simon as black. How appropriate that an African be appointed to help the Savior carry the burden of the sins of the world. For thousands of years, the African people (and those descended from them) have carried more than their fair share of the burdens of the sins of mankind.

Tests are supposed to be fair. I've been a teacher for twenty years. If I've learned anything about education I've learned that. If the instructor were to give different tests to different students based on what he thought each student needed, he'd be run out of the classroom by irate students and parents before the semester ended. The heavy burden placed on those of African descent in the Church by the priesthood ban doesn't seem fair. But I've also been a parent for almost fifteen years. And I know that wise parents adjust their rules and instructions for each child in their care based on their intimate knowledge of the child's needs and capacities.

Our Heavenly Father is the master teacher. But He is our Father before all else. As a Father, He is going to treat me differently than any of His other children because He knows perfectly my individual needs. What I need to learn from Him is different than the lessons and tests He has for anyone else.

When his brothers sold Joseph into slavery, he was unfairly abused and suffered tremendous pain, depravation, and humiliation. A child of covenant and promise was reduced to slavery and abuse. But the Lord allowed his suffering because He was preparing him to take his place among the kings of the earth, as well as among the kings and gods of eternity.

If the Lord's love is so inclusive and universal, why did those of African descent have to endure so much depravation for so long? Why're they still subject to so much discrimination and bigotry?

Perhaps it was the racism among members of the Church that prevented the Lord from giving the revelation sooner. Elder Marion D. Hanks of the Seventy said, "For me it was never that blacks [were unqualified but that] the rest of us had to be brought to a condition of spiritual maturity . . . to meet the moment of change with grace and goodness."[16] In other words, it may have been the "unreadiness of the Mormon whites"—our prejudices—that kept the Lord from extending the priesthood to blacks.[17] It's hard to figure out from my perspective why the Lord would allow our prejudices to deprive others of blessings. But then again, why were the Gentiles denied blessings of the gospel in Old Testament times and during Christ's life? When the Church was ready to accept change, the Lord prepared the Gentiles to come in and bless the Church.

But there are still so many unanswered questions here. As difficult as it has been for me to comprehend why God has set up a world where injustice and hatred are the norm, all I have to do is receive a confirmation of the Spirit that the Official Declaration 2 is inspired by God. Read, ponder, pray, and listen. Then I'll know He was in charge of things all along. Even though He isn't responsible for racism, hatred, and oppression—whatever and however things happened—the Lord has allowed them to fulfill His plan. If Joseph Johnson, Helvecio

Martins, and Darius Gray can still see the Lord's hand through all of their immense trials, then I can certainly trust Him as well.

And eventually, God will make up for all losses in the great resurrection.

Mormons as Christians

"Kindness is a language the blind can see and the deaf can hear."[1]
—Anonymous

My sister, Shoni, called me once after a troubling conversation with a friend of another faith. Her friend had told her emphatically that Mormons weren't Christians. Shoni stumbled through a defense of our belief in Christ the best she could, but she left the conversation feeling flustered and perplexed. She was flustered because she didn't feel like she was able to communicate her belief in Christ in a way her friend would understand. She was perplexed because she couldn't understand why anyone would be so adamant that we weren't what we say we are. Shoni sincerely wanted to know why we couldn't be Christians if we wanted to be.

Perhaps in all our attempts to convince others that we really are Christians, we haven't stopped to consider why they might want to say we aren't. Many years ago, James E. Talmage attended a conference on Christianity and was shocked to find so many people who were convinced that we weren't Christians. Instead of merely insisting that we were, he decided to figure out why they were making such a claim. This was his justification for listening to their claims:

> The man who cannot listen to an argument which opposes his views either has a weak position or is a weak defender of it. No opinion that cannot stand discussion or criticism is worth holding. And it has been

> wisely said that the man who knows only half of any question is worse off than the man who knows nothing of it. He is not only one sided, but his partisanship soon turns him into an intolerant and a fanatic. In general it is true that nothing which cannot stand up under discussion and criticism is worth defending.[2]

So before we start protecting our status as Christians, perhaps we should follow Elder Talmage's example and try to understand where our critics are coming from.

If we think about it carefully, we should be able to comprehend why someone would want to say, "You're not one of us." In the spring of 2008, our nation was preoccupied with a government raid on the Fundamentalist Church of Jesus Christ of Latter-day Saints (FLDS) in El Dorado, Texas. Their leaders were accused of teachings and practices that were abusive toward children, with young teenagers being forced into underage marriages. When the story broke in the news, Latter-day Saints spent months trying to convince people that the FLDS had nothing to do with us. It was urgent that we make sure no one confused us with the polygamist fundamentalists. Why? Could it be because we didn't want any of the censure being heaped on them to taint our own reputation? Right or wrong, we saw them as an undesirable cult that we didn't want anything to do with.

Considering that, we should be able to understand if some Christians see us in a similar light and as a similar threat.

Cults and Christians

Is Mormonism a cult? The false assumption many seem to make is that if Mormons are not a *bona fide* Christian denomination, accepted as brothers and sisters by the Catholic and Protestant communities, then we must be a cult to be feared, shunned, and fought against. The Oxford English Dictionary says that the word derives from the Latin *cultus,* meaning simply "worship." A cult, it goes on to say, consists of devotion to a particular person or principle as paid by a body of professed adherents or admirers. Using this inclusive definition, certainly Mormonism would qualify as a cult. Latter-day Saints profess devotion to Jesus Christ and the principles of his gospel. In fact, virtually any religion or system of worship could qualify.

But there's a more contemporary usage of the word *cult* that is not so flattering. We use it now to mean something like "a small group of strange zealots who blindly follow a charismatic religious leader." Some Protestants and Catholics want to use this kind of definition in labeling Mormons a cult to warn others to stay away from us. They see us as a small group of overzealous fanatics who blindly follow the teachings of Joseph Smith. Using this definition, however, we're clearly not a cult. There are over fifteen million members of the Church worldwide. We say Jesus Christ is the head of the Church and herald personal moral agency as one of the greatest gifts of God. Some renowned scholars and organizations have begun to recognize Mormonism as a world religion.[3]

So that brings up the question: If Mormonism is a separate world religion, how can we be Christians? In the end, that depends on how someone wants to define a Christian. To most Protestants and Catholics, a Christian is anyone who worships the Trinity and accepts the traditional Christian creeds (Apostles, Nicene, Athanasian, Westminster Confession of Faith, and so on). Latter-day Saints don't worship the Trinity, so we aren't Christian. With their definition, they're right. We don't accept the Trinity and we have little interest in the traditional creeds, believing they were created after the Christian Church fell into apostasy. So we don't qualify—by their definition—to be called Christians. We're out of the club.[4]

Still, we insist that we're Christians in another sense. Who were the Christians in the Bible? We learn from the Apostle Luke that "the disciples [of Jesus] were called Christians first in Antioch" (Acts 11:26). It was originally given as a derogatory label by nonbelievers but later was adopted by believers as being descriptive of their faith (see 1 Peter 4:16). Anyone who was a disciple of Jesus Christ was a Christian.

Latter-day Saints were first called Mormons by enemies of the faith because of our belief in the Book of Mormon. In 1981, the Church added a subtitle to the Book of Mormon—"Another Testament of Jesus Christ"—to clarify the nature of the book as complementary to the Bible and to emphasize the preeminent role of the Savior as the basis of our faith. The actual name of the church is The Church of Jesus Christ of Latter-day Saints. In the Book of Mormon, the resurrected Lord tells His disciples, "How be it my church save it be called in my name? For if a church be called in Moses' name then it be Moses' church; or if it be called in the name of a man then it be the church of a man; but if it be called in my name then it is my church, if it so be that they are built upon my gospel" (3 Nephi 27:8).

Because of that injunction, Latter-day Saints don't mind being called Mormons, but we do oppose any reference to being a so-called "Mormon Church." We insist there is no Mormon Church.[5] It is The Church of Jesus Christ. Disciples of Christ were called Saints in Paul's day. We see ourselves as Latter-day Saints—disciples of Christ in our day. In fact, according to the 2010 U.S. Religious Census carried out by the Association of Statisticians of American Religious Studies (ASARB), Salt Lake City is the most Christian major city in America with 72.5 percent of the population self-identifying as Christians! (Portland, Oregon, was the least Christian city in America with about 30 percent self-identifying as Christian.)[6]

Some critics want to argue that no matter how much we claim to be Christians, we aren't based on the traditional gospel of Christ and thus can't rightfully adopt the title. They quote Paul speaking to the Galatians: "But though we, or an angel from heaven, preach any other gospel unto you than that which we have preached unto you, let him be accursed" (Galatians 1:8). The angel here could be the so-called Moroni. The "other gospel" could be the Mormon message. But our reply is simply that the gospel of the Church is, in fact, the original Christian message preached by Paul, John, and Christ Himself. It's the "doctrine of Christ" that Paul refers to in Hebrews 6:1–2, which includes faith, repentance, baptism, laying on of hands for the gift of the Holy Ghost, resurrection of the dead, and judgment—doctrines that are fundamental in Mormonism. It's the gospel that John saw preached by the angel from heaven in the last days (Revelation 14:6).

We believe that there was a universal apostasy from the original gospel shortly after the deaths of Christ's Apostles, necessitating a restoration of the faith in the last days by another prophet, Joseph Smith. Paul said, "Let no man deceive you by any means: for that day [the Second Coming] shall not come, except there come a falling away first" (2 Thessalonians 2:3). The Church is neither Catholic (universal) nor Protestant (didn't break off from the Catholic), but rather was restored wholesale through angelic visitations to Joseph Smith. So Mormonism is a separate religion from traditional Christianity, but we see our faith as a restoration of the original biblical Christianity, descending all the way from Adam and Eve. "Our club came first and it's the best," as it were.

Godhead

Catholics and Protestants naturally are skeptical of Mormons wanting to call themselves Christians because many of our doctrines seem so different from traditional Christianity. A typical concern is the LDS belief in the nature of the Godhead. Most Christians worship the Trinity—the Father, Son, and Holy Ghost—as one being with three different manifestations. Latter-day Saints see them as three separate beings in a familial relationship. We believe we all lived with God in a premortal life as spirit children of heavenly parents. Jehovah was Jesus's premortal name and He was the firstborn spirit son of Elohim, or God the Father. Lucifer was also a spirit son of Elohim, as were all of us. For other Christians to hear that we believe Jehovah and Lucifer to be brothers is practically tantamount to blasphemy. From their view, to reject the Trinity is to reject the Christian God.

While I was serving as an institute director for Long Beach City College, I was approached by a campus student organization to speak at a "Three Religions, One God" symposium. The group was trying to foster harmony between Jews, Muslims, and Christians. They invited me to represent Christianity. My assignment was to speak for about twenty minutes on the development of Christianity and afterward field questions from the audience. Somewhat flattered that Latter-day Saints would not only be included in such a discussion but actually chosen to represent Christianity, I naively accepted the invitation. I might as well have accepted an invitation to tea!

I thought my presentation was well received, but then came the question-and-answer session afterward. Every question dealt with some aspect of the Trinity. I tried to respond the best I could, but I quickly realized how ill-equipped I was to answer detailed inquiries into a subject I didn't understand well, not to mention didn't believe in. After the event ended, one graduate student in comparative religions was so perplexed about my caricature of the Trinity that she came to one of the institute classes to find out more. At first I thought, *Great—a missionary opportunity!* But she was just curious to see if I really misunderstood the Trinity as much as it appeared I did at the symposium. Her suspicions were confirmed. Perhaps the occasion would've been better served if they would've had a Protestant minister representing Christianity. In general, we probably misunderstand other Christians' beliefs at least as much as they misunderstand ours.

Creation

The traditional Christian view of creation is that it was *ex nihilo*, or out of nothing. Latter-day Saints deny the notion. We see creation as the organization of preexisting spirit and matter. But that implies God isn't the ultimate author of all that is. That belief qualifies as blasphemy to traditional Christians. Latter-day Saints believe the Bible literally in that we are all children of a Father in Heaven. Moses referred to Him as the "God of the spirits of all flesh" (Numbers 16:22) and Paul referred to him as the "Father of spirits" (Hebrews 12:9).

We become adopted as children of Christ through our acceptance of His grace by repentance and baptism, but we're all literally spirit children of Heavenly Father, whether we accept Him or not. Paul said that "we are the offspring of God" (Acts 17:29). To us, that means we're of the same race as God, which again is alien enough of an idea for other Christians to count as blasphemy.

Salvation

The doctrine of being saved by grace is another point of contention. Many Protestants emphasize, as Paul does in his New Testament Epistles, that we're saved by grace. Latter-day Saints do agree, if the doctrine is put in context. Paul was writing against continued belief in the law of Moses as the source of salvation. The works required by the law of Moses were preparatory to receiving the gospel of Christ. That doesn't necessarily mean that accepting Christ's gospel requires no effort on the believer's part. It's God's grace, or gift, that saves us from sin and death, but we still must accept that gift by being worthy of it. We must allow God's power to work through us to change our sinful nature. We have the ability to block God's power and prevent His saving action in us if we choose. So Latter-day Saints believe that we are indeed saved by grace "after all we can do" (2 Nephi 25:23), and all we can do is to not get in the way of God's power. That's the work on our part required for salvation. James said that "faith, if it hath not works, is dead, being alone" (James 2:17) and "by works a man is justified, and not by faith only" (James 2:24). We don't see these references as meaning that we somehow earn our way to heaven, only that it isn't enough to *say* we follow Jesus. We must allow Him to work through us to do His bidding. This includes receiving all the ordinances of salvation (through which He refashions us in His image) and keeping the covenants that go with them.

A German Protestant minister named Dietrich Bonhoeffer wrote a book condemning what he saw as a Protestant perversion of discipleship he called "cheap grace." The book is entitled *The Cost of Discipleship* and was first published in Berlin in 1937. In it, Bonhoeffer outlined what he saw as the price that must be paid by a true disciple of Christ, even though and because Christ paid the price for our salvation. "It is costly because it costs a man his life."[7]

Bonhoeffer argued that a true Christian isn't one who says he follows Christ, but rather one who sacrifices all for His cause. He said it's too easy to say that Christ paid the price for me, thus excusing me from having to do anything myself. That simply will not do. It's counterfeit discipleship. Christ commanded His followers to take up their crosses and follow Him. "The only man who has the right to say that he is justified by grace alone is the man who has left all to follow Christ."[8] Latter-day Saints couldn't agree more.

Scripture

Another doctrinal point of departure between Latter-day Saints and other Christians is on the topic of scripture. Protestants and Catholics traditionally see the Bible as the inerrant and unique word of God and the only source of the message of salvation. We accept the Bible as the word of God "as far as it is translated correctly,"[9] but we also believe in the Book of Mormon as the word of God, on the same par as the Bible. We have other scriptures as well and believe in continuing revelation from God to man through a living prophet. Protestants and Catholics believe that the scriptural canon is closed and there isn't any more revelation from God. They often use a passage from the book of Revelation as their justification for this belief, which reads, "If any man shall add unto these things, God shall add unto him the plagues that are written in this book: and if any man shall take away from the words of the book of this prophecy, God shall take away his part out of the book of life" (Revelation 22:18–19). Clearly, they say, in bringing forth the Book of Mormon, Joseph Smith added to the Bible and thus deserves to be cursed.

Latter-day Saints see this passage differently. John wasn't writing the final chapter in the final book in the final word of God. He was just writing the conclusion for his book and his revelation. He knew that wicked priests and careless transcribers would come along and change things in his record and was warning them. There's no good reason to believe that John was prohibiting anyone from ever again receiving revelation from God. The New Testament wasn't compiled until a hundred years after John's book of Revelation. In fact, most Bible scholars say that John wrote his Gospel *after* he wrote the book of Revelation.[10]

Latter-day Saints point out that Moses wrote a similar warning about his writings a thousand years earlier. In Deuteronomy 4:2, he said, "Ye shall not add unto the word which I command you, neither shall ye diminish ought from it." If that were construed to mean no further revelation from God could be received or no further scripture could be added to the cannon, we'd have a much shorter Bible than we do today. But Latter-day Saints simply read Moses to be warning about those who would come along and deliberately alter his words, not that God couldn't continue to speak to man through a living prophet. Likewise, John wasn't restricting further prophetic activity. Latter-day Saints believe what Amos said in his book: "Surely the Lord God will do nothing, but he revealeth his secret unto his servants the prophets" (Amos 3:7). As long as God is actively participating in the affairs of the world, He's doing so through a living prophet. The prophet writes His words, and those writings can become scripture.

There's an intriguing passage in Jeremiah 36 that illustrates the relationship between prophets and scripture from an LDS perspective. The "word came unto Jeremiah from the Lord, saying, Take thee a roll of a book, and write therein all the words that I have spoken unto thee against Israel, and against Judah, and against all the nations, from the day I spake unto thee, from the days of Josiah, even unto this day" (Jeremiah 36:1–2). Jeremiah's scribe, Baruch, "wrote from the mouth of Jeremiah all the words of the Lord, which he had spoken unto him, upon a roll of a book" (verse 4). Baruch was then sent to the king to read the resulting book of scripture. The king rejected the revelation and burned it in a fire (see verses 20–23).

Yet the Lord continued to speak through His prophet: "Then took Jeremiah another roll, and gave it to Baruch the scribe, the son of Neriah; who wrote therein from the mouth of Jeremiah all the words of the book which Jehoiakim king of Judah had burned in the fire: and there were added besides unto them many like words" (Jeremiah 36:32). The Lord restored, through His prophet, what was lost and added many like words as well. The LDS belief is that the cannon of scripture is always open through a living prophet of God: "We believe all that God has revealed, all that He does now reveal, and we believe that He will yet reveal many great and important things pertaining to the Kingdom of God" (Articles of Faith 1:9). God has always led His people through a living prophet, whose inspired words become scripture. Because He never changes, why wouldn't He call such a prophet today?

We must certainly be on the lookout for false prophets as the scriptures warn, but the existence of false prophets shouldn't deter us from seeking true ones.

Testimony

That brings us to another somewhat exclusive LDS claim: the significance of personal testimony. Ever since Joseph Smith went on his quest to find the truth about religion, Latter-day Saints have been using James 1:5 as our inspiration for seeking personal revelation: "If any of you lack wisdom, let him ask of God, that giveth to all men liberally, and upbraideth not; and it shall be given him." This is a passage our missionaries read to potential converts to encourage them to pray for themselves about the truth of our faith. Other Christians take exception with our interpretation. They claim that James was originally writing to "the twelve tribes which are scattered abroad" (James 1:1), so they argue that his message applies only to those already of the faith. But why would God answer only the prayers of those who have already accepted His message? In Acts is the story of the first Gentiles converted to the Church of Christ. As Peter preached the gospel to them, "on the Gentiles also was poured out the gift of the Holy Ghost" (Acts 10:45). When those present saw how they'd felt the Spirit and knew the Church was true, Peter said, "Can any man forbid water, that these should not be baptized, which have received the Holy Ghost as well as we?" (Acts 10:47). The Gentiles were baptized.

The Book of Mormon contains a promise of a similar manifestation to those who read it: "And when ye shall receive these things, I would exhort you that ye would ask God, the Eternal Father, in the name of Christ, if these things are not true; and if ye shall ask with a sincere heart, with real intent, having faith in Christ, he will manifest the truth of it unto you, by the power of the Holy Ghost. And by the power of the Holy Ghost ye may know the truth of all things" (Moroni 10:4–5). Millions of Latter-day Saints have prayed and received just such an answer that it is true. It's understandable that Protestants and Catholics would want to say those answers all came from the devil or are self-delusions, but to those who feel they've received personal revelation, that explanation seems shallow. Paul said you can recognize what comes from the Spirit of God by its effects: "But the fruit of the Spirit is love, joy, peace, longsuffering, gentleness, goodness, faith, meekness, temperance" (Galatians 5:22–23). When one is basking in the love of Christ, he isn't terribly concerned about a naysayer on the sidelines claiming that he's suffering from a delusion. In fact, Latter-day Saints might wonder how much love, joy, and peace is spread by anti-Mormons' claims that all Mormons secretly worship the devil and are going to hell.

Still, we wonder why they won't accept our testimonies. When I was fifteen years old, I spent a summer as a soccer camp counselor at Pepperdine University in Malibu, California. My roommate was another counselor, who was a sophomore in college. Every night before going to bed, I'd read the scriptures and kneel to say a personal prayer. The last night of our week together, my roommate saw me pull out my scriptures as usual, but this time he interrupted my routine by asking me to bring them over to his side of the room. He was a born again Christian and said he wanted to ask me some questions about my religion. As a young, naïve seminary student, I was excited but nervous at what seemed like an opportunity to "share the gospel."

As it turned out, what he really wanted to do was Bible bash. One by one, he asked me questions about Mormonism and tried to shoot down my answers by quoting passages from the Bible. I frantically tried to keep up with him using scripture mastery scriptures from seminary and other references I could pull out of the Topical Guide, but he knew the Bible much better than I did and seemed to have an answer for any claim I tried to prove. When it became clear to me that he wasn't interested in any of the scriptures I found to establish my point or in any of the beliefs I shared except to tear them down, I decided there was but one thing left to do: I would bear my testimony to him. So I told him that I couldn't answer all his objections well, but I knew beyond a shadow of a doubt that Joseph Smith really did see the Father and the Son in a grove of trees and that the Book of Mormon he translated really was the word of God. I was even willing to die for my belief. There! Now I was sure I had him.

But in the end, it was his reply that got me. He said that in World War II, the Japanese kamikaze pilots were sure "beyond a shadow of a doubt" that if they crashed their planes into American warships that they'd go straight to heaven. They were so certain that they were willing to give their lives for their belief. Were they right?

He had me there. It took me years to realize that personal testimony is just that—personal. To use it to try to convince naysayers is usually a form of casting your "pearls before swine" (Matthew 7:6). It's not that pigs are so dirty, but that they don't know how to appreciate the beauty of pearls. Even if I had won the argument with my roommate (which I didn't), I never would've won a convert that way. For people to respond to my personal testimony, they have to at least have a "desire to believe," as Alma says in his famous discourse on faith in Alma 32:27. There's great truth in the classic wisdom of Dale Carnegie: "A man convinced against his will is of the same opinion still."[11]

Becoming Gods

Another Latter-day Saint doctrine that bothers Protestants and Catholics has to do with the idea of man becoming divine. This idea seems the height of blasphemy to many other Christians—and understandably so. The sin that Lucifer was punished for in premortality was his ambitious aspirations to godhood (see Isaiah 14:12–15). But the fact that Lucifer sought to become a god by proudly supplanting the Father and taking over His power doesn't mean that God couldn't graciously offer His power to those who seek it humbly.

After Adam and Eve ate the fruit of the tree of knowledge of good and evil in the Garden of Eden, the Lord said, "The man is become as one of us" (Genesis 3:22). In other words, by choosing to eat of the "forbidden fruit" and becoming mortal, Adam and Eve took one step closer to becoming like gods. The way the story is portrayed in our current Bible makes it sound as if Adam and Eve were going against God's plan in this. But modern scripture makes it clear that the Fall was actually a part of God's original plan and a necessary step in the progress of man (see Moses 5:10–11).

In Christ's day, the Pharisees took issue with Him over several doctrines, but none got under their skin more than his proclaimed relationship with God the Father. In John 10:30, Christ taught that He was the Son of God. The Jews started picking up rocks to stone Him. With a sense of humor even in the face of death, Jesus said, "Many good works have I shewed you from my Father; for which of those works do ye stone me?" They answered, "For a good work we stone thee not; but for blasphemy; and because that thou, being a man, makest thyself God" (John 10:32–33). This is similar to the charge of blasphemy hurled against Latter-day Saints today.

Christ's reply is instructive: "Is it not written in your law, I said, Ye are gods? [Here, He's referring to Psalms 82:6.] If he called them gods, unto whom the word of God came, . . . Say ye of him, whom the Father hath sanctified, and sent into the world, Thou blasphemest; because I said, I am the Son of God? If I do not the works of my Father, believe me not. But if I do, though ye believe not me, believe the works" (John 10:34–38). Even though in context He's justifying His right to call Himself the Son of God, Jesus also hinted here at the divine potential that lies in each of us. He seemed to be saying that since we're all in the same family, our behavior should testify of our relationship.

The Apostle Paul picked up this idea in his letters to the Saints. In Romans 8:16–17, he declared, "The Spirit itself beareth witness with our spirit, that we are the children of God: and if children, then heirs; heirs of God, and joint-heirs with Christ; if so be that we suffer with him, that we may be also glorified together." Latter-day Saints read this passage as saying because we're literally children of God, as Christ is, we're also heirs of the glory Christ inherited from the Father.

To the Saints at Philippi, Paul instructed,

> Let this mind be in you, which was also in Christ Jesus: who, being in the form of God, thought it not robbery to be equal with God: but made himself of no reputation, and took upon him the form of a servant, and was made in the likeness of men: and being found in fashion as a man, he humbled himself, and became obedient unto death, even the death of the cross. Wherefore God also hath highly exalted him. (Philippians 2:5–9)

In other words, because Christ as the Son of God was in the image of His Father, He didn't think it was blasphemy to aspire to become like Him. And we as literal children of God as well should follow His example. Yet, just like Jesus, Latter-day Saints are charged with blasphemy for this belief.

However, Latter-day Saints aren't alone in believing this biblical doctrine of man's potential to become like God. It was actually a doctrine of the early Christian Church. Clement of Alexandria, a bishop of Rome who lived around AD 150–215, wrote that "the Logos [Word] of God had become man so that you might learn from a man how a man may become God."[12] Augustine, one of the greatest and most influential early Christian figures (AD 354–430), declared that "God became man, that man might become God."[13] And Aquinas, the greatest of the Catholic theologians (AD 1225–1274), echoed Augustine: "God became man, that man might become God."[14] To these great early Christian theologians, the whole point of Christ coming to the earth in the flesh was to pave the way for humankind to follow Him back into the presence *and likeness* of God.

Eastern Orthodox Christians still hold this view of man's potential to become like God. They call it divinization, meaning man becoming divine. And even John Paul II, a recent popular Catholic pope, resonated with this idea:

> Ultimately, only God can save men, but He expects man to cooperate. The fact that man can cooperate with God determines his authentic greatness. The truth according to which man is called to cooperate with God in all things, with a view toward the ultimate purpose of his life—his salvation and divinization—found expression in the Eastern tradition in the doctrine of synergism. With God, man "creates" the world; with God, man "creates" his personal salvation. The divinization of man comes from God. But here, too, man must cooperate with God.[15]

And German Protestant theologian Dietrich Bonhoeffer wrote, "He [Christ] has become like a man, so that men should be like him."[16]

It's true that these Christian theologians saw a limit to our potential to walk in Christ's footsteps. In their view, we're children of God only metaphorically. There's still an infinite gap between God as creator and man as creature. Latter-day Saints take the scriptural teachings of God's fatherhood more literally. Because our spirits are in some sense procreated by God, we're literally His offspring—of the same race. There is no gap. And therefore, our potential for becoming like God is unlimited.

One True Church

There's at least one further point of contention that traditional Christians have with Latter-day Saints. We declare boldly—which to other Christians may sound arrogant—that the Church is the only true church on the earth. Meanwhile, many Catholics and Protestants talk ecumenically; they're trying to look past doctrinal differences to beliefs and goals they share in common. They're even accepting baptisms performed by other denominations.[17] Where do we fit into this movement? Well, we're willing to join forces with our Christian brothers and sisters on social issues and in humanitarian efforts, but that's largely the extent of our willingness to cooperate. We still claim emphatically that salvation is found in the fullest sense only within the LDS Church. That doesn't sound like a claim made by people who want to be included in the mainstream Christian club, as it were.

What's my point in highlighting these doctrinal differences as I have? It's to show that in some ways we share a lot with other Christians, but in other ways we're different. We indeed have many beliefs that are quite unorthodox to Protestants and Catholics. Of course that doesn't seem to be reason enough to us to reject Mormonism as a bizarre cult that should be shunned, feared, and fought against. Yet we should be able to see why, in many respects, we still appear odd to them.[18]

In the end, they're partially correct. While we'll go on calling ourselves Christians because of our strong commitment to following Christ, perhaps we shouldn't worry so much if traditional Christians don't want to include us as part of the label. We don't see ourselves as part of their club anyway. Here's how President Gordon B. Hinckley expressed it: "As a Church we have critics, many of them. They say we do not believe in the traditional Christ of Christianity. There is some substance to what they say. Our faith, our knowledge is not based on ancient tradition, the creeds."[19] It was Christ Himself who called us to be a "peculiar people" (1 Peter 2:9). So perhaps we shouldn't worry too much if others go on thinking we're a bit weird.

Our unique witness of the Savior as the literal Son of God will become more and more vital in a world where religion is becoming more and more watered down to meet the lowering expectations of society. And we'll have many opportunities to stand as witnesses of the living Christ, who is the answer to the world's growing problems.

Making Friends

As we talk with others about our faith, we'll encounter some who want to Bible bash or draw us into other caustic debates. We must learn to resist. In John 13:35, Christ taught His Apostles at the Last Supper how the world was going to recognize a true Christian. He said, "By this shall all men know that ye are my disciples, if ye have love one to another." To His disciples in America, as recorded in the Book of Mormon, the resurrected Christ appeared and put an end to the doctrinal wrangling that'd been going on in the name of religion.

He said that "there shall be no disputations among you, as there have hitherto been; neither shall there be disputations among you concerning the points of my doctrine, as there have hitherto been. For verily, verily I say unto you, he that hath the spirit of contention is not of me, but is of the devil, who is the father of contention, and he stirreth up the hearts of men to contend with anger, one with another" (3 Nephi 11:28–29). In other words, when we Bible bash, name call, or otherwise contend with those who understand Christ's message differently than we do, we exclude ourselves from being Christians. Perhaps I've fallen into this trap by writing a chapter about how we differ from other Christians instead of what we share in common. When we learn to look beyond doctrinal differences and treat each other as children of God, we begin approaching the true meaning of Christianity.

Joseph Smith tried to teach us how to handle these differences with our Christian neighbors. He said,

> If I esteem mankind to be in error, shall I bear them down? No. I will lift them up, and in their own way too, if I cannot persuade them my way is better; and I will not seek to compel any man to believe as I do, only by the force of reasoning, for truth will cut its own way. Do you believe in Jesus Christ and the Gospel of salvation which he revealed? So do I. Christians should cease wrangling and contending with each other, and cultivate the principles of union and friendship in their midst; and they will do it before the millennium can be ushered in and Christ takes possession of His kingdom.[20]

To attack, argue, criticize, name call, or humiliate was never part of the Prophet's agenda. Even as I try to be polite and share my beliefs with others, I'm tempted at times to allow a smug sense of superiority to separate me from those I try to teach. A member of the Seventy shared, in general conference, an encounter that illustrates this danger:

> I had an interesting experience years ago as we were returning from South America on a ship. Three ministers were on board, and soon each one came to me and asked if there might be an opportunity to talk together to learn what the Mormons believed. One was a Methodist, one a Presbyterian, and one a Disciple of Christ.
>
> We arranged a visit together and spent a pleasant hour, they asking questions and I giving answers. Our visit was warm, friendly,

> and congenial. After about the first ten minutes, they began to look at each other and say: "Isn't it interesting—he has an answer for every question." And they repeated this comment over and over.
>
> A day or two later the Methodist brother stopped to talk with me, saying, "I have been thinking of what you told us the other day. I think you know too much. I wonder if God wants us to know everything."[21]

Sometimes we can let the strength of our doctrine separate us unnecessarily from those we want to serve, teach, or befriend. We can be so sure of the powerful answers the restored gospel provides that we fail to appreciate the full weight of the questions it answers.

Danish philosopher and theologian Soren Kierkegaard was slow to label himself a Christian. He was afraid that, by lackadaisically labeling himself a Christian, he might paradoxically lose the chance to actually become one. Using the pseudonym Climicus, he wrote, "My idea is that if Christianity is the highest good, it is better for me to know definitely that I do not possess it, so that I may put forth every effort to acquire it; rather than that I should imagine that I have it, deluding myself, so that it does not even occur to me to seek it."[22]

For Kierkegaard, becoming a Christian wasn't about what someone professes but what he or she pursues. Perhaps rather than insisting to others that I really *am* a Christian, I could simply say that I'm trying to *become* one. I might make more friends that way. I might also better avoid the Lord's censure in Luke 6:46 where He said, "And why call ye me, Lord, Lord, and do not the things which I say?" And one of the primary things He says to all of us is to "love your enemies" (Matthew 5:44).

In 2007, a devout Mormon named Bryan Hall decided he had to learn to love his enemy, Ruben Israel. Israel was a street preacher among the protestors at Temple Square every general conference weekend. Hall had come to hate Israel as his enemy, but when Hall approached him to ask his forgiveness for harsh feelings towards him, they eventually began a dialogue that led to mutual understanding and a warm friendship. Now even though they still disagree adamantly on religious beliefs, they're friendly enough that Hall lets Israel stay with his family whenever he comes to Utah to preach.[23]

For Joseph Smith, religious discussion was all about cultivating this type of friendship. In fact, he once declared, "Friendship is the grand fundamental principle of Mormonism."[24] If we're going to become friends with other Christians, we're going to have to do a better job at understanding where they're coming from. My son Reese came home one day excited, having learned that one of his friends at school was a Jehovah's Witness. He asked how he should share the gospel with him. I told him to start by simply asking a lot of questions to find out what he believed—not so Reese could point out differences but merely try to sincerely understand his friend's religion.

After a few days, Reese came home even more excited because he was learning so much about Jehovah's Witnesses and getting to know his friend better. The next step was to ask if he could go with him to his church meeting. Of course, eventually he'd want to reciprocate and invite his friend to scouts and perhaps sacrament meeting. But my wife and I are trying to teach him that you can't make a difference in people's lives unless you genuinely care about them and their interests first.

In Plato's dialogue *The Lysis*, Socrates has a discussion with several questioners about the nature of friendship. Various definitions of friendship are alternately constructed and dismantled. The dialogue remains inconclusive at the end, but through the process of giving each other their accounts, they've indeed become friends.[25] Perhaps it's time that we as Latter-day Saints look for more ways to interact and have dialogue with Catholics, Protestants, Jews, Muslims, and so on—if not as members of the same club then as brothers and sisters. As friends.

Accepting the Gift of the Atonement

"In his plans for the human family, long ago God made ample provision for all mortal mistakes. . . . All His purposes will come to pass in their time."[1]

—Neal A. Maxwell

I have a friend who broke the law of chastity in high school. He confessed to his bishop, abandoned his former life of bravado and self-indulgence, and since then has fully dedicated his life to building the kingdom of God. He's felt the Lord's forgiveness many times, but in his darkest hours, he returns to beating himself up over his past mistakes. He wonders how he could ever make it to the celestial kingdom. Sometimes people (like my friend) paint themselves into a spiritual corner where they think they're beyond the Lord's reach and He can't rescue them anymore. They may withdraw from the Church and the gospel altogether, feeling like they'll just never be good enough. I must admit that I too have asked the question of my own life: If people could see into the darkest recesses of my past, would they be shocked at my sins and tempted to shun me? There just doesn't seem to be any way that I could ever make it as a celestial being.

The first step for me toward embracing the Lord's Atonement is to understand and believe that Christ *did* make it. He lived a life untainted by sin. He suffered in the Garden of Gethsemane, died on the cross at Calvary, and rose from the tomb on the third day. His overcoming sin and death is the Atonement. He did it for me, a sinner, so I could overcome sin and death as well and eventually become "at one" with Him and the Father.

The Atonement isn't limited to covering my intentional mistakes. Christ also overcame all the circumstances outside of my control. "And he shall go forth, suffering pains and afflictions and temptations of every kind; and this that the word might be fulfilled which saith he will take upon him the pains and the sicknesses of his people" (Alma 7:11). He not only paid for my sins, but He also absorbed all my obstacles. Alma said, "He will take upon him their infirmities" (Alma 7:12). Everything is covered, including my weaknesses, the trials that overtake me because of those weaknesses, and the consequences dumped on me because of the sins of others.

My biggest problem, though, isn't what's done to me; it's the evil I commit. I know what I should do, but I don't always do it. I fall short. I forget. I fall back into old patterns of selfishness. The Apostle Paul had a similar experience. He said, "For we know that the law is spiritual: but I am carnal, sold under sin. For that which I do I allow not: for what I would, that do I not; but what I hate, that do I. . . . For the good that I would I do not: but the evil which I would not, that I do" (Romans 7:14–15, 19). Instead of doing all the good things I *want* to do, I find myself doing all the dumb stuff I *don't* want to do. (At least I am in good company.) Not only did Paul feel the same way, but he also said this is the universal plight of humankind: "For all have sinned, and come short of the glory of God" (Romans 3:23). Solomon said, "For there is not a just man upon earth, that doeth good, and sinneth not" (Ecclesiastes 7:20). Solomon would know—he ended up marrying out of the covenant! If only good people ended up making it, the celestial kingdom would be a lonely place. None of us are all that good on our own.

All right, so I know that no one's going to make it without the Savior's Atonement, but don't I have to stop sinning and do my entire part first before He can do the rest? There's that passage in 2 Nephi 25:23 that says, "We know that it is by grace that we are saved, after all we can do." But I never do *all* I can do—I always could've done something better. It'd seem, then, that I can never be saved.

Maybe I'm misunderstanding the Lord's message. Perhaps it's not that I do all in my power first, and then the Lord does the rest. Rather, I'll receive the Lord's grace before, during, and after all I can do. Jacob taught that "it is only in and through the grace of God that ye are saved" (2 Nephi 10:24). The only variable is whether I'm letting the Savior's grace work in me or not. After everything I do, though, it's still only through Christ's power that I'll be saved. But His power is certainly enough if I let Him work His wonders in me.

In my quest for hope, I've been surprised to discover how freely the Lord forgives. The Lord seems to have no interest in condemning me when I mess up. I condemn myself by my actions. All the Lord wants to do is to forgive me, get sin out of my life, and help me get on with my eternal progress. "For God sent not his Son into the world to condemn the world; but that the world through him might be saved" (John 3:17). Christ spent His mission with prostitutes and cheats (among others), trying to help them see that they could repent and change. Surely He can help me do that as well. Joseph Smith taught, "Our . . . Father is more liberal in His views, and boundless in His mercies and blessings, than we are ready to believe or receive."[2] Are the Lord's views liberal enough and His mercies boundless enough to embrace and reform a sinner such as I?

Repentance and Forgiveness

I know the Lord has said that if I repent, I can be forgiven (Mosiah 26:30–31). But one of the steps in repentance is that I stop committing the sin, and I can't seem to do that. So it seems as if I can never be forgiven. Yet the scriptures teach that there are many other things I can do to receive the Lord's forgiveness short of perfect repentance. I can accept Christ's covenant (see Hebrews 8:10–12). I can pray for forgiveness (see 1 Nephi 7:21). "But I'm not worthy." Exactly! That's why we pray in the name of Christ; He *is* worthy. I can work in the kingdom (see D&C 31:5). I can have a broken heart and a contrite spirit (see 3 Nephi 9:20). I can accept the Lord's chastisement (see D&C 95:1). I can bear solemn testimony (see D&C 84:61; 62:3). I can stop rejecting the Lord (see Jacob 6:4–5). I can offer a sacrifice that He requests of me (see D&C 132:50). I can do missionary work (see James 5:20). I can forgive another person (see 3 Nephi 13:14).

I can receive a priesthood blessing (see James 5:14–15). I can move someone else to offer a sacrifice on my behalf (see Leviticus 4:20). I can trust Christ (see Luke 7:50). I can hear and accept Christ's word (see Mark 4:12). I can confess my sins (see 1 John 1:9). These are just a sampling of the activities the scriptures mention that, by themselves, can bring forgiveness through the Atonement.

How is that possible? Elder Bruce R. McConkie said, "Whenever faithful saints gain the companionship of the Holy Spirit, they are clean and pure before the Lord, for the Spirit will not dwell in an unclean tabernacle. Hence, they thereby receive a remission of those sins committed after baptism."[3] So anything I do to invite the Spirit back into my life will allow Him to cleanse me and make me whole. I need to resist the temptation to take credit for "being spiritual," however. Christ explained to the Nephites that "the Father giveth the Holy Ghost unto the children of men, because of me" (3 Nephi 28:11). So it's not because of some greatness on my part. It's still a gift, an act of grace, and all I can do is receive it.

Does this mean that anytime I feel the Spirit I'm forgiven? No. Sometimes the Lord sends the Spirit to prick my conscience and tell me I need to change. That's a different experience from having the Spirit return to bring me peace. After King Benjamin's address from the tower, his people were cleansed: "And it came to pass that after they had spoken these words the Spirit of the Lord came upon them, and they were filled with joy, having received a remission of their sins, and having peace of conscience" (Mosiah 4:3). Every time *that* happens, I can know I've been forgiven. Obtaining the Lord's forgiveness isn't hard; the hard part is allowing the Lord to change my nature. This is the dual purpose of justification and sanctification.

Justification and Sanctification

I've often read the passage in Doctrine and Covenants 20:30–31, which says, "We know that justification through the grace of our Lord and Savior Jesus Christ is just and true" and that "we know also, that sanctification through the grace of our Lord and Savior Jesus Christ is just and true." For years, though, I really didn't understand either doctrine well. Then one year, I was discussing these with my brother and we got excited about them. I couldn't believe I'd gone so long in my gospel study without appreciating these powerful truths. The next weekend was general conference, and to our mutual surprise and delight, Elder David A. Bednar addressed them as the topic of his talk.

Elder Bednar explained that the Lord wants us to do two things. He wants us to stop sinning, but He also wants us to allow Him to change our nature so we become like Him. Elder Bednar addressed these complementary doctrines as follows:

> The gospel of Jesus Christ encompasses much more than avoiding, overcoming, and being cleansed from sin and the bad influences in our lives; it also essentially entails doing good, being good, and becoming better. Repenting of our sins and seeking forgiveness are spiritually necessary, and we must always do so. But remission of sin is not the only or even the ultimate purpose of the gospel. To have our hearts changed by the Holy Spirit such that "we have no more disposition to do evil, but to do good continually" (Mosiah 5:2), as did King Benjamin's people, is the covenant responsibility we have accepted. This mighty change is not simply the result of working harder or developing greater individual discipline. Rather, it is the consequence of a fundamental change in our desires, our motives, and our natures made possible through the Atonement of Christ the Lord. Our spiritual purpose is to overcome both sin and the desire to sin, both the taint and the tyranny of sin.[4]

Christ paid the price for both the cleansing of our sins and the changing of our natures. Both justification (the covering up and erasing of our sins) and sanctification (the refashioning of our sinful natures into the image of God) are possible only through the Atonement. Christ's mercy is what cleanses us; His grace is what changes and empowers us. And they both come by receiving the Holy Ghost into our lives. Moroni said that those who are baptized are "wrought upon and cleansed by the power of the Holy Ghost" (Moroni 6:4). Being cleansed is justification; being "wrought upon" is sanctification. The Holy Ghost cleanses us each time He comes to be with us, and if we allow Him to stay, He begins refashioning our natures so that we lose the desire to sin and seek to do the Lord's will more completely.

After King Benjamin's famous address to his people from the tower, "the Spirit of the Lord came upon them, and they were filled with joy, having received a remission of their sins" (Mosiah 4:3). But even more than being forgiven by the Spirit, they were being transformed by Him. They said the Spirit "wrought a mighty change in us, or in our hearts, that we have no more disposition to do evil, but to do good continually" (Mosiah 5:2).

That feeling of never wanting to sin again doesn't last forever. The meetings end, my prayers conclude, and I have to return to the world of tantalizing temptations, and I fall again. Then what happens? Doesn't the Lord say that "unto that soul who sinneth shall the former sins return" (D&C 82:7)? I've been trying so hard to change, but I slip up and my whole past comes crashing down on me again?

I guess forgiveness is temporary. It doesn't wipe the hard drive clean; it just temporarily deletes the file by sending it to the recycle bin. I have to continue to strive daily to get and keep the Spirit in my life to "stay covered." That same Spirit that covers my past will also slowly bring about a change in my present nature, leading me to a fuller future. Unless I choose to extinguish it, that light will grow brighter and brighter until the perfect day—until the Lord plants in me a new heart, a fresh hard drive.

The Lord has given me a small vision of the kind of person the Spirit can make of me if I allow Him. Parley P. Pratt said,

> The gift of the Holy Spirit adapts itself to all these organs or attributes. It quickens all the intellectual faculties, increases, enlarges, expands, and purifies all the natural passions and affections, and adapts them, by the gift of wisdom, to their lawful use. It inspires, develops, cultivates, and matures all the fine-toned sympathies, joys, tastes, kindred feelings, and affections of our nature. It inspires virtue, kindness, goodness, tenderness, gentleness, and charity. It develops beauty of person, form, and features. It tends to health, vigor, animation, and social feeling. It invigorates all the faculties of the physical and intellectual man. It strengthens and gives tone to the nerves. In short, it is, as it were, marrow to the bone, joy to the heart, light to the eyes, music to the ears, and life to the whole being. In the presence of such persons, one feels to enjoy the light of their countenances, as the genial rays of a sunbeam. Their very atmosphere diffuses a thrill, a warm glow of pure gladness and sympathy, to the heart and nerves of others who have kindred feelings, or sympathy of spirit.[5]

I've certainly known people who radiate with this kind of love and power. Yet the Lord assures me that He will make such a person out of me—as long as I don't get in His way.

Tokens of Salvation

Will all this justification and sanctification be enough to overcome my wicked past and exalt me in the celestial kingdom? The Apostle Paul said that if we seek the Lord's blessings, He will give us the "earnest of the Spirit" (2 Corinthians 5:5). What is the earnest of the Spirit? Earnest money is something you give a homeowner as a token of your intention to buy their home. The earnest is the small proof you offer now to show that, in the end, you'll pay the entire amount. So what's the Lord promising to pay us with the earnest of the Spirit? Paul explained to the Ephesian Saints that it is "the earnest of our inheritance until the redemption of the purchased possession, unto the praise of his glory" (Ephesians 1:14). In other words, every time the Lord sends His Spirit to be with me, it's His way of assuring me that I'm on the right track. I'm going to make it to the end when He will give me all that He has (my inheritance), even the eternal life that He enjoys. When I sin and get frustrated and ask if I can ever make it, the Lord sends His Spirit time and again to assure me that I *am* going to make it and His promise is still intact. All I have to do is commit that, no matter how many times I sin and stray off the path, my only option is to repent and get back on. Then the Lord will send His Spirit again as a witness that I'm forgiven and I'm going to make it back to His presence. And as I continue to strive to keep the Spirit with me, I'll begin to go longer and longer between sinning and driving it away.

Even so-called "good" people have to go through this same process. Since "all have sinned, and come short of the glory of God" (Romans 3:23) and "the Lord cannot look upon sin with the least degree of allowance" (D&C 1:31), absolutely no one is going to make it without a total spiritual makeover by the Savior. This is perhaps why LDS scholar Hugh Nibley used to teach that to be righteous is simply to be repenting. He wrote, "Who is righteous? Anyone who is repenting. No matter how bad he has been, if he is repenting, he is a righteous man."[6] We're either trying to accept the Lord's help or we're not—that's the only divide.

The Lord is anxious to forgive us and help change our natures. He places symbols of His redeeming love everywhere. He knows that I'm quick to forget and to turn back to my old sinful life, so He's infused the entire universe with reminders of His powerful love to help me remember. He said, "I am the bread of life" (John 6:35) so that every time I eat I can remember His word will nourish me if I consume it daily. He said that He's the fountain of "living water" (John 4:10) so that every time I take a drink I can remember that He will send revelation by His Spirit that'll quench my thirsty soul. The Lord is my rock, so every stone I see could remind me of the surety of my foundation (Psalm 18:2). He places rainbows in the sky after storms to remind me of the forgiveness He offers after I sin (Genesis 9:16; Isaiah 54:7–9). Just as the clouds block out the hot rays of the sun, His mercy will block out my sins (Isaiah 44:22). The wind symbolizes God's power to protect and deliver us (Exodus 15:10). The rain represents the Lord's word, which gives life to the soul (Isaiah 55:10–11). Every song I sing can be a reminder that the Lord wants to redeem me (Isaiah 44:23). It could be a kind of prayer to invite His redeeming Spirit, if I use it to remember His mercy (D&C 25:12). Every fire is a testimony of the redeeming flame of mercy that'll purify me of sin and make me clean (Isaiah 66:15–16). Milk is a witness of the nourishment the Lord will give my soul if I let Him (Isaiah 66:10–11). Every car, bicycle, or other mode of transportation is a symbol of the Lord's redeeming power because each could carry me to the temple, where His redemption is found (Isaiah 66:20). Every house symbolizes the Lord, for He is our dwelling place (Psalm 90:1). Every skyscraper or tall building represents the Lord's towering presence and sheltering shadow (Psalm 61:3). All trees and plants can testify of the Lord's desire to cultivate us (Isaiah 61:3). Birds of every kind, from eagles (Deuteronomy 32:11–13) to swallows (Psalm 84:3) to chickens (3 Nephi 10:5–6), represent Christ's willingness to carry me to safety. Snow can remind me that the Atonement covers and purifies my sin-stained past (Isaiah 1:18). Every hill I see (Psalm 121:1–2), shady spot I find (Psalm 121:5), stone I throw (D&C 50:44), or sunrise I watch (Malachi 4:2) can remind me of the Savior. Even the waves of the sea bear testimony of Christ's love (Psalm 107:29).

Bread, water, milk, rocks, fire, rain, rainbows, clouds, wind, cars, houses, songs, snow, plants, birds, hills, shade, waves—all things bear witness of Christ and His redeeming power. They were *created* to bear record of Him (see Moses 6:63). Every time I see these objects in the course of my daily routines, I can try to see them as symbols and remember that the Lord offers me forgiveness and the power to change to become more like Him.

Meeting with Christ

The other day in sacrament meeting, we sang the hymn "We Love Thy House, O God." As we were singing, I thought seriously for the first time about the meaning of the second verse: "It is the house of prayer, / Wherein thy servants meet, / And thou, O Lord, art there, / Thy chosen flock to greet." Every meeting in the Church—from general conference to family home evening—is a reminder that Christ will return and meet with us again. And He wants to meet with us now. So why do I complain about having to attend so many meetings? It's probably because I don't feel the redeeming power of the Atonement at every meeting. But could I?

Gene R. Cook shared how changing our perspective can change a meeting: "President Kimball one time was asked, 'Elder Kimball, what do you do when you're in a boring sacrament meeting?' President Kimball thought a minute and then he gave a very profound answer. He said, 'I don't know; I've never been in one.' What he was really teaching, brothers and sisters, was about another meeting. If you're in this meeting with me—this one we physically see—you're not in the meeting yet. The real meeting is the meeting between you and the Lord. And if you want to really get in the meeting and have the Lord work upon your heart, that will be up to you."[7] All of our meetings are supposed to help us invite the Spirit back into our lives, which prepares us to meet with Christ.

Meeting Christ again is what the gospel message is all about. It's what the endowment ceremony in the temple is all about. It's what the scriptures are all about. Here's how the Lord explained it to Moroni: "And because thou hast seen thy weakness thou shalt be made strong, even unto the sitting down in the place which I have prepared in the mansions of my Father" (Ether 12:37). Moroni's feelings of weakness and unworthiness are the catalysts that prepared him for a greater glory to come. "And now I, Moroni, bid farewell unto the Gentiles, yea, and also unto my brethren whom I love, until we shall meet before the judgment-seat of Christ, where all men shall know that my garments are not spotted with your blood. And then shall ye know that I have seen Jesus, and that he hath talked with me face to face, and that he told me in plain humility, even as a man telleth another in mine own language, concerning these things" (Ether 12:38–39).

Moroni wants us to have the same experience he did: "And now, I would commend you to seek this Jesus of whom the prophets and apostles have written, that the grace of God . . . may be and abide in you forever" (Ether 12:41). The fact that we're trying to see the Savior will invite His power into our lives and prepare us for the experience the prophets refer to as "entering into the rest of the Lord" (Alma 60:13). The Lord calls this privilege of meeting Him someday "the great and last promise" (D&C 88:68, 69, 75).

Is it a realistic goal? After dedicating half of the record of the Jaredites to the experience that the brother of Jared had in seeing the Savior, Moroni assures us that this experience wasn't unique: "And there were many whose faith was so exceedingly strong, even before Christ came, who could not be kept from within the veil, but truly saw with their eyes the things which they had beheld with an eye of faith, and they were glad" (Ether 12:19). So they first have hope in Christ. They see with their mind's eye—the eye of faith—the fulfillment of the promise before it happens. Later, they truly see Christ. There are "many" who have had this experience. How many? In his discourse on how to overcome the world, Alma said there are "many, exceedingly great many, who were made pure and entered into the rest of the Lord their God" (Alma 13:12). It seems clear that this isn't a privilege for the prophetic few, but rather an offer extended to all faithful Saints, just as soon as we're ready to claim it. And many have.

In the Doctrine and Covenants, the Lord gives us instructions about how to come unto Him. "Verily, thus saith the Lord: It shall come to pass that every soul who forsaketh his sins and cometh unto me, and calleth on my name, and obeyeth my voice, and keepeth my commandments, shall see my face and know that I am" (D&C 93:1).

So the goal of true repentance and obedience is to see Christ. If every soul has that invitation, why haven't I seen Him yet? Am I just not a spiritual person? No, the Lord doesn't want me to get discouraged like that. He says reassuringly, "Ye are not able to abide the presence of God now, neither the ministering of angels; wherefore, continue in patience until ye are perfected" (D&C 67:13).

In a recent general conference address, President Henry B. Eyring characterized our search for Christ in concrete but patient terms: "Although His time is not always our time, we can be sure that the Lord keeps His promises. For any of you who now feel that He is hard to reach, I testify that the day will come that we all will see Him face to face. Just as there is nothing now to obscure His view of us, there will be nothing to obscure our view of Him. We will all stand before Him, in person. . . . We want to see Jesus Christ now, but our certain reunion with Him . . . will be more pleasing if we first do the things that make Him as familiar to us as we are to Him. As we serve Him, we become like Him, and we feel closer to Him as we approach that day when nothing will hide our view."[8] How do I prepare for such a meeting?

One Thing Is Needful

The more I meet with other Saints at Church, listen to our leaders in general conference, and learn from the prophets of old in the scriptures, the more I'm coming to see that it's all about learning to love. Mormon explained this in one of his last letters to his son, Moroni. "Wherefore, my beloved brethren, if ye have not charity, ye are nothing, for charity never faileth. Wherefore, cleave unto charity, which is the greatest of all, for all things must fail—But charity is the pure love of Christ, and it endureth forever; and whoso is found possessed of it at the last day, it shall be well with him" (Moroni 7:46–47). Nothing else will matter if I haven't learned to love.

How do I do that? "Wherefore, my beloved brethren, pray unto the Father with all the energy of heart, that ye may be filled with this love, which he hath bestowed upon all who are true followers of his Son, Jesus Christ; that ye may become the sons of God; that when he shall appear we shall be like him, for we shall see him as he is; that we may have this hope; that we may be purified even as he is pure. Amen" (Moroni 7:48). The kind of love I need is charity, and it comes only as a gift from Christ. I can't *do* charity; I have to *receive* it. If I strive to keep the commandments and humbly pray for charity, the Spirit will be able to accompany me and teach me what I need to do. It'll also refashion me to become more like Christ. Then, when the time arrives for me to meet Him, I won't have to shrink away in shame and remorse. I'll be like Him, so I'll be eager to embrace Him and be with Him.

Because I'm not like Him yet but want to become that way, it inspires me to learn from the examples of those who are. I read a story once about a woman who was preparing to teach her Relief Society lesson. Moments before the meeting was to begin, she realized that her baby had blown out his drawers and stained his outfit—and hers as well. With tears streaming down her cheeks, the mother ran into the bathroom and desperately tried to mop up the mess, knowing that her lesson now was doomed.

Just then, her visiting teacher came into the bathroom. She'd heard what had happened and was ready to help. She told the sister to take off her dress while she began to unzip her own. The sister just stared at her in disbelief, but the visiting teacher persisted. "Take off your dress and put on mine. I'll put on your dress, take your baby home, and clean him up. You put on my dress and go teach your class." In shock, the mother followed her visiting teacher's instructions. She zipped on the clean dress, fixed her makeup, and ran into the Relief Society room just in time to teach her lesson.

We talk a lot about charity, but this visiting teacher discovered a way to live it. Would I be so willing to sacrifice and help? I'd like to think so, but I'm not sure. When I go to church, am I the one who's looking for the visitor or the lonely person to sit next to, or am I the one who always finds "my pew" to sit in my comfort zone? Am I the one complaining that my neighbors never do anything together, or am I the one inviting them over for dinner? I know I can't simply make myself into this kind of person—only Christ could bring about such a transformation. But I'm praying for more opportunities to listen to the Spirit's instructions on how to try.

I have a friend who, together with his wife, raised many kids. When his oldest daughter was a young teenager, she began breaking every commandment her parents had ever taught her—including the law of chastity. She put them through a hard form of parental hell. She graduated from high school, packed her bags, and moved as far from home as possible. When she reached Jackson Hole, Wyoming, her money ran out. She was able to get a job at a dude ranch teaching children to ride horses. She spent half a summer there, miserable, running from her life.

One evening, this young lady sat in bed, unable to sleep, thinking about how much she resented her life. She hated her parents, she hated the Church, and she even decided she hated God. So she got out of bed, dressed, and walked to the men's dormitory across the ranch, fully intending to break the law of chastity again.

She got halfway across the ranch when she threw her fist up at the night sky and challenged God with this profound question: "Why don't you stop me?! You're supposed to love everyone, so why don't you stop me?"

She later said that she heard an answer in her mind. A gentle but firm voice said, "I cannot stop you. I love you too much to take away your agency. But if you will stop yourself and turn around, I will be there for you." She paused there in the darkness for a long time. She pondered, stewed, deliberated, and finally made a decision. Slowly, she picked up her foot and rotated it around to face in the opposite direction. She said that when she did, it felt like a blanket of love fell from the sky and wrapped her up. For the first time in years, she felt the Spirit again. She slowly made her way back to the women's dormitory.

When she returned, she lay in bed the rest of the night, unable to sleep. She thought about the course of her life and, in that fateful night, she made a decision to return. She arose early the next morning, packed her things, quit her job, and headed home. She found her parents and apologized profusely for all she'd put them through. She said she wanted to repent and get her life together. Her parents suggested that, with all she'd done, she should have to talk with the bishop, and she agreed. The bishop put her on probation for many weeks, and she couldn't take the sacrament while she worked on getting the Spirit back in her life through personal prayer, scripture study, and church attendance. She finally finished her probation, enrolled in an institute class, and eventually met a wonderful returned missionary. They were sealed in the temple and are now raising eight beautiful children in the gospel.

We could fret about what parents do in the name of love that sometimes drives their children to rebel against them and the Church, but that's not my point. My point is that there's a way back. When we choose to turn our lives over to the Savior and are willing to do anything He may require of us, His Atonement is sufficient to redeem and reform us—to buy us back from the slavery of our sins and refashion us in His image. He can even cleanse and purify those among us who have broken the law of chastity—but we have to *let* Him do it. He won't start a life makeover without our consent! The only thing that'll keep Him from doing it is if we decide to block His power. He says if you "come unto Christ," "deny yourselves of all ungodliness," and "deny not his power," then "is his grace sufficient for you" and, through the Atonement, He will make you "without spot" and "holy"—justified and sanctified (Moroni 10:32–33).

What'll I look like when the Lord has finished my spiritual makeover? The process of becoming more Christlike is becoming more childlike. "Except ye be converted," He says, "and become as little children, ye shall not enter into the kingdom of heaven. Whosoever therefore shall humble himself as this little child, the same is greatest in the kingdom of heaven" (Matthew 18:3–4). The last thing I want to become is child*ish*. I'm petty and selfish enough as it is. But the Lord intends me to become child*like*. King Benjamin listed those attributes: "Becometh as a child, submissive, meek, humble, patient, full of love, willing to submit to all things which the Lord seeth fit to inflict upon him, even as a child doth submit to his father" (Mosiah 3:19). More than anyone else, children know how to forgive, love, and accept others. Children want to please their parents and will try endlessly to measure up to expectations—even if they fail over and over. And so can I, knowing that the Savior's grace will bring about the changes in me and make up the difference until I become as He is.

Breaking the Law of Chastity

Could someone who's broken the law of chastity ever really change so much that they could one day become a celestial being? That just seems like too big of a leap, even for the Lord to accomplish.

Let's look at Alma the Elder. Even though he'd been a member of the Church and held the priesthood, under the wicked King Noah's rule he'd been led into a profligate lifestyle. He was one of Noah's wicked priests, who "were lifted up in the pride of their hearts" (Mosiah 11:5). They "were supported in their laziness, and in their idolatry, and in their whoredoms" (Mosiah 11:6). The dictionary says that whoredoms are illicit sexual indulgences. But we aren't left to our imagination to figure out what Alma and his fellow priests were up to. Mormon explained that "so did also his priests spend their time with harlots" (Mosiah 11:14). Alma, who grew up in the Church, was apparently as wicked and self-indulgent as they come. Yet what happened to him? He believed the testimony of Abinadi, repented, started a branch of the Church, and eventually became a prophet. Does anyone think Alma isn't going to the highest degree of the celestial kingdom?

And what about his son, Alma the Younger? As children of Church leaders sometimes do, Alma struggled with the faith of his father. In fact, he and the sons of Mosiah "were numbered among the unbelievers" (Mosiah 27:8). How bad did things get? Well, the record says he "became a very wicked and an idolatrous man. And he was a man of many words, and did speak much flattery to the people; therefore he led many of the people to do after the manner of his iniquities" (Mosiah 27:8).

Then, as if Mormon wanted to impress on us how bad a character Alma had become, he continued his description: "And he became a great hinderment to the prosperity of the church of God; stealing away the hearts of the people; causing much dissension among the people; giving a chance for the enemy of God to exercise his power over them" (Mosiah 27:9). Just in case we still didn't get how awful Alma was, Mormon kept on railing against him: "He was going about to destroy the church" and "he did go about secretly with the sons of Mosiah seeking to destroy the church, and to lead astray the people of the Lord" (Mosiah 27:10). Still not satisfied that we fully grasped what a wretch he was, Mormon added that "they were going about rebelling against God" (Mosiah 27:11). These were awful, nasty, rebellious people. Did their crimes include whoredoms like Alma's dad committed? It's possible.

And what happened to Alma the Younger? He was converted through the fasting and prayers of his father, the visit of an angel, and a born-again experience. He eventually followed in his father's footsteps and became the prophet of the Church. Will Alma the Younger make it to the highest degree of the celestial kingdom? Of course he will.

There's another link in this genealogical chain of sinners-turned-prophets. Alma the Younger had a son named Corianton. He was called on a mission to the Zoramites with his brothers, but he was distracted from his duty and ended up with the harlot Isabel (see Alma 39:3). Alma spent four chapters of the record reprimanding Corianton and cutting through his self-justifications. Alma left no doubt that Corianton really messed up and committed one of the worst sins we know of.

But his prodigal son returned! Corianton humbly set out to finish his mission with his brothers and apparently developed just as much power as they did: "And now it came to pass that the sons of Alma did go forth among the people, to declare the word unto them" (Alma 43:1). And "they preached the word, and the truth, according to the spirit of prophecy and revelation; and they preached after the holy order of God by which they were called" (Alma 43:2).

So what happened to Corianton? He ended up taking his place next to his brothers on Mormon's list of greatest missionary heroes: "Yea, verily, verily I say unto you, if all men had been, and were, and ever would be, like unto Moroni, behold, the very powers of hell would have been shaken forever; yea, the devil would never have power over the hearts of the children of men. Behold, he was a man like unto Ammon, the son of Mosiah, yea, and even the other sons of Mosiah, yea, and also *Alma and his sons, for they were all men of God*" (Alma 48:17–18; emphasis added). Corianton is listed with Mormon's heroes as one of the all-time greatest missionaries. This is high praise for a man who earlier as a missionary had committed fornication and brought so much misery to himself and embarrassment to the Church!

Alma the Elder, Alma the Younger, and Corianton all followed similar paths. They grew up knowing the gospel. They messed up, struggled with the law of chastity, and led many others astray. But they all repented and became great missionaries and leaders in the Lord's Church.

Wouldn't they feel horribly guilty for the rest of their lives for the awful things they'd done in their youth? I think Alma the Younger spoke for all three of these repentant sinners when he said, referring to the Savior's Atonement, "I could remember my pains no more; yea, I was harrowed up by the memory of my sins no more. And oh, what joy, and what marvelous light I did behold; yea, my soul was filled with joy as exceeding as was my pain!" (Alma 36:19–20). They still remembered their previous life of sin, but the pain, guilt, and embarrassment were gone. Now they simply rejoiced in the Savior's Atonement, which covered up and transformed the past into a glorious present and hope-filled future.

His Promises Are Sure

Here's my point: if these men could make it back and have a chance at the celestial kingdom, so can I. Sure, it would've been better to learn my lesson without making such awful mistakes. It would've been better for both Almas and for Corianton if they could've learned their lesson without being immoral. But the point is that they *did* learn their lesson, and so can I. And just as no one talks much about their pasts—except in discussions like this one where we're trying to learn from them—when the Lord is done with me, no one will talk much about my past either.

The Prophet Joseph Smith said this about Judgment Day: "If you do not accuse each other, God will not accuse you. If you have no accuser you will enter heaven, and if you will follow the revelations and instructions which God gives you through me, I will take you into heaven as my back load. If you will not accuse me, I will not accuse you. If you will throw a cloak of charity over my sins, I will over yours—for charity covereth a multitude of sins."[9] With Joseph Smith carrying me, I can certainly make it. The Lord continues to pour out His Spirit upon me as a witness that my past is forgiven, as a transforming power to refashion me into His image, and as a token of His promise that I'll make it back to His kingdom someday.

Like Nephi, I'll at times bemoan the undeniable fact of my sinfulness. I'll cry, "O wretched man that I am!" (2 Nephi 4:17). I'll feel at times that I can never make it "because of the temptations and the sins which do so easily beset me" (2 Nephi 4:18). But "I know in whom I have trusted. My God hath been my support. . . . He hath filled me with his love" (2 Nephi 4:19–21). I'll plead along with Nephi, "O Lord, wilt thou encircle me around in the robe of thy righteousness!" (2 Nephi 4:33). The pathetic robes of secrecy I try to hide my sins in are so full of holes that they'll always leave me exposed in the end. But the robes of *His* righteousness will not only cover but also transform the weak flesh underneath them. One day, after He's finished his work with me, He will dress me permanently in robes of royalty to reign in the house of Israel forever. I'll be at one with Him, ready for His work.

A Parable

I'll close this chapter by modifying an ancient Eastern parable. A man is running away from a tiger when he falls into a well. Halfway down to the depths below, the man becomes lodged on the branch of a vine growing out of the sidewall of the well. As his eyes slowly adjust to the darkness, he sees a small honeycomb at the end of the vine. Recognizing his hunger, he slowly inches his way to the edge of the branch and starts scooping the golden liquid into his mouth.

Presently, the man gets a glimpse of something that horrifies him. He vaguely makes out the outline of a gigantic crocodile curled up in the darkness below him, hungrily waiting for the man to fall to the bottom. Frantically, he looks toward the top of the well to see if there might be any way to crawl up the sides to safety. To his dismay, he sees the tiger ferociously glaring over the edge of the well, anxious to devour him. But it's the next sight that sends the worst chills of shock and dread. At the base of the vine he's so precariously perched upon, he sees two small mice—one black and one white—quietly but determinedly nibbling away at the vine. The man discerns in horror that it won't take long for them to gnaw through the vine, which will send the man to his certain demise in the jaws of the vicious crocodile below. Try as he might to swat them away, he simply can't reach the mice at the base of the vine without losing his balance and plunging to his death.

While contemplating the precarious and hopeless state of his predicament, the man's view is suddenly focused again to the sight of the golden honey at the end of the vine. Almost in spite of himself, he reaches out once more, scoops up a tasty glob, and smears it on his tongue. He savors the sweet nectar and momentarily forgets the horrors that seem to seal his awful fate.

All of a sudden, out of the darkness that encompassed the man, he sees someone has thrown a rope down to his rescue. His benefactor has chased away the tiger and now offers him a sure escape. But to reach the rope, the man will have to let go of the vine he sits perched upon. He'll also have to give up his feast of honey. All he has to do is grasp the rope and climb to safety and freedom. Yet the man has become comfortable in his pitiful little spot on the faltering vine. What will he do?

This parable can represent our own desperate plight of existence. The well we've fallen down is mortality. The vine is our short span of life. The crocodile that awaits us below is death and the tiger looming above us is our own sinful nature. The honey represents the worldly pleasures that taste so sweet and can be so distracting. The black and white mice that nibble away at our branch of life are the nights and days ticking away our hours to the certain conclusion of death.

The rope represents the Atonement. Christ offers it to us, along with the assurance of deliverance from sin and death. I'll have to sacrifice my little pleasure trap and allow Him to pull me to safety. Only I can grab the rope and cling to it through gospel covenants. But imagine the embrace awaiting me upon my arrival at the top.

Second Coming Surprises

"All the easy things that the Church has had to do have been done. From now on, it's high adventure."[1]

—Neal A. Maxwell

Thomas was my roommate in college. He was bright, thoughtful, and full of optimism about the future. One day, Thomas and I were discussing current events and I could tell something was troubling him. I asked him what it was, and he revealed what'd been on his mind. He asked me how I could believe in all the scriptural prophecies about the Second Coming that seem so outlandish to the modern worldview. The moon turning to blood, the stars falling from the sky, the battle of Armageddon—it all sounded more to him like a J. R. R. Tolkien novel than a realistic future to prepare for. I've thought about Thomas's concerns quite a bit. Is the Savior really coming back trailing clouds of glory? If so, when? And how can I be prepared?

One argument that Thomas had for not believing in a literal Second Coming was all the failed predictions of it in the past. Didn't I know that William Miller had used Daniel 8:14 to prophesy Christ's return on October 22, 1844? When it didn't occur, believers reinterpreted the prophecy to be Christ appearing in the heavenly sanctuary and the Seventh-day Adventists were born. Later, Charles Russell predicted the Second Coming was going to occur in 1873. When it didn't happen, he changed his explanation to be that Christ came invisibly, and thus began the Jehovah's Witnesses. In our century, one of the big predictions was for December 21, 2012, since that was supposedly the last day of the Mayan calendar. (How were the Mayans supposed to know when the world would end?) Every time someone makes a failed prediction of the end of the world or the coming of the Savior, it makes the whole idea seem a little less believable.

Ironically, the failed predictions of the Lord's coming are part of the signs. The Savior explained as much to His Apostles when they were asking about His return: "Then if any man shall say unto you, Lo, here is Christ, or there; believe it not. For there shall arise false Christs, and false prophets, and shall shew great signs and wonders; insomuch that, if it were possible, they shall deceive the very elect. Behold, I have told you before. Wherefore if they shall say unto you, Behold, he is in the desert; go not forth: behold, he is in the secret chambers; believe it not. For as the lightning cometh out of the east, and shineth even unto the west; so shall also the coming of the Son of man be" (Matthew 24:23–27). In other words, people will make all sorts of claims about His coming, but don't believe them. When He comes for the last time, everyone will see Him together and know He has arrived. He will leave no doubt.

One of the signs of the Second Coming is that even those who believed in the Savior will say the time is past. "And in that day shall be heard of wars and rumors of wars, and the whole earth shall be in commotion, and men's hearts shall fail them, and they shall say that Christ delayeth his coming until the end of the earth" (D&C 45:26). People will say, as they did before His first coming, "that it is not reasonable that such a being as a Christ shall come" (Helaman 16:18). And Peter foretold "that there shall come in the last days scoffers, walking after their own lusts, and saying, Where is the promise of his coming? for since the fathers fell asleep, all things continue as they were from the beginning of the creation" (2 Peter 3:3–4). This was precisely the attitude of my roommate, who didn't think believing in the Second Coming was reasonable—the world just seemed to be going on the same as it'd always been.

Literal or Figurative?

One way to view the signs of the Second Coming that'd fit in with modern sensibilities a little better would be to see them as figurative. Perhaps they're merely symbols of things we can apply to our own lives in the here and now.[2] That way, we could "liken all scriptures unto us, that it might be for our profit and learning" (1 Nephi 19:23) and not have to worry so much about literal events to come.

To suggest that the signs are only symbolic and not literal is to start down a slippery slope of "spiritualizing" the scriptures that ends in having nothing but powerful metaphors. Paul warned, "If in this life only we have hope in Christ, we are of all men most miserable" (1 Corinthians 15:19). If we see Christ's Resurrection and glorious return only as symbols to enrich our experiences with others in the here and now, eventually we'll be frustrated and left empty-handed. Other competing religious symbols may begin to lay claim to our allegiance. The symbolism by itself may lose its authoritative power to guide our lives. Either we keep the literal interpretations as a solid foundation for our faith to stand on or we run the risk of letting the symbolic ones float away as so much fluff.

Subtle Signs

The point of all the Second Coming signs in the scriptures seems to be that events are really going to happen out of the ordinary march of civilization, and we need to be prepared when they occur. But I do think we can get too caught up in the sensational nature of the prophecies—like earthquakes, wars, and chaos in the heavens—and miss some of the more subtle signs of the Savior's return.

One of those often-missed signs was pointed out to me by a friend and is found in the book of Zechariah. The ancient high priest of Israel wore a cap, or mitre, with a golden band across the front. Engraved on it in Hebrew were the words *holiness to the Lord*. Today, we have the plate of gold with those words written on the outside of every temple. Before the Second Coming, "holiness to the Lord" will be written on "the bells of the horses" and on "every pot in Jerusalem and in Judah" (Zechariah 14:20–21). It won't just be on our temples, but also on our places of residence. Symbolically, the point seems to be that we'll all need to sanctify our homes to become more like temples. My friend decided to take that sign literally as well as symbolically, so he hung a brass bell on his front door, on which he engraved "holiness to the Lord." It's there as an expression of his faith in the Savior's return and as a reminder of his need to be ready.

Another sign that's often missed is that of the rising and setting sun. Just as the sun rises in the east and sets in the west, Christ's return will be from the east. "For as the lightning cometh out of the east, and shineth even unto the west; so shall also the coming of the Son of man be" (Matthew 24:27). This is also why bodies in cemeteries are traditionally buried with the feet facing east. That way when the resurrection of the righteous occurs at the Second Coming, they can rise up to face the coming Lord.

In his letters to the early Church, Paul discussed another more subtle sign of the Second Coming: false doctrine that'd take over the intellectual landscape. "For the time will come when they will not endure sound doctrine; but after their own lusts shall they heap to themselves teachers, having itching ears; and they shall turn away their ears from the truth, and shall be turned unto fables" (2 Timothy 4:3–4). Paul warned that in the last days before the Savior's return, the people will be "ever learning, and never able to come to the knowledge of the truth" (2 Timothy 3:7). And he even prophesied what these intellectual elite will secretly be itching after in leading people away from the gospel truth: "For of this sort are they which creep into houses, and lead captive silly women laden with sins, led away with divers lusts" (2 Timothy 3:6). In other words, all their sophisticated arguments against traditional religion will be, in the end, merely a smokescreen to cover their true designs of inducing innocent young people to indulge in their sexual appetites. If I can convince you that your religion is irrational superstition, then perhaps I can also convince you that your moral code is merely childish prudishness.

Recently, one of my dear friends was sucked down this path. After spending hours on anti-Mormon websites, he allowed himself to become convinced that Joseph Smith's practice of polygamy was driven by his own licentiousness. Consequently, he abandoned his commitment to the Church and, along with it, his commitment to his family. Ironically, that left him free to indulge his own licentious impulses and pursue a relationship with a married woman he'd been flirting with at work. Neil L. Anderson of the Quorum of the Twelve warned about this latter-day sign: "The negative commentary about the Prophet Joseph Smith will increase as we move toward the Second Coming of the Savior. The half-truths and subtle deceptions will not diminish. There will be family members and friends who will need your help. Now is the time to adjust your own spiritual oxygen mask so that you are prepared to help others who are seeking the truth."[3] Am I prepared to defend Joseph as the Lord's great latter-day Prophet? Opposition to him and the work he began is going to heat up even more as we get closer to the Savior's return.

A closely related sign of the Second Coming is that society will embrace homosexuality. In 2 Timothy 3:1–3, Paul wrote to a young bishop describing what would come about in our day: "This know also, that in the last days perilous times shall come. For men shall be lovers of their own selves, covetous, boasters, proud, blasphemers, disobedient to parents, unthankful, unholy, without natural affection." Paul went on to warn that these people would have "a form of godliness, but denying the power thereof: from such turn away" (2 Timothy 3:5). Is it a form of godliness today for people to claim compassion and tolerance as their guiding star in defending the right of homosexuals to marry?

We should be more compassionate and tolerant of some things and honor the struggle of those who must deal with this issue. But that doesn't mean we should stop teaching God's law of marriage out of fear of offending people. The Lord has always guarded the powers of procreation and protected them within the bond of lawful marriage between a man and a woman. As society at large is growing more and more accepting of gay relationships and marriage, it'll require more and more faith and integrity to stand and defend the Lord's law. Elder Holland stated in general conference that it'll require both courage and compassion to stand up appropriately for our beliefs as society abandons those standards.[4] Those who do may find themselves increasingly alienated from mainstream society, but they'll be the ones prepared for the Lord's return.

Holy Places

One of the signs of the Second Coming is that, while the wicked shall be lifting up their voices against God and His plan, the Lord's people "shall stand in holy places, and shall not be moved" (D&C 45:32). What is a holy place? It's a place made sacred by the presence of a member of the Godhead. Many years before I met my wife, I went on a date with a spiritual young lady. Before we left for our activity, she asked if she could show me something she'd just read in the Bible Dictionary. Thinking that scripture study was a different but kind of cool activity for a date, I agreed. She turned to the entry under "Temple": "A place where the Lord may come, it is the most holy of any place of worship on the earth. Only the home can compare with the temple in sacredness."[5] So perhaps the two most distinctive places for the righteous in the last days will be the temple and the home. Of course, that doesn't mean the faithful won't go other places. The temple garment is a mini version of the temple. So if I'm wearing the garment and keeping my temple covenants, or if I'm wearing modest clothing that would cover and respect my garments as if I'd been to the temple, then wherever I go, I can be standing in holy places. My respect for the temple will invite the Holy Ghost to be with me—in a sense sanctifying the ground on which I walk.

The prophets connect many aspects of temple worship with the Second Coming. Paul said, "For the Lord himself shall descend from heaven with a shout" (1Thessalonians 4:16). Commenting on this verse, Lorenzo Snow explained his feeling that this'll be a great Hosanna Shout.[6] If so, then every Hosanna Shout at a temple dedication is practice for the great and terrible day of the Lord when the righteous will let out a great shout of welcome.

Another sign of the Second Coming is the special meeting at Adam-ondi-Ahman. Before Christ comes in all His glory, there'll be a sneak preview at a special meeting in northern Missouri. All the faithful Latter-day Saints will be invited somehow to participate. Whether we will all be gathered together already in Missouri or whether we'll participate through some sort of satellite broadcast across the globe, we will all participate. Daniel saw "ten thousand times ten thousand" (Daniel 7:10) faithful Saints gathered to greet the Savior there. All the great prophets of the past will be present as resurrected beings (see D&C 27:5–14). "Saints and angels" will sing together in this great sacrament meeting presided over by Adam himself.[7]

So I never want to miss a Church meeting I'm invited to attend. Each one is a preparation for the Second Coming. I'll not likely know ahead of time which one will be *the one*. The Lord said, "Behold, it is my will, that all they who call on my name, and worship me according to mine everlasting gospel, should gather together, and stand in holy places; and prepare for the revelation which is to come, when the veil of the covering of my temple, in my tabernacle, which hideth the earth, shall be taken off, and all flesh shall see me together" (D&C 101:22–23). Every time we get together in a Church meeting, we're preparing for the great "meeting" when Christ shall return in glory. Perhaps if I go, as the scriptures say, "seek[ing] the face of the Lord always" (D&C 101:38), one day I'll be at the right meeting at the right time, ready to enjoy His appearance.

Will the prophet call us all to move back to Missouri to build the New Jerusalem? I really don't know. But I hope I'll always be ready to move my family wherever I may be called to go. We'll always be mere pilgrims here on earth—this is not our true home (see Hebrews 11:13–14). Eventually, Christ will come and take us home, where many mansions are prepared for us.

In the meantime, we certainly must be doing our part to make our current homes into places of refuge. Before the Second Coming, the moral chaos of the world will become so extreme that the Saints will have to turn their homes into mini temples. "And the Lord will create upon every dwelling-place of mount Zion, and upon her assemblies, a cloud and smoke by day and the shining of a flaming fire by night; for upon all the glory of Zion shall be a defence. And there shall be a tabernacle for a shadow in the daytime from the heat, and for a place of refuge" (2 Nephi 14:5–6).

Commenting on these verses, Apostle Orson Pratt once prophesied in general conference. He declared, "The time is to come when God will meet with all the congregation of his Saints, and to show his approval, and that he does love them, he will work a miracle by covering them in the cloud of his glory. I do not mean something that is invisible, but I mean that same order of things which once existed on the earth so far as the tabernacle of Moses was concerned, which was carried in the midst of the children of Israel as they journeyed in the wilderness."[8] Just as the Lord led Moses and the Israelites through the Sinai wilderness by a cloud in the day and a pillar of fire at night to indicate His presence in the tabernacle, He will do it again before the Second Coming:

> But in the latter days there will be a people so pure in Mount Zion, with a house established upon the tops of the mountains, that God will manifest himself, not only in their Temple and upon all their assemblies, with a visible cloud during the day, but when the night shall come, if they shall be assembled for worship, God will meet with them by his pillar of fire; and when they retire to their habitations, behold each habitation will be lighted up by the glory of God—a pillar of flaming fire by night. Did you ever hear of any city that was thus favored and blessed since the day that Isaiah delivered this prophecy? No, it is a latter-day work, one that God must consummate in the latter times when he begins to reveal himself, and show forth his power among the nations.[9]

And so it's our business to be turning our homes into places apart from the world, like mini temples. Then the Lord will "light them up" with the power of His Spirit and one day protect them with a literal cloud of glory and pillar of fire.

Spectacular Signs

In highlighting some of the less familiar scriptural signs of the Second Coming, I don't mean to diminish the significance of any of the more spectacular ones. The most frequently mentioned sign is that "before this great day shall come the sun shall be darkened, and the moon shall be turned into blood, and the stars shall fall from heaven" (D&C 29:14). At least fifteen times in the standard works, prophets mention this. How could such intergalactic chaos be possible? According to both Joseph Smith and Brigham Young, when this earth was created, it was formed near Kolob, the throne of God. But when Adam and Eve fell and became mortal, so too did the planet. It fell from the Lord's presence and took up its current orbit in our solar system. But eventually, it'll be "rolled back into the presence of God."[10] I don't know how all this will happen. But it will happen.

The Last Great Sign

The scriptures are often ambiguous as to the exact order of the Second Coming signs. Will the waters be polluted with wormwood (see Revelation 8:10–11) first or will the gospel be preached in every nation (Revelation 14:6)? Are the two prophets killed in Jerusalem (see Revelation 11) before or after the temple is built in Jackson County (see D&C 84:3)? Where does the battle of Armageddon fit in (see Zechariah 11–14)? We're mostly left to ourselves to figure out the timing of the signs relative to each other. But we do know what the last great "sign of the Son of man" will be (Matthew 24:30). Joseph Smith taught that "then will appear one grand sign of the Son of Man in heaven. But what will the world do? They will say it is a planet, a comet, etc. But the Son of Man will come as the sign of the coming of the Son of Man, which will be as the light of the morning cometh out of the east."[11] People will think a comet is heading for collision with the earth, but it'll be the Savior Himself—the Light and Life of the World—coming back in all His splendor.

As dramatic as these last events shall be, I believe there are even greater signs of the Second Coming, and they're occurring right now. "For I, the Lord, have put forth my hand to exert the powers of heaven; ye cannot see it now, yet a little while and ye shall see it, and know that I am, and that I will come and reign with my people" (D&C 84:119). The Lord has already begun to part the veil and touch our lives. Every little miracle, every tender mercy, is a sign that He's with us now and will yet come in His promised glory. Today, if we harden not our hearts, we can hear His voice and know that He's on His way (see Jacob 6:6).

When?

What we all seem to want to know is when. When will He come? In high school, I had a few teachers who liked to give pop quizzes. You never knew when they'd have you take out a piece of paper, number one to five, and then quiz you on the reading assignment for the day. The point was that because we didn't know when it was coming, we'd always be up to date and prepared. Perhaps that's analogous to what the Lord is doing with us and the Second Coming.

The scriptures do provide an interesting clue though. In Joseph Smith—Matthew 1:33–34, the Savior taught His disciples that the generation that sees the sun and the moon darkened and the stars fall from the sky is the one that shall see the Second Coming. "This generation, in which these things shall be shown forth, shall not pass away until all I have told you shall be fulfilled" (verse 34). By then, it may be too late to do much preparing, like walking into class and seeing the pop quiz on the teacher's desk ready to be handed out.

Phil was a ninth-grade student who was as sharp as any I'd ever had. Before class one day, I asked Phil if he was excited to leave on his mission in a few years. His reply took me by surprise. He said he wasn't planning on serving one. When I asked why, he explained that a friend had recently received his patriarchal blessing, which said something about being called home from his mission to fight in World War III before the Second Coming. Since his friend was three years older than he was, clearly he wouldn't be serving a mission. I was frustrated. I hear these kinds of stories all too often. Still, I was grateful for the chance to intervene.

I began by reminding Phil that patriarchal blessings are personal revelation and are not to be shared with others. So anything that gets spread around from blessings should be disregarded. It's rarely reported accurately, and even if it were, again, it wasn't supposed to be shared with anyone else. To base decisions in your life on what you think you heard from someone else's blessing is folly to the nth degree. Get your own blessing and see what the Lord actually has to say to *you*. Fortunately, Phil did receive his own blessing and learned that the Lord had a mission in store for him. Four years later, he served faithfully and returned with honor.

We're so fascinated by the signs of the Second Coming that we're willing to listen to anyone's account of them—even fictionalized ones. Books and movies about the end of the world are extremely popular. Anyone who has more to add to the signs than what's in the scriptures is eagerly received.[12] It's as if we want to know when we finally have to take His return seriously because we don't want to worry about it too soon.

Preparation

The Savior has taught that His coming shall be as a thief in the night for the unprepared. No one knows the day nor the hour of His return, and the wicked will be caught off guard. Yet for the faithful who are watching and preparing, the Second Coming won't be a surprise. It "overtaketh the world as a thief in the night—therefore, gird up your loins, that you may be the children of light, and that day shall not overtake you as a thief" (D&C 106:4–5). In my study of the gospel, I've found several basic things I can do.

The first way to prepare for the Second Coming is to foster the Spirit in my life. Wilford Woodruff taught, "Who is going to be prepared for the coming of the Messiah? [Those] who enjoy the Holy Ghost and live under the inspiration of the Almighty, who abide in Jesus Christ and bring forth fruit to the honor and glory of God. No other people will be."[13] If I have the Spirit with me today and the Savior returns this evening, I'll be excited to see Him.

There are a few specific activities the scriptures mention as appropriate preparation for that great day. "And whoso treasureth up my word, shall not be deceived, for the Son of Man shall come" (Joseph Smith—Matthew 1:37). Daily feasting on the scriptures and the words of the prophets will do more to invite the Spirit into my life and prepare me to meet the Savior than anything else.

Of course, reading His word and not applying it in our lives will still leave us unprepared. The Lord says that "the great day of the Lord is nigh at hand. . . . Wherefore gird up your loins lest ye be found among the wicked. Lift up your voices and spare not. Call upon the nations to repent, both old and young, both bond and free, saying: Prepare yourselves for the great day of the Lord" (D&C 43:17, 19–20). To "gird up your loins" is scripture-talk for "get to work." The one who's busy working in the kingdom serving his or her family and neighbor, and inviting them to live the gospel message, is the one who will be prepared.

The scriptures emphasize at least one other activity that'll prepare me for the Second Coming. Joseph Smith made the connection between temple work and the Lord's return:

> Behold, the great day of the Lord is at hand; and who can abide the day of his coming, and who can stand when he appeareth? For he is

> like a refiner's fire, and like fuller's soap; and he shall sit as a refiner and purifier of silver, and he shall purify the sons of Levi, and purge them as gold and silver, that they may offer unto the Lord an offering in righteousness. Let us, therefore, as a church and a people, and as Latter-day Saints, offer unto the Lord an offering in righteousness; and let us present in his holy temple, when it is finished, a book containing the records of our dead, which shall be worthy of all acceptation. (D&C 128:24)

So the offering that'll prepare me for the Second Coming will be the temple work I've done to seal my extended family together. "For behold," explained Malachi, "the day cometh, that shall burn as an oven; and all the proud, yea, and all that do wickedly, shall be stubble: and the day that cometh shall burn them up, saith the Lord of hosts, that it shall leave them neither root nor branch" (Malachi 4:1). The wicked who are burned at the Savior's return are those who have neither roots (ancestors) nor branches (descendants) because they haven't been sealed to them in the temple. Family history and temple work are great preparations for His Second Coming.

Christ taught His disciples two powerful parables about preparing for the Second Coming. One was the marriage of the king's son. In this parable, to be prepared for the feast, you had to be wearing a wedding garment. One of the king's guests was found without the wedding garment and was cast out of the party. The feast is the Second Coming, and the wedding garment is the temple garment. Many are "called" (invited to come) but few are "chosen" (making and keeping temple covenants). The chosen are the ones who'll be prepared (see Matthew 22:1–14). How many will be ready? That's where the other parable comes in.

In the parable of the ten virgins, the wedding feast is again the symbol of the Second Coming. All were invited, but only five had enough oil in their lamps to keep them burning when the bridegroom arrived (see Matthew 25:1–13). The ten virgins represent the members of the Church. President Spencer W. Kimball used this parable to teach that, when the Savior returns, only half of the Church will be ready for Him.[14] Ask your bishop about it. In any given ward, how many are active temple worshippers? About half.[15]

So should we load our shotguns and hunker down for Armageddon? That'd be a mistake and a tragedy, because it'd miss the whole point.

The point is to build our families and Zion while we work on purifying our hearts. President Boyd K. Packer taught this to the youth in general conference: "Everything that I have learned from the revelations and from life convinces me that there is time and to spare for you to carefully prepare for a long life. One day you will cope with teenage children of your own. That will serve you right. Later, you will spoil your grandchildren, and they in turn spoil theirs. If an earlier end should happen to come to one, that is more reason to do things right."[16] But there's no need to get overly worked up about all this.

The Great and Dreadful Day

Every time we have a lesson in seminary or institute on the signs of the Second Coming, my students share the same two emotions: excitement and fear. It *is* exciting. Christ is coming back. But why are we afraid? "You also shall hear of wars, and rumors of wars; see that ye be not troubled" (Joseph Smith—Matthew 1:23). The Lord tells us about what's going to happen precisely so we won't have to be afraid. We'll know exactly what's going on and see each sign as bringing us one step closer to the Savior's glorious return. The great and dreadful day of the Lord is only dreadful for the wicked. For the righteous, it's glorious.

In December 2010, the historic Provo Tabernacle burned to the ground. When the destruction was over, nothing remained except the badly damaged outer walls of the building. Virtually everything inside burned to ashes. An original Minerva Teichert painting (worth three quarters of a million dollars) was completely destroyed in the flames. As the firemen were rummaging through the charred remains, they uncovered one of the few things that even partially survived the razing: a painting of the Second Coming. The entire painting was charred black except for a thin outline around the figure of Christ in the center.[17] It's difficult to look at photos of the near-complete destruction of the building and compare them with the saved image of the resurrected Lord returning in glory and not to wonder at the potential symbolism.

Throughout the ages, the prophets have foretold truly remarkable—nearly impossible—things to come before Christ's triumphal return. Yet the only question we really need to answer is this: Did

Christ actually, literally rise from the tomb two thousand years ago with a resurrected body? If He did, then that's the greatest miracle that ever has or will occur, and with God nothing shall be impossible. If He didn't, then the entire gospel message is lost in mere symbolism and metaphor, and the world and our future are pretty much just what the scientists tell us it is, so the only thing we really need to worry about is global warming. The testimony of fifteen men whom we sustain as prophets, seers, and revelators is that Christ really did rise from the dead and that He really is coming back with all the promised bells and whistles. That's my witness as well.

Facing Death and the Meaning of Life

"What you see with your eyes shut is what counts."[1]

—John Lame Deer

Not long ago, one of my fourteen-year-old students was dealt a devastating blow. Her father—her best friend in the world—died of a heart attack at age of fifty-five. Of course, the first question many wanted to ask was how God could allow this kind of heartbreaking tragedy to occur if He truly loves us and wants us to be happy. But after wrestling with the age-old problem of evil for a while, there's an even bigger question that sometimes haunts us: Is there really something more, or does death actually end it all?

Most of us don't like to talk much about death, and we certainly don't like to contemplate our own demise. I think it plain scares us. For all our professed religious beliefs, when it comes right down to it, many of us are still terrified at times of the possibility that this life is all there is. As one author wrote, "Though all men have to suffer death, like children at a party we all hate going to bed."[2] And so we lose ourselves in the fun and frenzy of the moment and try not to think about the reality awaiting us at the end of the day.

The Prophet Joseph Smith taught us a different approach to the subject. He said,

> All men know that they must die. And it is important that we should understand the reasons and causes of our exposure to the vicissitudes

> of life and of death, and the designs and purposes of God in our coming into the world, our sufferings here, and our departure hence. What is the object of our coming into existence, then dying and falling away, to be here no more? It is but reasonable to suppose that God would reveal something in reference to the matter, and it is a subject we ought to study more than any other. We ought to study it day and night, for the world is ignorant in reference to their true condition and relation. If we have any claim on our Heavenly Father for anything, it is for knowledge on this important subject.[3]

Wow! Most of us prefer to hide from death as much as possible and perhaps think about it only at an occasional funeral. But the Prophet said we should study this topic more than any other; we should study it day and night.

Why would he say that? Is it because death is an essential part of the plan? Could it be that, in some sense, death *is* the plan? Nephi called it "the great and eternal plan of deliverance from death" (2 Nephi 11:5). Perhaps it's death alone (through the Atonement) that gives meaning to life.

Immortality

For thousands of years, people have entertained the idea of living forever in mortality. In literature and film, quests for the Holy Grail or the Fountain of Youth symbolize this yearning to never die. But as much as we cleave to life like a child clinging to his or her sucker at bedtime, if we thought it through, would we ever really want endless mortality?

The movie *Tuck Everlasting*, based on a book of the same name, addresses this issue. The Tuck family discovers a spring of water that affords everlasting life to anyone who drinks from it. They're freed from aging, suffering, and dying. They spend their endless time traveling the world and seeing the sites. But the story shows the Tucks as being cursed by their immortality. It robs them of the significance of love, suffering, pain, growth, and hope. Father Tuck explains that what they have isn't everlasting life, but mere continuous existence: "There's no living without dying. Don't be afraid of death. . . . Be afraid of the unlived life." Later, he clarifies what he's learned, "You don't have to live forever; you just have to live." In the end, the smart ones are the ones who refuse to drink from the fountain and accept their mortality and all that comes with it.[4]

Another movie that teaches the value of death is *Shadowlands*. It's based on the true story of C. S. Lewis and his unusual romance and marriage with Joy Gresham. After finally embracing love and marriage late in life, Lewis has to come to grips with Joy's terminal cancer and impending death. Lewis spent his career teaching the purpose of suffering in mortality. But now he runs headfirst into the tragedy he has spent his life trying to make sense of theoretically. He is devastated. It's up to Joy to help him realize that "the pain then is part of the happiness now. That's the deal." The suffering we experience in losing a loved one is an essential element for the joy of our relationship with them in the present. As Lehi put it to his son Jacob, "There [must needs be] an opposition in all things" (2 Nephi 2:11). Though Lewis would prefer for all things, including their love, to simply go indefinitely "unpicked—like a bud," it's only the probability of Joy's imminent death that allows Lewis to appreciate what he has now with her and embrace it. It's the reality of our impending death that gives meaning and urgency to what we do now.[5]

If endless mortality would ultimately lead to boredom and meaninglessness, wouldn't we also get bored in eternity? Someone once said, "Eternity is very long, especially near the end."[6] Joseph Smith tried to reassure us that boredom won't be an issue: "That same sociality which exists among us here will exist among us there, only it will be coupled with eternal glory, which glory we do not now enjoy" (D&C 130:2). So if I took the best day I've ever experienced with family and friends and magnified it a hundred times, I'd barely begin to get a glimpse of what eternity will be like. But I still find that terribly hard to do, so the Lord reassures me that "eye hath not seen, nor ear heard, neither have entered into the heart of man, the things which God hath prepared for them that love him" (1 Corinthians 2:9). Somehow, I just have to trust the Lord when He says that He isn't bored.

What does the Lord do with His time? "For behold, this is my work and my glory—to bring to pass the immortality and eternal life of man" (Moses 1:39). God spends all His time helping us to become like Him, to enjoy the kind of life He enjoys. But then what? What will He do when we reach that? He said that He works for "their exaltation in the eternal worlds, that they may bear the souls of men; for herein is the work of my Father continued, that he may be glorified" (D&C 132:63). In other words, to paraphrase my friend who just had his twenty-fifth grandchild, God wants to be a grandpa to our spirit children someday and watch the whole plan continue with them! So what do gods do? They have spirit children, teach them, and watch them grow to become gods themselves and continue the cycle. Anyone who has ever had a child and taught them to create something beautiful knows that the excitement and satisfaction of teaching your own to succeed is potentially endless.

Perhaps death truly is a gift to look forward to. "Adam fell [became mortal with the inevitability of death] that men might be; and men are, that they might have joy" (2 Nephi 2:25). We're born to die, and death is an intimate part of eternal joy. Those who would eliminate the pain, suffering, or finality of death perhaps don't understand the Lord's purposes in sending us to earth. "Now behold, it was not expedient that man should be reclaimed [exempted] from this temporal death, for that would destroy the great plan of happiness" (Alma 42:8). The key to accepting it, though, is to understand that it's merely temporal, or temporary.

Job's Question

Many hundreds of years ago, Job struggled with the ultimate questions of death and the meaning of life. While Job was going through the loss of his fortune, the loss of his children, the deterioration of his physical health, and the rejection of family and friends, he began to wonder if life had any meaning left at all. He surmised that it all boils down to one question: "If a man die, shall he live again?" (Job 14:14). He'd somehow make sense of all the tragedies and sufferings of mortality if he could just be sure that this life of tears isn't all there is. There has to be something more or this life is just a waste.

The interesting thing to me about Job's question is that he apparently already had what we'd call a testimony of the Savior, the plan of happiness, the resurrection of the body, and life after death. He said, "I know that my redeemer liveth, and that he shall stand at the latter day upon the earth: and though after my skin worms destroy this body, yet in my flesh shall I see God" (Job 19:25–26). Perhaps it's possible to have a testimony of the gospel plan and still ask at times if it really is all true.

In Job's case, all he needed was an answer from the Lord that He was there and He cared about Job's plight. By the end of the story, God did answer him from the whirlwind and assured him that He's still in charge of the universe. That was enough for Job. He said, "I have heard of thee by the hearing of the ear: but now mine eye seeth thee" (Job 42:5). God's direct answer to Job's prayer assured him that God is real, that life has meaning despite all the unexplained suffering, and that there's an afterlife where all the injustices of this life will be straightened out. Three thousand years later, it all still comes down to the same ultimate question for us: Is there really something more than this life?

The American Dream

Times have changed a bit since Job's day. Our middle class American culture teaches quite persuasively what the meaning of life is now. You go to school to get good grades so you can go to more school and get a diploma. You get a diploma so you can get a good job, meaning a job that makes substantial amounts of money. You work hard for thirty or forty years so you can retire someday with a decent pension. Or better yet, you go into business for yourself so you can amass more wealth faster. Then you can enjoy the good life, which consists of nice cars, traveling to exotic places, eating at expensive restaurants, and lots of rest and relaxation. To be truly successful is to retire early so you can enjoy a life of endless travel, entertainment, and pleasure for a longer time. It's as if we all want to be a member of the Tuck family.

But the good life would get boring by yourself. Somewhere along the way, you try marriage and family. Because half of all marriages fail, you don't bank too much on any one person. Still, it'll be nicer enjoying the good life someday if you have a companion to do it with and a few grandkids to visit. So after your career is firmly established, you get married sometime in your thirties and have your one boy and one girl. But because family life is so hard, you don't count on it working out and maintain your independence as much as possible.

You'll need it should you divorce and have to face life on your own again. Divorce isn't the ideal life; it's just reality, so you prepare for it and learn to deal with it. In the end, life is all about rugged individualism and survival of the fittest.

This contemporary version of the American Dream is the subconscious motivator that seems to inspire Americans to get out of bed in the morning. Yet there's something that seems so, well, futile about it.

There's a parable about a businessman visiting a small coastal village in Mexico. He sees a fisherman pulling his small fishing boat up to a little dock with his modest catch for the day. The businessman asks the little fisherman how long it took him to make his catch. The fisherman replies, "Not long, señor."

The businessman asks what the fisherman does with the rest of his time. "Oh, I sleep late, play with my children, take a siesta with my wife, then take a stroll to the village where I play guitar with my amigos in the evening."

The businessman says he has an MBA and could help the fisherman be more successful. If he spent more time fishing, he could save up and buy a bigger boat. He could then reinvest his bigger profits and eventually buy a whole fleet of boats. He could qualify for a loan that'd allow him to buy a cannery, which would allow him to control the product, processing, and distribution. Of course, he'd have to leave his little village and move to Mexico City, then to Los Angeles, and eventually to New York City where he would become a multimillionaire tycoon.

"And then what, señor?"

"Then you could retire and enjoy the good life. You could move to a tiny coastal village, sleep late, play with your children, take a siesta with your wife, and play the guitar with your amigos in the evening."[7]

Of course, many people wear out their lives climbing this ladder of success only to discover in the end that their ladder was leaning against the wrong wall. In the musical *Man of La Mancha*, Miguel de Cervantes discovers this tragedy. He says,

> I've been a soldier and a slave. I've seen my comrades fall in battle or die more slowly under the lash in Africa. I've held them in my arms at

> the final moment. These were men who saw life as it is, yet they died despairing. No glory, no brave last words, only their eyes, filled with confusion, questioning "Why?" I don't think they were wondering why they were dying, but why they had ever lived. When life itself seems lunatic, who knows where madness lies? To surrender dreams—this may be madness; to seek treasure where there is only trash. Too much sanity may be madness! But maddest of all—to see life as it is and not as it should be.[8]

Perhaps this is why we fear death so much. We're afraid that when we come to that point, all the things we've dedicated our lives to—the accumulation of degrees, money, houses, toys, and pleasure—won't mean anything. They'll amount to trash that we've discarded along the journey.

In the Savior's parable of the sower, it's our preoccupation with worldly "cares and riches and pleasures" that choke the life out of us and "bring no fruit to perfection" (Luke 8:14). James has a similar warning: "Go to now, ye that say, To day or to morrow we will go into such a city, and continue there a year, and buy and sell, and get gain: whereas ye know not what shall be on the morrow. For what is your life? It is even a vapour, that appeareth for a little time, and then vanisheth away" (James 4:13–14). Death has a way of erasing all the accolades of mortality. There's an Italian saying that "after the game, the king and the pawn go into the same box." So what callings we had in the Church, how much money we made, how big the house was—none of this will matter. As someone once quipped, "What honor is there in being the richest man in the cemetery?" In the end, neither our achievements nor our shortcomings will matter all that much.

What, then, is life's journey really all about?

The Practice for Death

Mahatma Gandhi said, "Each night, when I go to sleep, I die. And the next morning, when I wake up, I am reborn."[9] If life gives me anything, it gives me daily opportunities to practice for death. Every night as the sun goes down, I slip into bed and I get to ask myself, like we sing in the hymn, "Have I done any good in the world today?"[10] Then I get to wake up the next morning and try again. One of these days, I'm going to lie down in bed and I'm not going to wake up the next day. If I'm confident I'll wake up on the other side of the veil and I'm confident I've dedicated my life to the pursuit of things that matter most, then I'll be ready when that day comes.

For the ancient sage Socrates, philosophy was all about preparing for the ultimate. "Is not the love of Wisdom a practice of death?"[11] In the same dialogue, Socrates said that philosophy is the "art of dying well."[12] So true wisdom is recognizing that wealth, fame, and pleasure are mainly the distractions of this life from what really matters most, which is the treasure trove of love and learning we take with us and the legacy that we leave behind us when we go.

Elder Russell M. Nelson described our situation this way: "We live to die, and we die to live again."[13] As we come to trust the Lord in *this* life, He will take us by the hand, show us how to walk successfully through the challenges of mortality, and lead us gently into the next life. This process of death and rebirth is what the Father's plan is all about.

Because I'm going to die and the materialistic aspirations of life are going to fade away in significance, it makes sense to focus now on the things that matter most. In his classic book *Life After Life*, Raymond Moody interviewed hundreds of people who professed to have had near-death experiences. They clinically died, were somehow revived, and later described the experiences they had in the spirit world without a body. Many of them got to review their life in a kind of Judgment Day experience. When they did, there were only two questions that seemed to matter: How much have I learned? How much have I loved?[14]

For us, the ultimate role model of living life each day with one's own death always in view is Jesus Christ. In 2 Nephi 26:24, Nephi explained that Christ "doeth not anything save it be for the benefit of the world; for he loveth the world, even that he layeth down his own life that he may draw all men unto him." He draws us to Him by sacrificing His own life for our welfare. In 2 Nephi 31:20, Nephi said that we too must "press forward with a . . . love of God and of all men," and then we can enjoy a small piece of eternal life, or God's life. God's life is to be maximally involved in the welfare of others.

The author Charles Dickens wrote about this truth and claimed that it's epitomized in Christmas: "I have always thought of Christmas time . . . as a good time: a kind, forgiving, charitable, pleasant time: the only time I know of, in the long calendar of the year, when men and women seem by one consent to open their shut-up hearts freely, and to think of people below them as if they really were fellow-passengers to the grave, and not another race of creatures bound on other journeys."[15] So the question becomes, How do I treat others today—when it's not Christmastime—like fellow-passengers to the grave?

C. S. Lewis said, "It is a serious thing to live in a society of possible gods and goddesses, to remember that the dullest and most uninteresting person you talk to may one day be a creature which, if you saw it now, you would be strongly tempted to worship."[16] How can I learn to see that *my* journey really is little more than to help another on his or her journey? "He that findeth his life shall lose it: and he that loseth his life for my sake shall find it" (Matthew 10:39). When I start to see the purpose of mortality this way, I start to enjoy a taste of divine life in the here and now. It all depends on how I relate with people.

This emphasis on relationships was the focus of a general conference talk by President Dieter F. Uchtdorf entitled "Of Things That Matter Most." He said, "As we turn to our Heavenly Father and seek His wisdom regarding the things that matter most, we learn over and over again the importance of four key relationships: with our God, with our families, with our fellowman, and with ourselves."[17] Prayer, scripture study, and temple worship bring us closer to God. Family meals, family prayer and scripture study, family night, and family fun time bring us closer to our families. If we want to have our families forever, we ought to be working on creating relationships with them now that they'd want to continue in eternity. Service and sacrifice bring us closer to our fellowman. President Uchtdorf counseled us to refocus on these essentials: "Let us simplify our lives a little. Let us make the changes necessary to refocus our lives on the sublime beauty of the simple, humble path of Christian discipleship—the path that leads always toward a life of meaning, gladness, and peace."[18]

This path that President Uchtdorf described appears to be all about seeing today as the most important day of my life and seeing the person in front of me as the most important person in the world. As Anne Morrow Lindbergh wrote in her classic book *Gift from the Sea*, "The light shed by any good relationship illuminates all relationships. And one perfect day can give clues for a more perfect life."[19] Christ went about doing good in the moment with those He was with, and so can we—in simple ways. Then we won't fear death when it comes for us or our loved ones, regardless of the circumstances.

Attitude Determines Altitude

Whether death is a tragedy or a blessing may depend more on our attitude and approach to it than on the circumstances that surround it.

A few years ago, a young man, Tom, came into my class one Monday with an amazing glow about him. I shook his hand and asked how he was doing, and he replied that everything was fine. During the course of the lesson, I asked the class if anyone had seen anything they would count as a miracle lately. A few students responded, and then Tom meekly raised his hand. He said that his father had a brain aneurism that past weekend. He said it shook their family, but they saw the hand of the Lord and he knew everything was going to turn out for the best. As Tom left after class, I noticed that his countenance was radiating a peaceful light. I thanked him for his remarks and shook his hand good-bye.

I found out from another student later in the day that Tom's dad had died that weekend from the aneurism. Whatever happened, his family had seen the hand of the Lord *in* their father's sudden, unexpected death. Tom hadn't even mentioned that his dad didn't survive the experience. Apparently for Tom, that wasn't the point. They still knew the Lord was in charge. What for the world was a tragedy was a miracle for them—evidence that the Lord was working in their lives. I'll never forget that look on Tom's face. It wasn't one of resignation, but rather one of rejoicing! How can I exchange my fear or even reticent acceptance of death for this attitude of rejoicing in it?

Near-Death Experiences

Nearly a hundred years ago, a young man named Hugh Nibley was growing up in the Church. He was a precocious genius preparing to embark on a lifelong journey of discovering and writing about history and the gospel. But when the bottom fell out of his world with the onset of World War I, he sank into despair. He had to know if there really was a life after death. He could accept all he'd ever learned about the Father's plan if he could just somehow be sure that death didn't end everything.

Then Nibley went to a stake conference. The visiting authority was Matthew Cowley, an Apostle famous in the Church for being in tune with the Spirit and performing miracles. After the meeting, Elder Cowley approached Nibley (whom he'd never met) and said, "Come with me, young man." He took Nibley into a small room and gave him a blessing. In the blessing, he promised that the Lord would give him an answer to the troubles of his heart immediately.

Within forty-eight hours, Nibley was admitted to the hospital for an appendicitis attack. On the operating table, he swallowed his tongue and clinically died. He said later that when he died, he passed over to the spirit world and immediately began to bask in all his heightened senses and abilities. He was invigorated by the transformation and continued working on intellectual puzzles. The doctors eventually revived Nibley and he carried on with his life. But he had the answer to his question. He knew for himself that death wasn't the end, so he could dedicate his life to building up the kingdom of God through his studies.[20]

Another near-death experience recounted in the annals of Church history occurred in the life of nineteen-year-old Ella Jensen, niece of Lorenzo Snow. When Lorenzo Snow received his patriarchal blessing from Joseph Smith Sr., he was promised that he'd have the gift of healing and would even one day raise the dead. Then in 1891, when President Snow was president of the Quorum of the Twelve Apostles, the opportunity came. On March 9, he was speaking in the Brigham City Tabernacle when he was handed a note, informing him that his young niece Ella Jensen had just passed away two hours earlier. He immediately excused himself from the meeting and took Rudger Clawson, the stake president, with him. They rode on horseback to the Jensen home.

Upon arriving, they found many of the family still grieving over Ella's body. President Snow observed a moment and surprised everyone by asking if there was any consecrated oil in the house. Some was brought, and he had President Clawson anoint Ella's body. He then sealed the anointing and pronounced a blessing. In the prayer, he commanded in a loud voice for Ella's spirit to return to her body. He said that her mission in life wasn't complete and that she'd yet live to raise a large family and perform a great work. Then he excused himself and President Clawson to return to their meeting.

A short while later, Ella shocked the entire family as she opened her eyes. The first thing she did was ask where the man was who had called her back from that beautiful place. She went on to describe the peaceful circumstances of the spirit world. She saw many of her deceased loved ones there. She saw her aunt, Eliza R. Snow, teaching a Primary class to children who had all recently passed away. But she was surprised to see one young member of her own Sunday School class there, Alphie Snow. She didn't know that he'd passed away that morning before she did. The family hadn't told her for fear that it'd upset her. Ella Jensen went on to marry in the temple and raise a large family in the Church.[21]

These kinds of near-death experiences—abundant both in and out of the Church—are a witness that there's life beyond the grave. But there's even stronger evidence.

Evidence of Something More

One of the greatest witnesses we have of the reality of life after death is the temple. President Thomas S. Monson taught, "Each of our temples is an expression of our testimony that life beyond the grave is as real and as certain as is our life here on earth. I so testify."[22] The temple is the focal point connecting mortality and eternity. Many of our temples (including Mt. Timpanogos, Bountiful, Las Vegas, Portland, and Kirtland) utilize the symbol of the circle and the square in their architecture. The circle represents the dome of the heavens and the square represents the four cardinal directions of the earth. The temple is where heaven and earth come together.[23] Every time I enter the temple and feel the Spirit, the Lord is assuring me that there's life beyond the grave. Perhaps this is one reason the Lord wants me there as often as possible, for each time I go, my convictions are strengthened as to the purpose of this life and the reality of the next.

The Twelve Apostles provide another witness of the next life. They're called to be "special witnesses of the name of Christ in all the world"

(D&C 107:23). According to Joseph F. Smith, that special witness is significant. "These twelve disciples of Christ are supposed to be eye and ear witnesses of the divine mission of Jesus Christ." He continued, "That is their mission, to testify of Jesus Christ and Him crucified and risen from the dead and clothed now with almighty power at the right hand of God, the Savior of the world."[24] If Christ really is still alive—as the Apostles testify at just about every opportunity—then there is a life after death for my loved ones and me. Paul described the connection this way: "If in this life only we have hope in Christ, we are of all men most miserable. But now is Christ risen from the dead, and become the firstfruits of them that slept. For since by man came death, by man came also the resurrection of the dead. For as in Adam all die, even so in Christ shall all be made alive" (1 Corinthians 15:19–22). Every apostolic testimony that Christ lives is also, by implication, a testimony that there's a life after death for all of us.

A third witness of life after death is the testimony of the scriptures. Alma teaches his son Corianton that "concerning the state of the soul between death and the resurrection—Behold, it has been made known unto me by an angel, that the spirits of all men, as soon as they are departed from this mortal body, yea, the spirits of all men, whether they be good or evil, are taken home to that God who gave them life. And then shall it come to pass, that the spirits of those who are righteous are received into a state of happiness, which is called paradise, a state of rest, a state of peace, where they shall rest from all their troubles and from all care, and sorrow" (Alma 40:11–12). When we die, we go to the spirit world and await the resurrection. Alma learned that doctrine from an angel, no less.

Joseph F. Smith provided another scriptural witness of the reality of the afterlife in his vision of the redemption of the dead: "I beheld that the faithful elders of this dispensation, when they depart from mortal life, continue their labors in the preaching of the gospel of repentance and redemption, through the sacrifice of the Only Begotten Son of God, among those who are in darkness and under the bondage of sin in the great world of the spirits of the dead" (D&C 138:57). And Jacob taught, "For as death hath passed upon all men, to fulfil the merciful plan of the great Creator, there must needs be a power of resurrection," and "O how great the plan of our God! For on the other hand, the paradise of God must deliver up the spirits of the righteous, and the grave deliver up the body of the righteous; and the spirit and the body is restored to itself again, and all men become incorruptible, and immortal" (2 Nephi 9:6, 13).

Every time I read the scriptures and feel the Spirit, that's the Lord's way of telling me they're true. Indirectly, it's also a confirmation that there's more to life than molecules in motion. Our spirits really will survive death. Only in knowing this greatest of truths can I figure out how to live my life in the present (see Ecclesiastes 6:12).

My Mother's Journey

I learned some of my most significant lessons about death, mortality, and the meaning of life while watching my mother pass away.

At the end of 2009, Mom's health had been spiraling downward for weeks. Each time her condition seemed to hit bottom, she'd ask for a priesthood blessing and she'd rebound. But we all knew her miraculously extended life couldn't go on forever. This was her third bout with cancer and chemotherapy.

One Sunday, my wife and I took dinner over to Mom and Dad and hung out with them for a while. Mom seemed weaker and less coherent than usual, pale and frail. The customary sparkle was gone from her eye. Her liver had been shutting down for months. Her arms and legs had swollen up with fluid, and she was even "bleeding" fluid through lesions on her skin.

That evening, I spoke with my sister Shoni, who was working in Kansas at the time, and told her I thought we'd come to the time when we couldn't take a single moment with Mom for granted. I'm so grateful for the prompting to have that conversation. The next morning, Shoni spoke with her supervisors and explained that she had to leave her assignment and go to her dying mother immediately. They understood and helped her arrange for a flight on Thursday morning.

Around the same time Monday morning, Mom was trying unsuccessfully to make it up the stairs from their basement apartment to the main level above. She told Dad she needed to go to the hospital. That was unusual because she never wanted to go there.

With all her dozens and dozens of prior trips to the hospital, it was almost always Dad's idea. But I think somehow this time she knew it was her time and she was going to need medical help to say good-bye to her family. She was right.

After spending a considerable amount of time in the emergency room, they admitted her to intensive care on Monday night. I visited with her and Dad on Tuesday and Wednesday after work. I think Dad must've known they had finally come to the end as well because he "withdrew to his cave" both evenings and went home early, whereas in the past he had rarely left Mom's side for anything.

Wednesday night, I had my last real conversation with Mom. She looked at Dad and then at me and said, "I love you both. Tell all the kids I love them!" (The last time she talked coherently with my sister-in-law, she asked for a piece of her favorite lemon pie.) I asked the nurse, Carol, to call me during the night if her condition changed at all. Then I went home and collapsed.

Sometime around two in the morning, I was awakened suddenly with a jolt. I heard a voice sounding like Mom's that said, "Call Carol!" But I wasn't panicked. I simply realized in an instant that we were all about to embark on an amazing journey together. I knelt down at the side of my bed and poured out my soul quickly to Heavenly Father. I simply asked Him to be with Mom and to help us all through this experience I knew was about to occur.

I got off my knees and calmly went to the bathroom and put in my contacts. I realized I wasn't going to be thinking clearly, but I needed at least to *see* clearly. As I came out of the bathroom, the phone rang. It was Nurse Carol. Mom had indeed just taken a turn for the worse. Her heart was racing and Carol thought we ought to come. I called my brother and told him to wake Dad and meet me there. On the way to the hospital, I asked the Lord to help Mom hold on long enough for everyone to say good-bye.

As I entered her room, I could see that she was highly agitated and not doing well. I sat by her side and took her hand. I said, "Hi, Mom. It's Chad. How are you doing?" All of a sudden, the glassy, glazed look in her eyes disappeared. The sparkle returned. She smiled, leaned forward, and declared loud and clear: "Grrreat!" Then she sank back down on her bed in pain. I tried to think of something

I could do to ease her suffering. So I started to sing her a song. But she quickly shook her head vehemently, expressing her desire that I cease and desist. I guessed my singing was adding to her pain. (Later, my sister said she was confident that Mom simply wasn't ready to say good-bye yet.)

Finally, my dad and brother arrived. The doctors were frantically trying to get her heart rate under control as she was flailing her arms in distress. We administered to her and promised her rest until she could say good-bye in her own way to all the family. Almost immediately, she went to sleep and rested peacefully until the end when she woke up to say good-bye.

My wife and sister-in-law brought the grandkids over to give their love. We called my brother in North Carolina so he could say good-bye and express his love. Mom mouthed words in response to his expressions, obviously recognizing him to some degree. The biggest concern was that Mom would stay around long enough for Shoni to arrive. She would've been devastated if she hadn't been able to say good-bye.

Shoni was able to leave her job amicably and arranged a flight out of Kansas City early Thursday morning. But she had to race through a blizzard going nearly seventy miles per hour for two and a half hours to make her flight. Several of the surrounding flights were canceled due to the weather, but hers miraculously made it out through the storm. She arrived at the Salt Lake airport and retrieved her bags, but my wife, Stacy, who was picking her up, was stuck in traffic. Knowing that her mother was dying in a distant hospital, Shoni couldn't do anything but pray and weep.

A woman—the only other person left in the baggage claim area—approached Shoni and asked if she could be of assistance. Shoni explained her dilemma and was amazed to discover that this woman from out of state was actually headed to the hospital where Mom was and she offered Shoni a ride. Stacy continued to the airport, retrieved Shoni's bags, and turned around and zipped back to the hospital.

Those last three hours with Mom were an amazing time of family bonding. We started out singing hymns, but Shoni decided we sounded too much like a funeral dirge already. So we switched to Neal Diamond and John Denver songs. We sang "Sweet Caroline" and "Take Me Home, Country Roads." Then we concluded with Mom's favorite song, "Amazing Grace." Music seems so essential in expressing the emotions that matter in life.

We consulted each other about artificial life support. Each of us expressed our independent feelings that she didn't want to be artificially kept alive for long. Then Dad made the final decision to let her go. From the moment he made that decision, I saw the Spirit rest with him. It was with us all so indelibly that morning. We asked the doctor to remove the oxygen mask and cut off the life-sustaining medications. I'm sure Mom was relieved we finally took off that mask. She was claustrophobic and hated it. At one point, she even slugged Nurse Carol for trying to put it back on!

Mom regained consciousness at the end for a little over an hour. We all got to say good-bye. We gave her one more blessing that she could depart now in peace. The doctor had explained that she could potentially last several days without her oxygen and medications, and we didn't want that. We were relieved when at 11:30 a.m. on Thursday, January 7, 2010, Mom finally slipped away in peace. We all cried, of course. It was the only time I ever remember seeing my Dad cry. But there was such a powerful spirit of peace and love in that room. I felt like I did in the temple the day I married Stacy. Time stood still and heaven was near. Perhaps there were angels among us.

My sister and I felt Mom's influence that entire weekend as we made arrangements for her burial and planned her funeral. I'll mention just one experience. As I sat down to write her obituary, I began with the intention of simply following the traditional outline. But the moment I started typing, I was led in a different direction. I wrote it in the first person, using Mom's optimistic, enthusiastic voice. It was as if Mom herself directed the words. It became an expression of her testimony and love of life and the family. She was one of the most Christlike people I've ever known—full of optimism, compassion, affection, faith, and dedication to a life of service. Many people later commented on how strongly her obituary affected them. Even in death, Mom was doing missionary work.

The funeral, burial, and few days we all spent together were filled with reminiscing about Mom, reenacting family traditions, and powerful, love-charged family bonding. Other than when Stacy and I were married, this was undoubtedly the most spiritually energizing week of my life. And from beginning to end, the only thoughts that any of us had were centered around the family. Surely, death teaches us that family is what life is all about.

I know that not everyone has such reassuring, faith-promoting experiences connected with their loss of loved ones. But my experience reconfirmed to me the reality of life after death and the central role of family love as the meaning of life. And even for those whose earthly family relationships have failed, what's left is a hope that there really is something more in the next life. There also remains the hope that, as Joseph Smith promised, if we endure to the end no matter how bitter that journey might be, "all our losses will be made up in the resurrection."[25]

At the End

What would I do today if somehow I knew that it'd be my last day on earth? Would I ride a bull named Fu Man Chu and try skydiving, as in the popular country song by Tim McGraw? Probably not. I think I'd read a little. I'd write a little in my journal. I'd try thanking loved ones around me for their kind attention. If I still had the strength, I'd sing and dance with my wife and children. I think I'd fast most of the day and perhaps eat one more simple meal of cucumbers and tomatoes out of my garden, trying to appreciate the tastes of each bite. None of the things I think I'd do would require much money. Paul said, "Having food and raiment let us be therewith content" (1 Timothy 6:8). I think I might ask my family to engrave something simple on my tombstone like, "See you on the other side."

But there's still something a tiny bit narcissistic about living every day as if it were going to be my last. A comic strip shows a businessman arriving at his office cubicle in his birthday suit, holding a briefcase in one hand and a coffee cup in the other. He says nonchalantly to his coworker, "If I'm going to live every day as if it were my last, why waste time doing laundry?" Even more important than to act as if it were going to be the last day of *my* life is to act as if it were going to be the last day for those whom I meet. Og Mandino expressed this principle clearly when he said, "Beginning today, treat everyone you meet as if they were going to be dead by midnight. Extend to them all the care, kindness, and understanding you can muster, and do it with no thought of any reward. Your life will never be the same again."[26] But am I going to wait until I'm old and gray and too tired to continue zipping up whatever ladder of success I'm on before I learn this lesson? President Uchtdorf warned, "I pray that we will not wait until we are ready to die before we truly learn to live."[27]

When my mother was thirteen, one evening she had a terrible altercation with her mother. Her last words to her mom before she went to bed were an angry "I hate your guts!" That night around midnight, her mother had a heart attack and passed away. Mom regretted that tragic last encounter for decades, but she learned her lesson. The rest of her life, she always seemed to treat people as if her only concern in the world was to care for their needs today because she might never get the chance again.

I'm not as afraid of death as I once was. I'm grateful now for the lessons it's taught me: To treasure each moment as if it were our last together. To focus on relationships with family and friends. To learn all that I can. To never leave undone an act of service that's within my reach. To leave something of lasting value for those who come after me. If the skeptics were right and death ended all, I would've at least met it meaningfully. But my conviction is that there is more—so much more. And I *will* see you on the other side!

Concluding Thoughts

I'm impressed that you've made it this far in my book. I couldn't even get my mother-in-law to read the whole thing, and she has as much charity and patience for me as anyone. I hope you understand that I don't propose to have answered all the questions I've addressed. I've tried to share some of my thinking and experiences pertaining to relevant topics for thoughtful Latter-day Saints. But living a life of faith is *not* dependent on having all the answers—even to the most pertinent issues.

While any thoughtful member of the Church can stumble upon curious questions that deserve at least some attempt at partial answers, sometimes doubt can be used as justification for not acting. The Protestant theologian and martyr Dietrich Bonhoeffer wrote, "Keep on posing problems, and you will escape the necessity of obedience."[1] And yet it's precisely in obedience to gospel principles that our hope lies.

President Harold B. Lee explained this truth: "It is not the function of religion to answer all the questions about God's moral government of the universe, but to give one courage, through faith, to go on in the face of questions he never finds the answer to in his present status."[2] And Elder David A. Bednar stated, "Devoted discipleship is the best and only answer to every question and challenge."[3] What I've tried to do in this book is merely help gospel seekers carry on the quest of discipleship in the face of imperfectly answered questions.

I've come to realize that discovering a testimony isn't an event that just occurs and establishes our gospel-based path for the rest of our lives. It is more like the ongoing result of staying the course. Christ said, "If any man will do his will, he shall know of the doctrine, whether it be of God, or whether I speak of myself" (John 7:17). We just need to try living life His way and we'll eventually discover that it really is the best way.

But that isn't the sort of answer we want. We desperately want some sign that we're going to be on the right path before we muster up the strength for the journey. The Lord doesn't make any such guarantees ahead of time. The signs come only along the road. That means we must be up and about our business. Heber J. Grant put it this way: "There is but one path of safety to the Latter-day Saints, and that is the path of duty. It is not a testimony, it is not marvelous manifestations, it is not knowing that the Gospel of Jesus Christ is true, that it is the plan of salvation. It is not actually knowing that the Savior is the Redeemer, and that Joseph Smith was his prophet, that will save you and me, but it is the keeping of the commandments of God, the living the life of a Latter-day Saint."[4] Strong testimony isn't going to save us. Christ alone can save. He does it as we do what He's asked us to do. This is the interactive journey of conversion.

As I've pointed out earlier, this doesn't mean that we have to follow blindly. Because we've felt of the Savior's love in the past, we can trust Him in the present and hope firmly in His promises to take care of our future. As Elder Bruce C. Hafen quoted Gilbert K. Chesterton as saying, "Love is not blind; that is the last thing that it is. Love is bound; and the more it is bound the less it is blind."[5] As our loyalty and faithfulness to the Savior grows, our capacity to see and understand His plan increases proportionately.

As long as we stay on that path of duty, there'll certainly be signposts that we're headed in the right direction. The presence of the Holy Ghost in our lives is the Lord's way of indicating that we're on the path. The prophet Isaiah said, "And thine ears shall hear a word behind thee, saying, This is the way, walk ye in it, when ye turn to the right hand, and when ye turn to the left" (Isaiah 30:21). If we feast on the scriptures and the teachings of the modern prophets, we'll learn the tongue of angels, which is the language of the Spirit.

Then, as we act on the gospel message and find ourselves in need of help, the voice of the Spirit will give us the direction we seek—or at least enough to keep us moving forward. The more we act on those promptings, the more we'll come to see the Lord working in our lives, helping us to succeed at times and to carry on in spite of failing at other times. Those promptings from the Spirit are the tokens along the way that we're still on the right track.

When Brigham Young took over as head of the Church after Joseph's death, he had the daunting task of leading thousands of Saints to their promised land. After trudging through the mud plains of Iowa and waiting for spring in the bitter cold Winter Quarters of Nebraska, Brigham was a bit discouraged. He took ill. One night, he became so sick that he actually died and his spirit left his body. He went to the spirit world and conversed with Joseph and Hyrum, but then he was sent back. The next morning, he couldn't recall any of the instruction he learned from his near-death experience and wanted desperately to remember.

The next night, he had a dream. In the dream (which he called a vision), he saw Joseph Smith. He begged Joseph to come lead the Saints to the promised land. Joseph said his mission was done and now it was Brigham's turn to lead the Saints. Brigham pleaded with Joseph to come preach one last sermon to the people to encourage them on their difficult journey. Joseph said he was too busy in the spirit world and Brigham would have to do the preaching now. Brigham then asked Joseph at least to tell him what to teach the Saints that'd help them make it through. Finally, Joseph consented. He said to teach the Saints to get the Spirit in their lives. They could overcome any challenge with the Holy Ghost as their guide.[6]

Brigham squared his shoulders and went to work. He led the Saints across the plains and spent the next thirty years of his ministry trying to do just what Joseph had told him—to teach the Saints how to stay on the gospel path by following the Spirit.

Any journey that isn't merely aesthetic has an objective. The prophetic promise is that one day all our diligent seeking will be rewarded with a glorious discovery: "And though the Lord give you the bread of adversity, and the water of affliction, yet shall not thy teachers be removed into a corner any more, but thine eyes shall see thy [teacher]" (Isaiah 30:20, footnote b). The great and last promise is that one day—in this life or the next—we'll see the Savior and rejoice in His presence. By staying on the path He's taught us, we will have become like Him and be ready to enjoy His permanent companionship. Then, at last, every question will be answered in Him. Or at least, we'll have the perfect guide for our continued quest. "Lord, I believe; help thou mine unbelief" (Mark 9:24).

Endnotes

Introduction

1. Jeffrey R. Holland, "Lord, I Believe," *Ensign*, May 2013, 94.
2. Dieter F. Uchtdorf, "Come, Join with Us," *Ensign*, November 2013, 23.
3. "Doubt," *The Compact Edition of the Oxford English Dictionary* (Oxford: Oxford University Press, 1971), 791.

Chapter 1

1. Carmella B'Hahn, "Be the Change You Wish to See: An Interview with Arun Gandhi," *Reclaiming Children and Youth*. Vol. 10, No. 1 (Spring 2001), 6. The authenticity of this quotation attributed to Gandhi by his grandson has been questioned, but if he didn't say those exact words, he certainly taught the principle.
2. Marvin J. Ashton, "The Tongue Can Be a Sharp Sword," *Ensign*, May 1992, 19.
3. Eugene England, *Why the Church Is as True as the Gospel* (Salt Lake City: Bookcraft, 1986).
4. Joseph Smith Jr., *Teachings of the Prophet Joseph Smith*, ed. Joseph Fielding Smith (Deseret Book: Salt Lake City, 1976), 183.

5. Martin Buber, *I and Thou* (New York: Scribner, 1987).
6. Thomas S. Monson, "Charity Never Faileth," *Ensign*, November 2010, 124.
7. Ibid., 122.
8. Boyd K. Packer, "The Choice," *Ensign*, November 1980, 21.
9. Dieter F. Uchtdorf, "Come, Join with Us," *Ensign*, November 2013, 23.

Chapter 2

1. William James was quoting Fitz-James Stephen in James's essay, "The Will to Believe," in Robert Paul Wolff, *Ten Great Works of Philosophy* (New York: Penguin Books), 480.
2. Dennis Rasmussen, *The Lord's Question: A Call to Come unto Him* (Provo: Keter Foundation), 4.
3. Martin Buber, *I and Thou* (New York: Scribner, 1987), 115.
4. Henry B. Eyring, "Trust in God, Then Go and Do," *Ensign*, November 2010, 73.
5. Howard W. Hunter, "Standing as Witnesses of God," *Ensign*, May 1990, 60.
6. Larry Kacher, "Trifle Not with Sacred Things," *Ensign*, November 2014, 105.
7. Howard W. Hunter, Conference Report, October 1960, 108.
8. Neil L. Andersen, "It's True, Isn't it? Then What Else Matters?" *Ensign*, May 2007, 74.
9. Richard G. Scott, "The Transforming Power of Faith and Character," *Ensign*, November 2010, 45.
10. Neil L. Andersen, "Never Leave Him," *Ensign*, November 2010, 41.
11. Richard Edgley, "Faith—the Choice Is Yours," *Ensign*, November 2010, 32; italics in original.
12. See Henry B. Eyring, "A Living Testimony," *Ensign*, May 2011, 127–28.

13. Jeffrey R. Holland, "Lord, I Believe," *Ensign*, May 2013, 94.
14. See, for example, Spencer W. Kimball, "Circles of Exaltation," address to religious educators, Brigham Young University, June 28, 1968, 8.
15. Parker Palmer addressed truth as "re-membering" as opposed to "dis-membering" in *To Know as We Are Known: Education as a Spiritual Journey* (San Francisco: Harper Collins Publishers, 1993), 103.
16. Edward Connery Lathem, ed., "A Masque of Mercy," *The Poetry of Robert Frost*, (New York: Holt Rinehart and Winston, 1969), 520; lines 716–25.

Chapter 3

1. "Talk: Habit (psychology)," *Wikiquote*, accessed February 27, 2015, http://en.wikiquote.org/wiki/Talk:Habit_%28psychology%29.
2. Mark Twain, *Roughing It* (NP: Providence Books, 2013), 76.
3. Boyd K. Packer, "Teach the Scriptures," *Charge to Religious Educators*, Third Edition (Salt Lake City: Church Educational System, 1994), 87.
4. David A. Bednar, "A Reservoir of Living Water," CES fireside for young adults, Febuary 4, 2007.
5. Henry B. Eyring, "Serve with the Spirit," *Ensign*, November 2010, 60.
6. Cheryl C. Lant, "My Soul Delighteth in the Scriptures," *Ensign*, November 2005, 76–78.
7. I realize the original context of this passage is slightly different than the way it reads in our current version of the scriptures. (See "Doctrine and Covenants/Oliver Cowdery and the 'rod of nature' " Fair Mormon Answers, accessed February 27, 2015, http://en.fairmormon.org/Doctrine_and_Covenants/Oliver_Cowdery_and_the_%22rod_of_nature%22). I have chosen to use the passage as it currently reads in our standard works.

Whether referring to a rod or a stone, the gift of Aaron was the ability to use a divinely approved object to assist in receiving revelation. The Lord through His prophets can and sometimes does change the official wording of printed revelations to apply them to more universal contexts than their original settings.

8. Dallin H. Oaks, "Scripture Reading and Revelation," *Ensign*, January 1995, 8.
9. Brigham Young, *Discourses of Brigham Young*, ed. John A. Widtsoe (Salt Lake City: Deseret Book, 1941), 243.
10. Vaughn J. Featherstone, "The Aaronic Priesthood Holder and Athletics," *New Era*, September 1975, 28.
11. Sheri L. Dew, *Women and the Priesthood* (Salt Lake City: Deseret Book, 2013), 158.
12. Austin Farrer, "The Christian Apologist," in *Light on C. S. Lewis*, ed. Jocelyn Gibb (New York: Harcourt, Brace & World, 1965), 26; as quoted in Dallin H. Oaks, "The Historicity of the Book of Mormon," *Historicity and the Latter-day Saint Scriptures,* ed. Paul Y. Hoskisson (Provo, Utah: Religious Studies Center, 2001), 238.
13. Brent Lee Metcalfe, ed., *New Approaches to the Book of Mormon: Explorations in Critical Methodology* (Salt Lake City: Signature Books, 1993).
14. *Review of Books on the Book of Mormon*, Vol. 6, n. 1, 1994 (Provo: Foundation for Ancient Research and Mormon Studies, 1994).
15. William James, *Pragmatism*, ed. Bruce Kuklick (Indianapolis: Hackett Publishing Company, 1981), 8.
16. James E. Faulconer, "Scripture as Incarnation," in *Historicity and the Latter-day Saint Scriptures,* ed. Paul Y. Hoskisson (Provo, Utah: Religious Studies Center, 2001), 17–61.
17. John W. Welch, "A Masterpiece: Alma 36" in *Rediscovering the Book of Mormon*, John L. Sorenson and Melvin J. Thorne, editors (Salt Lake City: FARMS and Deseret Book, 1991), 100–13.

18. Donald Parry, *The Book of Mormon Text Reformatted According to Parallelistic Patterns* (Provo, Utah: The Foundation for Ancient Research and Mormon Studies, 1992).
19. There are at least fifteen references to snow in the Old Testament before 600 BC, when Lehi's family left Jerusalem.
20. Jeffrey R. Holland, "Lord, I Believe," *Ensign*, May 2013, 94.
21. Ibid.
22. "President Kimball Speaks Out on Personal Journals," *Ensign*, December 1980, 61.
23. Joseph Smith Jr., *Teachings of the Prophet Joseph Smith*, ed. Joseph Fielding Smith (Deseret Book: Salt Lake City, 1976), 73.
24. Oliver B. Huntington in *The Young Women's Journal* 2:466, May 1891. Also in Hyrum L. Andrus and Helen Mae Andrus, *They Knew the Prophet* (Salt Lake City: Bookcraft, 1974), 65.

Chapter 4

1. Alice Calaprice, ed. *The Expanded Quotable Einstein* (Princeton: Princeton University Press, 2005), 319.
2. Eugene E. Campbell and Richard D. Poll, *Hugh B. Brown: His Life and Thought* (Salt Lake City: Bookcraft, 1975), 196.
3. Howard W. Hunter, Conference Report, October 1960, 108.
4. "Miracles," Bible Dictionary, The Holy Bible (Salt Lake City: The Church of Jesus Christ of Latter-day Saints, 1979), 732.
5. David Hume, *An Inquiry Concerning Human Understanding*, published in 1758, Section X, parts 1–2 in Robert Paul Wolff, ed., *Ten Great Works of Philosophy* (New York: Mentor, 1969), 254–72.
6. Richard L. Anderson, *Investigating the Book of Mormon Witnesses* (Salt Lake City: Deseret Book, 1981).
7. Howard W. Hunter, Conference Report, April, 1987, 19–20.

8. Spencer W. Kimball, Conference Report, April 1978, 48.

9. Gordon B. Hinckley, "Testimony," *Ensign*, May 1998, 71.

10. Boyd K. Packer, "The Witness," *Ensign*, May 2014.

11. Daniel H. Ludlow, ed., *Encyclopedia of Mormonism*, Vol. 2 (New York: Macmillan Publishing Company, 1992), 446–47.

12. Spencer W. Kimball, "The Significance of Miracles in the Church Today," *Instructor*, December 1959, 396. See also Dallin H. Oaks, "Miracles," *Ensign*, June 2001, 9.

13. Spencer W. Kimball, *Faith Precedes the Miracle* (Salt Lake City: Deseret Book Company, 1972).

14. Edward L. and Andrew E. Kimball Jr., *Spencer W. Kimball, Twelfth President of The Church of Jesus Christ of Latter-day Saints* (Salt Lake City: Bookcraft, 1977), 260.

15. *Church History in the Fulness of Times* (Salt Lake City: The Church of Jesus Christ of Latter-day Saints, 1989), 113–14.

16. David A. Bednar, "The Spirit of Revelation," *Ensign*, May 2011, 89.

17. C. S. Lewis, *The Weight of Glory and Other Addresses* (New York: Macmillan, 1980), 142.

18. Dennis Rasmussen, *The Lord's Question: A Call to Come unto Him* (Provo: Keter Foundation), 27–28.

19. Brent Hafen, et. al., *Behavioral Guidelines for Health and Wellness*, First Edition (Englewood: Morton Publishers, 1988), 36.

20. Elizabeth Maki, " 'A People Prepared': West African Pioneer Preached the Gospel Before Missionaries" *Pioneers in Every Land*, The Church of Jesus Christ of Latter-day Saints, created April 21, 2013, accessed February 27, 2015, https://history.lds.org/article/ghana-pioneer-jwb-johnson?lang=eng; In chapter eight, I discuss more about Joseph Johnson.

21. Rodolfo Acevedo, "President Hinckley in Chile marks largest LDS gathering; Chilean members eagerly greet President Hinckley," *Church News*, Saturday, May 8, 1999.

22. Robert D. Hales, "The Covenant of Baptism: To Be in the Kingdom and of the Kingdom," *Ensign*, November 2000, 6.
23. Joseph Fielding Smith, *Teachings of the Prophet Joseph Smith* (Deseret Book: Salt Lake City, 1976), 137.
24. Elizabeth Barret Browning, from "Aurora Leigh," Book VII, I, lines 821–22. Accessed March 2, 2015, http://www.bartleby.com/236/86.html.
25. Boyd K. Packer, "The Aaronic Priesthood," *Ensign*, November 1981, 32.
26. Quoted in Ronald E. Poelman, "Divine Forgiveness," *Ensign*, November 1993, 85. See also Bruce R. McConkie, *The Mortal Messiah: From Bethlehem to Calvary,* 4 vols. (Salt Lake City: Deseret Book, 1980), 3:40–41, n. 1.

Chapter 5

1. Quoted in Glen Cleeton and Charles Wilkins Mason, *Executive Ability: Its Discovery and Development* (Yellow Springs, OH: The Antioch Press, 1946), 81.
2. William Shakespeare, *Twelfth Night*, act 1, scene 5, *The Collected Works of William Shakespeare* (New York: Crown Publishers, 1975), 76.
3. Gordon B. Hinckley, "Life's Obligations," *Ensign*, February 1999, 2.
4. George D. Watt, et al., *Journal of Discourses* (London: Latter-day Saints' Book Depot, 1855–86), 2:314.
5. Richard G. Scott, "To Acquire Spiritual Knowledge," *Ensign*, November 2009, 8.
6. Boyd K. Packer, "The Candle of the Lord," *Ensign*, January 1983, 56.
7. Spencer W. Kimball, "Marriage and Divorce," BYU Devotional, 1976, 5.
8. Joseph Smith Jr. *The Words of Joseph Smith: The Contemporary Accounts of the Nauvoo Discourses of the Prophet Joseph*, comp.

Andrew F. Ehat and Lyndon W. Cook (Provo: Brigham Young University Religious Studies Center, 1980), 183.

9. Boyd K. Packer, *Eternal Love*, (Salt Lake City: Deseret Book, 1973), 11.

10. Bruce R. McConkie, "Agency or Inspiration?" *New Era*, January 1975, 40.

11. In Wilburn Talbot, *The Acts of the Modern Apostles* (Springville, Utah: Cedar Fort, Inc., 1985), 323.

12. See John D. Claybaugh, "Dating: A Time to Become Best Friends," *Ensign*, April 1994, 21.

13. Randy Hall, "The Importance of Maintaining Balance," *A Current Teaching Emphasis for the Church Educational System: In Service Training Video*, 2003.

14. Boyd K. Packer, *That All May Be Edified* (Salt Lake City: Bookcraft, 1982), 333–34.

15. Robert D. Hales, *Return: Four Phases of Our Mortal Journey Home* (Salt Lake City: Deseret Book, 2010), 237–38.

16. M. Russell Ballard, "Fathers and Sons: A Remarkable Relationship," *Ensign*, November 2009, 50.

17. B. H. Roberts, ed., *History of the Church of Jesus Christ of Latter-day Saints,* 7 vols. (Salt Lake City: Deseret Book, 1902–12), 6:248.

18. Spencer W. Kimball, *The Teachings of Spencer W. Kimball*, ed. Edward L. Kimball (Salt Lake City: Deseret Book, 1982), 292.

19. Gordon B. Hinckley, "A Prophet's Counsel and Prayer for Youth," *Ensign*, January 2001.

20. Spencer W. Kimball, "The Importance of Celestial Marriage," *Ensign*, October 1979, 5.

21. James E. Talmage, *Jesus the Christ: A Study of the Messiah and His Mission according to Holy Scriptures both Ancient and Modern* (Salt Lake City: The Church of Jesus Christ of Latter-day Saints, 1981), 548.

22. Heber J. Grant, "Comforting Manifestations: Excerpts from Funeral Sermon Delivered Recently," *Improvement Era*, Vol. 34, no. 4, February 1931, 189–90.

23. For a discussion on keeping marriages together, see chapter five.

Chapter 6

1. Ogden Nash, "A Word to Husbands," *Marriage Lines: Notes of a Student Husband* (Boston: Little, Brown and Company, 1964), 79.

2. Sheri L. Dew, "Are We Not All Mothers?" *Ensign*, November 2001, 96.

3. David A. Bednar, "The Powers of Heaven," *Ensign*, May 2012, 51.

4. Boyd K. Packer, "The Aaronic Priesthood," *Ensign*, November 1981, 32.

5. Melissa Merrill, "Sister Beck Shares Lessons from Relief Society History," *Church News and Events*, created on May 4, 2011. Accessed March 2, 2015, http://www.lds.org/church/news/sister-julie-b-beck-shares-lessons-from-relief-society-history?lang=eng.

6. Valerie Cassler, "I Am a Mormon Because I Am a Feminist," *Mormon Scholars Testify*, posted September 2010. Accessed March 2, 2015, http://mormonscholarstestify.org/1718/valerie-hudson-cassler.

7. Sheri L. Dew, "It Is Not Good for Man or Woman to Be Alone," *Ensign*, November 2001, 12–14. In a general conference address, Elder Dallin H. Oaks went even further than Sister Dew to emphasize gender equality in the priesthood. He drew on teachings by President Joseph Fielding Smith to argue that women hold priesthood authority as well as priesthood power (in the temple, for example) and that it is only priesthood keys and offices that are limited to men. See Dallin H. Oaks, "The Keys and Authority of the Priesthood," *Ensign*, May 2014, 50.

8. Richard G. Scott, *21 Principles: Divine Truths to Help You Live by the Spirit* (Salt Lake City: Deseret Book, 2013), 70.

9. "O My Father," *Hymns of The Church of Jesus Christ of Latter-day Saints* (Salt Lake City: The Church of Jesus Christ of Latter-day Saints, 1985), 292.
10. Wilford Woodruff, *The Discourses of Wilford Woodruff*, edited by G. Homer Durham (Salt Lake City: Bookcraft, 1969), 62.
11. Brigham Young, *Discourses of Brigham Young*, ed. John A. Widtsoe (Salt Lake City: Deseret Book, 1941), 51.
12. Valerie Cassler, "I Am a Mormon Because I Am a Feminist," *Mormon Scholars Testify*, posted September 2010. Accessed March 2, 2015, http://mormonscholarstestify.org/1718/valerie-hudson-cassler.
13. Gordon B. Hinckley, "Daughters of God," *Ensign*, November 1991.
14. Peggy Fletcher Stack, "Excommunicated Mormon to Tell How She Came Back to the Faith," posted July 2012. Accessed March 2, 2015, http://www.sltrib.com/sltrib/lifestyle/54514350-80/church-excommunicated-faith-hanks.html.csp.
15. Douglas E. Brinley, ed., *Eternal Companions: Advice from LDS Counselors and Educators on Building a Forever Marriage* (Salt Lake City: Bookcraft, 1995), 18.

Chapter 7

1. B. H. Roberts, ed., *History of the Church of Jesus Christ of Latter-day Saints,* 7 vols. (Salt Lake City: Deseret Book, 1902–12), 6:317.
2. Brian C. Hales, *Joseph Smith's Polygamy*, 3 vols. (Salt Lake City: Greg Kofford Books, 2013), 1:105.
3. Ibid., 1:109.
4. Ibid., 1:118–23.
5. Ibid., 1:105.
6. Richard Lyman Bushman, *Joseph Smith: Rough Stone Rolling* (New York City: Alfred A. Knopf, 2005), 439.

7. Brian C. Hales, *Joseph Smith's Polygamy*, 3 vols. (Salt Lake City: Greg Kofford Books, 2013), 1:426.
8. Ibid., 1:428.
9. Ibid., 1:354.
10. Ibid., 2:8, 17–18.
11. Ibid., 2:3, 20, 47.
12. Ibid., 2:290–300.
13. Richard Lyman Bushman, *Joseph Smith: Rough Stone Rolling* (New York City: Alfred A. Knopf, 2005), 440.
14. Brian C. Hales, *Joseph Smith's Polygamy*, 3 vols. (Salt Lake City: Greg Kofford Books, 2013), 1:523–24.
15. Ibid., 2:226.
16. George D. Watt, et al., *Journal of Discourses* (London: Latter-day Saints' Book Depot, 1855–86), 3:266.
17. Brian C. Hales, *Joseph Smith's Polygamy*, 3 vols. (Salt Lake City: Greg Kofford Books, 2013), 1:237.
18. Ibid., 2:61.
19. Ibid., 2:142–43.
20. Ibid., 2:65–66.
21. Ibid., 2:79.
22. Linda King Newell and Valeen Tippetts Avery, *Emma Hale Smith: Mormon Enigma* (Champaign, Illinois: The University of Illinois Press, 1994), 171.
23. Brian C. Hales, *Joseph Smith's Polygamy*, 3 vols. (Salt Lake City: Greg Kofford Books, 2013), 2:64.
24. Ibid., 2:92.
25. Richard Lyman Bushman, *Joseph Smith: Rough Stone Rolling* (New York City: Alfred A. Knopf, 2005), 496.
26. Brian C. Hales, *Joseph Smith's Polygamy*, 3 vols. (Salt Lake City: Greg Kofford Books, 2013), 2:129.

27. Ibid., 2:258.

28. "Comparison of Community of Christ and the Church of Jesus Christ of Latter-day Saints," *Wikipedia*, accessed March 3, 2015, http://en.wikipedia.org/wiki/Comparison_of_Community_of_Christ_and_The_Church_of_Jesus_Christ_of_Latter-day_Saints. The Community of Christ doesn't have an official public statement about polygamy.

29. Gracia N. Jones, "My Great-Great-Grandmother, Emma Hale Smith," *Ensign*, August 1992.

30. Brian C. Hales, *Joseph Smith's Polygamy*, 3 vols. (Salt Lake City: Greg Kofford Books, 2013), 2:101, 186, 438.

31. Ibid.

32. For a more detailed analysis of Sarah's polyandry, see Hugh Nibley, "The Sacrifice of Sarah," in *Abraham in Egypt* (Salt Lake City: Deseret Book, 1981), 343–81.

33. A helpful lecture vindicating the Prophet against the claims that he was just lusting after women is Brian Hales, "Controversies of Joseph Smith's Polygamy," YouTube, posted on September 12, 2012. Accessed March 3, 2015, https://www.youtube.com/watch?v=AciIEmqLUIc.

34. Brian C. Hales, *Joseph Smith's Polygamy*, 3 vols. (Salt Lake City: Greg Kofford Books, 2013), 2:155–56.

35. Cited in Stanley B. Kimball, "Heber C. Kimball and Family, the Nauvoo Years," *Brigham Young University Studies*, Vol. 15, no. 4 (1975), 461–62.

36. Bruce R. McConkie, *Mormon Doctrine*, Second edition (Salt Lake City: Bookcraft, 1966), 578–79.

37. Brian C. Hales, *Joseph Smith's Polygamy*, 3 vols. (Salt Lake City: Greg Kofford Books, 2013), 2:86.

38. He really said, "Marriage is a far better school for character than any monastery." See Ken Curtis, PhD, "Martin Luther: Monumental Reformer," *Christianity.com*. Accessed March 3, 2015, http://www.

christianity.com/church/church-history/timeline/1501-1600/martin-luther-monumental-reformer-11629922.html.

Chapter 8

1. Found in Ken Robinson, *The Element* (New York: Viking Press, 2009), 260. The authenticity of this quotation is up for debate, but the wisdom remains.

2. Trent Stephens and Jeffrey Meldrum, *Evolution and Mormonism: A Quest for Understanding* (Salt Lake City: Signature Books, 2001), 13.

3. Theodosius Dobzhansky, "Nothing in Biology Makes Sense Except in the Light of Evolution," in *The American Biology Teacher*, March 1973, 35:125–29. Quoted in ibid., 91.

4. *Inherit the Wind*, directed by Stanley Kramer (1960; Universal City, CA: United Artists).

5. Chris Irvine, "The Vatican claims Darwin's theory of evolution is compatible with Christianity," *The Telegraph*, December 11, 2013, http://www.telegraph.co.uk/news/religion/4588289/The-Vatican-claims-Darwins-theory-of-evolution-is-compatible-with-Christianity.html.

6. Charles Darwin, *On the Origin of Species* (New York: Penguin Books, 1958), 175.

7. "Darwin's Greatest Challenge Tackled: The Mystery of Eye Evolution," *Science Daily*, November 1, 2004, http://www.sciencedaily.com/releases/2004/10/041030215105.htm.

8. Charles Darwin, *On the Origin of Species* (New York: Penguin Books, 1958), 294.

9. Trent Stephens and Jeffrey Meldrum, *Evolution and Mormonism: A Quest for Understanding* (Salt Lake City: Signature Books, 2001), 151, 154.

10. Stephens and Meldrum suggest another interpretation of this scripture could be simply that "the prevailing conditions would have continued indefinitely, as they had for millennia." Trent Stephens and Jeffrey Meldrum, *Evolution and Mormonism: A*

Quest for Understanding (Salt Lake City: Signature Books, 2001), 134.

11. The First Presidency of the Church, "The Origin of Man," *Ensign*, February 2002, 30. See also Daniel H. Ludlow, *Encyclopedia of Mormonism* (New York: Macmillan Publishing Company, 1992), 4:1665–69.

12. See William James, *Pragmatism* (Indianapolis: Hackett Publishing Company, 1981), 26.

13. Bruce C. Hafen, "Neal A. Maxwell: An Understanding Heart," *Ensign*, February 1982, 10.

14. Dallin H. Oaks, *Life's Lessons Learned* (Salt Lake City: Deseret Book, 2011), 57.

15. Ibid., 59–60.

16. Boyd K. Packer, "Little Children," *Ensign*, November 1986, 18.

17. Boyd K. Packer, "The Law and the Light," from the Fourth Annual Book of Mormon Symposium, BYU, 1988, published in Monte S. Nyman and Charles D. Tate Jr., eds., *The Book of Mormon: Jacob through Words of Mormon, To Learn with Joy* (Provo: BYU Religious Studies Center, 1990), 6–7.

18. Ibid., 10.

19. Ibid.

20. Charles Darwin, *The Autobiography of Charles Darwin,* ed. Nora Barlow (London: Colline, 1958), 138–39; quoted in Boyd K. Packer, "The Law and the Light," from the Fourth Annual Book of Mormon Symposium, BYU, 1988, published in Monte S. Nyman and Charles D. Tate, Jr., eds., *The Book of Mormon: Jacob through Words of Mormon, To Learn with Joy* (Provo: BYU Religious Studies Center, 1990), 16–17.

21. Boyd K. Packer, "The Great Plan of Happiness and Personal Revelation," CES fireside, November 1993, published in Boyd K. Packer, *Things of the Soul* (Salt Lake City: Bookcraft, 1996), 45–60.

22. Paul R. Green, *Science and Your Faith in God: A Selected Compilation of Writings and Talks by Prominent Latter-day Saints Scientists on the Subjects of Science and Religion* (Bookcraft: Salt Lake City, Utah, 1958), 256–73.

23. James R. Clark, compiler, *Messages of the First Presidency*, Vol. 4 (Salt Lake City: Deseret Book, 1971), 206.

Chapter 9

1. Patrick Henry Hughes, *I Am Potential* (Philadelphia: Da Capo Press, 2008), 3.

2. *Preparing for an Eternal Marriage Teacher Manual* (Salt Lake City: Church Educational System, 2003), 18–21. https://www.lds.org/manual/preparing-for-an-eternal-marriage-teacher-manual/5-the-law-of-chastity?lang=eng.

3. Gordon B. Hinckley, "What Are People Asking about Us?" *Ensign*, November 1998, 71.

4. The Church of Jesus Christ of Latter-day Saints, "Church Responds to HRC Petition: Statement on Same-Sex Attraction," *Newsroom*, posted October 12, 2010, accessed March 3, 2015, http://www.mormonnewsroom.org/article/church-mormon-responds-to-human-rights-campaign-petition-same-sex-attraction.

5. Abby Ohlheiser, "How Many Americans Self-Identify as Gay, Lesbian, Bisexual or Transgender?" *Slate*, posted October 19, 2012. Accessed March 3, 2015, http://www.slate.com/blogs/the_slatest/2012/10/19/how_many_americans_are_gay_or_lesbian_gallup_survey_says_3_4_percent.html. See also "Gay Americans Make Up 4 Percent of Population," *ABC News*, posted April 8, 2011. Accessed March 3, 2015, http://abcnews.go.com/Health/williams-institute-report-reveals-million-gay-bisexual-transgender/story?id=13320565 and Simone Wilson, "How Gay Is America? UCLA Study Shows Only 3.5 Percent of U.S. Claims Rainbow—But 11 Percent Are Tempted," *LA*

Weekly, posted April 8, 2011, accessed March 3, 2015, http://www.laweekly.com/news/how-gay-is-america-ucla-study-shows-only-35-percent-of-us-claims-rainbow-but-11-percent-are-tempted-2392276.

6. Dallin H. Oaks, "Same-Gender Attraction," *Ensign*, October 1995, 9.

7. Edward Laumann, et. al., *The Social Organization of Sexuality: Sexual Practices in the United States* (Chicago: The University of Chicago Press, 1994), 299.

8. See, for example, www.mormonsandgays.org. The site uses "gay" as an adjective but not as a noun, while those interviewed use it both ways.

9. J. M. Bailey and R. C. Pillard, "A genetic study of male sexual orientation," *Archives of General Psychiatry*, Vol. 48:1089–96, December 1991.

10. Ty Mansfield, *Voices of Hope* (Salt Lake City: Deseret Book, 2011), 28.

11. Jeffrey W. Robinson, "Understanding Unwanted Same-Sex Attraction: A Context Specific Approach," *The Guard Rail*, accessed on March 3, 2015, http://theguardrail.com/files/Understanding_Unwanted_Same-Sex%20Attraction.pdf. See also Jeffrey W. Robinson, "Practical Advice from a Therapist for Responding to Same-Sex Attractions," Dennis V. Dahle, et al., ed., *Understanding Same-Sex Attraction (LDS edition)* (Salt Lake City: Foundation for Attraction Research, 2009), 249–78.

12. George D. Watt, et al., *Journal of Discourses* (London: Latter-day Saints' Book Depot, 1855–86), 9:150.

13. Boyd K. Packer, "Agency and Control," *Ensign*, May 1983, 66.

14. Ty Mansfield, *Voices of Hope* (Salt Lake City: Deseret Book, 2011), 17.

15. "Quotes falsely attributed to Mother Teresa and significantly paraphrased versions or personal interpretations of statements that are not her authentic words," *Mother Teresa of Calcutta Center*,

accessed March 5, 2015, http://www.motherteresa.org/08_info/Quotesf.html.

16. "Catholic Charities pulls out of adoptions" *The Washington Times*, posted on March 14, 2006, accessed March 3, 2015, http://www.washingtontimes.com/news/2006/mar/14/20060314-010603-3657r/.

17. See Brian Camenker, "What same-sex 'marriage' has done to Massachusetts," updated June 2012, accessed March 3, 2015, http://www.massresistance.org/docs/marriage/effects_of_ssm_2012/SSM_Mass_2012.pdf.

18. Pamela Openshaw, "Agenda behind gay marriage is destructive," *The Daily Herald*, October 14, 2014, A7.

19. *Fiddler on the Roof*, directed by Norman Jewison (1971; Beverly Hills, CA, MGM).

20. Edwin Markham, "Outwitted," *Holyjoe.org*, accessed March 3, 2015, http://holyjoe.org/poetry/markham.htm.

Chapter 10

1. Hugh Nibley, *Since Cumorah* (Salt Lake City: Deseret Book Company, 1967), 247.

2. I thank Marvin Perkins for helping me see the Book of Mormon in this light. See his video, "Mormon Doctrine on Blacks, Race and Priesthood" YouTube, posted October 30, 2012, accessed March 3, 2015, https://www.youtube.com/watch?v=7BATew0wqRs.

3. See blacklds.org.

4. "William McCary," *Wikipedia,* accessed March 5, 2015, http://en.wikipedia.org/wiki/William_McCary.

5. Address to the territorial legislature, January 16, 1852, recorded in Wilford Woodruff's journal of that date as reported in Lester E. Bush Jr. and Armand L. Mauss, eds., *Neither White nor Black: Mormon Scholars Confront the Race Issue in a Universal Church* (Salt Lake City: Signature Books, 1984), 70–72.

6. See Edward L. Kimball, "Spencer W. Kimball and the Revelation on Priesthood," *BYU Studies*, Vol. 47, no. 2 (2008), 19.
7. E. Dale LeBaron, "Steadfast African Pioneer," *Ensign*, December 1999, 45–49.
8. E. Dale LeBaron, "African Converts without Baptism," BYU Devotional, given on November 10, 1998, accessed March 4, 2015, http://speeches.byu.edu/?act=viewitem&id=361.
9. Ibid.
10. Ibid.
11. "Elder Helvecio Martins of the Seventy," *Ensign*, May 1990, 106.
12. See Edward L. Kimball, "Spencer W. Kimball and the Revelation on Priesthood," *BYU Studies*, Vol. 47, no. 2 (2008), 41.
13. Gordon B. Hinckley, "Priesthood Restoration," *Ensign*, October 1988, 70.
14. Bruce R. McConkie, "All Are Alike unto God," BYU Speeches, given 18 August 1978, accessed March 4, 2015, http://speeches.byu.edu/?act=viewitem&id=1570.
15. Edward Kimball, *Lengthen Your Stride*, working draft in *The Spencer W. Kimball CD Library*, 2006, chapter 24, 4.
16. Edward L. Kimball, "Spencer W. Kimball and the Revelation on Priesthood," *BYU Studies*, Vol. 47, no. 2 (2008), 28.
17. Ibid.

Chapter 11

1. This quote is often attributed to Mark Twain due to a citation in 1941, but it cannot be positively traced to any of his known writings. See "Kindness Is a Language Which the Deaf Can Hear and the Blind Can See," *Quote Investigator*, accessed March 4, 2015, http://quoteinvestigator.com/2013/10/26/kindness-see/.
2. Editorial quoted by James E. Talmage in "Christianity Falsely So-Called," *Improvement Era*, January 1920, 204.

3. For example, the National Conference for Community and Justice, accessed March 4, 2014, http://nccj.org and Jan Shipps, *Mormonism: The Story of a New Religious Tradition* (Illinois: Illini Books, 1987).

4. Ironically, with the exception of The Westminster Confession of Faith, which defines God as being "without body, parts, or passions," there isn't a lot in the Christian creeds that Latter-day Saints can't agree with. See Terryl Givens's discussion of this in his book, *The Crucible of Doubt* (Salt Lake City: Deseret Book, 2014), 86–87.

5. And yet now to communicate effectively with those not of our faith, the Mormon.org home page makes several references to the "Mormon Church." Technically and doctrinally there is no Mormon Church, but in practice we must still recognize that that's who we are to the world.

6. Jahnabi Barooah, "Most and Least Christian Cities In America," *Huffington Post*, updated October 8, 2012, accessed March 5, 2015, http://www.huffingtonpost.com/2012/10/08/most-and-least-christian-cities_n_1915050.html?utm_hp_ref=religion&ncid=edlinkusaolp00000009.

7. Dietrich Bonhoeffer, *The Cost of Discipleship*, translated R. H. Fuller (New York: Touchstone, 1995), 45.

8. Ibid., 51.

9. Articles of Faith 1:8.

10. Dating the New Testament, accessed March 4, 2015, http://www.datingthenewtestament.com/.

11. Thomas Michael Cornelius McGinnis in Dale Carnegie, *How to Win Friends and Influence People* (New York: Pocket Books, 1981), 117.

12. Clement of Alexandria, *Exhortation to the Greeks*, 1.8.4 in *The Oxford Dictionary of the Christian Church*, "deification," accessed March 4, 2015, http://www.oxfordreference.com/view/10.1093/acref/9780192802903.001.0001/acref-9780192802903-e-1957?rskey=4gKJx0&result=1973.

13. Ibid., Augustine, *De Nativatate Domini*, Sermons 22, 13.
14. Ibid., Thomas Aquinas, *Summa Theologica*, 3.Q.1. art. 2.
15. Pope John Paul II, *Crossing the Threshold of Hope,* translated by Jenny McPhee and Martha McPhee (New York: Alfred A. Knopf, 2005), 194–95.
16. Dietrich Bonhoeffer, *The Cost of Discipleship*, translated by R. H. Fuller (New York: Touchstone, 1995), 301.
17. "Historic Ecumentical Move," *Keep the Faith Ministry*, posted February 14, 2013, accessed March 4, 2015, http://orkut.google.com/c119671965-t66e137fdc45cb155.html.
18. In a 2006 *BYU Studies* article, David Paulsen outlines several doctrines that mainstream Christian theologians have begun to write about in ways that sound more and more like the Mormon "heresies" first emphasized by Joseph Smith in the Restoration: the three person Godhead, man becoming God, the possibility of new scripture, a Mother in Heaven, eternal progression, and salvation for the dead. See David L. Paulsen, "Are Christians Mormon? Reassessing Joseph Smith's Theology in His Bicentennial," *BYU Studies*, Vol. 45, no.1 (2006), 35–128.
19. Gordon B. Hinckley, "We look to Christ," *Ensign*, May, 2002.
20. Joseph Smith Jr., *Teachings of the Prophet Joseph Smith*, ed. Joseph Fielding Smith (Salt Lake City: Deseret Book, 1976), 313–14.
21. William Grant Bangerter, "The Quality of Eternal Life," *Ensign*, November 1988, 81.
22. Soren Kierkegaard, *Concluding Unscientific Postscript*, translated by Howard Hong and Edna Hong, (Princeton: The Princeton University Press, 1992), 340.
23. Jenny Spencer, "An Unlikely Friendship," *LDS Living*, March 2014, 40–49.
24. Joseph Smith Jr., *The Words of Joseph Smith: The Contemporary Accounts of the Nauvoo Discourses of the Prophet Joseph*, comp.

Andrew F. Ehat and Lyndon W. Cook (Provo: Brigham Young University Religious Studies Center, 1980), 234.

25. I have my friend David Grant to thank for this insight about Socrates in *The Lysis*.

Chapter 12

1. Neal A. Maxwell, "Put off the Natural Man, and Come off Conqueror," *Ensign*, November 1990, 15.

2. Joseph Smith Jr., *Teachings of the Prophet Joseph Smith*, ed. Joseph Fielding Smith (Deseret Book: Salt Lake City, 1976), 257.

3. Quoted in Ronald E. Poelman, "Divine Forgiveness," *Ensign*, November 1993, 85. See also Bruce R. McConkie, *The Mortal Messiah: From Bethlehem to Calvary*, 4 vols. (Salt Lake City: Deseret Book, 1980), 3:40–41, n. 1.

4. David A. Bednar, "Clean Hands and a Pure Heart," *Ensign*, November 2007, 80–83.

5. Parley P. Pratt, *Key to the Science of Theology* (Salt Lake City: Deseret Book, 1978), 61.

6. Hugh Nibley, *Approaching Zion* (Salt Lake City: Deseret Book, 1989), 301–2.

7. Gene R. Cook, "Teaching by the Spirit and Learning How to Receive Blessings from the Lord," CES seminary and institute meeting, 30 June 1989, 1–2.

8. Henry B. Eyring, "Where Is the Pavilion?" *Ensign*, November 2012, 74.

9. B. H. Roberts, ed., *History of the Church of Jesus Christ of Latter-day Saints*, 7 vols. (Salt Lake City: Deseret Book, 1902–12), 4:445.

Chapter 13

1. Quoted in Linda K. Burton, "Wanted: Hands and Hearts to Hasten the Work," *Ensign*, May 2014, 122.

2. This is C. Michael Wilcox's approach in his book, *Who Shall Be Able to Stand? Finding Personal Meaning in the Book of Revelation* (Salt Lake City: Deseret Book, 2003).
3. Neil L. Anderson, "Joseph Smith," *Ensign*, November 2014, 30.
4. Jeffrey R. Holland, "The Costs—and Blessings—of Discipleship," *Ensign*, May 2014, 6.
5. "Temple," *Bible Dictionary* (Salt Lake City: The Church of Jesus Christ of Latter-day Saints, 2013), 734.
6. Quoted in Daniel H. Ludlow, ed., *Encyclopedia of Mormonism*, Vol. 2 (New York: Macmillan Publishing Company, 1992), 659.
7. See "Adam-ondi-Ahman," *Hymns of The Church of Jesus Christ of Latter-day Saints* (Salt Lake City: The Church of Jesus Christ of Latter-day Saints, 1985), no. 49.
8. Orson Pratt in George D. Watt, et al., *Journal of Discourses* (London: Latter-day Saints' Book Depot, 1855–86), 16:82–83.
9. Ibid.
10. Joseph Smith Jr., *Teachings of the Prophet Joseph Smith*, ed. Joseph Fielding Smith (Salt Lake City: Deseret Book, 1976), 181.
11. Ibid., 287.
12. See, for example, John Pontius, *Visions of Glory* (Springville: Cedar Fort, 2012).
13. *Teachings of the Presidents of the Church: Wilford Woodruff* (Salt Lake City: The Church of Jesus Christ of Latter-day Saints, 2004), 258.
14. Spencer W. Kimball, *Faith Precedes the Miracle* (Salt Lake City: Deseret Book, 1972), 252–53.
15. "What percentage of Mormons regularly participate in temple worship?" Mormon Social Science Association, posted January 19, 2012, accessed March 4, 2015, http://www.mormonsocialscience.org/2012/01/19/q-what-percentage-of-mormons-regularly-participate-in-temple-worship/.

16. Boyd K. Packer, "To Young Women and Men," *Ensign*, May 1989, 59.

17. "Provo Tabernacle Fire—Unburnt Picture of Christ" *LDS Resources*, posted December 2010, accessed March 4, 2015, http://www.ldsresources.net/provo-tabernacle-fire-unburnt-picture-of-christ/.

Chapter 14

1. John (Fire) Lame Deer and Richard Erdoes, *Lame Deer, Seeker of Visions* (New York: Simon and Schuster, 1994), 161.

2. Hugh Nibley and Michael D. Rhodes, *One Eternal Round* (Salt Lake City: Deseret Book, 2009), 32.

3. B. H. Roberts, ed., *History of the Church of Jesus Christ of Latter-day Saints*, 7 vols. (Salt Lake City: Deseret Book, 1902–12), 6:50.

4. *Tuck Everlasting*, directed by Jay Russell, (2002; Burbank, CA: Walt Disney Pictures).

5. *Shadowlands*, directed by Richard Attenborough (1993; Savoy Pictures).

6. Possibly by Maurice Frot, "Talk: Woody Allen," *Wikiquote*, accessed on March 4, 2015, http://en.wikiquote.org/wiki/Talk:Woody_Allen.

7. Heinrich Böll, "The Story of the Mexican Fisherman," the Positivity Blog, accessed on March 4, 2015, http://www.positivityblog.com/index.php/2007/04/04/the-story-of-the-mexican-fisherman/.

8. *Man of la Mancha*, directed by Arthur Hiller (1972; Rome, Italy: Produzioni Europee Associati).

9. "Mahatma Gandhi Quotes," GoodReads, accessed March 4, 2015, https://www.goodreads.com/quotes/26601-each-night-when-i-go-to-sleep-i-die-and.

10. *Hymns of The Church of Jesus Christ of Latter-day Saints* (Salt Lake City: The Church of Jesus Christ of Latter-day Saints, 1985), 223.

11. Plato, *Phaedo*, 81a.
12. Ibid., 67e.
13. Russell M. Nelson, "Face the Future with Faith," *Ensign*, May 2011, 34.
14. Raymond A. Moody Jr., *Life After Life: The Investigation of a Phenomenon—Survival of Bodily Death* (New York: Harper Collins, 2001).
15. Fred (Scrooge's nephew) in Charles Dickens, *A Christmas Carol* (London: Bradbury & Evans, 1858), 6.
16. C. S. Lewis, *The Weight of Glory* (New York: Harper Collins, 1976), 45.
17. Dieter F. Uchtdorf, "Of Things That Matter Most," *Ensign*, November 2010, 21.
18. Ibid., 22.
19. Anne Morrow Lindbergh, *Gift from the Sea* (New York: Pantheon Books, 1983), 99.
20. *The Faith of an Observer: Conversations with Hugh Nibley*, directed by Bruce R. Capener (Covenant, 1985). Transcript available at http://www.bhporter.com/Hugh%20Nibley/The%20Faith%20of%20an%20Observer%20Conversations%20with%20hugh%20Nibley.pdf.
21. Thomas C. Romney, *The Life of Lorenzo Snow* (Salt Lake City: S.U.P. Memorial Foundation, 1955), 406.
22. Thomas S. Monson, "The Holy Temple—A Beacon to the World," *Ensign*, May 2011, 94.
23. Hugh Nibley, "The Circle and the Square," *Temple and Cosmos: Beyond This Ignorant Present* (Salt Lake City: Deseret Book, 1992), 139–73.
24. Joseph F. Smith, Conference Report, April 1916, 6.
25. Joseph Smith Jr., *Teachings of the Prophet Joseph Smith*, ed. Joseph Fielding Smith (Deseret Book: Salt Lake City, 1976), 296.

26. Og Mandino "Og Mandino Quotes," BrainyQuote, accessed March 5, 2015, http://www.brainyquote.com/quotes/quotes/o/ogmandino106300.html.
27. Dieter F. Uchtdorf, "Of Resolutions and Regrets," *Ensign*, November 2012, 24.

Concluding Thoughts

1. Dietrich Bonhoeffer, *The Cost of Discipleship*, translated by R. H. Fuller (New York: Touchstone, 1995), 73. In a brilliant and instructive address entitled "Helping a Student in a Moment of Doubt," President Henry B. Eyring goes even further than Bonhoeffer. He uses Helaman 6:33–34 to show that "doubt is a natural consequence of choices, just as faith is." Henry B. Eyring, *To Draw Closer to God* (Salt Lake City: Deseret Book, 1997), 153.
2. Harold B. Lee, Conference Report, October 1963, 108.
3. David A. Bednar, "Faithful Parents and Wayward Children," *Ensign*, March 2014, 33.
4. Heber J. Grant, Conference Report, April 1915, 82.
5. Bruce C. Hafen, "On Dealing with Uncertainty," *Ensign*, August 1979.
6. Juanita Brooks, ed., *On the Mormon Frontier: The Diary of Hosea Stout, 1844–61* (Salt Lake City: University of Utah Press, 1982), 237–39.

About the Author

Chad P. Conrad grew up in Manhattan Beach, California, and served his mission in Mexico City. He graduated with a bachelor's degree from Brigham Young University and a master's degree from Boston University, both in philosophy. Chad has taught full-time for LDS seminaries and institutes of religion for twenty years and has taught philosophy at BYU. He married Stacy in the Manti Temple, and they're now being raised by eight children in Orem, Utah.